Book 3 of the Cordell Dynasty

The Prodigal Brother

Longhorn: Book III
The Prodigal Brother
Copyright © 2007
By Dusty Rhodes
All rights reserved.

Cover art: Holly Smith
Book Skins
Copyright 2007 ©
All rights reserved.

Published and Printed in the U.S.A.

The characters and events in this book are fictional, and any resemblance to persons, whether living or dead, is strictly coincidental.

All rights reserved. No part of this book may be reproduced or transmitted in any form by any means, electronic or mechanical, including photocopying, recording, scanning to a computer disk, or by any informational storage and retrieval system, without express permission in writing from the publisher.

ISBN: 978-0-9815795-8-0

Other Books by Dusty Rhodes

Man Hunter

Shiloh

Jedidiah Boone

Death Rides a Pale Horse *

Shooter

Vengeance is Mine *

Longhorn I: The Beginning **

Longhorn II: The Hondo Kid **

Longhorn III: The Prodigal Brother

Dusty Rhodes

Part 1

Chapter I

The dead and dying littered the dusty street of Trinidad, Colorado. Blood pooled under and around twenty men, Arlis Higgins's hired killers. They came to burn the town and slaughter everyone in it. Instead, they lay where they fell, cut down by a hailstorm of buckshot from angry townspeople.

One of the raiders, severely wounded with half his face blown away by the heavy pellets, clawed at the dirt, trying desperately to pull himself along on his stomach. A bloody trail followed his slow progress. In a last desperate gasp, his time ran out. Death won another victory.

One by one the townspeople began to emerge. Soon more and more ventured from their place of battle into the street. Ed Hamilton approached Cody and Juliana. He cradled a twelve-gauge shotgun in the crook of an arm. As he passed, he paused briefly and glanced down at Arlis Higgins.

"Real sorry about your pa, Juliana. I hope you can understand we couldn't let him burn the town and kill our families."

"I know. I just don't know what got into him. I would never have thought he would do something like this."

"Glad to see the town had a change of heart," Cody told the storekeeper.

"Yeah, well, after you said your piece and left the meeting in the church, we all agreed that if you was man enough to take on a bunch of killers single-handed we ought to be men enough to side you and fight for what's ours. Sorry we were a little slow in coming around."

"Well, the important thing is, you did."

"Far as we can tell, only one got away. Last we saw of him, he was riding hell bent for leather out of town. He's likely halfway to Denver by now."

O. J. Goodson, the judge/undertaker/doctor, and Miss Molly strode up. He, too, carried a shotgun over a shoulder. Molly carried a blanket that she spread over the body of Juliana's father.

"Looks like I've got a lot of work to do," Goodson said.

Molly wrapped an arm around Juliana's shoulder and pulled her close.

"Why don't you come on over to the house with me, child? Mr. Goodson and the men folk need some time to take care of things here. I've got a big pot of hot coffee already made. I reckon you've got lots of things all bottled up inside. Might be good to get it all out. We can talk woman to woman."

As they walked away, Juliana glanced over her shoulder at Cody. Their gazes met. Juliana offered a weak smile. Cody smiled back sadly and nodded.

Working together, the men of Trinidad had the bodies all gathered up and carried over to Mr. Goodson's place in less than an hour. Several pitched in to help make wooden coffins. Others went to work digging graves in the *boot hill* section of the local graveyard. By sundown, most of the hired killers had been buried in unmarked graves.

Snow began falling by mid-afternoon. It fell like a pure-white blanket and the large flakes quickly covered the bloodstained street. It was as if the gods were ashamed of what happened in Trinidad and wanted to hide the shame.

Arlis Higgins would be taken by wagon back to his ranch for burial.

It was still snowing heavily at dusk when Cody walked out the door of his office just as Ed Hamilton and a delegation of the town council hurried up.

"Got a minute, Marshal?"

"Reckon so," Cody said. "Just heading over to Miss Molly's for supper. Step inside out of the weather. What you men got on your mind?"

The councilmen stomped snow from their boots and stepped into the office. They gathered around the pot-bellied stove and held their hands out to the warmth.

"We just wanted to tell you what a fine job you're doing," Hamilton said. "We just had a little get together over at the store and decided you deserve a raise. As of now, you'll be making a hundred-fifty a month."

"I'm much obliged."

"The way you stood up to those killers was proof enough for all of us that you are the man for the job as marshal of Trinidad. We just wanted to show our appreciation."

"Well, to tell it like it is, I wouldn't have had a chance if you and the townspeople hadn't helped."

"We'll run along. We don't want to keep you from supper."

"Like I said, I'm obliged for the raise. I'll do the best job I know how."

The council members trooped out and Cody headed for Miss Molly's.

Juliana was helping Molly carry heaping bowls of food

from the kitchen when Cody walked in. Three other boarders sat already sipping coffee and waiting.

"Pull up a chair, Kid," Molly said in her usual booming voice. "We'll have supper on the table before you can say scat. What with all that's been going on I'm running a tad late, but Juliana has been a lifesaver. She jumped in and helped me or it might have been breakfast time before you fellows got supper."

Juliana's eyes looked red to Cody, like she had been crying. He supposed that would be natural, seeing how she had just lost her father. As she placed a supper plate on the table in front of Cody, he grasped her hand and squeezed it for a brief moment. He saw her lips quiver before she turned and hurried back into the kitchen.

She didn't return to the dining room until supper was over and the others had left. Cody sipped coffee and waited. She finally walked in slowly.

"Could we go for a walk?" she asked, her face sad. "I need to talk."

"Of course." He pushed from his chair.

They walked through the falling snow along the street leading away from town. Neither spoke. Cody sensed that she had things on her mind, but wasn't quite ready to talk about them.

The night was cold. Juliana pulled a white shawl she had borrowed from Miss Molly tighter around her shoulders. Cody shoved both hands into his pockets and hunched deeper into his sheepskin coat.

"I'm so confused," she finally said, her voice breaking. "So heartbroken. I still can't believe my father would do such a thing."

Cody said nothing. He simply listened, his heart aching for her.

"First my brother, then Mother, and now my father. Seems like my whole world has fallen apart, all within a few weeks. What am I going to do? Everyone I've ever loved is gone."

He reached a hand to brush snowflakes from her hair and encircled her shoulders with a strong arm. That simple touch seemed to open the floodgates of her pent-up emotions. She turned to him and buried her face in the hollow of his shoulder and wept. Her body shook with wracking sobs. He held her close until the weeping softened, which took a while.

It was a cold, gloomy day for a funeral. Snow stopped sometime during the night, but several inches covered the ground. A coffin containing the body of Arlis Higgins was loaded into a wagon. O. J. Goodson drove and Juliana sat on the wagon seat beside him. A long line of wagons, buggies, and horsemen followed. Cody rode Cincinnati and led the procession.

They arrived at the Higgins ranch by mid-afternoon. All the hands of the ranch had heard of the events in town and were gathered with hats in hand when the wagon containing the coffin pulled to a stop at the little family graveyard.

Juliana felt like she was living a nightmare. She was aware of Cody being there. She felt his hand helping her from the wagon. Molly and Cody walked beside her. She moved on shaky legs to stand near an opening in the ground beside her mother's fresh grave.

The coffin was placed on two ropes held by four ranch hands. She became vaguely aware of the minister from town speaking, but she didn't comprehend a word he said. In her mind lay a tangle of twisted emotions, of questions with no answers, of overwhelming guilt. *Is all this my fault? Maybe if I had been more understanding with Father. Maybe if I had talked to him more. Maybe . . .*

Her thoughts were cut short by the preacher stepping up to her and extending a hand and soft whispers of comfort. She nodded. A seemingly endless line of folks approached, offering words of sympathy, most of which she didn't hear.

As Miss Molly and Cody helped Juliana to the house, she glanced back to see the ranch hands lift the coffin over the hole and slowly lower it. She tore her eyes away from the sight.

After the funeral, Cody and the townspeople from Trinidad headed back to town. Juliana went to her room where she stayed for the next three days. During that time alone, she came to grips with her feelings of guilt. She decided there wasn't anything she did or didn't do to cause what had happened.

She also came to the realization that the entire responsibility of the ranch now rested squarely on her shoulders. There had never been a need for her to be involved in the business dealings of the ranch since her father made all the decisions. It dawned on her that she didn't even know how large the ranch actually was or how many cattle and horses the ranch owned. *Surely Father must have kept records. I'll see what I can find tomorrow, s*he decided.

A typical Saturday night reigned in Trinidad. Cody broke up two fights and arrested a miner for drunk and disorderly conduct.

It was well after midnight. The drunk was sleeping it off in one of the two cells in back and the rowdies had all ridden back to wherever they called home. Cody decided it was time to call it a day.

I'd better make the rounds before I head to Miss Molly's. Pulling the door to his office closed behind him, he strode down the street.

The town was quiet, the street dark. Citizens of Trinidad had long since retreated to warm beds. The only light to be seen was the lamp at Miss Molly's at the edge of town. She always left the lamp on until Cody got home. Its yellow glow cast a splash of light across the snow-covered ground.

Traffic from horses and wagons had turned the single street into a quagmire, but elsewhere the recent snow still covered the ground and clung stubbornly to the rooftops and trees.

Cody pulled the collar of his coat up around his neck against a chilling wind coming down from the mountains. He trudged slowly along the narrow boardwalk, his gaze sweeping the street. He didn't expect anybody in their right mind would be out on a night like this, but it was his habit to always be on alert anyway.

Pausing, he checked several doors to make sure they were locked. All seemed well, at least until he passed Hamilton's mercantile store. A soft sound from inside the store reached his hearing. He stopped and listened, but heard nothing more. *Probably Ed's big black cat he let stay in the store to catch mice and rats.* Still, he decided he better check.

He stepped over to the large glass showcase window where Hamilton always displayed the latest ladies' dresses and pressed his cupped hands against the frosted window, but could see nothing but darkness inside.

Turning, he stepped off the boardwalk into the snow-covered ground beside the store. When he rounded the corner and reached the back door he found it ajar. Somebody had pried the door open. He slipped his Colt from its belly holster and thumbed back the trigger.

Pressing his back against the side of the building, using his left hand, he slowly pushed the door open. Inside the store a gun exploded! The bullet splintered the doorframe only inches from Cody's face.

"Whoever you are inside," Cody called out, "throw your gun out and come out with your hands up!"

He listened, but no sound or movement could be heard from inside the store. He waited, knowing whoever was inside wasn't going anywhere and the shot would most likely bring help.

The sound of heavy footsteps running along the boardwalk told Cody help had arrived. Ed Hamilton rounded the corner of his store, cautiously followed by Blackie Bishop, the owner of the Silver Nugget, and Pete, the blacksmith. All three carried shotguns.

"What's the shooting about?" Hamilton asked, hunkering down against the side of the building behind Cody.

"Somebody's inside the store. Whoever it is took a shot at me. Couple of you cover the front. Ed, stay here in case he gets by me. I'm going in."

"Be careful, Marshal."

Cody swung a quick look around. A stack of firewood sat piled along the outside wall. He scooped up a piece, took a deep breath, and tossed it as far as he could through the door into the room.

It must have hit a glass display case because the sound of crashing glass was followed immediately by a shot. Cody dove through the open door and landed flat on his belly on the wooden floor.

The afterglow from the intruder's shot still lingered, outlining the shooter's silhouette clearly. He was crouched behind the wooden counter with only his head and shoulders showing.

Cody snapped off two quick shots aimed just below the

intruder's fading form. He heard his heavy .44 slugs tear through the thin wood of the counter and heard the familiar slapping sound when they struck man.

A loud grunt, followed by the sound of a body hitting the floor, told Cody his bullets found their mark. He cautiously climbed to his knees and then to his feet, all the time watching and listening for any movement from the direction of the counter.

"Come on in, Ed," he called. "I think I got him. Where's a lamp or lantern?"

"The lamps right over here. I'll light it."

Cody kept his gaze fixed in the direction of the counter while Ed lit the lamp. Light filled the large room with a dull glow. Cody peered over the counter. A man lay on his stomach in a growing puddle of blood. He didn't move and appeared to be dead.

Ed Hamilton approached cautiously, carrying the lamp. Cody walked around the end of the counter and turned the man over onto his back.

"It's Harvey Jessup," the storekeeper said. "He's the no-good husband of Juliana's childhood friend, Mary Ann. I ain't surprised. He's been a thief for years. Looks like his thieving days are over."

"I reckon I better go tell his wife what happened," Cody said.

"I'll go with you."

As Cody and Hamilton were leaving the store, the undertaker hurried up.

"Got another customer, O. J.," Hamilton told him. "He's inside. It's Harvey Jessup. Me and the marshal are on our way to tell his wife what happened."

"So Jessup finally got caught, eh? I doubt there'll be much grieving on his account."

"Reckon you're right about that," Ed said.

* * *

The Jessup place was dark when Cody and Ed Hamilton rode up. They dismounted and walked through the cluttered yard to the front of the house. Ed knocked on the door. He repeated his knock twice before a lamp lit up inside.

A young woman opened the door a crack with a lamp in her hand and peered out.

"Who is it?" she asked in a weak voice.

"It's Ed Hamilton from the store and the town marshal. We need to talk with you. Could we come in?"

"What's wrong?" she asked, opening the door wider and stepping aside.

Hamilton and Cody climbed the rickety steps and stepped inside. The place looked like a pigsty. What little furniture occupied the room was broken and looked like salvage from the town dump.

Cody took one look at the woman and cut a glance at Hamilton. The storekeeper shook his head sadly.

Mary Ann Jessup had been beaten to a pulp. Her lip was cut and swollen and one of her eyes was black and blue, swollen shut. The thin gown she had on barely covered her body. Dark bruises on her arm showed plainly even in the dim light.

"Did Harvey do that to you?" Hamilton asked.

"He didn't mean to. Is something wrong?" she asked, her voice taking on a frantic tone. "Has something happened to Harvey?"

"I'm afraid so, Mary Ann," the storekeeper told her. "He broke into my store tonight. The marshal caught him and Harvey tried to shoot him. Harvey's dead. I'm sorry."

Mary Ann's eyes went wide. She covered her mouth to stifle a scream. Tears burst from her eyes and her frail body shook with sobs. Ed gathered her in his arms and held her until the weeping subsided. She looked up at him through tear stained eyes.

"What will I do? Where will I go? How can I survive without Harvey?"

"Why don't you get the children up and let us take you to Miss Molly's until we can work something out?" Ed suggested.

The next day, Juliana spent all morning pouring over the books and records she found in her father's desk. She also found a short-barreled Colt in the desk drawer. Juliana was no stranger to weapons. According to Rafael, the aged Mexican that had taught her to shoot, she could outshoot half the hands on their ranch. She checked to see if the gun was loaded. It was. She replaced it in the middle desk drawer.

She discovered that the Higgins Ranch encompassed six thousand acres. According to the figures she found, their cattle herds added up to something over three thousand head.

In her searching, she also found the combination to the large safe that set in the corner of the den. It took several tries, but the handle finally turned and the heavy door swung open. Inside, she found a stack of official looking papers and a metal box. Inside the box were two large bundles of money, lots of money.

Juliana sent one of the young Mexican boys, who did odd jobs around the ranch, to find Roy Self, the ranch foreman, and tell him she wanted to see him. Within minutes he entered the den.

"You wanted to see me?" he asked, pausing at the door with hat in hand.

"Yes, come in and have a seat."

"I'm real sorry about your pa, Miss Juliana," he said as he folded into a chair in front of the desk.

"Thank you, Roy. How long have you been with us here on the ranch?"

"About fifteen years, I reckon. Went to work for your pa when I was still wet behind the ears. He took me in and gave me a job when I didn't know beans about ranching. The ranch has been my home most of my life. Never worked nowhere else. Never wanted to."

"Roy, I know my father sent you to Denver under the pretext of buying a breeding bull. But that's not what you really went for, was it?"

The foreman dropped his head and stared at his boots for a long moment before answering.

"No, ma'am, it wasn't."

"What was the *real* reason you went?"

Roy raised his face toward the ceiling and took a deep breath. He circled the hat in his hand between his thumb and fingers. He let his breath out in a long sigh.

"He told me to hire twenty gun hands."

"Did he tell you why?"

"No, ma'am, not exactly. Not until I got back."

"Did you ask him?"

"Yes, ma'am. But he got real upset and threatened to fire me and get somebody else to do what he wanted done. Like I tried to tell him, I'd worked for him fifteen years and never once questioned what he told me to do, but what I figured he had in mind wasn't right. I'd never seen him like that before."

Juliana nodded her head in agreement.

"I know. I think losing Trace was more than he could deal with. He wasn't himself those last few weeks. One more question. Why didn't you go with them when they raided Trinidad?"

"I finally got enough sand in my craw to tell Mr. Higgins that what him and the others were fixin' to do was wrong and that I didn't want no part in it. He got madder than a wet hen and told me he would deal with me when he got back. I've already got my gear packed. I figured that's why you wanted to see me. If you don't want me to stay I'll move on."

"Nonsense. I want you to stay. I can't run this ranch without you. What does my father pay you?"

"Seventy-five a month. But it ain't about money. This is my home. Has been more'n half my life."

"You'll always have a job here as long as I have anything to say about it. As of now, you'll be drawing a hundred a month."

Roy's eyes saucered wide. "I'm much obliged, Miss Juliana."

"How many do we have working for us on the ranch?"

"We got twenty-four cowboys, not counting the Mexican workers that take care of the house and stuff like that. As you know, some of our hands have been with us a long time. We got a real good crew, Miss Juliana. I hope we can keep them on, too. A few of them's got families that live in the shacks down by the river."

"Yes, I know. I haven't been down there since I returned from Denver. I want to ride down tomorrow. What do we pay our ranch hands?"

"Same as always, forty a month and found."

"I'm raising their wages to fifty a month starting today. How many cattle does the ranch have?"

"In the neighborhood of three thousand, give or take a few. That will go up when the spring calf crop comes in. Right now, they're spread out in valleys all over the ranch. We need to start gathering them in closer before hard winter sets in."

"How much land do we actually own?"

"Last I talked to Mr. Higgins about it, he owned six thousand acres. But he's got a lease arrangement with the Mountain Ute Indians for grazing rights to almost twenty thousand acres. Him and their chief, an Indian named *Tusabe'*, signed it a year or so ago."

"I see. Tell me, Roy, if this were your ranch, what would you do that we aren't doing?"

"Hmm, hard question. When I was in Denver, I heard the market for beef was strong. The cattle brokers are paying forty-five dollars a head delivered in Denver. We've been selling our cattle mostly to the mining camps scattered all over this part of Colorado, but we don't get but twenty a head for 'em.

"I think you'd be smart to try to buy some cattle from some of the small outfits scattered around that don't want to winter them. We got more grazing land then we need for our herds. I figure we could get them pretty cheap. Then come spring, I'd drive a herd of the older ones to the Denver market."

"Could we do that with the hands we have now?"

"We could get by with hiring a few more."

Juliana thought on Roy's suggestion for a few minutes. "I'll let you know in a day or two. Would that be soon enough?"

"Yes, ma'am. I'm gonna have some of the boys start gathering our stock and moving them in closer so we can keep an eye on 'em during the winter."

"Good. Anything else?"

"Not that I can think of."

Juliana stood up and stuck out her hand. "Thank you for coming, Roy. If you ever need to talk to me about anything, I'll always be willing to listen."

"Obliged, ma'am," the foreman said, standing and leaving the room.

* * *

Juliana pored over the records the rest of the day and far into the night. Lamps had been extinguished long ago and still Juliana worked, absorbing the many legal documents and endless columns of figures.

The big grandfather clock in the hallway just struck two o'clock when the sound of a door opening reached her hearing. *Who could that be?* She looked up from the documents in front of her with curiosity. *Who would be up at this time of night?*

Her answer came when a complete stranger opened the door of the den and stepped inside. The side of his wool coat was blood-soaked and his left arm hung slack. He had been shot. He clutched a gun in his right fist.

"Who are you?" Juliana demanded. "What do you want?"

As he staggered toward the desk she suddenly recognized him as one of the men she had seen around the campfire the night before the raid on Trinidad. He was one of her father's hired killers. She remembered Ed Hamilton telling them that one had escaped. This had to be the one.

"I want my money. That's what I want. Higgins promised us five hundred apiece. I want it. All of it!"

"I don't know what you're talking about. Get out of my house!"

She saw the man's gaze cut towards the open door of the safe in the corner. "Maybe I'll just kill you and help myself," he slurred, starting toward the safe. His right hand with the gun in it clutched his left shoulder.

"One shot and every man on the ranch will be in here in half a minute," Juliana threatened.

The evil-eyed outlaw stopped in his tracks, obviously thinking about what she had said, and replaced his gun in the holster. He withdrew a long hunting knife from a belt scabbard and turned toward Juliana. Lamplight reflected from the wide blade and flashed across the room as he stalked toward her.

Suddenly it dawned on her. He was going to kill her. She gasped. Her heart pounded, as she looked frantically around for a way to escape. Her mind raced, searching for an answer. *I have to do something, but what? Should I scream? Should I try to run?*

CHAPTER II

Buck sat alone in the den. It was late. Rebekah and little Cody had long since gone to bed. He leaned back in the large upholstered chair and stared at the ceiling with unblinking eyes. He was worried.

All the money we had was in that Del Rio bank. Now it's gone. All we got left is a few thousand dollars here in the safe. That's only a drop in the bucket for what it takes just to meet the ranch's payroll, let alone pay the bills and for the cattle the Mexican ranchers will be delivering come spring.

Shore hope Chester and the marshal can find Dawson and his bunch. Mexico's a big country. It'll be like looking for a needle in a haystack. I'm afraid, unless they're able to get that money back, the Longhorn Ranch is a goner. Don't see how we could come up with enough money to keep it going.

Worse comes to worse, we could sell our brood herd, maybe even El Toro, but that still wouldn't be enough to keep us going until we could catch enough longhorns out of the thickets to put together a trail herd.

We should've hung Clayton Dawson when we had the chance. That two-bit outlaw's been a thorn in our side from the git-go. With all the security we had around the bank, who would've thought he'd figure out a way to rob it?

Buck's thoughts scattered as Rebekah slipped into the den. His troubled gaze softened as he watched her pad barefooted across the room toward him. She wore a white nightgown. The cream-colored robe over it was open in front.

Light from the single lamp reflected off her red hair and seemed to set it ablaze in flaming color. Buck never ceased to be amazed at her beauty.

"What are you doing up this time of night?" he asked, opening his arms to wrap her in a long bear hug.

"I woke up and you weren't in bed beside me. I was worried about you and couldn't go back to sleep. What's wrong, Buck? I know you well enough to know something's wrong. What is it?"

"Just thinking about the bank robbery. All our money was in that bank. If Chester and the boys don't find Dawson and his gang and get our money back, we're in a heap of trouble. But it's nothing for you to worry about. We'll make it."

"Of course, I'll worry. Anything that concerns you concerns me, too. We're in this together. What can I do to help?"

Buck hugged her closer. For a time, they held one another. The soft crackle of the fire in the fireplace was the only sound to disturb the silence. The side of his face was pressed against her chest. He could hear her heart beating. Love overwhelmed him and he slowly shook his head.

"What?" she asked.

"Just thinking how much I love you," he whispered. "Let's go to bed."

* * *

A fiery-red sun ball peeked above the eastern horizon as Chester, Bud Cauthorn, and twenty Longhorn security men left the tiny village of *El Sueco,* Mexico. People from the village stood and watched them go, lifting their arms in a friendly farewell.

A single wagon, the same one Dawson used to haul the stolen money, rolled across the desert sand, pulled by two mules. Chester and Bud led the procession. The Longhorn riders flanked the wagon that hauled the money from the bank. The marshal slanted a sideways look at Chester riding beside him.

"That was a good thing you did back there," he said. "Giving the villagers part of the money like that."

"Least we could do."

"Still in all, it'll go a long way toward making their lives a little better. I can't imagine living like they do way out here in the middle of nowhere."

"Some places are better than others, but everybody's gotta live someplace. Seemed to me they're happier than most."

"I reckon. That sounds like something Buck would say. How long you and him been saddle pards?"

"Rode with him all through the war. He was a captain. I was his corporal. We've been through thick and thin together. Except for my pa, Buck's the best man I ever knew. I'd take a bullet for him in a heartbeat."

"Fellow don't meet many men like that in a whole lifetime," Bud said.

"You shore got that right."

* * *

Rebekah pored over the stack of invoices that needed to be paid. She had just finished posting them in an expense ledger and adding them up. She was shocked at the total.

Buck's right, she thought. *Without the money the outlaws stole from the bank, there's no way we can meet our obligations.*

She looked up as little Cody burst into the room, followed closely by his father. The small bundle of energy flew across the floor as fast as his tiny legs could carry him. Rebekah turned in her chair and opened her arms. Her son leaped into them. She hugged him close.

"We're going for our morning walk," Buck said from the doorway.

It had become a daily ritual that Buck and little Cody took a walk around the compound together. It was part of their *alone time,* as Buck called it.

"How about I finish up here and meet you two in the chow hall for lunch?" Rebekah suggested.

"It's a date. Come on, son, we've got some exploring to do."

Rebekah watched with pride as her son hurried to his father's side. He reached a tiny hand and grasped Buck's extended finger. As they walked away, Buck glanced back over his shoulder and winked. Rebekah smiled and winked back at him.

Buck strolled along slowly. Even so, little Cody's tiny legs struggled to keep up. As they walked, an endless stream of questions from his son kept Buck explaining this or that. It seemed to Buck that Cody's inquisitive mind was like a limitless sponge, soaking up everything in sight.

It had become their daily custom to swing by the new corral that held *El Toro*. For security reasons they moved the big bull inside the compound.

Weird as it seemed, little Cody was fascinated by the monster bull. Just the sight of the huge animal sent cold chills up the spine of most grown men, but not so with Cody. He tugged on Buck's finger as they neared *El Toro's* corral, almost dragging Buck toward the thick rail fence.

"El Toro!" the young child screamed happily, lifting a hand to point.

"El Toro," Buck repeated, scooping the boy up so he could get a good look at the monster bull.

Pappy emerged from the nearby barn and walked over.

"Morning, Buck," the bush-popper greeted. "See you and the boss-hoss are taking your morning walk."

"Yep. Never answered so many questions in my life. That bull calming down any?"

"Not that I can tell. He's a killer. Rankest bull I ever seen in all my born days. Ain't a man on the ranch that will dare crawl into the corral with him, and that includes me."

"He might have killer blood in his veins, but he shore sires some prime calves."

"Best I ever saw," Pappy agreed.

"We better be getting along," Buck said, setting little Cody down and sticking out his finger for the boy to grasp. The boy took Buck's finger, but strained to look over his shoulder at *El Toro* until the corral was out of sight.

Buck, Rebekah, and little Cody were having lunch when the guard in the gate tower sounded the bell announcing a visitor. Buck rose and walked to the door of the chow hall to see who had arrived. He recognized the Pinkerton agent from San Antonio. His heart leaped into his throat.

Maybe, just maybe they have found my brother, Buck thought, as he rushed to meet his visitor.

Mel Sloan dismounted and stuck out his big hand as Buck approached.

"Hope your visit brings good news," Buck said, shaking the Pinkerton agent's hand.

"Maybe. We don't know for sure yet. We've got what we think is a good lead. We're checking it out now."

"We were just having lunch," Buck said. "Come on in and join us."

"Much obliged. Don't mind if I do. It's been a long ride from San Antonio."

They walked together to join Rebekah and little Cody in the chow hall. Buck introduced his wife to the Pinkerton man.

"And this is little Cody. We named him after my brother you're looking for."

Sloan reached out to grasp the outstretched hand of the small boy.

"Mighty proud to meet you," the Pinkerton man said, shaking Cody's small hand.

Jewel brought a heaping plateful of food and set it in front of the agent. Another Mexican girl poured him a cup of coffee.

"Tell me what you've found out," Buck said anxiously.

"Well, it seems there was a big shoot-out in a little town in Colorado called Trinidad. Twenty or so gun slicks were hired to burn the town to the ground. Instead, they all ended up in boot hill. The story about it spread all the way to Denver.

"As the story goes, the town marshal stood in the middle of the street and braced the whole gang. That town marshal is a young fellow who calls himself The Hondo Kid. Two of our agents are on their way to Trinidad, Colorado right now. They'll report to me by telegraph just as soon as they find out something."

Buck nodded in silent contemplation.

"Sounds like him," Buck finally said. "At least from all I've heard about him."

"I'll let you know just as soon as I hear something."

"I'd be obliged."

"Heard about the big bank robbery in Del Rio. I understand it was the Dawson gang?"

"Yep. They skee-daddled across the river into Mexico. The Del Rio marshal and some of my men went after them. Haven't heard from them yet."

"Well, let's hope they catch them. Clayton Dawson and his kind has been a scourge on Texas for way too long. Reckon I better be getting on. Got some business down in Laredo to take care of."

"I'm much obliged for bringing me the news. I'll be hoping to hear from you again when you learn something more."

"You can count on it," the Pinkerton agent said, pushing from the bench and fixing his flat-brimmed Stetson in place. "You folks take care now."

Buck stood and shook Mel Stone's hand and walked with him out to his horse.

Three days came and went and still no word from Chester. Rebekah could tell her husband was growing increasingly concerned. She couldn't help noticing the long spells when her husband sat in his den, staring off into space at nothing, or the long rides when he would be gone for hours at a time.

She wanted to help, to take him in her arms and hold him, to reassure him that things would work out and that no matter what, she and little Cody and his friends would always be there for him.

It was near noontime. Little Cody was running through the house playing, in and out of the den where Rebekah worked on the books. Marie Garcia, the middle-aged Mexican nanny who watched after Cody, was trying hard to keep up with the energetic young boy, but wasn't having much luck.

Rebekah finished her work on the books and was just putting them away when Marie passed the open doorway of the den. Rebekah called to her.

"Marie."

"Yes, ma'am?"

"Make sure Cody has his jacket on. I'm going to take him over to the chow hall to have lunch with his father."

"Isn't he with you?" the Mexican woman asked, sudden concern evident in her voice.

"No, I haven't seen him for several minutes," Rebekah said, rising quickly. "I assumed he was with you."

Rebekah jumped to her feet. Both women hurried through the spacious house, calling out to the young boy, but got no response. That's when Rebekah noticed the front door slightly ajar. Running to the door, she jerked it open and rushed outside. She spotted Cody immediately. He was halfway across the compound, running as fast as his little legs could carry him. Rebekah's look darted in the direction her small son was headed and her breath caught in a sharp gasp. Her heart leaped into her throat. Fear raced north from her belly and lodged in her chest.

Cody was making a beeline for the corral that held *El Toro!* Rebekah let out a scream and broke into a run.

Out of the corner of her eye, she saw Buck and Ray Ledbetter coming out of the chow hall.

"Buck! Catch Cody!" she screamed at the top of her voice. "He's headed for the corral!"

Rebekah raced to catch her son. Her heart pounded thick

and loud beneath her ribs. Her lungs wrung raw and labored. Tears blurred her vision and panic sliced through her like a knife as she realized that she could never get to him before he reached the corral.

Pounding boots on hard-packed ground told her others were racing toward the corral too, but she had no time to look, her gaze was locked on only one thing. Her son.

The young boy reached the corral and stopped. He twisted his head toward Rebekah.

"Look, Mama, *El Toro*," the boy cried out, lifting an arm to point at the monster bull inside the corral.

"Cody!" she screamed. "Come here!"

But the boy seemed not to hear. He turned and easily slid his small body between the heavy timbers of the corral and started walking slowly toward the huge animal.

Pappy must have heard Rebekah's screams because he rushed from the nearby barn. Rebekah spotted him as she raced nearer the corral fence.

"Pappy! It's Cody! He's inside the corral!"

The bush-popper broke into a run. He was closer to the corral than Rebekah and reached the fence before either Rebekah or Buck. Pappy didn't even slow down when he reached the fence; he planted a foot on the second rail and vaulted the high fence in one movement.

Inside the corral, the monster bull swung its massive head toward the intruder of his domain. Its blazing eyes fixed upon the boy. It let out a loud snort. White, foamy lather bubbled from its flaring nostrils. The huge hooves pawed the ground, throwing dirt upward in a dusty cloud.

Rebekah reached the corral fence at the same instant Buck and Ray pounded up. Buck planted a boot on the second rail and climbed the fence, pulling his large frame over the top rail and dropping to the ground inside the corral.

"Cody!" both Rebekah and Buck called out frantically. But the small boy's attention was set on *El Toro*. The bull's loud snort seemed to startle Cody. For the briefest moment he stopped. It seemed the boy and the bull's gaze locked on one another.

Rebekah's heart stopped when she saw the bull lower its massive head. Sunlight bounced off the shiny black eight-foot horns with razor-sharp tips. It let out a deep, rumbling bellow from the depth of its chest and charged!

Rebekah screamed at the top of her voice.

"Cody! Come here! Run to Mommy!"

El Toro was thirty yards from little Cody when it charged. Rebekah let out a frantic scream. She stood staring between the timbers of the fence, unable to do anything to save her son. Her fingers bit into the heavy wooden rails of the fence until blood oozed from her fingertips. She teetered on the very precipice of panic, a helpless observer of the tragedy unfolding before her very eyes.

The monster bull was breaching the short distance between itself and the boy, bearing down upon Cody like a runaway train. Rebekah couldn't bear to watch and yet couldn't tear her eyes away.

With only a few short feet before the bull reached little Cody, a figure darted between them. It was Pappy.

The impact of the bull's enormous bulk and speed drove the bush-popper's body forward and upward like a rag doll being flung through the air. *El Toro* wheeled quickly as Pappy's body came down and hit the hard-packed ground. The monster bull was upon the helpless man, goring, smashing and stomping the very life from him.

In the same instant, Buck snatched little Cody up into his arms and raced for the corral fence. Ray Ledbetter jerked the heavy bar up and swung the gate open. Buck hurried through to safety.

Two mounted vaqueros arrived and spurred their horses through the open gate into the corral. With their heavy-braided *reatas*, they were able to quickly secure the bull to the center post in the corral.

Ray rushed to the bush-popper. He knelt to the ground beside Pappy and felt his pulse. He slowly looked up with tears oozing from his eyes and shook his head sadly. It was too late. Pappy was gone.

Rebekah rushed to Buck's side. Together they hugged their son between them for several minutes. Hot tears of thankfulness for little Cody's rescue and safety were tempered by the realization that Pappy had sacrificed his life to save their son.

CHAPTER III

Bud Cauthorn, Chester, and the twenty security men from the Longhorn Ranch splashed their tired horses across the Rio Grande River. Someone spotted them and shouted the news. In seconds, townspeople rushed from stores and homes to welcome the returning posse.

"Did you catch them?" Sam Colson asked anxiously, as he hurried to meet the weary riders.

Chester nodded to his father. "We caught them. The money's in the wagon."

A large smile broke the features of the banker's face. *"Thank goodness.* The whole town's been worried sick."

Happy handshakes and slaps on the back greeted members of the posse as they dismounted.

"I knew if anybody could catch them scoundrels, you fellows could do the job," John Walker said, pumping Bud Cauthorn's hand.

"The money's in those sacks there in the wagon," the marshal told him.

"We rebuilt the bank building while you were gone," Sam said. "It's even stronger than before. Doubt even a cannonball could bust through that wall now."

"Buck in town?" Chester asked.

"Nope, ain't seen him for several days," Sam told his son.

"What about Selena, is she all right?"

"She's fine. Stopped by the house just yesterday. For a woman in the family way, she shore Junes around. Didn't have time to sit down. Said she had a lot to do down at her mother's café. She works too hard, Chester."

"That's just the way she is, Pa. No use wasting words trying to get her to slow down. Is she still in town?"

"Don't think so. She said something about needing to get back to the ranch before dark."

"I'll leave a few of the men in town to help get the money back where it belongs," Chester told the marshal. "I'm gonna ride on out to the ranch. I expect Buck will be anxious to hear about the money."

"We'll see it gets done," Bud assured him.

It was dusky-dark when Chester and the Longhorn riders reined their horses through the gate of the Longhorn compound. The bell sounded announcing their arrival.

Buck heard the bell and rushed to the door, hoping against hope that it was Chester and the men returning with good news. His heart leaped as he saw his friend swing a leg over the saddle and step to the ground. Their gazes met. Chester broke a tired grin and lifted a gloved thumb into the air. Buck let out a long sigh of relief.

Chester turned the reins to his mount over to one of the Longhorn men and strode to meet Buck. Their hands clasped in a strong handshake.

"You been gone a while," Buck said. "I was getting a mite worried."

"It's getting harder and harder to get our money back," Chester said, smiling at his friend and partner.

"Come on, you can tell me all about it over coffee. I'll send someone to let Selena know you're back. She'll be anxious to see you."

"Not near as much as I am, I expect."

As they headed toward the chow hall, Buck broke the news about the loss of Pappy. Chester was stunned. He ducked his head and gritted his teeth.

"He was a good man," Chester said sadly. "Without a doubt, the best I ever saw at what he did."

"Yeah, he was. We're sure gonna miss him. We buried him day before yesterday."

"What you gonna do about the bull?" Chester asked.

"Don't know. Haven't decided yet. What's your thinking?"

"He's a killer, sure enough. He's proved that twice now. You thinking about putting him down?"

"Like I said, don't know yet. Let's think on it a few days or so before we decide."

It didn't take long for Chester to fill his partner in about the recovery of their money.

"I gave that little village five thousand dollars," Chester told his partner. "Figured it was the thing to do."

"Glad you did. So you stretched Dawson's neck, huh? Least we won't have to worry about him and his gang anymore."

"Not unless he figures out a way to come back from the grave."

"You done good, partner," Buck said, clamping a big hand on his friend's shoulder. "You done real good."

Rebekah and Selena hurried in. Chester rose and gave his wife a long hug.

"I missed you," Selena told him.

"I missed you, too," Chester said, patting his wife's protruding stomach. "Looks like our son is growing fast."

"You mean our *daughter*," Selena laughed, pressing Chester's hand tightly against her.

"If it is, she's gonna take a lot of ribbing about having a name like Dakota."

"So you've already decided on a name?"

"Yep."

"Well, we'll see," she said smiling and lifting a look to gaze deep into her husband's eyes.

"Chester was just telling me they recovered the bank's money," Buck told the ladies. "Maybe we can rest easier now, but what would you all think about transferring part of our resources to the San Antonio Bank, just to be safe. Might be better not to have all our eggs in one basket."

Rebekah and Selena looked at one another and then at their husbands. They all nodded approval. "Sounds like a good idea," Rebekah agreed.

"Good," Buck said. "I've got to ride into town tomorrow. I'll talk to Sam about it."

It was early March, 1869. The Longhorn Ranch was a beehive of activity. The ranch's brood herds were moved to make room for the large deliveries of longhorns from the Mexican ranchers that would be arriving within two weeks. Mountains of supplies for the twelve trail crews were arriving daily. Chuck wagons were checked and re-checked, harness repaired, and green mustangs, fresh off the range, broken for the long trek to Kansas.

Buck and Chester sat their saddles and watched the cowboys going about their work.

"We've got a good crew," Chester said.

"Sure do. We need to pick somebody to take over Pappy's job in the thickets. Got anybody in mind?"

"Kinda thinking about Pedro Sedillo. He's maybe the best vaquero on the ranch. He's tough as wang leather, but gets along with the other workers. He's pretty much been running the catching crews across the river since Pappy's been working with *El Toro*."

"He'd be my pick, too. You want to talk to him and see what he thinks about taking the job?"

"Be glad to. When you got to go back to Austin?"

"Late April. I'll be leaving a couple of weeks after the first trail drive pulls out."

"Know how long you'll be gone this time?"

"No more'n a few weeks. The wheels of government turn slow."

"Ain't it the truth."

Their conversation was interrupted by the arrival of Ray Ledbetter and Wade Thomas, head of the Longhorn's security. They reined their mounts to a stop with grim looks occupying their faces.

"We got trouble, Boss," Ray told Buck and Chester. "One of our line riders rode across some wagon tracks, got curious, and followed them to a box canyon. Somebody rounded up some of our brood cattle, penned them in the canyon, and peeled the hides off half of them. Looked like they got a wagonload of hides and hauled them someplace to sell. There's still forty or so of our cattle there. Should we herd them back to our range?"

"*Hide peelers*," Chester said with disgust, spitting out the words like they tasted bad. "They're lower than a snake's belly."

"No, leave the cattle where you found 'em, but put some men nearby in case they come back for another load. I want to look these low-lifes in the eyes when we hang 'em."

***

Wade Thomas and half a dozen Longhorn security men crouched behind rocks and waited. It had been three days. The security foreman began to believe the hide peelers weren't coming back for another load of hides.

"Seems like such a waste just to take the hides and leave the carcasses for coyotes and buzzards," one of the security detail told the others crouched nearby. "Looks to me like they'd take the whole cow and butcher it for meat."

"Cow hides fetch a good price, especially across the river in Mexico. They're almost as valuable as the whole cow and a lot easier to steal. I figure these fellows are Mex."

"Well, I wish they'd come on if they're coming. My behind's tired from sittin'."

The rattle of a wagon wheel on rocks echoed up the canyon and reached their hearing.

Wade Thomas jacked a shell into his Spencer carbine and motioned for his men to hunker down.

Soon a wagon with a dirty canopy rolled into sight pulled by two slat-ribbed mules. The driver was a huge bear of a man with long, dirty whiskers. His clothes were ragged and filthy. His shifty eyes flicked from side to side under the brim of a floppy black hat.

Three outriders rode beside the wagon. Each carried a rifle in the crook of an arm; all four were Americans. The stench of the men and wagon was overwhelming even from a distance of forty yards.

At Thomas's signal the Longhorn security men stood up from behind their rocks, their Spencer carbines tucked against their shoulders and leveled at the hide peelers.

"First man that moves is a dead man!" the security foreman hollered.

One of the outriders swung his rifle up and levered a shell. It was the last mistake he would ever make. Six rifles barked in unison. The man was blown from his saddle with six bullet holes in him.

The remaining three men threw their hands into the air. Their rifles clattered to the rocky ground. The big fellow on the wagon seat glared at the Longhorn men.

"Who ar' ya?" he demanded in a bullfrog voice.

"We're the last men on earth you wanted to run into," Thomas said. "Tie 'em up," he told his men.

Several security men hurried forward and quickly had the three hide peelers tied securely.

"What ya want with us? We ain't done nothin'."

"You skinned a wagonload of hides off our cattle. Now shut your mouth. The boss wants to see you or I'd shoot you right here."

"Don't know nothin' about skinned cattle. We're jest out huntin'."

"Save your breath. You're gonna need it. Some of you men throw them in the wagon."

The Longhorn men walked them to the back of the wagon and were about to lift them inside.

"Hey, Boss. You better come and take a look at this," one of the Longhorn men said.

Wade Thomas walked over and flipped up the edge of the dirty canopy. A young Mexican girl looking to be no more than twelve, or thirteen, was lying on the floor of the wagon. Her hands and feet were tied with strips of rawhide.

"Untie her and get her out of there," Thomas ordered.

Two Longhorn men climbed into the stinking wagon and untied the girl, lifting her gently to another security man on the ground. Her frail young body was nothing but skin and bones. Her bare feet were badly cut and bruised. The ragged dress barely covered her. A rope was tied around her neck that had obviously been used to pull her behind the wagon. She had been beaten unmercifully.

Wade set his jaw. He ground his teeth together. Hot anger rose inside him and he felt his face flush red. He swung a hard look at the big leader. His look was met with a defiant stare.

How could grown men treat a young girl the way this girl has been treated? Wade thought.

"Changed my mind," the security foreman told his men. "Scum like these don't deserve to ride. Drop a rope around their necks and slip their boots off, then tie them to the back of the wagon. We'll give them a taste of their own medicine. They'll walk or be dragged the twenty miles back to the ranch."

The Longhorn men washed and doctored the girl's bruised and swollen face and bloody feet as best they could. They wrapped her in a blanket and made a pallet for her in the wagon before striking out for the ranch.

It was a long trip, especially for the three hide peelers. Sharp rocks and cactus cut their bare feet to shreds. As the miles passed underneath the wheels of the wagon, the three men stumbled more and more often. When they fell, they were dragged behind the wagon until they managed to climb to their bloody feet.

They cursed, pled for mercy, and cursed some more. But their pleadings fell on deaf ears. The Longhorn riders had no sympathy for them.

Daylight turned to darkness. Still, the wagon and detail of security men continued southward toward the ranch.

"We gonna stop for the night or keep going?" one of the Longhorn men asked.

"We ain't stopping," Wade told his men. "I want to get

that girl some help soon as we can. It's a wonder she's still alive as it is. I figure if we keep rolling, we can be there by sunup."

All through the long night, the wagon rolled on. One of the hide peelers gave up. He could no longer climb back to his feet. The rope stretched tight. It choked the last remaining shred of life from him as his heavy body was dragged along behind the wagon.

His two partners saw what happened and were quicker to climb back to their feet when they fell.

The first hint of a new day colored the eastern horizon. Buck ate his breakfast with Chester and twelve foremen when the bell in the guard tower sounded. Somebody rushed into the chow hall with the news that the security detail had returned.

Buck and his crew of foremen hurried out to meet the Longhorn men as they pulled a wagon through the front gate. Wade Thomas swung a leg over his saddle and stepped to the ground.

"What you got here, Wade?" Buck asked, eyeing the bloated and bloody remains of a man lying behind the wagon. Buck's gaze followed a bloody trail in the dirt as far as the eye could see. Two other men collapsed and remained motionless where they fell.

"You said bring them back alive if I could," the security chief told his boss. "I reckon two is all I could manage. There's a young girl in the wagon who needs tended to. She's in pretty bad shape. I'll tell you all about it after we get her to Miss Jewel."

Thomas climbed into the wagon and lifted the young

girl. He handed her to waiting arms. They rushed her to the small room in the back of the chow hall set aside for treating injuries.

"Put these two in the barn until we decide what to do with them," Buck instructed the crowd of Longhorn cowboys who gathered around. "Watch them close. I wouldn't want them to miss their party. Their *necktie* party."

It took only a few minutes for Wade Thomas to relate the details surrounding the capture of the four hide peelers. Buck and Chester listened closely. As the head of security explained how the young girl had been abused, Buck glanced up at Chester. He saw his partner and friend set his jaw. He saw a look on Chester's face he had seen only a handful of times in all the years they had ridden together. It was a frightful look. It was a look that made cold chills race up the spine of even Buck.

Without a word, Chester rose from the chow hall and strode quickly from the building.

"We're obliged for the report, Wade," Buck told his security man, as they both stood to their feet and shook hands. "You and your men did a fine job."

Buck hurried to find Chester. He found his friend leading the two prisoners from the barn. The stableman followed, leading Chester's horse and two extra.

"Let me handle this one," Chester said as Buck approached. The anger in Chester's voice reminded Buck of stories he had heard of the rumblings deep inside a volcano just before it explodes.

The finality of his friend's words stopped Buck in his tracks.

"What you got in mind, partner?"

"You don't want to know. Do me a favor. Just let me handle it."

Buck said nothing more. He shook a single nod and turned on his heels. As he walked toward his house he glanced back over his shoulder. Both Chester and the hide peelers were mounted. Chester had the reins to the prisoners' horses in one hand and two coiled ropes in the other. Buck watched as they rode through the open front gate toward the hanging tree.

CHAPTER IV

Recognition sizzled along Juliana's nerves, the certainty of what was about to happen. This stranger intended to kill her. The thought shocked her and swelled the barely controlled panic lodged beneath her ribs. She felt her fear spiraling. It seemed she could smell the fear seeping from her pores. Juliana's heartbeat thundered, reverberating against the wall of her chest. She froze, near motionless, straining, quivering.

The snarling killer stalked toward her, now only feet away. A cold hatred blazed in his dark eyes.

By lightening instinct, rather than plan, she jerked open the drawer of her desk. Her hand grasped the short-barreled Colt she discovered earlier. The weapon exploded once, twice, three times. The sound was deafening in the stillness of the night.

Shock rounded the killer's eyes. The snarl on his lips turned to surprise as his mouth dropped open. He staggered backwards, his boots searching for firm footing, and found it. For a long moment, he wavered unsteadily. His gaze lowered. Blood gushed from three fresh holes in his chest and formed a crimson puddle at his feet.

As Juliana watched, the man's legs buckled under him and he collapsed to the floor. A piercing scream erupted from her lips. She muffled it with a hand.

Suddenly the room was full of people. Half-dressed cowboys, with belted holsters in one hand and a cocked gun in the other, searched the house for other would-be intruders.

Roy Self, the ranch foreman, was there. He took the gun from her shaking hand and placed an arm around her shoulders and helped her to a chair. One of the Mexican house girls spread a blanket over the dead outlaw.

"What happened?" Roy asked once Juliana collapsed into the chair.

It took a minute before she could get her breath, and words came out.

"It was one of my father's hired guns, the one that got away. He came back for his money. I've never shot anyone before. *I killed a man. It was awful."*

"It's okay, Miss Juliana. You did what you had to do."

"He was going to kill me."

"I know. I found the knife lying beside him. I'll send someone into town for the marshal, come morning. He'll straighten it all out."

"Yes, yes. Do that."

"Probably best we not move the body until the marshal takes a look around. Why don't you go on upstairs and get some rest? We'll take care of things here."

It was a cold, frosty morning. The streets of Trinidad were mostly deserted, even though it was nearly noon. Only a few hardy citizens ventured out, bundled up against an icy north wind. Snow clouds drifted in over the mountains to the northwest.

Cody glanced up at the clouds and hunkered deeper into his sheepskin coat as he trudged along the snow-covered street. *Looks like we're in for a real humdinger.*

A galloping horse and rider coming in from the east caught Cody's attention. *What kind of fool would run his horse on icy roads like this?*

The rider raced past Cody and reined up in front of the marshal's office. He leaped to the ground and barely slowed down before opening the door and rushing inside. Cody wheeled and trotted back to his office. The man was on his way out when Cody opened the door.

"What's your hurry?" Cody asked the breathless cowboy.

"Oh, Marshal, I didn't recognize you. It's Miss Juliana, she sent me to get you. She shot a man. She wants you to come quick."

"Juliana? She shot somebody? Who was it? Who did she shoot?"

"It was that fellow who got away after the raid. He came to the house late last night. He tried to kill Miss Juliana. She shot him. She says to come quick."

"I'll get my horse."

Cody trotted down the street to the livery stable. On the way, he decided maybe he ought to take the undertaker's buggy, since he figured he'd need to bring the body back to town for examination and burial.

"I've got to ride out to the Higgins ranch," Cody explained to the liveryman. "A man's been shot and I'll likely need to haul the body back to Mr. Goodson. I'm gonna take the long bed buggy he uses to haul coffins. Let him know for me, will you?"

"Shore will, Marshal. Who was it that got shot?"

"One of the ranch hands rode in to get me. Seems like that hired killer that got away the other day showed up at the Higgins ranch. He tried to kill Miss Juliana. She shot him."

It took only a minute for Cody and the liveryman to hitch the undertaker's team of horses to the buggy. Cody climbed into the seat and popped the horses on their rumps with the long reins.

"I need to tell Ed Hamilton where I'm going," Cody hollered, as he rode past the cowboy from the ranch. "It won't take a minute."

Ed must have seen the Higgins rider barrel through town, because he was standing on the boardwalk in front of his store when Cody drove up.

"What's going on, Marshal?" the city councilman hollered above the whistling wind.

"That fellow who got away after the raid showed up at the Higgins ranch last night. He tried to kill Juliana. She shot him. She sent her rider to get me. I should be back late tonight or tomorrow."

"Don't worry about things here. I doubt anybody will be out looking to make trouble in this kind of weather. Be careful. Looks like we got a humdinger of a storm blowing in. Is Juliana all right?"

"Think so, but can't say for sure. Tell Mr. Goodson why I took his buggy and team."

Cody popped the reins again and headed up the street. The Higgins rider rode right behind him. As they left town, they met the stagecoach from Denver rolling in. Cody nodded a howdy to the driver as they passed each other.

As Cody and the Higgins ranch hand rode, the weather worsened. Before they went a half dozen miles, heavy snow began falling. The temperature plummeted. The north wind picked up and swept down the mountainside with a fury, sweeping the snow ahead of it in horizontal sheets. The flakes were as large as the end of a man's thumb. Within an hour it was so thick he could hardly see, a whiteout. Cody had never seen it snow like this.

"Hope you know the trail better than I do," Cody shouted to his companion, but the wind snatched his words and swept them off into the storm. He twisted in the saddle and motioned for the Higgins rider to take the lead.

Regis Maxwell stepped down from the stagecoach and stood aside as his partner, Wally Fletcher, climbed down.

"Like I told you fellows before," the burly stage driver said as he unloaded their duffle bags from the leather boot on back of the Concord stage, "Ain't a whole lot to see in Trinidad. Closest thing to a hotel is Miss Molly's boarding house up the street."

"We're obliged," the one called Maxwell said, in his usual soft voice.

"Storm blowing in. Reckon I best pull on down to the livery and switch teams so maybe I can get through the pass before the storm hits. Heard the stationmaster back in Denver say you fellows are Pinkertons. What'cha doing way out here in a one-horse town like Trinidad?"

"Looking for somebody," Maxwell said, picking up his duffle and turning away, ending the conversation.

"Don't know about you," the one known as Wally Fletcher said, clearing his throat and spitting. "I could sure use a stiff drink."

They headed for the nearest saloon, the Golden Nugget.

Down the street, the driver pulled the stage to a stop outside the corral. Pete sauntered out to meet him.

"In a hurry this trip, Pete. Want to get over the mountain before the storm hits."

"Can't say I blame ye," the liveryman said, spitting a long stream of tobacco juice. "Looks like a bad 'un. I'll get a new team out and have you hooked up in a jiffy."

"Hauled a couple of Pinkerton fellows in. Said they was looking for somebody. Reckon who they'd be looking for in Trinidad?"

The liveryman stopped and twisted a long look at the stage driver. *Yeah, who could they be looking for in Trinidad?* he wondered. The first one to pop into his mind was their new town marshal. *I always figured he had somebody on his trail. He's way too handy with that gun not to have made some enemies somewhere down the line. Maybe I ought to let Ed Hamilton know about this.*

"Where'd them fellows go?" he asked the driver as they hooked the trace chains in place.

"You talkin' about them Pinkerton fellows? Last I saw, they was headed toward the Golden Nugget."

As soon as the stage rolled out, Pete made a beeline for Hamilton's Mercantile. He burst through the door, breathless.

Hamilton looked up from a ledger book when the liveryman hurried in.

"What's got you in such an all-fired hurry, Pete? I ain't seen you move that fast in years."

"The stage driver told me he dropped off a couple of Pinkerton men a little bit ago. He said they told him they was looking fer somebody. Reckon it could be the 'Kid they're looking fer?"

Hamilton rubbed his chin as he considered Pete's suggestion.

"Wonder what they want him for?" the councilman thought out loud.

"Got no idea, but shore would hate to lose the 'Kid as our marshal. You ask me, he's the best we ever had."

"Yeah, me too. Listen Pete. Don't say nothing about this to nobody. I'm gonna nose around some."

Ed Hamilton grabbed his heavy coat from the peg on the wall and sleeved into it. He snatched his hat from another peg and clamped it on his head.

"Go on back to the livery, Pete, and keep what you just told me under your hat until we see what's what."

The Golden Nugget was mostly deserted when Ed walked in. He stamped the snow from his feet and walked to the bar.

Besides Blackie, the owner and bartender, the only others in the saloon were two well-dressed businessman types. They both wore greatcoats with fur collars over black business suits. One wore a black derby hat and the other wore a flat-brimmed black Stetson. Both wore gun belts that showed through the opening in front of their coats.

"Morning, Ed. Looks like a storm moving in," Blackie Bishop said, setting a glass on the bar, and pouring Ed's favorite drink. "This'll warm your insides."

Ed tipped the glass and swallowed the fiery golden-colored liquid in one gulp. As he set his glass back on the bar he crooked a look at the two men leaning against the bar.

"You fellows just get off the stage from Denver?"

The one called Maxwell turned his head to look at Ed.

"Yep."

"I'm Ed Hamilton. I'm president of the town council. You fellows passing through or staying with us a while?"

"Depends. We're with the Pinkerton Detective Agency. I'm Agent Maxwell. This is my partner, Agent Fletcher. We're here looking for somebody."

"Oh? Well, like I say, I'm head of the town council. I

know most everybody in Trinidad. Maybe I can help you. Who is it you're looking for?"

"Young fellow who calls himself the Hondo Kid. We heard he was the town marshal here. You know anybody by that name?"

Ed thought on it a minute before he answered the question. *That's what I was afraid of. They're after the 'Kid for something, no telling what. Don't seem right that a fellow's past would dog his trail like a hungry wolf. Everybody deserves a chance, a new start. Especially after what the 'Kid did for our town.*

I figure that's why the 'Kid came here, to start over. The most out-of-the-way place he could find. Somewhere where nobody could find him, but they did.

Suddenly an idea burst in his mind like a stick of dynamite going off. *It's crazy, but it might just work.*

"Yeah, I knew the 'Kid. To be so young, he was quite a man."

The Pinkerton agent's head jerked around. A questioning look swept across his face.

"You said, *was*."

"What?" the town councilman asked, trying to sound innocent.

"When you said you knew the Hondo Kid, you said *was?*"

"Oh, well, I figured you knew. The Hondo Kid was killed in the big raid we had not long ago. Yes, siree, that young fellow was something, sure enough. Why, he stood right out there in the middle of the street while twenty hired killers bore down on him. He had a shotgun in each hand, blazing away. Killed several of them too, before they cut him down. Riddled his young body with more bullet holes than we could count. Ain't that right, Blackie?"

Ed shot a quick glance at the saloon owner. Blackie

quirked his eyebrows with a puzzled look on his face. Hamilton winked.

"Oh, yeah, that's right," the bartender agreed. "That's just the way it happened."

"Yes, sir. It was a sight to behold, it was. Never seen anything like it. Most likely never will again. He's buried right up there in the town cemetery. Wish we could have given him a better send-off, seeing as he saved our town and all.

"Them fellows had orders to burn our town to the ground and kill every man, woman, and child in it. The Hondo Kid saved us. Soon as the weather clears some, the towns gonna put up a monument for him. Ain't that right, Blackie?"

The saloon owner had now figured out what was going on and got right into the spirit of the charade.

"We sure are. If anybody ever deserved a monument, it's the Hondo Kid."

The Pinkerton men looked at each other. Both nodded their heads.

"Do you have an undertaker in this town?" one of the Pinkerton agents asked. "We'd like to talk to him, not that we're doubting what you say, you understand. We just have to have several witnesses, that's all."

"We sure do. Mr. O. J. Goodson is the judge, doctor, and undertaker. You fellows just finish your drinks and I'll get him right over here for you."

Ed turned and hurried out the door. He made tracks to the Judge's office. In less than five minutes, Hamilton filled Goodson in on what was going on and they were on their way to the saloon.

"Judge, these fellows are Pinkerton agents from Denver. Mr. Maxwell and Mr. Fletcher. They're here looking for the Hondo Kid. I told him about the tragic end the 'Kid met with, but they need a few more witnesses to swear to what happened."

"How can I help you gentlemen?" the judge asked, swallowing the drink Blackie had set in front of him.

"We understand you're the undertaker hereabouts?"

"Sure am."

"And you oversaw the burying of the Hondo Kid?"

"Yep, buried him right up there in the town cemetery."

"And you'll sign an affidavit to that effect?"

"Be glad to. If you fellows are staying in town, I can draw up that paper and have it for you by tomorrow."

"Well, from the looks of that storm brewing, it ain't likely we'll be going anywhere anytime soon. When's the next stage come through going to Denver?"

"Supposed to be day after tomorrow, but with the weather like it is, don't see much chance of that."

"I understand there's a boarding house here?"

"Sure is. Miss Molly'll take right good care of you fellows. Her place is up the street a ways."

"We heard the ''Kid rode a black and white pinto. Think we might take a look at that horse, just to tie up any loose ends, you understand?"

"Don't see why not," Hamilton told them. "I reckon his pinto's still down at the livery, that's where the 'Kid kept him. Talk to Pete Cox, he owns the livery. By the way, never heard you say why you were looking for the 'Kid?"

"Don't reckon it matters now," Agent Maxwell said.

"Yeah, don't reckon it does at that. Well, I've got to be getting along," Hamilton said quickly.

"You fellows have another drink on the house before you go," Blackie said, as Ed Hamilton hurried out the door.

Ed headed down the street to the livery. It took only a few minutes to fill Pete in on the story they had told the Pinkerton men. He then practically ran up the street to Miss Molly's and found her in the kitchen. He rushed in panting and out of breath.

"Land sakes, Ed, you're too old to be running around like that. Where's the fire? I tell you, folks now days are always in such—"

Hamilton cut her off in mid-sentence. "There's two Pinkerton men on their way here right now. They'll be here any minute. They're looking for the 'Kid. We all got together and cooked up this cock-and-bull story about the 'Kid being killed in the big shootout the other day."

"O. J. told them we buried the 'Kid up in the graveyard. I'm not sure why they're looking for him, but we figured after what he done for all of us, we ought to give him a chance to get away if we could."

Molly was nodding her agreement.

"Molly, for once in your life, don't say no more than you have to. We've got to convince them the 'Kid was killed in that shootout."

A knock on the front door interrupted them.

"I'm going to slip out the backdoor. Soon as you get the chance, tell your other boarders what's going on. Get them to go along with it. Be sure to talk to Mary Ann, too."

"I will, don't you worry none. We'll have them fellows shedding tears over the 'Kid before they're gone."

Ed made a circuit of several businessmen in town and asked everybody to come to the church that night for a secret meeting.

It was slow going.

By the time Cody and the ranch hand reached the Higgins ranch an eerie, premature dusk had swallowed daylight. The snow was knee-deep on the horses as they pulled up to the barn. A Mexican stableman took charge of the horses.

"Alonzo will see to the horses," the Higgins rider told Cody. "Miss Juliana will be up to the house. She'll be expecting you."

Cody hunched deeper into his coat and made his way to the main house. A Mexican house girl he remembered as Louisa opened the door to his knock.

"I'm the town marshal. Is Miss Higgins available?"

"Yes, sir. Miss Juliana is expecting you. Come this way."

Cody followed the girl down a wide hallway, past the closed door to the den, and into the toasty warmth of a spacious living room. Juliana was sitting on a large sofa in front of the fireplace. She leaped to her feet and rushed into his arms when Cody entered.

"Oh, I'm so glad to see you," she told him. "I'm sorry you had to make the trip in this weather, but I'm glad you're here. I didn't know what else to do."

"You did right. Let's sit down. Start at the first and tell me exactly what happened."

Louisa brought coffee and poured them both a cup. Cody sipped on the steaming liquid and listened intently as Juliana related the events of the night before. As she talked, it was as if she was reliving the nightmare all over again. She seemed breathless. Her voice began to quiver.

Cody reached to still her shaky hand.

"Take your time. It's all right. No one's gonna hurt you now."

When she finished, she buried her face in her hands and wept unashamedly. Cody moved closer and took her in his arms. Juliana seemed to calm down and regain control of herself.

"Roy said we should leave things in the den just as they were. We didn't move anything. He...that man is still there."

"I'll take a look in a bit. Something's happened in town

that you should know about, too. We caught Harvey Jessup in Hamilton's store night before last. He tried to shoot it out. He was killed. Your friend, Mary Ann is staying at Miss Molly's until we can figure out something."

"*Oh, my.* I can't say truthfully I'm sorry about her no good husband. She should never have married him in the first place. With those two small children, there's not much she can do. I begged her to come and live with me, but she wouldn't leave him. As soon as the weather clears up, I'll go get her and the children and move them here to the ranch."

After Cody looked over things in the den and found them to be just the way Juliana said, he spread the blanket back over the attacker and went to find the Higgins foreman. He found Roy Self in the bunkhouse playing poker with several of the ranch hands. They all shook hands.

"Any chance of getting some of your boys to move that fellow's body out of the den?" Cody asked the foreman. "I think it might make Miss Juliana feel better if it was gone."

"Sure can, Marshal. We'll move it to the barn. We can put together a wooden coffin, too, if you want."

"That'd be good. Soon as the storm lets up, I'll haul him back to town to be buried. I doubt they'd want him buried here on the ranch."

"Not likely. Bob, take a couple of boys and move that fellow's body to the barn. Looks like this storm's set in for the night. You ain't thinking about trying to make it back to town tonight, are you Marshal?"

"Not if you've got an extra bunk I could use."

"Got plenty. Just throw your bedroll on an empty one and make yourself to home."

"I'd be obliged," Cody told him. "I need to go tell Miss Juliana we're moving that fellow and I'll be back in a bit."

The storm was raging with no let up in sight. Waist-high drifts piled high by the strong winds. Large flakes peppered his face as he made his way back to the main house.

He stomped snow from his boots and stepped inside. He found Juliana still in the living room and sat beside her on the sofa.

"I talked to your foreman. Some of the men are moving that fellow to the barn. They'll put together a coffin and I'll haul his body back to town to be buried. I didn't figure you'd want him buried here on the ranch."

"Thank you."

He reached to take her hands in his. "Juliana, you did exactly what you had to do. You shouldn't feel bad. He was a bad man. He tried to kill you. You had every right to defend yourself."

"I know. It's just the thought that I actually *killed* someone. It's hard to accept."

"Sometimes we have to do things we're rather not do."

"They say you've killed several men. Doesn't it bother you?"

"Yes, ma'am, it does, but I've never killed anybody that wasn't trying to kill me."

"You aren't thinking about going back to town tonight, are you?"

"No, ma'am. If it's all right, I'll bed down in the bunkhouse with your men until the storm breaks."

"We have extra bedrooms, you're welcome to stay here in the house."

"I reckon it'd be best if I stayed in the bunkhouse, but I'm obliged for the offer."

"Will you have breakfast with me in the morning?"

"It'd be a pleasure, I'll look forward to it all night," he

said, standing to his feet. She stood also. His gaze met hers. For a long moment their gazes locked and held.

The light in Juliana's eyes and the glow on her face gave him pause. He saw his own deep yearnings reflected in her eyes. He felt a familiar longing surge through him. He was sorely tempted to take her in his arms, to hold her, to claim the fantasies that haunted him since the first time he laid eyes on her.

Instead, he clamped his hat in place and swallowed before the words would come.

"Goodnight, Juliana."

Chapter V

Buck spent most of the day playing with little Cody and spending time with Rebekah before going to the chow hall to check on the Mexican girl's condition. It was late afternoon. The sun was dipping toward the western horizon.

"She will heal," Jewel told him. "At least on the outside. I'm not sure she will ever get over what she suffered on the inside."

"I can't even imagine," Buck said. "Well, do the best you can. See she has anything she needs."

Buck was leaving the chow hall when Ray Ledbetter rode through the front gate, spotted Buck, and rode over.

"Is Chester all right?" Ray asked.

"I reckon. Why?"

"I rode past the hanging tree this morning and again just now. He's got them two fellows sitting their horses under the tree. They got ropes around their necks, but they're just sitting there. Have been all day.

"Chester was propped against the tree like he was on a

Sunday picnic. It just looked strange. Thought you ought to know."

Buck decided he ought to make sure Chester was all right. He quickly saddled his horse and headed for the tree that since the beginning of the ranch had come to be the place where Longhorn justice was carried out.

As he rode near, sure enough, it was just as Ray had said. The two hide peelers sat astride saddled horses, their hands tied behind their backs, sitting beneath a sturdy limb, with nooses knotted around their necks.

Chester sat with his back against the trunk of the tree with one leg propped over the other. His hat was pulled low on his forehead and a long stem of grass protruded from his lips. He was the picture of relaxation.

Buck reined up nearby and stepped to the ground.

"Thought I better check on you. Seemed to be taking longer than usual just to hang two men."

Chester looked up and shrugged his shoulders.

"The hanging won't be until sundown. I wanted this scum to have all day to think about what they did and what's gonna happen come sundown. Sometime the wait is the worst part."

Buck nodded. "It's almost sundown, so if you have no objections, I'll wait with you."

Chester crooked his neck to glance up at the sinking sun. It was nearing the horizon. The two condemned men sat facing west. Their heads were hatless. Sunlight burned into their faces.

The knotted nooses hung snug around their necks, the knot resting against their left ear. Chester lazily climbed to his feet and walked over to stand in front of them.

"Almost time," he said.

Neither man spoke. Obviously, they finally figured out their cursing and begging for mercy was falling on deaf ears.

Chester walked around behind the two horses. He stood quietly, watching the sun as it slid lower and lower.

Buck glanced at the condemned. They, too, were watching the sun as it seemed to speed its descent, as if it, was anxious to get the execution over with.

Buck's gaze flicked back and forth between the faces of the hide peelers and the giant sun ball. The blazing sun kissed the rim of the horizon. He saw the two men's eyes widen. The sun quickly buried half of itself behind the distant mountains, then three-quarters, and then only a thin sliver was visible.

When the last sight of the giant ball disappeared from view, Chester swatted the rumps of the horses with a leather quirt. They leaped forward.

One of the men, the smaller of the two, gulped in a gasp of air so loud Buck could hear it. The other fellow, the biggest and leader, opened his mouth wide in an ear-piercing scream. The horses' forward motion dragged the men from their saddles. Their bodies dropped toward the ground.

The scream was cut short abruptly when the big man hit the end of the rope. The bodies swung back and forth. Their feet thrashed the air in a futile last effort to find footing.

Cody awoke to the sound of somebody building a fire in the big potbellied stove. He pulled his blanket higher around his neck and snuggled deeper into the cozy warmth. Somebody coughed. Somebody else cursed. The voice of the foreman brought men crawling from their blankets and grumbling under their breath.

"Off your bunk and on your feet, we got work to do today."

Cody rolled to a sitting position on the edge of his bunk.

It reminded him of many mornings at the Brazos River Ranch down in Texas. *Wonder how Lefty and the boys are doing?*

Suddenly remembering that he was supposed to have breakfast with Juliana, he quickly pulled on his pants, stomped into his boots, and buttoned his shirt. He strapped his gun belt and holster in place and sleeved into his sheepskin coat.

"Coffee will be ready in a bit," Roy Self, the foreman said, as Cody walked over.

"I'm obliged, but Miss Juliana asked me to breakfast."

"I hear she sets a good table. Storm blew itself out. Looks to be clearing off."

"Good. Maybe I can head back to town today."

"Doubt that. Some drifts are waist deep. Might want to wait another day. Looks like the sun's coming out, maybe it'll melt some of this stuff off."

"Might be right," Cody said, clamping his hat in place and turning for the door.

"Miss Juliana's a fine woman," Roy added. "She's been through a lot lately."

Cody swung a look over his shoulder at the foreman. *Was there a hidden meaning in the foreman's words?* Cody wondered.

"Yeah, she has. I figure she needs all her friends more than ever right now."

The foreman was right. The snow was hip-high as he trudged his way to the main house. He climbed the steps and knocked on the front door. Juliana opened the door and greeted him with a wide smile that sure looked good on her.

"Good morning," she said, stepping aside to allow him entry. "I've been up for an hour waiting on you. Coffee's hot and breakfast is almost ready."

"You're mighty chirpy this morning," Cody told her, as she closed the door.

"Mother use to say, *no use crying over spilt milk.* So, I decided last night, what's done is done and there isn't a thing I can do to undo it. Starting today, I'm going to be a happy person."

"I figured you were always a happy person," Cody said, as they made their way to the dining room.

"I usually am, but so much has happened in such a short time, it just threw me for a loop. But I'm okay now. You are looking at the *new me.*"

"I kinda liked the *old you,* too."

Juliana stopped and looked at him for a long moment. "Did you? Like me, I mean?"

Cody swallowed, and then swallowed again, searching for the right words.

"I kinda figured you could tell."

She laughed happily. "I could. But a girl needs to hear it said sometimes. Just sit yourself down and I'll pour some coffee to keep you occupied while I get breakfast on the table."

Cody removed his hat and hung it on the back of his chair. He sipped the hot coffee she poured him and looked around the room. It was nicely furnished. A large rich looking buffet sat against one wall.

A tall, glass-fronted china cabinet sat against another wall. It was filled with expensive dishes. Two large, upholstered chairs occupied the third wall. Pictures of floral arrangements hung on the walls.

It was the fanciest house he had ever been in.

Juliana finally finished bringing food from the kitchen and sat down directly across the table from him.

"Well, that's all of it," she laughed, as Cody sat motionless, making no move to fill his plate. "You'll have to make do with what's on the table."

He grinned, felt a little embarrassed, and glanced quickly at the platter full of eggs, cured ham, and hot biscuits.

"Your foreman was right. He said you set a good table."

"Don't know how he'd know. You're the only man I've ever invited to breakfast."

"Reckon that makes me special, then."

"Yes, it does. You *are* special."

Cody felt his face flush hot. He dropped his head and forked some egg to his mouth so he wouldn't have to reply. He couldn't reply.

Regis Maxwell and Wally Fletcher climbed into the stagecoach. The two Pinkerton agents were the only passengers.

"Be glad to get back to Denver," Fletcher said, putting fire to the long cigar between his lips. "This was a wasted trip."

His companion was silent. He sat staring out the window at the storekeeper standing on the boardwalk in front of his store. As he looked he saw the judge, O. J. Goodson, walk up. They said something to each other and looked toward the stagecoach.

"I ain't so sure," Maxwell said.

"What'cha mean?"

"Didn't it seem like they tried a little *too* hard to convince us the Hondo Kid was killed in that fight?"

"Not to me. They gave us everything we asked for."

"Yeah, but something just doesn't feel right."

"Don't go looking for trouble. We talked to a dozen or more witnesses that saw it. We got a sworn affidavit from the judge and undertaker. His horse was right there in the stable. His belongings were still in his room at the boarding house. They showed us his grave. What more could you want?"

"Guess you're right. Still..."

His words were drowned out by the stage driver's shout to his four horses.

"Hee-yaw! Get up in there!"

The stagecoach jerked into motion and rolled up the snowy street. Trinidad was quickly left behind.

Chapter VI

Juliana convinced Cody to stay at the ranch two more days. It didn't take much convincing. Besides, he reasoned, *the snow is still pretty deep.* During that two days Cody and Juliana drew closer and closer.

They spent long hours talking, laughing, going on long walks in the snow, and even made a snowman with a corncob pipe. They were on one of those long walks in the snow and Juliana walked backwards in front of Cody.

"I know what let's do," Juliana said excitedly. "Let's make some snow ice cream."

"I've never had snow ice cream before," Cody told her. "We didn't have snow where I grew up."

"You've never had snow ice cream? Your education is seriously lacking, *Mr. Hondo Kid.*"

"It's Cody."

Juliana wrinkled her forehead in a questioning look. "What?"

"My name's Cody. Cody Cordell."

"I don't understand," she said.

They stopped. Cody took both of her hands in his. He looked deep into her eyes and swallowed.

"Only one other person in the whole world knows my real name. It's a long story, but I want you to know the truth. You deserve to know."

He began with the slaughter of his parents. He told of burying them and his trek through the desert. He told about finding *El Diablo* and living in the cave with him for a year, about learning to use a gun, and about all the gunfights he had survived.

Sometime during the telling, they began walking slowly. Juliana listened silently. Cody related his whole story, leaving nothing out.

"It started when I told that liveryman in San Antonio my name was the Hondo Kid. I was afraid I might get in trouble for killing those three Indians and taking their horses.

"As I traveled around, there were more gunfights. Like I said before, I never killed anybody who wasn't trying to kill me, but sometimes, folks see things differently. I was afraid the law might be looking for me, so I just kept using the Hondo Kid name.

"I know the Pinkerton's are on my trail. I don't know why, but they've been asking about me in several places I've been. That's one of the reasons I came to Trinidad. I figured nobody would find me way up here.

"I like it here, especially now that I've met you. I hope I can stay here forever, but sooner or later somebody is gonna hear about the shootout, or some gun fighter is gonna stumble into me. When that happens, bad as I hate to, I'll have to move on."

"Cody." She said the name slowly, as if she hadn't heard a word he said and as if she was trying it out on her tongue. "Cody Cordell. Yes, the name fits you. I like it."

"It feels good, you knowing my real name, I mean. I've wanted to tell you since the first time I met you, and I've felt guilty because I hadn't. Can I ask you something?"

"Of course. You can ask me anything."

"Does it make a difference in the way you feel about me?"

"Why should it? You're the same person, just a different name, that's all."

Cody breathed a long sigh of relief.

"Come on, let's go make that snow ice cream," Juliana said, turning and racing ahead of him.

Ed Hamilton and Doctor Goodson watched the stage roll out of Trinidad and disappear from sight.

"Think they bought our story?" Goodson asked.

"Not sure the one called Maxwell did, the other one swallowed it hook, line, and sinker."

"It was hard to keep a straight face when they was looking at that grave we told them was his, and then Miss Molly showed up and put those home-made flowers on it. I thought she was gonna cry."

They both chuckled.

"Whose grave was that anyway?"

"Just one of them fellows we killed in the raid. I slipped up there and put a marker with the Kid's name on it before we took them to the graveyard. When you reckon the 'Kid will be back from the Higgins Ranch?"

Hamilton glanced up at the sky. "Well, since the storm's blowed over and the sun's melting things off, I figure he'll be back any time now."

"Sure would hate to lose him as our marshal. The whole town's taken a liking to him. Think the 'Kid'll stay on since he knows the Pinkertons are after him?"

"Don't know. Doubt it. But I figure he already knew they were looking for him. Most likely the reason he came here, thinking he could shake them off his trail."

Cody drove into Trinidad just shy of noon. He pulled the buggy to a stop in front of the undertaker's office. Goodson came out to meet him. Ed Hamilton hurried up as Cody was climbing down from the buggy.

"Who you got in the coffin?" Hamilton asked.

"It's that fellow from the raid that got away. He showed up at the Higgins Ranch. Tried to kill Juliana. She shot him."

"Is she all right? Was she hurt?"

"She's fine. I got snowed in. Took me longer than I thought."

"No use unloading him here," the undertaker said. "I'll have somebody pull the buggy on up to the graveyard."

"We had some visitors come to town while you were gone," Hamilton told Cody. "Couple of Pinkerton men from Denver."

Cody's head jerked around. "What'd they want?"

"Said they heard about the big shoot-out way up in Denver. They heard you was our town marshal. They come looking for you."

"Don't know why the Pinkertons would be looking for me. Did they say?"

"Nope, didn't say. But you might not have to worry about them no more."

"Oh? How come?"

"They think you're dead. We told them you were killed in the big shoot-out. The whole town swore to it. You've even got a grave up yonder in the cemetery with a marker and everything."

Cody was dumbfounded. *Why would the Pinkertons be looking for me? Must be something to do with one of my gunfights. Maybe another rich pappy out for revenge like the one in Missouri. One thing for sure, I can't let them catch me. I'd end up swinging from a tree or spending the rest of my life rotting in a prison somewhere.*

Maybe the Pinkertons will give up now that the townsfolk did what they did for me. Sure was nice of them trying to throw the Pinkertons off my trail like that.

I like it here. I was hoping maybe I could settle down. These are nice folks. Fact is, I like Juliana; I like her a lot. I hate to go, but it'd be best. I don't want to cause these folks any more trouble.

"Mr. Hamilton, you folks have been mighty good to me. I'm obliged for what you all tried to do. I don't know why the Pinkertons are hunting me and that's the gospel truth, but I reckon it's time for me to move on."

"We was afraid you'd say that. Sure hate to see you go, 'Kid, but I reckon a man's gotta do what a man's gotta do. When you figure on pulling out?"

"Right away, I reckon. Them Pinkerton fellows might have a change of heart and come back. There'd likely be trouble. Lord knows you folk've had more'n your share of that already. I wouldn't want to bring more on you."

"Well, just remember, you've always got a place here if you change your mind."

The goodbyes took awhile. Miss Molly cried and nearly smothered Cody with a bear hug. The townsfolk lined the boardwalk as Cody rode slowly up the street, followed closely by his packhorse on a lead line.

He nodded acknowledgements to the waves and touched the brim of his hat to the ladies. A huge knot lodged in his throat that no amount of swallowing dislodged.

Seems like I'm always saying goodbye.

El Diablo warned me it would be this way, though. He tried to tell me the life of a gunfighter was the loneliest life a fellow could choose—always on the move—always looking over your shoulder. But it's the life I chose. Now I reckon I have to live with it or die with it.

For three years I've carried my whole life in my saddlebags. Reckon I best get used to it.

I've got to tell Juliana what's happened. I've got to tell her goodbye. This will be the hardest goodbye I've ever had to say.

He pushed up a long sigh from deep inside and pointed Cincinnati's nose toward the Higgins Ranch.

Juliana and Roy Self stood in the runway of one of their big barns watching some of the hands fill wagonloads of loose hay.

"Think we'll have enough hay to last us through the winter, Roy?"

"Believe so. We laid in extra last summer in case we had a bad winter. We'll need more feed, though. I'll send some wagons into town in a day or two."

"I've been thinking about what you said we ought to do, about buying up cattle from some of the smaller ranches. Do we have enough hay to winter a larger herd?"

"Yes, ma'am. I figure we could handle another five hundred head or so without much problem."

"Where would you start to look?"

"Last time I was in town, I was talking with Mr. Hamilton at the store. He mentioned Ben Oliver was having trouble wintering his herd. He's got a small place about forty miles south. Don't know for shore, but I figure he runs a couple hundred head or so."

"Why don't you ride down and talk to Mr. Oliver. See if he'd be interested in selling and how much he'd want for his herd."

"Yes, ma'am. I could ask around, too. When the word gets out you're buying, I figure they'll be lining up to sell."

"Rider coming in," somebody hollered.

Juliana shielded her eyes with a hand and swung a look toward the west. Her heart skipped a few beats. It was Cody. Excitement surged through her, followed closely by a fluttering question.

Is something wrong? Why would he be back so soon, and with a packhorse loaded with trail supplies?

She ran to meet him.

Cody must have seen her coming. He reined to a stop and stepped to the ground. Juliana saw a worrisome look on his face.

"Is something wrong?" she asked anxiously.

Cody nodded.

"Could we talk? Just the two of us, I mean. Some place private."

"Of course. Come on up to the house. What is it? What's wrong?"

They walked side by side to the house. Cody didn't answer her question until they were seated in the den in front of a roaring fire.

"It's the Pinkertons. They showed up in Trinidad just like I was afraid they would. They heard about the raid and that I was the town marshal. They came looking for me.

"The folks in town made up this story that I was killed in the raid. They even fixed a marker on a grave and told them it was mine. The whole town swore to it."

"Do you think they believed it? Are they still in town?"

"No, they left town. Mr. Hamilton thinks one of them believed the story, but he said the other one seemed to have some doubts. Anyway, I figured there was a chance they might come back so it'd be best if I moved on."

Juliana felt a wave of disappointment sweep through her.

"You mean you're leaving Colorado, or just Trinidad?"

"Colorado. I've got to find out why the Pinkertons are looking for me. Got some other things I've got to get cleared up, too."

"Stay here. They'd never think of looking for you here on the ranch."

"I couldn't do that. It wouldn't look right. Besides, sooner or later word would leak out and they'd come looking, them or some gunfighter looking to build his reputation."

Juliana was on the edge of panic.

"But you can't leave now," she almost pleaded, forcing the words past the knot in her throat.

Unwelcome tears breached her eyelids and coursed down her cheeks. She swiped them away with the back of her hand and choked back a sob.

Cody took her in his arms and gathered her to him. She folded against his strong shoulder and pressed her face against his chest.

Neither spoke. For a long space of time they held one another. Juliana tingled from his nearness. Color warmed her cheeks. Her heartbeat flickered and picked up speed.

Again, silence fell. She felt her stomach flutter. Her hands went damp. She knew what she wanted to say, but didn't know if she had the nerve to say it. She lifted her face and gazed deep into his eyes.

She saw weariness on his face, a look of one who was very much alone and lonely.

Juliana felt a boldness born of desperation. She wanted to reach out to him. She wanted to soothe away the tension gathered between his eyes, the loneliness she sensed at the core of his being even now. She wanted to find a way to make him whole. She knew it was dangerous; she would have to risk emotions she had never felt before.

I can't lose him. I won't.

"Cody, I'm afraid. My heart wants to believe you will come back, but reason tells me if you leave now I may never see you again. I couldn't stand that. I don't want to lose you.

"For perhaps the first time in my life I understand how fragile and precious every moment is. Cody, you have brought joy back into my life. You have given me something back I thought was lost forever.

"I love you, Cody. There was a time not long ago when I would have never thought of saying those words, but you've proved in a hundred ways what a good and honorable man you are. I've finally realized that life must be lived to make dreams come true."

She saw his face soften, saw the sudden look of hope in his eyes, saw the tension melt away like snow under a warm sun.

His hand reached her face. His knuckles grazed her cheek, and with that simple touch, unfamiliar longings rose full and warm in her stomach and raced through her like a runaway train. She caught her breath at the suddenness. Barely breathing, she lifted her lips to meet his, taking his wide, warm mouth with her own.

Chapter VII

Buck was taking little Cody for their morning walk when the bell sounded announcing an arrival. He swung a look and immediately recognized Mel Sloan, the Pinkerton agent from San Antonio.

Sloan reined his horse to a stop and stepped from the saddle, but not before Buck saw the look on the Pinkerton agent's face.

"Morning, Mr. Cordell."

"Mr. Sloan. I hope that look on your face don't mean what I think it means."

Sloan dropped his head and fiddled with the reins in his hand a long moment before answering.

"Afraid I got bad news, Buck."

"Let's hear it."

"Well, like I told you earlier, we got word about a big shootout in a little one-horse town called Trinidad, Colorado. Seemed the town marshal was a young fellow who called himself the Hondo Kid.

"I sent two of my agents from Denver to investigate. I just heard from them. Seems this town marshal killed the son of a local rancher that throws a wide loop in that part of Colorado. He hired twenty men to get revenge by burning the town and killing everybody in it.

"Word is the folks in Trinidad couldn't find the backbone to defend their own town or families, so the Hondo Kid was gonna take the whole gang on all by himself. He planted himself in the middle of the street with two shotguns and faced them head on.

"The townsfolk finally found nerve enough to help him. But not before the raiders had cut him down. According to the undertaker, he had more bullet holes in him than a watering trough on Saturday night.

"My agents saw his grave and got sworn affidavits from the undertaker and the head of the town council. He's a local hero. They're talking about erecting a statue in his honor. I'm sorry. Buck, but I'm afraid your brother is dead."

Buck felt like he had been kicked in the stomach by a mule. He gulped a breath of air. His face lifted toward the sky. His eyes slammed shut. He felt like part of his heart had just been ripped from his chest.

For a long moment he couldn't move. Memories flooded his mind: memories of a small, tow-headed boy following in the furrow as Buck plowed the field and how Cody's small legs struggled to keep up.

He remembered the times he took his little brother hunting and how excited Cody was when he killed his first turkey. All these memories, and more, flashed through his mind like a lightning bolt.

"Papa. What's wrong, Papa?" A small, sad voice broke through his thinking. "Papa, why are you crying?"

Little Cody's concerned questions and the small hand jerking on Buck's pants leg brought him back to the present.

Reaching down, he lifted his son into his arms and held him close.

I wanted so much for my son to get to know my brother. Now he's gone. My whole family is gone. Why couldn't I have found him before...?

Mel Sloan's words scattered Buck's thoughts.

"Buck, I'm sorry. We did everything we could to find your brother."

"I know. It's not your fault. I'm obliged for you riding down to tell me personally."

The Pinkerton agent toed a stirrup and swung into his saddle.

"Next time you're in San Antonio, stop in and say howdy."

"I will."

Sloan reined his mount around and rode through the gate. Buck turned and walked slowly toward the house. He dreaded having to tell Rebekah.

One look at Buck's face when he walked into the house told Rebekah something terrible had happened.

"Mommy, Papa was crying," little Cody announced, concern still evident in his small voice.

"Buck, what's wrong? What's happened?"

Buck had to clear his throat twice before he could squeeze the words past the knot in his throat.

"Mr. Sloan, the Pinkerton agent, just left. He..." Buck choked up and couldn't finish.

"Oh, no." Rebekah said. "Cody?"

Buck nodded slowly.

"Oh, Buck, I'm so sorry. Where? How?"

It took a minute before he could continue.

"Little town up in Colorado. He was the town marshal. He was killed defending the town folk from some hired killers that was gonna burn the town and kill everybody in it."

Rebekah stepped to him and hugged him close. Buck's voice frayed and his tears wet her shoulder as he wept silently.

"I know how bad you wanted to find him, wanted to see him again."

"Maybe if I'd been here. Maybe if I hadn't gone off to the war. Maybe none of this would have happened."

"Buck, you can't blame yourself. You did what you thought you had to do at the time. How many times have you told me *what's done is done, you can't undo it?*"

"I know."

He looked down at little Cody. The boy clung tightly to Buck's shirt and shifted his concerned gaze back and forth between Rebekah and Buck. For a fleeting moment, Buck saw the echo of his small brother from years past: the same wheaten hair, the same pale blue eyes, the same stubborn stamp to his jaw, even the beginning of that powerful broadshoulder build that Cody had.

"I'll be okay. I just need some time to think. I'm gonna take a ride. I won't be long."

Buck hugged Rebekah and mussed Cody's hair before turning and walking from the room. He walked to the stable, saddled his black gelding, and toed a stirrup.

He was vaguely aware of the ranch hands' nodded greetings as he rode from the ranch compound. He rode slowly, his mind a swirl of troubled thoughts.

The age-old question that always haunts those who lose loved ones flashed again and again through his mind.

Why?

Time and miles crawled by. Without even realizing it, Buck found himself sitting on top of the flat butte overlooking the Sycamore River valley, the same spot where he, Chester, and their old friend, Eli Hoyt, had first glimpsed their new land.

Buck slowly swung a leg over the saddle and stepped to the ground. He ground hitched the gelding and chose a rock overlooking the vast river valley and sat down. For a long while he stared with unseeing eyes at the valley below. His mind struggled with a hopeless maze of thoughts and grief. An overwhelming feeling of guilt gnawed at his soul. Time stretched.

The sun slid slowly on a downward arch toward a destiny with the western horizon.

My brother's gone. Nothing I can do's gonna change that. But I won't allow his memory to die. It will live on in my heart, right alongside Ma and Pa, just like they were right here with me.

I've been lucky. By everything that's fair and right, I ought to be lying in a shallow grave somewhere in Virginia right alongside hundreds of my fellow soldiers. Still can't figure out why the good Lord took all my family and saw fit to spare me.

Don't reckon I believe in all that talk about reincarnation, but who knows, maybe the big man upstairs gave me little Cody to take the place of my brother. Now I've got a family of my own. I've got to get hold of myself and look after them.

With that firmly settled in his mind, Buck swung into the saddle and pointed the black gelding's nose back toward the ranch and to his family.

CHAPTER VIII

Three weeks passed. It was the best three weeks of Cody's life. During the day he worked alongside Roy Self, the Higgins Ranch foreman, and the rest of the ranch hands, but come sundown, Juliana always had supper waiting.

After supper they spent hours sitting in front of the fireplace talking, laughing, and eating popcorn. The hardest part of the day was saying goodnight before Cody headed for the bunkhouse.

One night as they sat in front of the fire, Juliana asked Cody what he thought of the ranch.

"You've got a good spread here," he told her. "Lots of grazing land and plenty of water. It's no wonder your cattle are doing so good."

"Roy thinks we ought to be running more cattle than we are. What do you think?"

"Well, you could handle more than you got, that's for sure."

"Let me ask you. If this was your ranch, what would you do that we aren't doing?"

Cody thought for a long moment before answering.

"Well, for starters, I'd separate the herds into two groups. One herd with nothing except the older stuff and one as a brood herd. I'd think about getting some better bulls and upgrade the brood herd and, come spring, sell off all your cows over four years old. Just my opinion, mind you, but you've got too many cows that ain't producing for you.

"I've heard the cattle buyers are getting more particular. Time not long ago when they'd buy most anything that could walk, but that's changing. The big Texas ranchers are bringing larger and larger herds to market and as the supply gets saturated, the buyers are getting more selective. Won't be long until they'll be contracting for only the best and paying higher prices for 'em. When that happens the regular run-of-the-mill cattle won't sell at any price. Everybody's gonna have to upgrade their stock. The ones who get the jump on the competition will make the most money."

"Roy suggested buying some cattle from the smaller outfits scattered around and drive them to market in Denver in the springtime. What do you think about that?"

"Roy's a good man. I think he's hit the nail on the head. That would give you the funds to start upgrading your herd, too. But I still think you need a high powered bull or two."

"Where would I get them?"

"They ain't easy to come by and they won't come cheap."

"Nothing worth having comes cheap."

"Reckon that's true. I'll keep my ears open. If I hear of a good bull I'll let you know."

As the days wore on, Cody became more and more uneasy and caught himself looking over his shoulder, sweeping the horizon with a searching gaze, on edge every afternoon as they rode into the ranch yard, watching for strange horses.

He knew he couldn't live this way; it wouldn't be fair to

either himself or to Juliana. Yet he hated to face what he knew he had to do. He had to move on, couldn't take the chance of involving Juliana in his troubles. He needed to get the thing with the Pinkertons settled.

On top of all that, he was nothing but a man on the run with nothing to offer a lady like Juliana.

He made up his mind and decided this was the night he was going to tell her. He felt nervous. All through supper he picked at his food and stared, absent-minded, at his plate.

"Cody, what's wrong?" Juliana asked, concern thickening her voice. "You've hardly eaten a bite."

"I'm, worried. I need to talk to you."

Her eyebrows slid closer together and wrinkled her forehead.

"What is it? What's wrong? Have I said or done something wrong?"

"No, it's nothing like that. It's just me. I'm afraid the Pinkerton agents are gonna come back looking for me, or some wannabe gunfighter is gonna stumble onto me and I don't want you to be involved.

"Juliana, I don't want to, but I've got to leave, at least until I can get this all straightened out."

The look that swept over her face hurt his heart. She closed her eyes and shook her head from side to side. Tears welled up and breached her eyelids. Her lips quivered.

"But I don't want you to leave," she choked the words out, her voice on the edge of panic. "I want you to stay here with me. You'll be safe here. Stay here and help me run the ranch. Together we could build it into something special. I, I love you, Cody."

Her words shook him to his foundation and swelled his heart. He gathered her into his arms and pulled her close.

"I love you, too. I've never said that to anyone except my ma."

"Then stay with me."

"Nothing in this world would make me happier, but I can't. Not until I've settled. I've done some mighty hard things in my life, Juliana.

"The day I found my folks after the Comanche got through with them was a hard time. Then the day I had to bury them with nothing except my coat to cover them with, that was a real hard time. But the thought of having to leave here, to leave you, is the hardest thing I've ever had to do. "

The drop of her shoulders and the long sigh told him she had resigned herself to his leaving.

"Will you come back?" she asked with a shaky voice.

"I'll be back. That's a promise. You can count on it."

"And I promise I'll be here waiting for you. No matter where you are, just remember I'll be here waiting for you. When will you leave?"

"Come first light."

As the gray of dawn seeped over the horizon and pushed back the darkness, Cody led Cincinnati and his loaded packhorse up to the main house. He looped the reins over the hitching rail and climbed the steps. The front door suddenly opened and Juliana stood there.

She wore a light blue robe tied at the waist over a snow-white nightgown. Her long hair was fresh-brushed and her eyes were red from crying. She forced a thin smile.

No longer able to hold back the reservoir of tears, she rushed into his arms as the dam broke and allowed the pent up tears to burst forth.

"I'm so scared," she said through the sobs. "I don't want to lose you."

"I'll be back," he finally managed to squeeze past the knot in his throat.

Cody relived that goodbye over and over for the next two weeks as the miles passed under Cincinnati's hooves. At night he camped beside a mountain stream and spent hours staring into the campfire and poking it idly with a stick.

As far as the Pinkertons know, the Hondo Kid is dead and buried. Maybe it's time I buried him, too. Why can't I? What's to keep me from becoming who I really am, Cody Cordell?

I could cut my hair, get rid of my serape, and I've still got that gun rig I took off that gunfighter back in Las Cruces. I could replace my belly holster with that one. That ought to change my looks enough so I wouldn't be recognized.

He nodded to himself and pulled the holster and gun belt from his saddlebags. He inspected the Remington and worked the hammer a few times.

With some practice, this might fill the bill.

He strapped the gun belt around his waist and tied the holster to his leg. For the next hour he practiced drawing the heavy .44 weapon. At first it felt awkward compared to his Colt, but after a while it began to feel more comfortable.

Cody followed the Arkansas River for weeks, finally arriving at newly established Fort Dodge, Kansas. The fort hugged the north bank of the river and was built in the shape of a horseshoe. The soldiers' quarters were nothing more than holes dug into the twelve-foot bank of the river. It seemed to Cody to be a mighty sorry excuse for a fort and he didn't linger long. He was able to replenish his trail supplies from the small store, get a haircut, and have both horses re-shod before moving on. It was early March, 1869.

From Fort Dodge, Cody swung southeast into the badlands of Oklahoma Territory. He hadn't traveled an hour before he saw two hard looking hombres sitting their horses in the middle of the trail up ahead. Cody figured them for highwaymen waiting for a victim to happen by to rob. He thumbed the traveling loop off the hammer of his Remington. The two men eyed him as he approached.

Both were filthy and unkempt. Their full beards were matted with tobacco stains. As bad as the men looked, the horses they rode looked worse. Both were slat-ribbed and looked half starved.

"Where you be headed, sonny?" one of the men questioned.

"Yonder-way," Cody replied, pointing south with the flat of his hand before allowing it to rest on his leg, only inches from his holstered gun.

"This here land belongs to me and my brother. We don't let strangers pass through without paying. You got money to pay, sonny?"

"It's a free country. I travel where I want."

"Not without paying, you don't. The way I figure it, those two horses ought to jest about cover what you owe us. We'll strike a trade. Your two horses fer ours and you can go your way."

Cody nailed the two men with a look. He knew what was coming.

"And if I don't?"

Both men went for their guns. The second fellow was a mite slower than the one doing the talking. Cody shot the talker first. His two heavy .44 slugs knocked the man over backwards out of the saddle. He swung the nose of his Remington toward the second robber. The second man was slower than molasses. His gun was just clearing leather.

"Drop it or die." Cody ordered.

The man dropped it and raised his hands shoulder high. He sat wide-eyed and open mouthed as if he expected a bullet to tear into him the next instant.

"You fellows live around here?" Cody asked.

The man pointed with a nod of his head toward the west.

"We've got a dugout a few miles over that-a-way."

"Climb down and shuck your boots and start walking. Looks like you could use the exercise."

"But, but I can't walk that far barefooted."

"Not my problem. Now move before I just go ahead and shoot you."

As the man tip-toed away barefooted, Cody gathered up their weapons, shoved them into one of their saddlebags, and tied the reins of their horses to the tail of his packhorse.

Buck buried himself in the busy activities of getting the first herds ready for their long trek to Abilene, Kansas. Every hand on the Longhorn Ranch worked from dark till dark. The hard work kept Buck's mind occupied and, for a time at least, off the loss of his brother.

"Looks like things are coming together pretty good," Chester said, as he and Buck rode together to check on the first herd that was scheduled to pull out in two days.

"Yep," Buck replied.

"When you leaving for Austin?"

"Week from today."

"Sure wish I could go with the trail herds," Chester said, "but my life wouldn't be worth a plug nickel if I wasn't here when the baby comes."

"How's Selena doing?"

"She's fine. If it weren't for her paunchy stomach you'd never know she was expecting. Been meaning to ask you. You thought any more about what we need to do about *El Toro*?"

"Yeah, been thinking about it. What would you think about hobbling him? It would let him move around, but wouldn't let him get out of control and charge whoever ventures into the corral with him."

Chester nodded his head slowly as he considered the suggestion.

"Might work. Just might work. I'll get one of the boys to put together a heavy-duty set of hobbles and put them on him. Our cows we bred to him ought to be dropping another calf crop any day now."

"How's our new sales program coming along?" Buck asked.

"We've got twenty-one of his calves from two years ago ready to sell this spring. We offer them for sale when they reach fertility at eighteen months."

"What'll they bringing us?"

"Five thousand apiece and we've got buyers standing in line for them. We're getting contacts from ranchers all over the country."

"Sounds like *El Toro's* gonna make us some money."

"You can say that again. That big bull is worth his weight in gold."

It's a long ride from Colorado to Waco, Texas, Cody thought, as he stepped stiffly from the saddle in front of the Waco Café.

He looped Cincinnati's reins around the hitching rail and

stomped the stiffness from his legs as he glanced up and down the dusty street. He didn't see any visible changes; the town looked just like it did when he rode out of it. He used his hat to brush dust from his long duster and stepped up on the boardwalk.

Ellen Richardson had a line of plates full of food balanced on her left arm when Cody stepped through the door. She swung a glance. She stopped and stared for a minute or two before her eyes went wide. A large smile split her lips and she come near dropping the plates.

"Well, look what the cat dragged in," she exclaimed happily. "I almost didn't know you. Have a seat if you can find one, 'Kid, I'll be right with you."

"Take your time," Cody replied, spotting an empty table and heading toward it.

As quickly as Ellen could set the food in front of her patrons she hurried toward Cody. He stood and opened his arms. Ellen filled them. They hugged for a long moment.

"It's so good to see you," she said softly, lifting her face to look deep into his eyes.

"It's good to see you, too."

"I was beginning to think you was never coming back. Are you here to stay?"

Cody shook his head.

"No, just got lonesome to see you."

"Well, now, that's encouraging. Let me look at you. You're all grown up. You've changed. You look so different. You left a boy and came back a full grown man."

"I've ridden a lot of miles since I saw you. Seen anything of the marshal lately?"

"Yes, he was in for lunch and just left a few minutes ago. He'll be anxious to see you.

"Wish I had more time to visit with you, 'Kid, but I've

got customers waiting on their food. Will you be around for supper? I'm having your favorite, fried chicken."

"Wouldn't miss it."

Cody pushed up from the table and left the café. He left his horses where they were and walked across the street to the marshal's office.

Marshal Henry Bell looked up from some wanted posters when Cody pushed open the door. For a long moment he stared, apparently not recognizing Cody right off.

"Well, lookee here," the marshal said, jumping from his chair and grabbing Cody's outstretched hand. "How are you, 'Kid?"

"I'm fine, Marshal. Just fine. Come to ask a favor."

"If it ain't against the law, I'll shore try my best to do it."

Marshal Bell folded into his chair and motioned Cody toward another. "What can I do for you?"

"The Pinkerton agents have been dogging my trail lately. Don't know why. Can't think of anything I've done to cause them to be looking for me, but I need to find out for sure. I'm trying to start a new life and I need to get whatever this is about straightened out. Is there some way you could find out why they're trailing me?"

Marshal Bell rubbed his chin in thought. Finally, he nodded. "I know a fellow who use to work for the Pinkertons. Let me see if I can locate him and see what I can find out. You gonna be in town awhile?"

"I'm gonna ride out to the Brazos River Ranch and visit with the boys, but I'll be back in a day or two."

"There's been a half-dozen or more gun slicks through here off and on looking for you. Most of them two-bit wannabe gunfighters, but a couple big names came by, too. You remember Vance Longley, the gunfighter I chased outta town before you left?"

"Yeah, I remember."

"He rides through real regular looking for you. Said he's got a score to settle with you and wouldn't stop looking till he finds you, so watch your back trail. He's a dangerous fellow. Maybe one of the best gunfighters I've ever seen. I'll send my friend a telegram and see what he can find out."

"I'd be much obliged."

"Where you been keeping yourself?"

"Oh, here and there. Spent some time as marshal in a little town called Trinidad, Colorado. The Hondo Kid was killed there in a big shootout."

The marshal's forehead wrinkled. "Can't say I understand. What you mean, you was killed?"

Cody spent the next half hour telling the story. When the telling was over, Marshal Bell shook his head in wonder.

"So then, what do I call you now?"

"My *real* name is Cody Cordell. Always has been."

"I see. Well, that could be a good thing. You've wanted to shake the gunfighter image for a while, maybe this is a way to do it. Ain't likely anybody's gonna recognize you without that belly holster rig and the serape. I didn't know you myself for a minute there."

"I'm hoping so."

"Me, too, son. Me, too. Ain't no wanted fliers come across my desk for you, leastwise not in Texas. I don't always get the ones from other states."

"I'll stop by in a day or two," Cody said, pushing to his feet.

"Do that. I'll try to have something for you."

Cody saw to his horses and spent most of the afternoon in the bathtub down at the local barbershop. He got himself a haircut and bought a change of clothes. His others were trail-worn and about used up. He felt like a new man when he stepped through the door of Miss Ellen's café.

"Well, would you look at you," she exclaimed. "Don't you look handsome."

"Don't know about that, but I sure do feel better."

Ellen poured them both a cup of coffee and sat down at the table with him. It was too early for supper and there were no other customers in the room.

"I've thought a lot about you and wondered where you were," she said, staring down into her coffee cup. "I was hoping you'd come back to stay."

"I've been up in Colorado. I was the town marshal there for awhile."

"You going back there?"

Cody nodded his head.

"You met someone there, didn't you?"

Again he nodded.

"I was afraid of that. Tell me about her. She must be something special."

Cody nodded. "Yeah, she is. I love her, Miss Ellen. Soon as I get some things straightened out I'm gonna ask her to marry me, if she'll have me."

"Oh, she'll have you, sure enough. What girl in her right mind wouldn't?"

"Something else I need to tell you. My real name is Cody. Cody Cordell. Some Indians killed my friend and I killed them and sold their horses. I was afraid to use my real name, so I told the liveryman my name was the Hondo Kid because I was from Hondo, Texas.

"As time went on, I just kept using it. The townsfolk in Trinidad, Colorado, where I was the town marshal, made up this story that I was killed in a big raid and told it to some

Pinkerton agents who came looking for me. They even had a grave with my name on it and everything.

"I figured this would be a good time to bury the Hondo Kid forever, so I changed the way I looked, best I could anyway. That's why I look different."

"Why were the Pinkerton agents looking for you?"

"That's the thing about it. I haven't figured that out yet. Marshal Bell knows somebody who use to work for them. He's trying to get hold of his friend now and see what he can find out. He says there ain't no wanted posters, so far as he can tell.

"That's one reason I came back here. I've got to get all this straightened out before I can really bury the Hondo Kid and start a new life as who I really am."

"Is there anything I can do to help?"

"I'm obliged, Miss Ellen, but just being my friend is the most important thing you can do right now."

"I'll always be your friend, Cody."

The Brazos River Ranch hadn't changed a bit. As Cody reined his pinto up into the yard several of his old friends were loading hay into a wagon. His friend Lefty was there. They all stopped working and leaned on their pitchforks as they stared at him with blank expressions.

Sudden recognition swept across Lefty's face and he broke into a wide grin.

"Well, I'll be a monkey's uncle," Lefty said, hopping down from the wagon and hurrying to meet his friend.

Cody stepped from his saddle and met Lefty's outstretched hand with his own in a firm handshake.

"Howdy, Lefty. Howdy, boys," Cody greeted. "Good to see you again."

"Well, it's shore-nuff you, all right," Lefty said. "But I didn't recognize you at first. You don't look the same. Your pinto gave you away."

"Been a lot of miles since I left here; they tend to do that to a fellow."

"You come looking for a job?" Lefty asked hopefully. "Bet you could have your old one back."

"No, but I'd like to see Del, if he's still the foreman here."

"Course he's still the foreman. This ranch couldn't operate without him. He rode out to the east range, but he ought'a be back any time now."

"You boys go ahead with your work, don't mind me. I'll just hang around and watch you. Be good to see you boys do some work for a change."

That brought some laughter and funning comments from the hands.

Del Horton rode up on his buckskin and reined to a stop near the corral. Cody walked over as the big foreman swung to the ground.

"Howdy, Del."

"Should I know you? Well, if it ain't the Hondo Kid. How are you, 'Kid?"

"I'm fine, sir."

"Hope you had a change of heart and come to get your old job back?"

"Well, no, sir. Just passing through and thought I'd stop and say howdy. Got to be moving on in a day or two."

"Still chasing that rainbow?"

"Something like that. Reckon we could talk over a cup of coffee?"

"Sure as shootin'. Let's walk up to the chow hall. Bet old Swede's still got some coffee left."

It took two cups of coffee and an hour for Cody to relate the events in Trinidad. Del listened intently, nodding his head often.

"So you're trying to bury the old life and start a new one?"

"Yes, sir. That's what I'm hoping."

"Well, it won't be easy, but if anybody can do it, you can."

"A friend of mine up in Colorado is wanting to upgrade their herd. They need a high-powered bull or two. Know where they might find one?"

"Matter of fact, I might. The boss was telling me just last week about this outfit down on the Rio Grande that's got this monster longhorn bull. They say this critter's more'n twice the size of a normal bull. They're selling his offspring. We're thinking about buying a couple of them ourselves. Might be something you'd want to look into."

"How much they asking?"

"Five thousand apiece."

"Boy! They're sure proud of them, ain't they?"

"Yeah, but they ain't having no trouble selling them. I hear the King Ranch is buying all they can get their hands on."

"What's the name of this outfit?"

"The Longhorn Ranch. It's just downriver from Del Rio, Texas where the Sycamore River joins the Rio Grande."

"Who owns it?"

"The boss didn't say."

"I'm obliged, Mr. Horton. Mind if I hang around a day or two and visit with the boys?"

"Be glad to have you. Stay as long as you want."

Chapter IX

Juliana felt devastated when Cody rode away. She thought she had found the one man in the entire world she wanted to spend the rest of her life with.

Now he was gone and half her heart went with him. She didn't know when, or even *if,* she would ever see him again. But instead of moping around, she threw herself into her work. She was determined to build the ranch into something both she, and hopefully one day, Cody could be proud of.

Her first priority was riding down to the workers' cabins located about two miles from the main ranch house. She hadn't been there since she returned from school in Denver.

Juliana was shocked at what she saw. The line of small, rundown shacks lined the riverbank. The slat board structures looked as if the smallest puff of wind would flatten them.

Goats and chickens scrounged for food. Women bent over washtubs doing the weekly laundry and small children ran about, seemingly unaware of the squalor they called home.

Women stopped to stare and lift a hand in greeting. Juliana was ashamed.

This is disgraceful, she thought. *I won't have my workers living like this.* She reined her horse around and galloped all the way back to the ranch.

"Hitch up the buckboard," she told the old Mexican stableman. "I'm going into town."

The man nodded his understanding and hurried to comply with her instructions. By the time she returned from the house a few minutes later, the buckboard was hitched to a matching pair of spirited horses and waiting for her.

She propped her loaded rifle against the springboard seat and took up the long reins.

It was mid-afternoon before she reached Trinidad. She was tired after the long drive, but not wanting to waste time, she went directly to Ed Hamilton's Mercantile.

"Afternoon, Miss Juliana," Hamilton greeted with a wide smile. "Haven't seen you in town in awhile."

"No, I've been busy at the ranch. Do you know someone I could hire to build some cabins?"

The storeowner scratched his chin in thought.

"What kind of cabins you got in mind?"

"I was thinking about log cabins. Know anybody like that?"

"Yep, Ian Fritz is your man. He's the best I ever seen, if you can get him. You know him?"

"No, can't say I do. Where could I find him?"

"Him and his two boys live on the south side of Big Piney Mountain, about halfway up. How many cabins you wanting to build?"

"Probably a dozen. They're for my workers."

"I see. I could get Wilbur to ride up and tell Fritz you need to see him. You staying in town tonight?"

"Yes, I'll be over at Molly's."

"Good. I'll ask Wilbur to ride up to the Fritz place and see if he'll come down and talk with you. See anything of Hondo' before he left?"

"Yes, he stopped by and spent a few days."

"He is a good man. Don't reckon we'll find a marshal that good to replace him. Sure hated to see him go."

"Yes, me too. One more thing I need to ask you. You supply most of the feed to the cattlemen in this area, don't you?"

"Only place there is within a hundred miles."

"I'm interested in buying some cattle. Any idea where I might look?"

"That's an easy one. I can think of half-a-dozen small outfits that would jump at the chance to sell their stock to keep from winter-feeding. Go see Cy Johnson. His place is about ten miles east of town. Might want to talk with Merv Gillette, too. He lives out that way."

"Thanks, I will."

From the store, Juliana drove her buggy to Molly's boarding house.

"Land sakes, child, if you ain't a sight for sore eyes. Where you been keeping yourself?" the large woman asked as Juliana walked in. "Me and Mary Ann was just wondering about you yesterday, I think it was. I said to her, 'I wonder why Juliana hasn't been to town lately? It ain't like her not to come in once a month or so.'"

"I've been pretty busy with the ranch and everything. Where is Mary Ann?"

"She's most likely upstairs making beds and cleaning. I tell you, I don't know how I got along without her. Men are the messiest creatures God ever put on the face of the earth. They just drop their dirty clothes where they pull them off and expect somebody to pick up after them. I'm getting too old and stove up to do it anymore. Thank the good Lord, He sent Mary Ann to help me. She's a good worker. And those two little darling children are so precious. I just love them to pieces."

"I think I'll go up and see if I can find her. I need to stay in town tonight. Do you have an extra room?"

"Sure do. The Hondo Kid's room is still empty. You can stay in there. I tell you, I sure miss that boy. Never seen a nicer fellow in all my born days. Still can't figure why those Pinkerton fellows were after him. Can't imagine Hondo' doing anything bad. You see anything of him after he left?"

"Yes, he stopped by and stayed several days," Juliana said, as she headed up the stairs. Molly still didn't stop talking; she just raised her voice higher and higher as Juliana climbed the stairs.

Juliana found Mary Ann making a bed in one of the boarders' rooms. She was dressed in a clean, flowery dress. Her hair was fresh-combed and braided. She smiled broadly as Juliana walked in.

"Hey, how's the little housekeeper?"

They hugged one another.

"How are you?" Juliana asked her friend.

"I'm good. I'm happy. Miss Molly has been so good to me and the kids, like a mother."

"Then I'm happy for you. I came to see if you are ready to come to the ranch and live with me like we talked about before."

"Oh, I couldn't leave Miss Molly now. She needs me. This is our home now. We have a nice room, plenty to eat, and I help with the housework, washing, cooking, and stuff. Besides, there's a man who lives here that really likes me and I like him. His name is Sammy. He's a little older than me, but that's okay. He's very nice."

"I see. Well, as long as you're happy, that's all that matters."

"You staying here tonight?"

"Yes, I'm supposed to meet with a man to see if he could build some log cabins for my workers. Mr. Hamilton is sending Wilbur up the mountain to get him now."

Mary Ann clapped her hands. "Good!" she said excitedly. "I want you to meet Sammy. I just know you'll like him."

"I'll look forward to meeting him."

Juliana followed her friend around as she worked steadily. They laughed and talked girl-talk for the next two hours.

"I've got to go help Molly fix supper," Mary Ann said. "Come on, we can visit in the kitchen."

"If Molly's there, I doubt we'll get much visiting done," Juliana laughed.

"Yeah, she does talk a blue streak, don't she? But I just love her to pieces. I can't wait for you to meet my Sammy."

"Oh? He's already *your* Sammy, huh?"

"Well," her friend giggled. "You know what I mean."

Mary Ann was right. Juliana did like Sammy Schroeder. He was a little shy, but she liked him immediately. He was a big young man, with wide shoulders and blond hair. Sammy was an immigrant from Germany. He spoke very broken English, but Mary Ann said she was teaching him.

Supper at Miss Molly's was a joyous occasion. There was enough food on the table to feed Cox's army. The gold miners who boarded there seemed like a happy lot. They took delight in kidding Sammy constantly about Mary Ann. Of course, Mary Ann loved it. She giggled, dropped her head, and shot quick glances at Sammy.

After supper was over and the dishes were done up, Mary

Ann and Sammy went walking. Juliana stayed with Molly and played with her friend's two small children.

Later, when Juliana blew out the lamp and climbed into bed, her first thought was of Cody. She immediately felt a special closeness to him. She reached a hand and moved it softly over the pillow.

Cody slept right here, in this very bed. He probably laid his head on this pillow. These sheets cuddled his body. A warm sensation surged through her and she snuggled deeper under the covers and dreamed sweet dreams.

They had just finished breakfast and were lingering over a second cup of coffee. The boarders were already on their way to work. A heavy knock on the front door turned their heads.

"Who in the world could that be this early," Molly said.

"I'll get it," Mary Ann offered, jumping up and hurrying toward the front.

Juliana and Molly could hear talking.

"Who is it?" Molly hollered.

"It's someone to see Juliana."

Juliana rose, set the baby in Molly's lap, and walked to the front door. The giant who stood there was fully bearded, wore heavy work clothes and held a floppy black hat in his hands.

"I'm looking for Miss Higgins. I'm Ian Fritz. They said you wanted to see me."

"I'm Juliana Higgins. Come in and have a cup of coffee with us. We can talk there."

The big man reluctantly stepped through the door and followed Juliana down the long hallway into the dining room. Mary Ann poured the man a cup.

"Mr. Hamilton, down at the store, said you were the best cabin builder in these parts. I need some log cabins built for my workers to live in. I own the Higgins Ranch about twenty miles northwest. I wanted to talk with you and see if you would be interested in building them for me?"

"How many you thinking about, missy?"

"At least a dozen, maybe more."

"How big you want 'em?"

"One large room for living, two smaller rooms for sleeping."

The man nodded slowly. "You got plenty of timber nearby?"

"Yes, sir."

"Cost ye three hundred apiece."

"When can you start?"

"Me and my two boys could be there and get started day after tomorrow, if that's soon enough?"

"Agreed," Juliana said, reaching to shake his hand and seal the bargain.

Mr. Fritz swallowed the rest of his coffee with one long gulp, rose, and headed for the front door without another word.

"That sure didn't take long," Mary Ann said, coming in from the kitchen.

"No, he's a man of few words. I've got to drive out to a couple of ranches south of town and see about buying some cattle. I ought to be back before sundown. Tell Molly I'll be staying tonight, too."

"I will. Be careful."

Juliana arrived at the Johnson Ranch just after noon. It was a nice little spread that had obviously been neglected. After she met Cy Johnson, she understood why.

He was about used up. He limped from the barn carrying a hammer and bucket of nails. His snow white hair stuck out from under a worn out hat. He wore bib overalls with one shoulder strap hanging loose. His sun-cooked skin was dry and cracked from years of hard work and wind.

"Are you Mr. Johnson?"

"That's me, what's left of me anyway."

"I'm Juliana Higgins. I've got a ranch twenty miles northwest of Trinidad. I'm interested in buying some cattle. Mr. Hamilton at the store said you might be willing to sell a few head."

"How many head would you be looking for?"

"As many as you're willing to sell."

"I'm all stove up and can't take care of what I got. Had to let all my hands go, so it's just me and the wife and neither one of us is able to do much of anything anymore. I've got a hundred-twenty head, all grass-fed and healthy, far as I know. Feed's so blaming high a man can't afford to winter cattle anymore."

"What would you need to have for the whole herd?"

Johnson studied on the question for a minute.

"Take ten dollars a head."

"Sold. Write me out a bill of sale and have it ready. I'll have my foreman and some of the hands pick them up in a few days. He'll pay you then. Fair enough?"

"Fair enough. Want to come in the house and meet the wife? I 'spect she's still got the coffee pot warming."

"I appreciate it, but I wanted to stop by the Gillette place while I was out this way. Can you tell me how to find it?"

"Just keep on going the way you was. Merv's place is another five miles. You can't miss it."

"Think he might have some cattle to sell?"

"Wouldn't be surprised. He's kinda fallen on hard times lately, too."

"Well, good-day to you, Mr. Johnson."
"Good day to you, too, Miss Higgins."

Juliana saw him when she rounded a curve. He was sitting his horse crosswise in the middle of the road. She immediately judged him to be a saddle tramp and had a bad feeling about him. She reached down and levered a shell into the Henry rifle leaning against the seat within easy reach.

Heavy bushes hugged both sides of the narrow road and there was no way to drive around him. She reined her team to a stop a few feet from the man.

He was dirty, heavily whiskered, and his clothes should have been trashed years ago. He sat staring at her with a look that made Juliana very uneasy.

"Is this the road to Trinidad?" the man asked in a gravelly voice.

"Yes, about twelve miles."

"What's a pretty thing like you doing way out here all by your lonesome?"

"Excuse me, but I'm in a hurry. Would you mind moving your horse?"

"Well, now. That ain't exactly a sociable attitude."

"I don't feel sociable. Now move your horse so I can pass."

Instead, he stepped his horse in front of her team and leaned over to grasp the bridle of one of her horses. While he was distracted, she picked up her rifle and leveled it squarely at the man's chest.

"I asked you nice, now I'm telling you. *Move* your horse!"

"Whoa, I've got myself a real she-cat here. Bet you'd be a real wild one. Why don't you just put that rifle down and lets you and me get to know one another."

"Mister, if you don't think I'll use this, you're making a big mistake. Now ride on while you still can."

"And if I don't, what you gonna do?"

"I'm gonna blow you outta your saddle."

The man stared at her for a long moment. She silently hoped he didn't notice her shaking hands or the quiver in her voice.

Finally, he turned loose of the team's bridle and reined his horse to one side. Juliana popped the reins to her team with one hand and kept the rifle pointed at the man with the other. The buggy pulled alongside him.

"I was just funnin' ye," he said. "No offense intended."

She didn't bother answering, but twisted around in her seat to keep her rifle on him until he disappeared from sight. Only then did she pull her team to a stop and bury her face in her hands.

Would I have killed him? Could I have killed him?

Merv Gillette's ranch was a direct contrast to Cy Johnson's. Juliana was impressed at first sight. The road leading to the main house passed underneath a cross-timber gate with a carved sign identifying the Merv Gillette Ranch.

A large, white, two-story house sat on a hill surrounded by a white picket fence. The barn and corral were well maintained and a large herd of cattle grazing nearby looked fat and healthy. She didn't hold out much hope of these folks wanting to sell their cattle.

A ranch hand near the barn told her the boss was up at the *big house*. Juliana climbed down and walked toward the house. She lifted the latch on the gate in the picket fence and strolled up the path to the front door. It opened immediately to her knock.

A tall lady in a starched gingham dress smiled a welcome.

"Good afternoon, ma'am," Juliana said. "I'm Juliana Higgins. I have a ranch west of Trinidad."

"Welcome to our home, Miss Higgins. I'm Evelyn Gillette. Won't you come in?"

Juliana stepped inside and was ushered into a spacious, well-furnished living room. A distinguished gentleman rose from a sofa.

"This is my husband, Merv Gillette. This is Juliana Higgins."

"Aw, yes, Miss Higgins. I heard about your tragic loss. Allow me to offer my condolences."

"Thank you, Mr. Gillette."

"Please be seated," Evelyn invited.

"After seeing your beautiful ranch, I've probably come for no reason. Mr. Hamilton, at the mercantile store in Trinidad, thought you might have some cattle for sale. Obviously he was mistaken."

"No, matter of fact, we do have some cattle we would consider selling. Would you be interested?"

"Depends on the price of course, but yes, I might be interested."

"To be perfectly frank, Miss Higgins, our herd has grown to the point that we are unable to maintain them. The winter has already depleted our feed supply and we still have two or three months before spring."

"How many would you be willing to sell?" Juliana asked.

"I'm running over two thousand head. I'd be willing to sell half of them."

"What would you need to have for them?"

"I'd take twelve dollars a head."

"I'm sorry, Mr. Gillette. I'd be willing to pay ten, but twelve is out of my price range. I'd have to winter them, too."

Merv Gillette silently nodded his head. Juliana rose to leave.

"Thank you for your hospitality, Mrs. Gillette. I need to be going. If you folks are over my way, I hope you will stop for a visit."

"You drive a hard bargain, Miss Higgins," Mr. Gillette said. "Ten dollars a head it is, if you will take the entire thousand head."

"Then we agree," Juliana said, offering her hand. Gillette took it and they sealed the agreement with a handshake.

"My foreman and some of my hands will pick up the cattle in a week or so. He'll deliver your money then. Is that acceptable?"

"It is. I'll have a bill of sale drawn up and waiting."

"You've been very kind," Juliana said, rising to her feet. "But I need to be going."

"This ranch of yours," Gillette said. "Are you gonna be running it yourself now that your folks are passed on?"

"Well, I have an able foreman and good workers. Yes, I suppose I will be."

"Mighty big undertaking for a young lady, but good luck to you."

Her business with the Gillettes had taken longer than she expected and as she hurried to her buggy, she glanced anxiously at the sun. It was just disappearing behind the western horizon. *I can't possibly get back to town before dark.* She immediately remembered the saddle tramp she had encountered earlier. *Will he be waiting somewhere along the road?* That thought sent cold chills racing up her spine.

Pushing the worry aside, she climbed quickly into her buggy and popped the reins. The matched set of horses leaped into a fox trot. Fading light slanted along the narrow road, making elongated shadows. Trees and thick undergrowth crowded the road on both sides.

She suddenly realized how vulnerable she was. Being

alone out here on a lonely road in broad daylight was bad enough, but in the darkness it was unthinkable.

She lashed at the horses' rumps with the tail end of the long reins, causing them to burst into a full gallop. The small buggy bounced along the narrow lane, it's wheels sliding around the curves. Fear gripped its ugly talons around her heart. She reached for her rifle, levered a shell, and laid it on the seat beside her. Juliana squinted to examine every bush, every rock, and every shadow that might hide the evil drifter. The night closed in around her. Full dark settled in quickly, only dim light from the stars lit the trail.

The horses raced belly to the ground and full out, yet Juliana lashed their rumps, urging them to even greater speed. She had never been so terrified in her life. She fully realized the chance she was taking, racing her horses at such speed on a narrow, curvy road in the dark, but right now she was willing to take that chance.

Suddenly, something loomed ahead. A large deadfall log blocked the narrow road.

She braced her feet against the dashboard and tugged back on the reins with all her might.

"Whoa!" she screamed at the top of her voice, but immediately realized she couldn't possibly get the racing horses stopped in time.

She could feel them already measuring their long strides, preparing to jump the log. The horses could clear the obstruction, but the buggy wouldn't. Already the buggy was sliding around the curve on two wheels. She knew instinctively that if it hit the log at this speed and tilted, it would be smashed to smithereens, and her with it.

Just as the horses left the ground for their leap, Juliana grabbed the rifle from the seat beside her and leaped from the buggy.

Chapter X

The first herd of the year's driving season began their long trek to Kansas on April 1, 1869. Buck sat his saddle with little Cody in his arms. Rebekah, Selena, and Chester sat their horses, beside him. They gazed down at the bawling, rebellious mass of longhorns gathered in the valley below.

What had become a yearly ritual for the kickoff of the driving season was about to be replayed for the third time. The large herd gathered in the valley below waited for Buck's signal to begin the first drive.

Wash's chuck wagons were fully loaded and ready. The large remuda of extra horses under the control of the horse wranglers, were bunched. The twenty drovers, assigned to the first herd, sat their horses with coiled ropes in hand.

Every eye was fixed on the small group on top of the hill and focused on the big man on the black horse holding his small son in his arms. The boss. Not a step would be taken until the signal came.

Their overall trail boss, Ray Ledbetter, rode up the hillside and reined down near Buck.

"Looks like everything is set to go, boss. All we need is your signal to move 'em out."

Buck's chest swelled as he lifted a hand and removed his big Stetson. He lifted it high in the air and circled it.

Down below, a chorus of cowboy yelps and yells echoed like a wave up the hillside. Smokey released the rangy old bell cow that would lead the herd on their long journey halfway across the country to Abilene, Kansas.

The drag riders rode along the backside of the herd, swatting the reluctant longhorns into movement. The drive had begun.

"Look, Papa!" Little Cody yelled and pointed an arm as the cattle began moving.

Buck glanced down at his son through tear-blurred eyes. He swallowed hard.

"Yes, son, take a long look. That's a sight I hope you'll never forget. This is one of those events that happen in one's life worth remembering. What you are witnessing down there is the birth of a nation.

"Immigrants from all over the world are flocking to our shores with hopes and dreams of building a new and better life. These cattle, and tens of thousands more like them, are the lifeblood that will supply the energy to build this young country.

"Right now these newcomers are located mainly in the north so we have to take our cattle to feed the hungry hordes. One day soon they will migrate south and the railroads will quickly follow. When that day comes, scenes like this will disappear forever. So hold onto what you are seeing down there today."

Chester, Rebekah, and Selena were staring wide-eyed at the eloquence of Buck's words.

"Well said, pardner," Chester told him. "You're already

beginning to sound like a politician. I reckon that's more words strung together at one time than I've ever heard in all the years I've known you."

Rebekah touched Buck's arm and squeezed it.

"I'm proud of my politician and even more proud of my *husband.*"

Later that night, alone in their large, sunken bathtub, Buck and Rebekah lay together in one another's arms for a long time. She snuggled deeper into the hollow of his broad shoulder and whispered, "I love you, Buck Cordell."

Candles flickered and painted dancing shadows on the ceiling. Buck gazed down at her, trying to soak up the depth in her soft whispers of love, the gleam of her hair in the candlelight, the silky softness of her skin against him. He wanted to close his hands around those moments, to hold them fast, to cling to the memories.

His arm drew her closer. "And I love you, Rebekah Cordell."

"I think I've loved you since the first time you walked into the store and into my life," she whispered softly. "I would never have believed one could fall so totally in love so instantly, at first sight. You swept me completely off my feet, cowboy."

"Well, can't rightly say I know what I did or how I did it, but I'm shore glad I did."

After a long moment she turned her face up to him and whispered, "Me, too."

Buck stirred and drew her closer still. His lips captured hers in a kiss that was both tender and passionate. Together, they were caught up and gloried in unbridled emotions and ecstasy, in total surrender and sweetness. They clung to the other as wonder and exultation swept them away to limitless heights of love and commitment neither of them could have imagined.

Chester lay beside his wife, his face was turned toward her. Her eyes were closed, but her breathing told him she was still awake. He loved to watch her sleep, amazed that she was here and was his wife.

Suddenly her eyes popped open wide. A look of shock swept across her beautiful face.

"What is it?" he asked anxiously. "What's happening? Are you all right?"

Selena slanted a look at him and smiled broadly.

"Want to feel your son kick his mother?"

Chester reached an awkward hand and placed it on her bulging stomach. She took his hand and moved it in place.

"It is!" Chester near shouted. "I felt it! I actually felt him kick. Why that little rascal," he said laughing.

That brought a happy smile to Selena's face. "Maybe you were right after all. Maybe you will get your son, but will you be disappointed *if* it should be a girl?"

Chester lifted her hand to his lips and kissed it tenderly before lying back and staring silently at the ceiling. "Dakota Colson. Yeah, that's the perfect name for our son, *or our daughter.*"

The first week on the trail went good, too good to suit Ray and Smokey. After as many herds as the two of them had taken up the trail, they both knew the danger signs of slipping into complacency.

Their worries proved justified on their eighth day out.

It began late that afternoon. Ray glanced up at the gathering clouds and didn't like what he saw. Growing dark clouds bumped shoulders from horizon to horizon.

"I purely don't like the looks of them clouds," he told Smokey, as they rode stirrup to stirrup behind the seemingly endless line of longhorns. "If them thunder-busters ever join up, we're in for a real humdinger."

"Fraid you're right. For sure we'll get rain, wind, thunder, and lightning. The thing that concerns me is we're caught out here smack-dab in the middle of the flattest prairie in Texas. Ain't a chance we could find a canyon or someplace to shelter the herd."

Again they lifted concerned looks at the sky.

"I look for it to hit us sometime before midnight." Smokey guessed. "That your thinking?"

"Sounds about right. We might as well circle the herd and try to get 'em bedded down. It's liable to be a long night. Tell the boys to keep a saddled horse close tonight."

"I'll pass the word," Smokey said, heeling his horse and riding off to tell the drovers.

By the time they had the herd circled, darkness had swallowed the light. Darkening and dangerous clouds rolled and boiled overhead. At first, the far away, deep rumbling sounded so distant it was almost imperceptible. As it grew closer, it intensified and sounded like an unrelenting barrage of cannon fire.

The cattle milled about nervously, bawled and bellowed loudly, but refused to bed down, even after a twelve-mile day. By halfway to midnight, the lightning started. Continuous flashes burst from the deep depths of the treacherous clouds swirling overhead.

Within minutes the wind picked up, and with the wind,

the heavens opened up and the rains came. It was rain like few of them had ever witnessed. It fell in great sheets and was driven sideways by the raging winds.

Every cowboy was in the saddle, sleeving quickly into heavy rain slickers and tying their hats in place with their bandanas.

"Won't take much to set 'em off," Ray shouted above the driving wind. "When they go, let 'em run, especially if they're headed north."

Smokey nodded his head to let his boss know he understood.

Lightning bolts shot from the approaching clouds and lit the night as if it were day. Some far off target, unlucky enough to be the tallest item in the vicinity, would be instantly disintegrated.

Then it happened. It happened so suddenly it caught them by surprise, even though they had been expecting it.

A huge, jagged lightning bolt burst from a nearby cloud. *It streaked directly toward them.* A gnarly old mesquite tree on the backside of the herd exploded with an ear-splitting boom. It instantly burst into flames and the entire herd erupted into a dead run.

The thundering sound of ten thousand hooves rose even above the noise of the storm. The earth seemed to tremble. A frightening sound.

The seasoned cowboys knew there was no chance of stopping twenty-five hundred longhorns deadset on stampeding. All they could do was stay a safe distance away and let them run themselves out, especially since they had broken northward.

The weaker and slower among them would have little chance of surviving; they would be overrun and trampled under the churning hooves of the stronger and swifter.

The cowboys raced their horses alongside the herd, careful not to get trapped in the stampede. They knew if that happened and their horse went down, they were done for.

The breakneck run lasted a long while, but finally the herd seemed to lose both their fear and the strength to run and finally began to slow to a trot, and eventually to a walk. When that happened, the cowboys moved in and slowly forced the leaders into a tighter and tighter circle.

The violence of the storm had long passed, leaving only the rain. In less than an hour the herd collapsed to their knees, and then to their bellies, with tired legs tucked comfortably under equally tired bodies, and there they stayed until well after a new day dawned.

Daylight brought with it the full, tragic truth of the stampede. Dead cattle, or what was left of them, lay strewn for miles along the path of the stampede. The final count shocked Ray to his core.

Of twenty-five hundred longhorns he left the ranch with only a week before, less than two thousand remained. They still had over a thousand miles to reach their destination and already they had lost twenty percent of their herd, more than twice the normal ten percent one expects to lose for the entire drive.

"Last night's stampede cost the ranch more'n twenty-two thousand dollars," Ray told Smokey, as they squatted near the campfire, sipping on a steaming cup of coffee. "I might be looking for another job after the boss hears about this."

"There weren't nothing else we could do. Buck would've done the same as us if he'd been here."

"Yeah, but still and all, that's lots of money. We're likely to lose another ten percent before we get to Abilene."

"I say we do the best we can and let the chips fall where they fall."

Ray nodded slowly, and swallowed the last of his coffee. "We'll let the herd rest another hour or so before we get 'em up and get 'em moving. There's water a few miles up ahead. They'll likely be plenty thirsty by the time we reach the Middle Concho River near San Angelo. We'll drift them until then."

Smokey nodded his agreement.

All too quickly the days slipped by. The day both Buck and Rebekah dreaded to see, arrived. As Buck handed his leather travel bag to the Longhorn security man that would serve as his driver, Rebekah stood nearby, toeing tiny lines in the dirt with her boot.

He turned to face her. She finally lifted her eyes to gaze deeply into his. Large tears seeped from the corners of her eyes and trailed down her cheeks. She sleeved them away and offered a weak smile.

"How long will you be gone?"

"Not one minute longer than I have to," he mumbled, holding her gaze with his in a long look of love.

"I'll miss you," she whispered, her gaze still locked with his.

He jerked a slow nod and opened his arms. She filled them. For a long moment the extended hug molded them as one. Buck brushed her lips with a soft kiss before turning and stepping quickly into the waiting buggy. He looked back only once, just before the buggy pulled through the front gate, and lifted a hand.

Rebekah stood motionless, staring after half her soul disappearing through the gate, followed by two mounted and heavily armed security men. She managed to choke back the sobs until she reached the privacy of their home. Once inside, the floodgates burst and the tears stored up over the last few weeks gushed forth.

The trip to Austin was long and tiring, but uneventful. Buck arrived at his hotel and checked him and his two security men in before hurrying to his office in the capitol building.

Just as he knew she would, Mrs. Johnson had his busy schedule all laid out, right down to the minute, for the next week before the official opening of the Congress. She handed him the schedule as he strode into his cramped office. He glanced quickly down the long list of meetings. His eyes paused at an eleven p.m. meeting, on Friday. It was circled in red ink, but there was no name attached to the meeting.

"What's this one listed for Friday evening at eleven?" Buck questioned. "That's pretty late for a meeting isn't it?"

"There's a private letter in your folder. The meeting is with General Phillip Sheridan in the private suite he maintains at the Mayflower. Very hush-hush. No one is supposed to know he is in town. His letter explains it in more detail."

"Reckon what that's all about?"

"I suppose you'll find out on Friday."

"You're too efficient to be a secretary," Buck told her, as he closed the folder.

"That's why you pay me the big bucks," she joked, picking up her note pad and pen. "Now let's stop the back-patting and get down to work. We've got a lot of ground to cover and not much time to do it."

"Slave driver," he cracked, as he shook out of his coat and sat down behind his desk. "Has somebody figured out how to shrink this office even smaller? It's not even as big as I remembered."

"Your skimpy office doesn't reflect your position, Congressman."

"I know, but I made a promise there wouldn't be *any* office reshuffling under my leadership and that includes me."

"But nobody in Congress expects you to keep that promise, with the possible exception of J. W. Wentworth, and a promise to him shouldn't count."

"Does to me."

"Are your cattle as stubborn as you?"

"You have no idea. We're burning daylight jawing at one another. Let's get down to business."

It was well after midnight when they finally locked the door and made their way through the deserted building. When they reached the front door, one of the guards unlocked the large double doors.

"Would one of you see Mrs. Johnson gets home safely? It's too late for a lady to be walking the streets alone," Buck requested.

"That's not necessary," his secretary protested.

"Of course it is. You are far too valuable to me for something to happen. One of the guards will be glad to see you home, won't you?" Buck said, turning a look upon the larger of the two.

"Of course, sir. I'd be glad to see the lady home."

"Goodnight then," Buck said, touching a curled finger to his hat brim. "I'll see you bright and early in the morning."

"Goodnight, Congressman, and thank you."

As Mrs. Johnson and the burly guard walked away, Buck overheard the guard comment,

"Congressman Cordell is way too nice to be a Congressman."

"That he is," his secretary replied. "But he can be hard as nails when he needs to be."

"Big as he is, I can believe it."

When Buck arrived at his office before seven the next morning, Mrs. Johnson was already busy at work.

"Good morning," he said. "You're up early."

"Good morning, Congressman. I usually get here by six."

"Six until midnight. Them are mighty long hours," Buck said. Opening his briefcase, he pulled out a picture of Rebekah in a gold frame and sat it on his desk.

"Well, I have a demanding boss. Is that your wife?" she asked, picking up the picture and staring at it.

"Yes. Her name is Rebekah."

"She's very beautiful."

"Yes. Yes, she is, thank you."

His archenemy, J. W. Wentworth, hadn't caused any open confrontations, but the hostility still remained just below the public surface, waiting to erupt.

Again that day, and the day after that, it was near midnight before they finished for the day and left the office. Buck seldom got back to his lonely hotel room before midnight.

The busy days were jam packed with non-stop meetings: committee meetings, procedural meetings, planning meetings, and meetings about meetings. It was now a regular part of the guard's duty to see Mrs. Johnson safely home. Judging by the new smile on the big guard's face, it seemed to Buck the man was beginning to enjoy that part of his duties.

The week slipped away quickly. When Friday evening came, Buck had all of his reports and talking points prepared for the meeting with General Sheridan. He had been given no indication what the hush-hush meeting was about, but he wanted to have the answer to any question the general might ask.

Buck arrived at the Mayflower Hotel precisely at eleven. The sprawling hotel wasn't one of the newer in Austin, but was equal to any in terms of elegance.

He climbed the stairs and located the proper door easily because of the two, no-nonsense looking guards standing on either side of it. Their manner told him they were both military, but they wore civilian clothes. A bulge under their coats told him they both wore shoulder holsters. *Strange.*

"I'm Congressman Buck Cordell."

"Yes, sir, Congressman. The general is expecting you. I'm afraid we're required to search you for weapons before you enter."

"I understand. I'm not wearing a sidearm, but there's one in my briefcase. I'll leave it with you until I leave."

He opened his solid leather briefcase and handed the security man his Colt. The other man tapped lightly on the door and opened it when the invitation was heard from inside.

General Sheridan rose quickly from a sofa and strode across the large room with his hand extended.

"It's good to see you again, Buck. Thanks for meeting with me at such a late hour."

"How are you, general?"

"I'm fine. How is your lovely wife? Rebekah, isn't it?"

Buck was somewhat surprised that a man with as much on his mind would remember Rebekah by name.

"Yes. My wife is doing well. We have a small son now. He's going on three."

"Yes. Cody, isn't it?"

Again, Buck was surprised.

"You seem to know quite a lot about my family."

"Well, I've learned over the years that it's prudent to know all you can about your friends, as well as your enemies," the general commented, motioning Buck toward a large chair near the sofa.

"May I ask which of those categories I might be in?"

The general hesitated before answering. He fixed Buck with a look.

"There was a time when both of us would have considered the other an enemy. Buck, I'm well aware of your activities while you fought for the south. I commend you for the manner in which you carried out your assignments. You served the Confederacy well. To be perfectly candid, you and your unit were a pain in our backside.

"The incident you were involved in that happened in Virginia after the war was over was unfortunate, but that's all water under the bridge. Fate and circumstances have brought us together for a purpose, I believe, and I'm pleased to call you my friend. Politics sometimes makes strange bedfellows.

"Obviously I trust you, or you wouldn't be here. With the air cleared of the past, can we speak of these things no more and get down to more pressing issues?"

Buck was in a state of shock. *All this time the general has known about my involvement in the ambush and could have had me hung or at the least thrown in prison. It's an open secret that he's in hot water in Congress because of his harshness in dealing with former Confederates that fought against the Union. Instead, he appoints me to Congress. Very puzzling.*

"One question?" Buck requested.

"Of course," the general agreed.

"Why did you choose not to pursue charges against me once you discovered my involvement? You certainly could have."

"Yes. Yes, I could have, but what would have been gained? Revenge? Retaliation?

"It wouldn't have changed what happened. It wouldn't have brought all those men back. Besides, you were far too valuable to our country, and particularly to Texas, to waste another life. My underlying goal is restoring Texas to the Union. To accomplish that, we must drastically increase the

Longhorn III: The Prodigal Brother

population, particularly in southern and western Texas. That's where you come in. Your leadership abilities, stature, and influence can expedite that process."

"I can see why you are a general."

"I've asked that you keep this meeting in strictest confidence. The fact is, I'm not even supposed to be in Texas. Some of my old enemies have succeeded in having me removed from my position with regard to our reconstruction efforts in Texas. I've been reassigned to Chicago and placed in command of the Department of Missouri.

"But regardless, the settlement plans for populating this part of south Texas must not be abandoned. You have moved swiftly, just as I knew you would. In the short time you have been in office, you have accomplished even more than I could have hoped for. Even now I have no authority in Texas. I'm afraid I must leave this political hot potato entirely in your hands.

"This will likely be our last meeting together. I have been given the assignment of putting an end to the Indian problems in the southwest once and for all. I've been ordered to round up the hostiles and place them on reservations or destroy them. I've been placed in command of seven regiments. Even as we speak, my force is being organized. The campaign in this part of Texas will be underway within weeks.

"The Comanche in this part of Texas are particularly troublesome. As you well know, they are perhaps the most ruthless, bloodthirsty of the lot. They raid, rape, kidnap, and slaughter innocent men, women, and children. I met recently with *Tosawi*, war chief of the Comanche. He had the gall to say, 'Me Tosawi. Me good Injun.' I told him, *The only good Indian I ever saw was dead.* They must be stopped. I intend to do just that.

"Buck, when one rises to a position of influence, any

position of influence, he gives birth to enemies along the way. From what I know about your dust-up with our friend, Wentworth, I suspect you already know what I am talking about. You handled the situation well and I commend you, but very shortly others will raise their heads in opposition against what we are trying to accomplish. Their influence is growing rapidly. They are utterly ruthless and will stop at nothing to prevent the re-admission of Texas to the Union. They can see no farther than the end of their noses. You are a man of vision. That's why I chose you to continue the work we've begun.

"As I'm sure you are aware, Washington is in a state of turmoil. It appears as though President Johnson has survived the efforts to have him impeached, nonetheless, our plans may still be in jeopardy. By the way, I've managed to get authorization from the Department of Defense to add three new forts in south Texas. I wanted more, but budget restraints and all the turmoil at the Defense Department wouldn't allow it."

"I'm obliged for your confidence, general. I'll do my best."

"One can ask no more of a man than that."

It was well after midnight when Buck left the meeting and made his way through the deserted streets of Austin to his hotel. He had plenty of time to think during the lonely walk.

Politics is a dangerous occupation, he decided.

Chapter XI

Cody spent the best part of four days visiting with his old friends at the Brazos River Ranch. It brought back lots of good memories. They hashed and re-hashed most of the things that happened while Cody worked there, but it was amazing how the stories had grown from the way he remembered them.

"Yep, good partner," Lefty told him as they all sat around the potbelly stove in the bunkhouse. "You were a real rip-snortin', ring-tailed gunfighter, and that's for sure and certain. Never seen anybody that could hold you a candle."

"Well, they say there's *always* somebody faster," Cody said meekly, wishing they could change the subject.

"One thing for shore," his friend pushed on. "You ain't met him yet. And far as that goes, I ain't for sure there *is* anybody faster."

* * *

Cody saddled Cincinnati and rode out before first light the following morning. When he arrived in Waco, he tied his pinto up in front of Marshal Bell's office and walked inside. His lawman friend was pouring himself a cup.

"Morning, 'Kid. How'd you find things out at the Brazos?"

"Nothing's changed, far as I could see. You find out anything?"

"Well, yes and no. I got hold of my friend I was telling you about. He's the town marshal up in Abilene now. He made some inquires. I got a telegram from him just yesterday. All he found out was that there had been, what they call, a *search contract* out for you. He said the case was closed after they verified that you were dead."

"A *search contract*? What's that mean?"

"Got no idea. Don't sound like nothing criminal or nothing to me."

"Then I ain't wanted for nothing?"

"Not as far as I can tell. Something else I gotta tell you, though."

"What's that?"

"Vance Longley rode into town last night. He's put up over at the hotel. You still got time to ride out before he finds out you're in town."

Cody shook his head.

"Wouldn't do any good. Seems he's dead set on settling whatever *score* he thinks he's got to settle. He'd follow me wherever I go. Just another one of those things I've got to get settled before I can put the old life behind me, I reckon."

"I can run him outta town like I did last time."

Again, Cody shook his head. "No. I'm obliged, Marshal,

but here's as good a place as any to settle it once and for all. I'm tired of running."

Cody left Marshal Bell's office and walked across the street to the Brazos café. It was busy as usual. Miss Ellen saw him walk in and motioned him to an empty table. Cody scraped out a chair and sat down. Ellen brought a cup and poured it full from a large coffee pot.

"Begin to think you had left without saying goodbye," she said.

"I wouldn't do that."

"How's Del?"

"He's about the same. Nothing's changed at the ranch."

"When you leaving?" she asked.

"Soon. Got something to get settled before I go."

"Does that *something* have anything to do with Vance Longley? I just heard he rode in last night."

Cody stared down at his steaming coffee. It was hot, black, and strong. He blew the steam away and tried it before he slanted a look up at her.

"I was afraid of that. Are you actually thinking about *fighting* him? No, Cody, please don't. They say he's killed more than twenty men."

"Got no choice, Miss Ellen. He seems to think we've got some sort of *score* to settle. He won't let it drop. It's just another of them things I've got to get settled before I can start a new life."

"Please, Cody. I'm begging you. Please don't fight him. You can just ride away."

"I'm sorry, Miss Ellen, but I can't do that. What sort of man would I be to run away? I can't start a new life having to look over my shoulder all the time. No, I've decided. It's gonna be over one way or another. When I leave here, I'm gonna leave as who I really am, Cody Cordell. Win or lose, it's gonna end right here."

"Whoever she is, she's one lucky lady. You're quite a man."

Cody rose with hat in hand. For a long moment he stood silently. Ellen took a tentative step toward him, lifted to her tiptoes, and kissed his cheek, even as her customers stared at one another with questioning looks.

Without another word, Cody turned, clamped his hat in place, and walked from the room without so much as a look back. He strode across the street to his horse and pulled his familiar belly holster and Colt from his saddlebag.

Marshal Bell emerged from his office as Cody was strapping his holster in place.

"Now just hold on there, son. I hope you ain't planning on doing what it looks like."

"Like I said before, Marshal, I'm gonna settle this once and for all. You're a good man. You're the best lawman I've ever met, but I'm asking you, stay out of this one."

"You're gonna get yourself killed, boy. Vance Longley ain't some snot-nosed kid fresh off the farm. He's a gunfighter, maybe the best there is. Last count, I heard he's killed twenty-four men in standup fights. You're good, I ain't saying you ain't, but he's a natural born killer. Do yourself a favor and ride out."

Cody shook his head firmly. "Sorry, Marshal, but I can't do that."

Pulling his well-worn serape from his saddlebag, he slipped it over his head and adjusted it in place. He removed the custom-made Colt from his belly holster and thumbed six fresh cartridges into the empty chambers before replacing it in the fat-slick holster.

Turning to the marshal, he stuck out his open hand. Marshal Bell took the hand and they shared a firm handshake.

"Good luck, Kid."

Turning, Cody walked determinedly toward the hotel.

He stopped dead center of the street in front of the small, two story, box-like building with his back to the red sun just beginning its journey toward its zenith.

"Vance Longley!" Cody shouted.

He saw a window curtain pushed aside in an upstairs window. Inside the window he could make out the vague form of a man through the dirty glass.

He waited. He didn't have long to wait. The front door of the hotel opened and the dapper gunfighter stepped onto the boardwalk and stopped.

For the crowd of onlookers that gathered along the boardwalk and whose faces could be seen peering through every window along the street, it must have been the ultimate contrast.

Vance Longley, the famous gunfighter known far and wide, stood there in his fancy, black three-piece suit with a solid gold watch chain dangling in front. A flat-brimmed, black Stetson set low on his forehead shaded his eyes from the sun.

His black suit coat was open in front revealing a black leather holster tied low on his right leg.

Casually, Longley reached a hand to his inside coat pocket and extracted a long, thin cigar.

He bit the tip from it, ran his tongue along the entire surface before sticking the end of it between his lips and putting fire to it. He drew in a long intake without removing his cold, hard eyes from Cody and then let the blue arrow of smoke out in a long, thin slide.

"I hear you been looking for me," Cody said, surprising even himself at how calm his words came out, considering his stomach was doing flip-flops.

"Well, well. If it ain't the famous Hondo Kid himself. Where you been hiding, 'Kid?"

"I'm here."

A thin smile surrounded the cigar in Longley's lips.

"Didn't think you had the sand to face me."

"I'm full of surprises."

Longley slowly sleeved out of his suit jacket and laid it carefully across the hitching rail in front of the hotel. The pearl handled Colt resting in the black, cutaway holster looked deadly. *Twenty-four men. Marshal Bell said Longley had killed twenty-four men with that gun.*

Casually, the gunfighter moved sideways along the boardwalk up the street toward the east, into the sun.

He's trying to out-maneuver me to get the sun to his back and into my face, Cody recognized. To counter Longley's move, Cody slid sideways along the middle of the street, refusing to give up his position.

"I can see you ain't no greenhorn," the gunfighter said, conceding the position issue and stepping to the middle of the street.

"You're good, but you ain't good enough to take me, 'Kid,'" Longley said, his voice low and menacing.

"Reckon we'll see."

Longley stopped in the very center of the dusty street. He spread his legs slightly apart and faced Cody squarely. He tilted his head slightly to shield his eyes from the blinding sun.

Cody slowly reached his left hand and flipped the corner of his serape back over his right shoulder, exposing the heavy, silver, bone handled Walker .44.

"Nice looking gun," Longley said casually. "Might just keep that one after I kill you."

"Ready when you are," Cody said.

Time seemed to stop.

* * *

Juliana flung herself through the air into the unknown darkness. Instinctively, she kept enough presence of mind to hold tightly to her rifle.

She landed with a bone-jarring jolt, tumbled over and over, and came to rest against a large boulder. She was stunned into stillness. A sharp pain shot through her left shoulder, but she tried to put the hurt out of her mind.

Deliberately she suppressed her loud breathing, aware that if the saddle tramp was nearby, she wanted to make it hard for him to locate her in the almost total darkness.

Off in the distance, she could hear the sound of her galloping horses dragging whatever remained of the buggy, fading away into the night.

She lay quietly. Listening. Her heart in her throat, but strangely calm. Silence lengthened.

"Where are ye, Miss Prissy?" The saddle tramp's taunting voice called from the darkness. "I know you're out here somewhere. The shoe's on the other foot now, ain't it?"

Juliana quietly hunkered closer to the large boulder. Her hand made sweat on the handle of her rifle as she swung the nose toward the sound of the man's voice. She had trouble lifting her left arm to balance the rifle.

"Might just as well come on out. We got all night. We're gonna get to know one another *real* good before this night is over."

She could hear the man's soft footsteps searching through the thick underbrush, drawing closer to her position with each step.

She was shocked to discover she could actually *smell* the man as he drew ever nearer, the way a horse can scent water at the end of a long, thirsty ride. The stale body odor wafted through the darkness and turned her stomach.

Chills rippled down her spine. She lay motionless, barely breathing, muscles trembling, her heart hardly daring to beat.

Then he was there, the vague outline of his form framed against the scattering of stars in a velvety black sky. His foot touched her.

"Ah, there you are."

Juliana closed her eyes and pulled the trigger.

The buck of her rifle sent shock waves up her arm into her injured shoulder. The blast from her shot blossomed in the darkness and lit the surroundings with an orangey-red glow.

The loud grunt told her the shot had found its target. The bulky form above her tumbled backwards, crashing into the underbrush at her feet. Like a startled rabbit, she sprang to her feet and headed toward where she imagined the road was, only to discover quickly that she was disoriented, and obviously was running deeper into the woods rather than toward the road.

Behind her, she heard a string of curses from her attacker. She ran into a tree, bounced off and sprawled headlong in the tangled underbrush. Scrambling to her knees, and then to her feet, she stumbled on through the darkness.

Behind her, she could hear her pursuer crashing through the underbrush, cursing with each step. In her confused state, she nonetheless realized that she was running the wrong way and began a wide circle, stopping often to pinpoint her attacker's location, and then moving on.

Branches slapped at her face and she stumbled, but caught herself and plunged on. Briars tore at her legs. She dodged a large tree that loomed up, before tripping and rolling down a steep bank and banging into a large boulder at the bottom.

She lay still, panting, her lungs burning, trying to be quiet. Listening fearfully above her chest pounding, her teary eyes blurred.

How long she ran, she had no idea. Her legs trembled and threatened to give way. Her shoulder throbbed, her breath came in gasps, and still she struggled on.

The sound of her pursuer faded, and then melded with the night. She stopped for a time and collapsed to her knees, finally having the presence of mind to lever another shell into her rifle.

Again she listened intently, but heard absolutely nothing except the night birds. Struggling to her feet, she staggered onward.

Suddenly the road stretched before her. She stepped cautiously from the thick underbrush and peered both directions through the darkness. Turning left, she started walking as quickly as she could in her weakened condition.

A sound reached her. It came from the direction of town. Horses. Several horses. *Who can it be?* she wondered. To be safe, she stepped off the road into the bushes and stood beside a large pine tree, holding the rifle firmly just in case.

She saw them coming at a gallop through the murky darkness. There were three horses and riders. One of the riders was a woman. *It's Mary Ann.* They had come to find her.

"Mary Ann!" she yelled, stepping quickly into the road.

The horses reined quickly to a stop. Mary Ann leaped from her mount and ran to meet her. They embraced.

"Are you all right?" Mr. Hamilton asked, with concern in his voice. "What happened? Your team ran into town dragging the tongue from your buggy. I got hold of Mary Ann. She told me where you had gone. Mary Ann and Sammy came with me to find you."

"What happened?" Mary Ann asked.

"It's a long story. There's a man back there somewhere; a saddle tramp. He tried to kill me. He pulled a tree across the trail and wrecked my buggy. I think I wounded him."

"It's almost daylight. We'll find him," Sammy Schroeder drawled in his German accent. "Mary, take your friend back to town. We'll stay here and find him. He won't get away."

As Cody stood in the middle of the dusty street, facing the most deadly gunfighter alive, the words of his old blind Mexican mentor, the man who taught him everything he knew about the gunfighter profession, flashed from his memory.

First, you pick the time and place to fight. If daytime, keep your back to the sun. If there is no way out of the fight, the only thing left is to kill him before he kills you. Last, and most important of all, watch his eyes and face. A nervous eye flicker, a tightening of the lips, clenching of the mouth, bulging jaw muscles. Any of these natural actions will be your warning that your opponent is about to draw.

That will give you a split second warning. Use it. It could make the difference in living and dying.

This was the defining moment of the endless hours of instruction and practice. This was the apex of his entire life. Cody's mind, senses, and body focused their total energies on one thing and one thing only: *the moment.*

His hearing shut off all sound. His mind rejected any distraction. His hands and arms were relaxed and ready. His eyes locked on Longley's eyes like a beacon with a fixed, unwavering, and unblinking stare.

For a small slice of eternity, time stood still.

Then it came.

The slightest hint of a thin smile wrinkled one corner of Vance Longley's top lip. In that instant, Cody's practiced hand moved instinctively. The bone handled Colt, that had become a mere extension of his hand, leaped from the greased holster.

His thumb instinctively raked back the hammer, his finger feathered the trigger, and the weapon bucked in his hand. Once, twice, three times, the jarring explosion radiated past his hand, journeyed up his arm, and rocked his shoulder. All this in less than an eye blink.

But what was wrong? Vance Longley was still standing! Cody was puzzled. How could he have missed at point-blank distance?

The famous gunfighter stood there, not twenty-feet in front of him, his pearl handled Colt in his hand. Blue smoke curled like a serpent from the nose of the barrel that was pointed toward the ground.

No, this can't be possible, Cody's mind screamed. *He's too fast. There must be some mistake. I don't understand.*

Then he saw it again, that same thin smile. The one he had seen just before the draw. Longley's eyes suddenly glazed and went foggy. His gaze dropped to his chest. A shocked, unbelieving look crept across his face at the sight of three thumbnail-size holes. He lifted a weak, confused and questioning gaze up into Cody's face.

Slowly, as if kneeling in prayer, he sank to his knees, still staring at Cody. Then, as if in slow motion, he toppled onto his face in the street. A small puff of dust feathered around where he fell.

Chapter XII

As the time grew closer for Selena to deliver her baby, Chester met with the Longhorn trail foremen each morning and took time to see the latest herd off, otherwise he was like a mother hen, hovering nearby, never more than hollering distance away.

Meanwhile, Selena was taking the upcoming birth in stride, going about her normal daily duties, at least insofar as Chester would allow.

"Are you feeling all right? Are you having any pain?" he asked constantly. "Be sure to let me know if you feel something happening."

"I'm fine, Chester. Stop worrying about me so much."

"I don't mean to be, it's just that this is my first baby."

She laughed. "It's *my* first one, too."

"Oh, yeah, that's right, I reckon." They both shared a laugh.

In the deepest part of the night Selena shook her husband awake.

"Go get Jewel," she instructed.

"Is it coming?" he shouted, as he jumped from the bed and pulled his pants on.

"The pains are just beginning. It will be a while yet, but I need Jewel here to help me."

Chester stomped into his boots.

"Will you be all right until I get back?"

"I'll be fine."

Chester hurried from the room. He returned in minutes with the black cook, who had become the unofficial Longhorn midwife.

She immediately took charge boiling hot water, placing towels and sheets nearby, and counting the time between the pains. When the time grew near, and over Chester's objections, she chased him from the room.

He paced the hallway outside the bedroom door, stopping often to listen for any sound from inside. Finally, his persistence was rewarded by a shrill cry from inside. His heart leaped inside his chest.

After a bit, the door opened and Jewel invited him inside.

Selena lay in the bed in a fresh in a white nightgown looking tired, pale, but happy. She looked up at Chester and smiled. In the crook of her arm lay a blanket wrapped baby.

"Want to see your new *daughter*?" Selena asked, smiling from ear-to-ear.

"*Daughter?*" Chester asked. "It's a girl?"

"Yes, I hope you aren't disappointed."

"Disappointed? Of course I ain't disappointed. Are you all right? Is the baby all right?"

"We're both fine."

Chester pulled the blanket from around the baby's face and gazed down at his daughter for the very first time.

"She's so beautiful. Just like her mother."

"Have you decided what you are going to name her?" Selena asked.

"Just like I said before, her name is Dakota Selena Colson."

Congressman Cordell gaveled the Texas State Congress into session on April 21, 1869. It took half the day to wade through the introduction of bills, endless motions and counter-motions.

Finally, late in the day, they got down to the business at hand.

"Mr. Speaker," one of the congressmen Buck had been working with rose and addressed the congressional body. "I'd like to introduce bill number 0012. It allows for the disbursement of up to one-hundred sixty acres of set aside land previously allocated, to any immigrant willing to settle on said land and render sustained improvements in accordance with the agreement."

"The bill is accepted for consideration, discussion, or amendments," Buck said.

J. W. Wentworth rose from his seat.

"For what purpose does the gentleman rise?" Buck asked.

"I rise to protest this outrage! We fought a war recently for the land we are talking about. Some of our young men died for that land. Now you want to just give it away to some squatter from Germany, or Ireland, or God knows where else, who waltzes in here and takes a notion to settle down? This is Texas land we're talking about. We don't need a bunch of foreigners coming in here."

A few nodded their heads, agreeing with Wentworth. Most sat stone-faced, waiting to see how this was going to play out.

Buck let the congressman finish and sit down before speaking.

Longhorn III: The Prodigal Brother

"With all due respect to the congressman, if Texas is going to be the great state we're all working to make it, we need people. We need people to plow the fields, plant and harvest crops. We need people to raise cattle and build communities and schools and churches.

What difference does it make if those people come from Georgia, or Tennessee, or Alabama, or Germany, or Ireland? I found that people are pretty much the same wherever they hail from.

"They come looking for the same thing you and I look for, a place to put down roots, to feel like they belong to something bigger than themselves. Give them a little time and they'll be proud to be called a Texan. Someday, if need be, they and their sons and grandsons will fight and die for the very land they'll be settling on."

With no further discussion, the bill passed with only one dissenting vote, that of J. W. Wentworth.

Ray Ledbetter rode into Wichita, Kansas on May 30, 1869. He left the first herd, or what was left of it, on the grassy plain a couple of miles out of town.

He rode directly to a small office located next door to the Drover's Cottage and dismounted. A quick rap on the door drew a welcome from within. Ray opened the door and stepped inside.

"Howdy, Ray. Figured it was about time for you boys to show up."

"Howdy, Harvey. How're things? Still buying cattle, I hope."

"All I can get my hands on. Hope you boys got a lot of longhorns for me coming up the trail."

"Yep, about like last year and maybe more. Got the first

herd outside town. Another will be here in a day or two, then two herds a week for the rest of the season."

"Buck or Chester come along?"

"Nope. Buck's all tied up with politics, Chester's fixing to be a daddy for the first time."

"You don't say."

"How's the market looking these days?" the trail boss asked.

"Strong. Good stock is bringing forty-four dollars a head."

"About time we got some good news. We had a stampede a ways back. Our first herd's gonna be short."

"When you wantta bring 'em in?"

"Sooner the better. I need to head back down the trail and check on the other herds."

"I'll send my boys out this afternoon and start bringing them in. You staying over at the hotel?"

"No, like I said, I need to be heading back down the trail."

"Then we'll get with your foreman on the counts and handle payments just like before. Tell Buck and Chester not to be strangers."

"I'll shore do it," Ray said, as he rose to leave. "Looks like Abilene's growing."

"Yep, with all the trail crews coming in looking to blow off steam, the town's getting wild. We've got a brand new sheriff, fellow named Ben Hickman. Ever hear of him?"

"No, can't say I have."

"He's tough as wang leather, just the kind we need right now."

" Well, some of these trail hands can be real cantankerous when they get liquored up."

Ray rode back to the herd and informed Smokey that Harvey Owens riders' would be coming to take the herd to the stockyards for counting.

"I'm gonna head on back down the trail and check on the upcoming herds. You know how to handle things here."

"We'll take care of it, boss," Smokey assured him.

Ray had gone only a few miles when he encountered Slim Hopkins and the second herd. He reined up beside the foreman.

"How's it going, Slim?"

"We've had a good drive. Way I figure, we've lost less than a hundred head."

"Sure beats what we done with the first herd. We had a bad stampede back down the way and lost lots of cattle."

"Yeah, we saw what was left of 'em, which wasn't much. Any of the crew get hurt?"

"No. We was lucky on that score. Smokey and his herd are camped a few miles north. I'm heading on back down the trail."

"Ride careful, boss."

A week later, Ray met Link Stone and his herd and spent the night. After supper Ray and the foreman squatted near the campfire and sipped coffee for a spell.

"I've been posting extra nighthawks around the remuda," Stone told him. "We've had Indians dogging us for the last three days. I figure they're looking for a chance to steal some horses."

"More'n likely. How many are in the bunch?"

"We never see more'n two or three. But you know yourself, they're like rattlers; where you see one, there's usually more pretty close. We just get quick glimpses of them, and that's usually on some hillside a ways off."

"Well, sounds like you're doing right by posting extra guards. Can you spare a packhorse and some trail supplies? I'm planning on checking on all the crews all the way back to the ranch."

"Sure can. I'll ask Cookie to saddle one up and pack it with supplies."

"I'd be obliged."

"How's the price of cattle holding up?"

"Strong. We're getting a bit more than last year. I think the boss will be pleased about the price, just don't know how he's gonna cotton to us losing so many this trip."

"That's just part of it. He knows we all do the best we can."

"I reckon," Ray said, downing the last swig of coffee. "Well, think I'm gonna hit the sack. I'll be pulling out before first light."

"Ride careful, boss."

The trail cook was up and had the coffee going when Ray stomped his boots on and donned his hat. Everybody else was still sawing logs.

"Got your horse all saddled and ready, Mister Boss," the cook said, handing Ray a steaming cup of coffee. "Packed plenty of supplies on a packhorse for you, too."

"Much obliged, Cookie," Ray told him, as he gathered the reins and booted a stirrup. "Looks like a clear day."

"Yes, sir. Sure do."

Ray did a half hitch around the saddlehorn with the lead rope to the packhorse and kneed his big roan gelding forward.

He blew steam from the coffee and chanced a sip as he reined his mount southward along the well-worn cattle trail.

He rode steady all morning, stopping a time or two at a creek to slake the thirst of his animals. At one watering stop, he had a strange feeling he was being watched. He searched the horizons with a slow gaze, but saw nothing.

It's most likely nothing. Maybe I'm just a little on edge, thinking about the Indians Link was telling about.

He made camp that night in a small clearing on the bank of the Cimarron River. A thick growth of willows hugged the river on both sides. The small clearing opened to the water. He watered and tied his horses on a picket line stretched between two sturdy trees. He built a small fire and put water on to heat for coffee.

When the water came to a boil he dumped in a handful of coffee and sliced strips of bacon into a frying pan from a slab of salt pork he found in his pack. He cut a small green willow stick and laid it across the top of the coffee pot to keep it from boiling over and poured in some cold water to settle the grounds. When the bacon was about done, he opened a tin of beans from his pack and dumped half the tin into the frying pan on top of the bacon.

After supper, he poured another cup of coffee and settled his back against the upturned saddle.

He glanced casually up at a star-filled sky. *Don't have to worry about rain tonight, looks like.* The moon still hadn't made an appearance. It was a peaceful night. He relaxed and sipped his coffee.

Orange flames from his small campfire licked toward the sky and offered cozy warmth on a chilly spring night. Sparks drifted lazily upward.

One of his horses nickered. He had company.

Instantly, Ray reached for his Spencer carbine that lay nearby. His quick glance swept the jagged circle of light from the campfire, but couldn't penetrate the darkness beyond.

A soft swish sped through the darkness, like a sparrow in flight. Something slammed into his leg. A sharp, piercing pain shot through his left leg.

He glanced quickly down. An arrow protruded from his thigh, just above the knee.

A movement captured his attention. A half-naked Indian emerged from the darkness racing toward Ray. The attacker hurtled toward him with an upraised tomahawk in his right hand.

Ray swung the carbine and fired point-blank into the chest of the oncoming attacker. Another movement behind the first Indian jerked Ray's head around. A large Indian with a painted face was notching an arrow. Ray levered a shell and shot the savage in the chest. A third attacker emerged from the darkness, but quickly turned on his heels and disappeared.

Ray levered another shell and hunkered down. He waited. Time inched by. Finally convinced that the third Indian had given up and left, Ray pitched some sticks on the campfire and by the light of the leaping blazes, examined his leg.

The leg throbbed with each heartbeat. Blood was oozing steadily from around the arrow and had soaked his britches wringing wet. He drew his long hunting knife from its belt scabbard and used it to cut away the pant leg.

The arrow had sunk deep just above the knee. Judging by the length of the arrow shaft, but mostly guessing, he figured the arrowhead lay at least four inches inside his leg.

He twirled his neckerchief into a tourniquet and wrapped it around his leg just above the arrow shaft. He cut a small stick and used it to twist the tourniquet, hoping to slow down his loss of blood.

He knew the arrow had to come out, but how? It would take him two days to catch up with Link's herd even if he could ride, which he seriously doubted. It would be close to a week—at the very least, four days—before the next herd came by. *I can't last a week with this arrow sticking outta my leg.*

Chapter XIII

Cody said his goodbyes and rode out of Waco, Texas just as the sun was sinking behind the western horizon. In his saddlebag was the rolled-up gun belt, hand tooled holster, and pearl handled Colt formerly belonging to the late Vance Longley.

Now that he felt the Pinkertons were no longer looking for him, maybe he could put his gun fighting days behind him and live a normal life. Once again, the serape and belly holster lay tucked safely in his saddlebags. He hoped he would no longer be recognized as the Hondo Kid.

He rode until the stars told him it was near midnight, made dry camp, rose, and rode again. As the miles passed beneath Cincinnati's hooves, Cody became more and more anxious to get back to Colorado. His mind was saturated with thoughts of Juliana.

Ever since he left Colorado, she was the last thing on his mind before he went to sleep and his first thought every morning. He felt sure Juliana loved him and there was no doubt that he loved her, but she was a wealthy ranch owner, he was a nobody. His pride wouldn't tolerate him asking for her hand until he made something of himself, it wouldn't be right.

By the fifth day he arrived at the Red River. Just across the river was the Indian Territory. A large herd of Longhorns was making the crossing as Cody reined up on the Texas side of the river. He hooked a leg around his saddlehorn and watched the Texas drovers as they worked the cattle, forcing the long line of longhorns across the wide crossing.

A Mexican vaquero rode up on a midnight-black horse. He reined up near Cody.

"I am Carlos Rodriguez."

"They call me the Hondo Kid," Cody said without thinking. He had used the name for so long it was second-nature. "This your herd?"

"I am the trail boss, *señor.* The cattle belong to the ranch I work for."

"Must be a big ranch to trail a herd this size."

"*Si,* it is. This herd is but one of twenty-four we will take to Kansas this year."

Cody's mouth dropped open.

"You're driving twenty-four herds this size to Kansas this year? What's the name of this ranch?"

"It is called the Longhorn Ranch. It is on the Rio Grande River just across from Mexico."

"The Longhorn, huh?" Cody repeated. "I've heard of it. Somebody told me they have some high-powered bulls for sale."

"*Si,* they are sired by *El Toro* and are the finest bulls one can find anywhere."

"Where you headed with the herd?"

"Abilene, Kansas."

"Long way."

"*Si,* I must be going. *Adios, señor.*"

Cody touched his hat brim as the trail boss reined his horse around and followed the last longhorns that were just climbing from the river into Indian Territory.

Making some mental calculations, he figured there must have been at least two thousand head in the herd that just crossed. The trail boss had said they took twenty-four herds a year up the trail. *That's 50,000 head of cattle! I can't even imagine a ranch that big.*

He shook his head in wonder and heeled his pinto toward the northwest.

When Mary Ann and Juliana arrived back in Trinidad, Molly met them at the door.

"Are you all right, child?" the boarding house owner asked frantically. "Come on in here to the dining room. Let me take a look at you. You're all scratched up and no telling what all else."

They helped Juliana into the dining room. Molly lit a second lamp and set it on the table close by.

"Oh, my," Molly exclaimed, as she saw the cuts and bruises. "Mary Ann, run and get the doctor."

"It's not that bad," Juliana protested.

Mary Ann hurried out the door to fetch the doctor.

"You poor child," Molly continued, as she hurried to the kitchen to heat some water. "We was worried sick when they found your horses dragging part of your buggy. We didn't know what had happened to you. Did you wreck your buggy or what?"

"It was a saddle tramp. He tried to kill me."

"Oh, my goodness!" Molly shouted from the kitchen. "What in the world is this world coming to when a decent woman can't drive down the road without being attacked by some no-good. Did they catch him yet?"

"I don't know. Mr. Hamilton and Sammy were looking for him. Mary Ann brought me back to town."

"Well, I sure hope they catch him. Going around attacking decent women. A man like that ought to be horsewhipped before they hang him. You met Sammy, didn't you? Ain't he a nice young man? Him and Mary Ann are making eyes at one another. I tell you, he sure beats the no-good she had before."

Mary Ann and Doctor Goodson hurried in. The doctor set his black bag on the table next to Juliana and opened it.

Molly came in carrying a pan of hot water and some towels.

"Let's take a look at you," the doctor said, lifting Juliana's arms to inspect the deep scratches and bruises. "Hate to ask, but I'll need you to remove your shirt so I can tend to all these injuries."

Juliana reluctantly removed her shirt. She felt embarrassed to sit there in a man's presence with only her petticoat top to hide her.

Doctor Goodson took his time. He examined her arms, shoulders, and knees. He carefully cleansed the scrapes with a wet towel, wiping the blood away, and withdrew a bottle from his doctor's bag and opened it.

"This is alcohol. I'm going to cleanse these scrapes with it to keep them from getting infected. This is going to burn."

He was right. Juliana winced when the doctor applied the alcohol. He applied some kind of salve and then bound up the scrapes and cuts with clean white bandages.

"I believe that will take care of it," Doctor Goodson told her. "Keep those bandages on for a few days."

After the doctor left, and at Miss Molly's insistence, Juliana explained in detail the events of the night. By the time she finished daylight had crept into the house.

"Oh, my goodness," Molly exclaimed. "Here it is daylight and I haven't got breakfast yet. The boarders will be up and hungry before I can possibly get it ready."

"I'll help," Mary Ann told her, rising and heading for the kitchen.

"I'll help, too," Juliana volunteered.

"No," Molly said firmly. "You go on to your room and get yourself in bed. You need some rest. Me and Mary Ann will handle the breakfast."

Juliana nodded and headed for her room, Cody's room. Just the reminder brought memories flashing through her thoughts: memories of their long walks in the snow, memories of their talks in front of the fireplace, memories of their quiet, intimate moments holding hands.

Will I ever see him again?

She lay across Cody's bed. Her body cried out for rest. She quickly drifted off to sleep with foggy pictures of Cody filling her mind.

After Juliana and Mary Ann left for town, Ed Hamilton and Sammy Schroeder hurried their horses farther down the narrow road. They quickly found the tree that had been pulled across the road and caused Juliana's buggy to wreck.

They reined their horses to a stop. Hamilton crossed his lips with a finger asking for silence. They were rewarded within a few minutes when they heard a horse approaching through the underbrush. Both men slid rifles from their saddle boots and levered shells.

A horse and rider emerged from the bushes no more than forty yards farther down the road.

"Just you hold it right there, mister!" the storekeeper shouted.

The surprised man jerked his head around. Hamilton kept the man covered while Sammy hurried his horse up beside the stranger.

"Get down off your horse!" the young German ordered.

"Who are ya?" the saddle tramp demanded. "Why you bothering me? I'm jest passing through."

Hamilton rode up, his rifle still pointed at the tramp.

Sammy dismounted and roughly pulled the saddle tramp off his horse and snatched the gun from the man's holster.

"Tie his hands," Hamilton said, pitching a rope to his young companion.

"Mister, don't know how they treat men who molest ladies where you come from. Here in Trinidad, we hang 'em."

"I ain't bothered nobody!" the tramp shouted.

"Save your breath for the trial."

Juliana awoke with a start. She hurt all over. She blinked her eyes at the brightness. *How log have I slept?* she wondered, as she climbed stiffly from the bed. She splashed water on her face and dried on the towel hanging nearby.

She found Molly and Mary Ann in the spacious living room. Mary Ann was breast-feeding little Marilyn, her youngest. Molly sat in a rocking chair crocheting a baby blanket.

"What time is it?" Juliana asked sleepily.

"It's about three o'clock," Molly told her. "Did you get some sleep? How you feeling?"

"I sure did, but I'm sore all over."

"Sammy and Mr. Hamilton caught the saddle tramp," Mary Ann told her. "He's locked up down at the jail. He said they were gonna have his trial tomorrow. He said you'd need to be there to testify against him."

"Thank goodness."

"Wonder what in the world made him think he could get away with what he did?" Molly asked. "I tell you, some men are no better than animals."

"Well, I'm glad they caught him." Juliana said, hoping her friends would drop the subject.

"Sammy said the fellow still had a slug in him when they caught him." Mary Ann told her.

"I thought I hit him, but I wasn't sure. He just kept coming after me like a crazy person."

"Well, if you ask me, he can't be none too bright, doing what he did." Molly added. "You two go ahead and visit. I've got to get supper started. Those boarders will be coming in before long, hungrier than wolves."

Molly left and headed for the kitchen. Mary Ann finished feeding the baby and placed her on her shoulder to burp her.

"I appreciate Sammy coming with you to rescue me," Juliana said. "Where is he? I'd like to thank him."

"He went on to work after they got back with the tramp. Sammy's a hard worker. He says he's gonna hit a silver vein in his mine and when he does, we're gonna get married. But working his mine all by himself, it's real slow."

"He sure seems like a good man. So he has his own mine?"

"Yes. Right now it's nothing but a hole in the side of a mountain, but someday he's gonna hit that silver vein. I just know it."

"I hope you're right," Juliana said. "I think I'm going to walk down to Hamilton's store and talk to Mr. Hamilton. I'll be back before suppertime."

"Yeah, the baby's asleep so I'm gonna help Molly get supper."

Juliana draped a crocheted shawl around her shoulders and walked toward the store. Several men touched finger and thumb to their hat brim as she made her way along the street. She nodded her greeting.

Mr. Hamilton and Wilbur, his helper, were busy loading a wagon with sacks of feed. She browsed around the store while she waited for them to finish.

The store was spacious and well stocked. Floor-to-ceiling shelves held most anything and everything one could imagine. She fingered through the dresses hanging on a rack, but found nothing of interest.

"Find anything I can help you with?" Hamilton asked, as he came in the back door.

"No, sir, I was just killing time."

"Reckon you heard we caught that fellow?"

"Mary Ann told me. She said something about having a trial tomorrow?"

"Yep, we decided nothing would be gained by waiting. Judge Goodson said he couldn't think of no reason to wait, so we're having it tomorrow."

"Mary Ann said I'd have to testify."

"Yes, since you're the one he tried to kill, we'll need you to tell what happened."

"I suppose so."

The trial was held in the largest building in town, the church. The building was packed. Since the town still hadn't found anyone to replace Cody, Ed Hamilton served as the prosecutor, and the preacher, Reverend Bishop, reluctantly acted as the man's attorney. Juliana sat with Molly, Mary Ann, and Sammy in the front row.

It took only a few minutes to choose twelve local citizens as jurors from the fifty or so that raised their hands to volunteer. They sat in chairs on the platform behind the pulpit.

The judge sat behind a small table on the left of the raised platform.

When the jury was in their seats, two men brought the accused in wearing handcuffs and leg irons. He was placed in a chair on the right side of the platform.

"Your honor," Ed Hamilton said, rising to his feet. "Ladies and gentlemen of the jury. We intend to show that this fellow sitting right here," Hamilton said, lifting an arm and pointing a finger at the saddle tramp, "attacked and attempted to molest and kill Miss Juliana Higgins yesterday on a road west of town."

"Call your first witness," Judge Goodson said.

"I call Miss Juliana Higgins."

Juliana rose from her seat and made her way onto the platform, where she sat down in the chair pointed to by Mr. Hamilton.

"We all know who you are, but for the record, tell us your name?"

"Juliana. Juliana Higgins."

"Tell us in your own words, what happened yesterday on the road west of town?"

Juliana told the story exactly as it happened, leaving nothing out. It took a while. As she talked, she avoided looking at the saddle tramp. When she finished, Mr. Hamilton sat down.

"You want to cross-examine her, Reverend?"

"No, your honor."

"Then you can step down, Miss Higgins," the judge told her. "Call your next witness, Ed."

"I call Sammy Schroeder."

Sammy rose and stepped onto the platform and sat down in the witness chair.

"Tell us your name?"

"Samuel Schroeder."

"What is your occupation, Mr. Schroeder?"

"I'm a silver miner."

"And did you have occasion to go with me out on the road west of town early yesterday morning?"

"Yes, sir."

"Tell us what happened."

Sammy explained, in broken English with a German accent, that Mary Ann was getting worried because it was after dark and Juliana still wasn't back from visiting some ranches west of town. He explained that he walked down to see if Mr. Hamilton had seen or heard from her.

While they were talking, Juliana's team of horses galloped into town dragging the tongue of her buggy. They caught the horses and immediately saddled their own mounts and went looking for her. Mary Ann insisted on going with them.

He explained they had found her on the side of the road west of town and that she was cut up and bruised something terrible. He said Juliana told them somebody tried to kill her and that he was still in the woods.

He told about sending Mary Ann and Juliana back to town while he and Mr. Hamilton looked for the man. He said the man came out of the woods and they captured him on the road.

"Is that man in the court room?" Hamilton asked.

"Yes, sir," Sammy said, pointing directly at the saddle tramp.

"You got any questions for this witness?" Judge Goodson asked the preacher.

"No, Your Honor."

"You got any more witnesses, Ed?"

"No, Your Honor. The prosecution rests its case."

"Very well. Reverend, you want to call any witnesses?"

"Yes, Your Honor, I'd like to call Otis Scrubbs to the stand."

The saddle tramp struggled from his chair. He had trouble shuffling onto the platform in his leg irons. He slouched into the witness chair.

That was the first time Juliana had heard his name.

"Tell us your name."

"Otis Scrubbs."

"And where are you from, Mr. Scrubbs?"

"Here and there. No place in particular."

"You heard the testimony of the two witnesses. Was it you they encountered on the road west of town night before last?"

"It was me, but what they said was all a pack of lies."

"Then tell us *your version* of what happened."

"Well, I was on that road, sure, but all I did was ask that lady how far it was to town. She got all huffy and pulled a gun on me, so I rode on down the road."

"And did you see her again later that afternoon?"

"Yeah, I did. A tree had fallen across the road and I was gonna pull it off the road out of the way. I figured folks would be passing and I wanted to do the right thing. I rested awhile before I done it, though. I was in the bushes relieving myself when I heard this buggy flying up the road like a bat outta ...well, you know.

"Anyways, before I could get my britches up I heard a crash. I ran to see if anybody was hurt, but couldn't find anybody. I started searching through the bushes when all of a sudden somebody shot me.

"It took me awhile to get myself together and find my horse. First thing I knew, these two fellows rides up and puts me under the gun and ties me up and here I am. I didn't do nothing to that woman. What she said I done is a lie."

It took the jury less than five minutes to find the defendant guilty of attempted murder.

"You got anything to say before I sentence you?" Judge Goodson asked the saddle tramp.

"I said my piece."

"Very well. Then I sentence you to be hung by your neck until you are dead. The sentence will be carried out as soon as we can get a gallows built. This court is adjourned."

Chapter XIV

Ray lay beside his campfire with the arrow sticking out of his leg and considered his options.

If I try to ride two or three days to catch up with Link's herd, I'll most likely bleed to death before I could reach them.

If I stay here and wait four or five days for the next herd to come through, infection will set in and likely kill me.

What's left? That arrow's got to come out or I'm a goner. Not much choice. Looks like I'm elected. But should I wait until daylight so I can see what I'm doing?

No, the longer I wait the more blood I'll lose and the more chance I'll have for infection to set in. No, I've got to do it and I've got to do it now. A man's gotta do what a man's gotta do.

Having made his decision, he reached out and placed the blade of his hunting knife in the flames of the campfire. His canteen lay attached to his saddle within easy reach. *I'll need something to bandage the leg after I get the arrow out.* He pulled his shirt off and tore it into strips.

Figuring the knife blade was as sterile as it was gonna be, he reached it into his hand.

If I can run the blade down the path of the arrowhead on both sides, it ought to clear a path for the barbs of the arrowhead to come out. Easier said than done, but if that arrowhead comes off and stays in my leg, there's no way I could get it out. I've got to clear a path for it to come out.

Positioning the point of the knife beside the shaft of the arrow, he took a deep breath—and shoved the knife blade as hard as he could, and with the same stroke, withdrew the knife blade.

An involuntary scream erupted from his throat. The pain was beyond belief. He bit the next scream off by clamping his teeth together like a vise. His whole body shook with the intense pain. Great drops of sweat popped out on his forehead and ran down into his eyes.

He gasped wildly for breath. His head spun like a child's toy top. He blinked his eyes to clear his vision. Pain radiated up his leg and spread throughout his body.

He collapsed back against his upturned saddle.

Can I stand to do the same thing again on the other side of the arrowhead? I've got no choice. It's got to be done.

He rested for a long moment, sorely tempted to postpone what he knew had to be done.

Finally accepting what he had to do and setting his mind to it, he again positioned the point of the knife on the other side of the arrow. This time, he placed a small green stick between his teeth, then shoved the knife with all his remaining strength.

He couldn't stop screaming. He muffled them with a fist, but the pain was so overwhelming the screams kept coming out. Finally they subsided to a steady groan. He gasped for breath. The world around him was spinning crazily. He glanced down through hazy eyes at the arrow. He rested for several minutes.

I've still got the hardest part left to do. Will I have the strength left to pull the arrow out? I'm not sure.

He reached for his canteen and took a long swallow. *I better put my gloves on so I can grip the shaft of the arrow better,* he decided.

Pulling on his gloves and placing his hands side-by-side as low on the arrow as he could, he breathed a silent prayer that whoever the Indian was who made the arrow knew what he was doing. If the arrowhead separated from the shaft and remained inside his leg, his chances of survival were slim and none. He gripped the shaft with all the strength in his work-hardened hands and jerked with every ounce of power left in him.

Chester's feet barely touched the ground for the next few days. He spent long hours sitting in the big rocking chair beside Selena's bed with little Dakota in his arms.

"She's going to be spoiled rotten and it's all your fault," Selena said, smiling at her husband.

"I want her to be spoiled," Chester replied. "I want my daughter to have the best of everything I'm able to give her."

"I've been in this bed long enough. I'm ready to get up and get to work."

"Nope, Jewel said you are to stay in bed two more days. She says you need time to get your strength back."

"But I'm getting lazier by the minute."

"There ain't a lazy bone in your beautiful body," he said.

"But right now, I need to go check on the herd that's supposed to leave in the morning. I'll be back before supper."

He gently laid the baby in her mother's arms and leaned down to kiss his wife.

"I love you," he whispered in her ear after the kiss.

"I love you, too, Chester. Thank you."

He drew back and looked confused.

"For what?"

"For loving me," she told him, smiling.

"You're sure welcome, ma'am. It's a pleasure."

He left the house and walked across the compound to the corral. The old stableman hurried out.

"Do you want me to saddle your horse, *señor?*"

"No, I'll do it. Much obliged, anyway."

He caught his horse and slipped the bridle in place and then led it into the barn. He positioned the saddle blanket and pulled down his saddle from the hanging strap, then placed the saddle on the sorrel's back and threaded both belly girths.

When he had both straps tightened, he toed a stirrup and swung into the saddle.

He headed for the valley they used to hold the herds getting ready for the long trek to Kansas. The Longhorn trail crews had been with the ranch long enough that they knew what had to be done and did it without being told. They needed little direction from the foremen.

Chester mentally went over the men they had chosen to head up the many operations that made up the Longhorn Ranch. They had twelve trail crews, each a separate, self-sustaining entity. Each crew was made up of twenty drovers, two chuck wagons, and a utility wagon used to carry extra supplies. Yet each crew was part of the whole. He thought of it all as being like his hand. Each finger had it's own function, and yet it worked together as a hand.

Their growing herd of stock cattle and bulls would be the basis for sustaining the ranch long after the trail drives ceased.

Their sales of *El Toro's* offspring were growing beyond belief. The first crop of eighteen-month old bulls was already sold and most of those that wouldn't be ready for another year were reserved. Ranchers from far and wide were contacting them weekly about buying one of the monster bull's offspring.

The day-to-day operation of the ranch was yet another operation in itself. At last count, they had near three hundred on the Longhorn payroll. All those hands had to be sheltered, fed, and provided for. That was a monumental task in and of itself.

No question about it, the ranch had grown far beyond anything me or Buck could have imagined.

Chester reined up on the hill overlooking the holding valley, the sea of longhorns below seemed endless. He watched the experienced cowboys work the herd, in essence, training them for the upcoming drive. His heart swelled inside his chest.

Jody Brown rode up beside him. The former bronc buster had proven himself and been promoted to oversee the preparation of the herds for the trail.

"Howdy, boss."

"Howdy, Jody. How're things going?"

"This herd's almost ready. We're working with the next herd over in the east valley too."

"Any problems?"

"None we can't handle."

"That's always good to hear. You're doing a good job, Jody. Keep up the good work."

"Thanks, boss. How's that new baby?"

"Prettiest girl ever born."

Jody laughed. "Spoken like a proud papa."

"Thought I'd ride out and look our brood herd over. They still in the pasture upriver?"

"Yep. Huey Horne ought to be around there somewhere."

"I'm obliged," Chester said, heeling his sorrel.

A galloping rider coming from the direction of the ranch caught Chester's attention. He reined up to wait for him. As he drew near, Chester recognized the rider as Charley Bean, one of Bud Cauthorn's deputies from Del Rio.

"They told me at the ranch I might find you out here," the deputy said. "Bud wants to know if you could ride into town? We've got a jasper locked up he wants to talk with you about."

"Reckon so. Who is this fellow?"

"He told us his name was Bridger. He's been loud mouthing around town that he was gonna kill you. Said you killed two of his brothers. Bud threw him in jail and sent me after you."

"Tell the marshal I'll ride in this afternoon."

"Yes, sir, Mr. Colson. This hombre's a slick one. Looks like a gunfighter to me."

The deputy touched his hat brim with a thumb and finger and reined his horse around.

Bridger, huh? So there was another brother. Somehow they just keep coming outta the woodwork. Reckon I better ride in and have a talk with this fellow.

Chester rode back to the ranch. He wanted to let Selena know where he was going.

"I've got to ride into Del Rio," he told her, as he leaned over and brushed her forehead with his lips. "Want me to tell your mother anything?"

"No, she just left day before yesterday."

"I may have supper with my folks before I come home so I might be a little late. Don't wait up for me."

Chester rode into Del Rio and reined up in front of the marshal's office. He stepped down and tied his horse to the hitching rail. The door to Bud's office stood open.

"Howdy, Chester," Bud greeted, rising from the chair behind his desk and sticking out his hand.

"Howdy, Bud." Chester took the offered hand.

"Have a seat. Charley told you about our guest, didn't he?"

"Yep. He said you had a fellow named Bridger locked up."

"You know him?"

"Don't reckon I do, but I figure he's another brother to the two I killed a while back."

"He rode into town yesterday asking about you. He started mouthing off about how you had killed two of his brothers and he was here to set things right. He's a cool cucumber. Wears two Colts in gunfighter rigs. We got the drop on him with a couple of shotguns and I still thought we was gonna have to kill him to lock him up."

"Let's take a look at this mean hombre," Chester said.

Bud took a large key ring from peg near the door that separated his office from the jail itself. He unlocked the heavy door and swung it open. There were two cells. Inside the second one a man rose from a cot and walked to the front of the barred cell.

Chester judged the man to be pushing thirty, although his weathered, pockmarked face suggested more. He was slim-waisted, with wide shoulders. His arms looked unusually long for his height.

"I'm Chester Colson," he said, stopping in front of the

bars, no more than a few feet from the man. Only the thick bars separated them. "The marshal said you was asking about me?"

For a long moment the man didn't answer. He just stared at Chester with coal-black, unblinking eyes, hard eyes. When he spoke, it was no more than a hoarse whisper, shoved from his throat between clenched teeth.

"You gunned down two of my brothers. I come to set things right."

"Wrong. I hung one of your brothers because he was a no-good horse thief who hung a helpless old man. Your other brother, Wade, I believe his name was, fancied himself a gunfighter like yourself. He thought he was fast. Turned out he wasn't fast enough."

"I'm gonna kill you, Colson. Mark my word. They can't keep me locked up in here forever. When I get out, I'm coming for you."

"Let me give you a piece of advice, Bridger. Don't ever corner something that's meaner than you are. I won't be hard to find."

Chester and Bud Cauthorn walked back into the office.

"I'm gonna have supper with my folks over at the café. Just before sundown, turn Bridger loose. Tell him I'll be waiting."

"No offense, Chester, but you sure about this?"

"I don't want to have to be looking over my shoulder worrying about getting shot in the back. I'd rather pick the time and place."

"If that's what you want."

"That's the way I want it."

Chester walked from the marshal's office to the bank. He returned the teller's greetings with a nod and made his way to his father's office. He paused outside the frosted-glass door that read, *SAM COLSON-PRESIDENT*. The sign made Chester proud. He tapped on the door before opening it and stepping inside.

Sam Colson sat behind a large, highly polished desk. A wide grin crossed his face when he saw Chester.

"Howdy, Pa. Hope I'm not interrupting anything."

"Nonsense. It's good to see you. Thanks for stopping by. How's my new granddaughter?"

""Pretty close to perfect. When you gonna get a chance to come out and see her?"

"Soon. Real soon. I've been so busy here I haven't had time to sneeze."

"Wondering if you and Ma could have supper with me over at the café later this afternoon?"

"Don't see why not. Any special occasion?"

"Nope, just like to have supper with my folks, that's all. All right if we eat kinda early, say three o'clock? Maybe we'll beat the crowd."

"Three's fine. I'll get word to your mother. She'll like that."

"I've got some things to take care of in town. See you at three."

Chester left the bank and walked up the street to Walker's General Store and Feed Company. It was the busiest place in town. Wagons were lined up four deep waiting to load feed. Three clerks waited on a dozen customers.

"Where could I find John?" he asked the nearest clerk.

"Mr. Walker will be out in the feed warehouse," the lady replied without even looking.

Chester walked from the store and made his way back to the long warehouse. Three men wheeled sacks of feed from inside to the dock. Others stacked it onto wagons backed up to the dock.

"John Walker?" Chester asked one of the men wheeling

out feed. The man jerked his thumb over his shoulder toward the inside. Chester made his way inside.

Feed sacks of all kinds were stacked from floor to ceiling in row after row from one end of the building to the other. Chester spotted Walker directing the men who were moving the sacks from inside to the dock. Walker saw Chester and handed a clipboard to a young man standing nearby.

"*Chester.* It's good to see you. What brings you to town?"

"Having supper with my folks. Got some business to take care of. Did you get that shipment of new feed you were expecting?"

"Sure did. It's supposed to be something special. It's fortified with molasses and ground-up corn. They tell me it will put weight and muscle on your cattle quicker'n anything on the market."

"How much you got for us?"

"Just ordered two ton to start with. See how you like it. If it works for you, I can get all you want."

"I'll send in some wagons to pick it up."

"How's that new baby?"

"Pretty as a picture."

"Congratulations."

From Walker's store, Chester stopped by the barbershop for a leisurely haircut and shave. From there he went by the saddle shop and ordered two dozen double-girded saddles and then, glancing up at the sun, decided it was time to meet his folks. He stopped by the marshal's office and led his horse up the street to Selena's café.

Mrs. Rodriguez greeted him pleasantly and a young Mexican girl showed him to a table near the back of the spacious dining room. She brought coffee and poured. Chester blew steam from the black liquid and waited for his folks to arrive.

Well, here I go again. Another gunfighter relative crawls out of their hole. Seems like there's no end to 'em. I didn't like the way this one looked. He's too sure of himself, too cold. This one scares me.

His thoughts scattered as his folks walked in. His mother made her way directly to Chester's table while Sam Colson took time to visit with the few early customers in the café.

"How's it going, Mom?"

"Good. How are you, son? How's the baby?"

"She's fine. You need to make Pa bring you out to see her before she's grown."

"I know. I've been after him about it. We'll be out in the next day or two. He's always so busy at the bank."

"I know, but he needs to take time out to see his new granddaughter."

"I'll see to it."

Sam finally joined them. They ordered, sipped coffee, and visited until the food came. It was a good time with his parents.

"We need to do this more often," Kathleen said.

"Let's do," Chester agreed. "You got the bank looking good, Pa."

"Our business is booming. The whole town is booming. Most of the credit goes to you and Buck and the Longhorn Ranch."

"It's good for everybody."

"Well, let's run along, Sam," Kathleen said. "Can you take the rest of the day off? There's something at the house I need you to do."

"I suppose. Take care, son. We'll be out to see that new granddaughter in a day or two."

"That would be good."

Chester sipped coffee and waited. When the sun shadows

stretched out long on the street, he swallowed the last of his coffee, paid for their meals, and stepped outside. The sun was just sinking behind the horizon.

Chester stepped to his horse and flipped open a saddlebag. He withdrew his ten gauge, sawed-off shotgun and a handful of double-aught buckshot shells. Flipping open the shotgun, he thumbed two shells into the chamber and closed it with a flip of his wrist. He thumbed back both hammers and waited.

He didn't have long to wait.

Down the street, the door to the marshal's office opened and Bridger stepped through the door onto the boardwalk. He paused and strapped on his guns. Stooping, he tied each holster low on his legs.

He withdrew each Colt and checked the load and then spun the weapons back into their holsters. Only then did his gaze swing up and down the street.

Chester stepped from behind his horse and began walking down the middle of the street toward the gunfighter. Bridger saw him and moved to the middle of the street. Marshal Cauthorn stepped through the door onto the boardwalk.

When Bridger reached the middle of the street he stopped. His feet were spread apart in a gunfighter stance. Only about thirty yards separated the two men. Chester kept walking. His long steps picked up speed. His right hand holding the shotgun hung at his side.

It was clear when the gunfighter spotted the shotgun. His eyes saucered wide. His eyebrows skewed together.

"Just you hold it right there," Bridger said.

Chester walked even faster, his eyes locked on the gunfighter's face.

"I said, stop where you are!"

Chester kept walking.

The look on Bridger's face had suddenly changed from total confidence to uncertainty and confusion.

Only twelve feet separated them.

Chester kept walking.

"But, but this ain't fair! You're not supposed to use a shotgun!"

"Life ain't fair, Bridger," Chester told him, spitting the words through clenched teeth. "You threatened to kill me. Either draw or I'll kill you where you stand."

The gunfighter lost it. His face went chalky-white. Great drops of sweat popped out on his forehead. The look of fear on his face gave way to terror. His eyes bugged out. His lips quivered uncontrollably. His mouth dropped open. The front of his britches were suddenly wet and a puddle formed in the dust at his feet. He suddenly threw his hands shoulder-high. Both hands were shaking wildly, a broken man.

"Marshal! Do something!" he shouted. "You can't just let him kill me in cold blood! Stop him!"

"Nothing I can do," The marshal said. "You made your threats. Either back them up or unbuckle that gun belt."

"Okay. Okay. Don't shoot. I'm unbuckling my gun belt."

Chester watched as Bridger nervously unbuckled his belt. With his left hand he slowly untied the tie-downs and let the weapons drop into the street.

"Bridger, I'm gonna say this once. I ever lay eyes on you again, I'll kill you. Are we clear on that?"

The gunfighter nodded his head again and again.

Chester swung the shotgun with all his might. The blow caught Bridger just above his left ear. The gunfighter dropped like a sack of feed into the dusty street.

Chester turned on his heels, walked back up the street, mounted, and rode out of town.

***

How long he was unconscious, Ray didn't know. He knew it must have been a while because the campfire had burned down to glowing coals. The pain had reduced to a throbbing mass that shook his body with each heartbeat.

Did it come out? He wanted desperately to look down at his leg to see if the arrowhead had come out with the shaft, but he was afraid to. He wanted to know. He had to know. He tried to force his eyes to look, but fear prevented it. *If the arrowhead didn't come out, I'm a dead man.*

He took a deep breath, gritted his teeth, and looked.

Clutched in his bloody hand was the arrow. *The arrowhead was there.*

Ray's emotions gave way. Tears burst from his eyes and he broke down. His body shook with wracking sobs. The sobbing finally subsided and logic broke through the cobwebs of his mind.

He glanced down at the gaping wound. It was bleeding profusely. A large puddle of his life-liquid had formed a growing pool under and around his leg.

I've got to stop the bleeding, but how?

Instinctively he knew. *I've got to cauterize it.* The moment the thought flashed into his mind it repulsed him. His stomach rebelled at the mere thought.

I've gone this far. That's the only way I know to stop the bleeding and improve my chances not to get infection. I've got to do it.

Before he had a chance to change his mind, he wiped the bloody blade clean with a strip of his shirt and stuck the blade into the fire. It took only a few minutes for the knife blade to turn a bright cherry red.

Again, he placed the green stick between his teeth. *This may be the worst part of the whole ordeal.*

Clamping his teeth down on the green stick, he grabbed the knife and in one swift move jammed the glowing-red blade against the gaping wound.

The scream was ear splitting. His entire body shook uncontrollably. Still, he held the blade against the wound. He could hear the skin cooking. The sickening stench of burning flesh turned his stomach. Things were getting dark. He blinked his eyes wildly. The world around him grew foggy. A darkening shroud settled over him.

The hurting stopped.

He floated. Drifted slowly through a foggy darkness. Awareness was an elusive quest that seemed always just beyond his grasp.

Consciousness came slowly. Gradually, the darkness was pushed aside by light. He shook his head to clear his thinking. He blinked his eyes wildly to clear his sight. But with consciousness came the pain.

He looked down. The bleeding seemed to have stopped. The wound looked ugly, but he didn't see the redness or streaks that would have meant infection. *That's the first good news I've had in awhile*.

The stench of burned flesh hung in the air. He would never forget that smell. He reached his canteen and took a long swallow. His dry throat was raw from screaming. The liquid felt soothing.

He picked up one of the strips from his shirt and doused it with water and then carefully wrapped the wound to keep the insects away.

One of his horses snorted, reminding Ray that they were tied to a picket line nearby. They would need water, but there was nothing he could do about it right now. He knew if he moved he would likely open the wound and it would start bleeding again. He was as weak as a kitten. He knew it was from all the blood he had lost.

He lay back against the saddle. It was light, then dark, and then light again. He drifted in and out of consciousness, more out than in. During one of the times he was half-conscious, one of the horses snorted loudly. They were tugging at the picket line that held them. It reminded him that the two horses had been without water since the attack. *How long has it been?* He couldn't even guess. One thing he did know, the horses had to have water.

If I move it's a good bet I'll break open that wound and start bleeding again. But if the horses don't get water, they'll likely die.

He looked around for something, anything to give him answer. A sturdy stick about six foot long lay nearby within reach.

If I could use that stick as a crutch, I just might make it to the horses. If I fall...well, that's just a chance I'll have to take.

Leaning as far out as he could, he was able to reach the stick. He pulled it to him. Using the stick to help him get up, he discovered he was even weaker than he thought.

Finally, he was able to get upright without using his wounded leg.

It was a good thirty feet to the horses; it looked like a mile. Slowly, holding his wounded leg as straight as possible, he took hopping, baby steps toward the horses.

His head spun. He became dizzy. He stopped and waited for the dizziness to subside. It took a while. He was exhausted, and he hadn't gone ten feet. *Maybe I've bitten off more'n I can chew. Maybe I better turn around while I still have a chance to get back to my pallet.*

His big roan swung its head and looked at Ray. It seemed those big, dark eyes were pleading with him not to give up.

Ray nodded his head and took another baby step onward.

He stopped every few feet to rest and clear his head. Finally, he reached the horses. He reached a hand and untied first one, and then the other. They made a beeline for the water.

It took time, a long while, but he finally made it back to his pallet. Carefully, slowly, he lowered himself down. Casting a worried look, he saw that the wound had not broken open. There was no fresh blood. He lay back against his saddle and slept, awoke, and slept again.

Chapter XV

After Cody encountered the Longhorn herd at the Red River crossing, he traveled northwest through the Indian Territory. He rode careful, knowing that the territory was widely known as an outlaw haven. Few lawmen dared venture into this lawless land.

He rode three days and figured he was nearing the Kansas line. He made camp just before sundown on the bank of a small, clear running stream.

After caring for his two horses, he picketed them close by and scrounged up wood for a supper fire. Dark settled in by the time the coffee was boiling. He opened a tin of beans and sliced some salt pork into the pan. He poured himself a cup and sat down for supper. A voice called out.

"Hello the camp!"

Cody thumbed the traveling thong off the hammer of his Remington sidearm.

"Who are you?" he hollered.

"Smelled your coffee. Me and my brother would be obliged if you could spare a cup."

"Unbuckle your gun belts and hang 'em on your saddle horn, then you're welcome to ride in."

After a minute, from the depth of darkness, a horse with two riders aboard stepped into the circle of light from the campfire. Two gun belts hung on the saddle horn.

"You're a mighty careful fellow."

"Live longer that way."

"Smelled your coffee a ways back. You're looking at two mighty thirsty travelers."

The talker was a big man, half-a-head taller than Cody. He looked to be thirty-something with several days beard. His clothes were surprisingly clean for a traveler. His eyes darted around the circle of light and came to rest on Cody.

The second man looked to be about the same age. His clothes were well worn. He had long, blond, stringy hair and a cruel look about him.

Cody judged them both to be untrustworthy. He decided to keep a close eye on them. They climbed from the horse and squatted near the fire. Cody pitched his only extra tin cup to the talker.

"Only got one cup. You'll have to share."

The older man caught the cup and poured it full from the pot.

"Traveling alone, are ye?"

"For now."

"Where you headed?"

"Yonder way."

"Uh-huh," the man said, slanting a darting look at his brother.

The talker blew the steam away and took a long sip of coffee before handing the cup to his brother.

"I didn't catch your name?" the older said.

"Didn't give it."

"Well, sonny, here's the way it is. We're in bad need of

another horse. Couldn't help noticing you've got an extra. We'd like to buy it from you, providing the price is reasonable, of course."

"Ain't for sale."

"Well now, if that's the case, then we've got ourselves a problem."

"And what would that be?"

"Like I said, we need that horse. You get my meaning?"

"Reckon not."

"Then let me put it this way. When we leave, that horse goes with us one way or another."

Cody had seen the bulge in their britches legs about boot high. It could be nothing but hideaway guns they slipped into their boots before riding in.

Now he saw the long haired one slowly slipping his pants leg up without letting on. Cody waited until he pulled the gun from his boot and was in the process of raising it. The older one was also tugging his hidden weapon from his boot.

Cody drew his Remington and shot both of them twice in the chest. He quickly stepped over and kicked the weapons away from the downed men. He touched a finger to their necks and found them both dead. It had all happened so quickly.

He went through their pockets and found three double-eagle gold pieces and a wanted poster. He unfolded it. Staring back at him were the two men he had just killed.

Seems they were the Cobb brothers, Ed and Junior. The poster said they were wanted for murder and robbery. There was a one thousand dollar reward for each of them.

Cody rode into Abilene, Kansas five days later. Two horses followed on lead lines. Tied belly-down on the horses were the two bloated bodies of the Cobb brothers.

Cody reined up in front of the jail. He tied Cincinnati to the hitching rail and stepped to the door of the office.

The lawman sitting behind the desk was tall, slim, and stone-faced. He had a *lawman* look about him. *This fellow's been up and down the trail a few times.* He swung pale green eyes at Cody.

"You the sheriff?"

"Ben Hickman. What can I do for you, young fellow?"

"I'm Cody Cordell. Got a couple fellows outside that's in bad need of a quick burying."

Cody pulled the wanted poster from his shirt pocket, unfolded it, and handed it to the lawman. Hickman studied the poster for a minute before cutting his eyes up at Cody.

"You saying the two men you got outside are the Cobb brothers?"

"Yep."

"Let's have a look," Hickman said, pushing his tall frame from the chair.

They walked outside. Before the sheriff got close to the bodies he wrinkled his forehead and grabbed his nose.

"How long they been dead, for crying out loud?"

"Reckon it's five days now."

The sheriff grabbed a handful of hair and lifted the head of first one, and then the other before retreating a safe distance away.

A small crowd had gathered a short distance away from the awful smell. The lawman called to one of them.

"Billy, lead these two horses over to the undertaker's. Come on inside, young fellow."

Cody followed the lawman into the office. After they were seated, Hickman fixed Cody with a questioning look.

"You're too young to be a bounty hunter. How'd you come to kill these two?"

Cody started at the first and told the lawman exactly how it all happened.

"I tried to find someplace closer to drop them off, but most places I stopped didn't even have a lawman. Is that poster right? Is that reward still good?"

"Far as I know now, it is, but I'll have to send a telegram to Fort Smith to the United States Marshal. He's the one who will have to authorize it before you can collect the money."

"How long will that take?"

"Can't say. I'll get the telegram off right away, but then we'll have to wait for a reply before anything else can happen. Off hand, I'd say two, maybe three days. A week at the most."

"That long, huh? Well, I'll be over at the hotel. Would you let me know if you hear anything?"

"Sure will."

Cody left the sheriff's office and walked over to the undertaker's business. The bodies had already been unloaded. He collected his three horses and walked them down the street to the biggest and fanciest livery he had ever seen. There must have been a hundred stalls in the sprawling building.

A black man dressed up like a butler came out to meet him as he walked his horses into the wide entrance of the livery.

"Might I help you, sir?"

"Well, I wanted to stall my horses, but looking around, I might ought to ask the price first."

"They'd be two dollars a night. Feed's extra."

"Is the two dollars for each horse?" Cody asked, shocked at the price.

"Yes, sir."

"How much if you want feed?"

"If you want 'em fed, it's three dollars a night."

"Who would I talk to about selling the bay mare?"

"You'd need to talk with Mr. Blue. You'll find him in that office right yonder. You want me to stall your animals?"

"Not yet."

Cody left his horses and walked to the office the black fellow had pointed out. He found Mr. Blue tipped back in his chair sipping coffee.

"I got a mare for sale. The fellow outside said I should talk to you."

"What kind of mare you got?" the man asked, sounding totally disinterested.

"Little bay."

The man rocked to his feet, stretched, and swallowed the last of his coffee.

"I'll take a look, but not much market these days."

Cody could tell right off the man was a horse trader. He was already laying the groundwork for a small offer. They walked out to the runway where Cody's three animals waited.

The man circled the bay slowly, his searching gaze taking in every detail of the mare. He ran his hand up and down the front legs and lifted the animal's top lip to look at her teeth.

"'Bout four years old, is she?" he asked.

"Couldn't say," Cody replied.

"You got a bill of sale on her?"

"Nope. She use to belong to two fellows who tried to kill me. Now she belongs to me."

The man crooked a sideways look. Cody saw a new respect in the man's eyes.

"Obviously, they came out on the wrong side of that argument. Okay, I'll work something out on the bill of sale. I'll give you thirty dollars for the bay if you'll throw in the saddle and bridle."

Cody shook his head. "I'm obliged, but with the saddle and all, I figure it's worth fifty."

"Fifty!" the horse trader near shouted. "I could buy a racehorse for fifty. No, thirty is the best I can do."

"Reckon I'll keep her, then," Cody said, turning to gather the reins of his three animals.

"Okay, okay. Against my better judgment, I'll give you forty for the lot."

"Throw in stall and feed for my other two for three nights and you got a deal."

"That's eighteen dollars worth right there. That comes out to fifty-eight dollars," the man protested. "I can't do that"

"Then good day to you," Cody told him as he walked his three horses away.

"All right, all right. I'll give you thirty and stall your other two for three nights. That's forty-eight dollars."

"Deal," Cody said, handing the reins to the three animals to the black man.

"Come on in the office and I'll get your money. Don't know what business you're in, but you ought to be buying and selling horses."

Cody left the livery with thirty dollars in his pocket. He slung his saddlebags over a shoulder and, with his rifle in hand, headed toward the hotel next door.

The *Drover's Inn* was the biggest hotel he had ever seen. It was a large, two story, box-like structure with wide steps leading up to a front porch that spanned the entire width of the building. The hotel was painted dark green with beige trim.

Folks of every description strode in and out. Cody climbed the steps and stepped through the double doors.

If he thought the outside was impressive, he was amazed

at the inside. He could actually see himself in the polished wood floor. Upholstered sofas and chairs were scattered around the large lobby, occupied by several men and women engaged in deep conversation.

Cody spotted a high counter he took for the check-in desk and headed that way.

"May I help you, sir," a stiff-collared, baldheaded fellow asked curtly, eying Cody up and down with obvious disdain.

"I'd like a room."

"Do you have a reservation?"

"No, didn't know I needed one. Just rode into town."

"Normally we are full this time of year, but I do have one room available on the second floor. How many nights would you be staying?"

"Don't know for sure, most likely three."

"Just sign your name in the book," the man instructed, sliding a key across the desk. "It will be eighteen dollars, please."

"Eighteen dollars?" Cody questioned, looking up from the registration book.

"Yes, sir. Our regular rooms are six dollars a night. *In advance.*"

Cody fished out the money the horse trader had just paid him and laid a double-eagle on the counter. He picked up his change and the key.

"You'll be in room number sixteen. Up the stairs and at the far end of the hall."

Cody touched his hat brim to a lady as he headed toward the stairway. She offered a thin smile.

He climbed the stairs and walked the length of the hall to room number sixteen. He tried the knob and found the door unlocked. He pushed the door open and stepped inside and locked the door behind him.

The room was small, but comfortable. There was a bed with a pink bedspread on it. A dark-colored dresser hugged one wall with a white wash pan and pitcher on it. A mirror hung on the wall behind the dresser. A single, upholstered chair sat near the bed. A window with a thin white curtain opened to the street. Cody pushed the curtain aside and was amazed at the traffic on the dusty street below.

I've got my horses seen to and a roof over my head for the next three days. Might just as well take it easy and rest up, I reckon.

He hung his saddlebags over the back of the chair and propped his rifle against the wall near the bed. He unbuckled his gun belt and hung it over the headboard. Then he pried off his boots and lay down on the bed. He was asleep within short minutes.

Juliana arrived back at the Higgins Ranch just before sundown. Roy, her foreman, saw her riding in and hurried to meet her.

"I was getting a mite worried," he said, holding onto her mount's bridle as she dismounted.

"How are you, Roy? A lot has happened since I've been gone. I'll tell you all about it first thing in the morning. Right now, I'm beat. I'm going to take me a long hot bath and get a good night's sleep. Oh, one thing. There'll be three men coming, probably in the morning. I've hired them to build new cabins for our workers."

"Our men will be happy to hear that. We've been needin' them for a long time."

"I know. I feel awful that our people have been living like that for so long. One more thing, I bought two herds of cattle. I'll need you to take some of the men and pick them up. I'll tell you more about it in the morning."

She left her horse with the foreman and walked up to the house. Maria, her housekeeper, was sweeping the floor of the living room.

"Welcome home, Miss Higgins," the housekeeper greeted happily.

"Thank you, Marie, it's good to be home. How is your family?"

"My family is good. It's good to have you back home."

"Would you mind asking a couple of the young boys to carry water and heat it for a bath?"

"Yes, ma'am. I'll see to it right away."

"Thank you, Marie."

While she waited for the water to heat for her bath, she went to the den, opened the safe, and counted out the money to pay for the herds of cattle she had bought.

In less than an hour, Juliana lay back in her bathtub. The warm water soaked into her tired, bruised, and aching body and felt so good. She was exhausted. She leaned back, closed her eyes, and let her thoughts wander. As usual, during quiet moments, Cody popped into her mind.

Wonder where he is? Wonder what he's doing right now? Wonder if he might be thinking about me? Wonder if I'll ever see him again? These and a thousand other thoughts flashed through her mind.

Juliana awoke with a start after drifting off to sleep. The water was cold so it was clear she had slept awhile. She climbed out of the tub, dried herself, and padded barefooted over to the bed. She crawled in, snuggled up against her pillow, and was sound asleep in minutes.

* * *

Juliana was up, dressed, and had breakfast almost ready when Maria arrived. She asked the housekeeper if she would go to the bunkhouse and invite Roy to come to the house for breakfast. He arrived a short time later with hat in hand.

"I'd like for you to have breakfast with me if you could." she told the surprised foreman. "We need to go over some plans I've been thinking about. I want your input on them. Have a seat. I'll pour us some coffee."

He looked nervous as he took a seat. Maria served the breakfast and Juliana began to lay out her plans as they ate. Roy listened closely. When they finished eating, Maria poured them a second cup of coffee.

"As I mentioned last night," Juliana told her foreman. "I've bought two herds of cattle from some local ranchers as you suggested not long ago. I'd like you and some of the hands to ride over to the Cy Johnson Ranch. It's about ten miles west of Trinidad. I bought a hundred-twenty head of cattle from him. I told him I would ask you to pick them up and pay him. I bought them for ten dollars a head."

She pushed a small leather drawstring pouch across the table. "Here's twelve hundred dollars to pay for them."

"Down the road past the Johnson place, you'll find the Merv Gillette Ranch. I bought a thousand head from him. Pick them up and pay him the ten thousand dollars, which is also in this pouch."

"Yes, ma'am. I'll get a crew together and head out first thing this morning," he said, rising. "We ought'a be back by tomorrow sometime. Is there something else, ma'am?"

"No, I guess that covers it unless you have something."

"No, ma'am, 'cept I'd like to say you're doing a mighty fine job running the ranch."

"Thank you, Roy."

"You're welcome, ma'am," he said, picking up his hat and turning to leave. Then he stopped, fidgeted with his hat a moment, and said. "You shore are easier to work for than your pa."

Before noon, Ian Fritz arrived with his two boys to begin work on the cabins. He awkwardly introduced them as Klaus and Gustav. Both boys were just a bit shorter than their father, but were heavily muscled and seemed awful shy. They both bowed when they were introduced.

The builder had two wagonloads full of tools, chains, and ropes. Teams of large mules pulled both wagons.

"I'll saddle my horse and show you where I'd like the cabins built."

Juliana rode in the lead. Ian Fritz and his two wagons followed. Juliana reined up near the little settlement and sat her saddle. The builder reined his team of mules to a stop beside her.

"That's the Apishapa River. It starts in the high mountains west of here and winds through half of Colorado into Kansas. It never floods, so I want our cabins built along the bank so my workers and their families will have easy access to the water.

"As you can see, there is plenty of timber. Take what you need, but I want nice, sturdy cabins like we talked about. If you need anything, just let one of my workers know and I'll see you get it. If it's agreeable with you, we'll settle up when the job is finished. Is that satisfactory?"

"Yes'em. That will be good."

Juliana rode down and visited with some of the workers'

wives for awhile. She explained what she was doing and they were excited. Fritz and his boys pulled their wagons a short distance away and went to work setting up their small tent and camp.

It was dusky-dark when Cody woke. He stomped on his boots, stretched, and headed downstairs. His stomach growled like a hungry bear. He by-passed the fancy dining room in the hotel, hoping to find one more to his liking along the busy street.

It seemed the saloons outnumbered all the other businesses combined. As he walked, he counted ten just on one side of the street. He meant to avoid the saloons, if possible, knowing the chances of him being recognized would be greater among the rowdy element.

He found a small café near the far end of the street and went inside. Only two of the six tables were occupied. The place looked clean and the aroma wafting from the kitchen smelled wonderful. Red and white oilskin tablecloths covered the tables. A heavyset woman emerged from the kitchen, wiping her hands on a dishtowel. She greeted him with a happy smile.

"How you doin', cowboy? I got beef stew and cornbread. It's hot, spicy and guaranteed to chase away the hungries."

"Sounds good."

"I 'spect you're a coffee drinking man?"

"Yes, ma'am."

"Coming right up," she said, hurrying into the kitchen and returning with a heavy, white coffee mug and a coffee pot. She poured his cup full and fixed him with a look.

"You just come in with a herd?"

"No, ma'am. Just passing through. I'll only be staying a few days."

"Hope you'll eat with me while you're in town. You're a clean-cut looking young fellow. Not like most of the cow nurses we get."

Cody blew the steam from his coffee and didn't bother answering. He chanced a sip. It was still too hot to drink,. burned his top lip.

"Sure a lot of cowboys in town. Is it like this all time?"

"Yeah, we get a passel of 'em. It's early in the season yet. Won't be long before you won't be able to walk down the street."

She turned and headed for the kitchen to get his supper.

He swept the room with a slow gaze. An older couple sat at one table. Four men sat at the other table. They weren't dressed like the typical cowboy. He judged them to be hard men. Men who wouldn't stoop to nurse cows. One of them cast long looks in Cody's direction.

The lady brought a heaping bowl of beef stew and cornbread and set it in front of him. He split the square of cornbread with a knife and spread a generous layer of butter on it. Then he picked up the big spoon and tasted the stew. It was delicious.

During his meal, he flicked quick glances at the fellow who was staring at him. When he scraped the bowl for the last spoonful and sopped the bowl with the last of his cornbread, the fellow from the other table rose and walked over to Cody's table.

The man was short, thin, and ugly. A long scar ran from his left ear all the way to his chin. He had shifty, mean eyes and wore a tied-down Colt in a butt forward holster.

"You look familiar," the man said, staring hard at Cody. "I've seen you somewhere before. Where was it?"

"Your guess is as good as mine. I never seen you before in my life," Cody said, looking up at the man and sipping on his coffee.

"I know you. I never forget a face. You from Texas?"

"Nope. Colorado."

"Ever been to Texas?"

"Look mister. I don't know you and I ain't looking for trouble. How about we just drop it?"

The man didn't reply. He just stood staring at Cody, refusing to let it go. Suddenly his eyes saucered wide with recognition.

"*Waco.* That's it. It was Waco. You're the Hondo Kid. I saw you gun down Billy Pike. I'm right, ain't I?"

"I don't know what you think you saw. My name's Cordell, Cody Cordell. Now leave me be."

The man was shaking his head from side to side, refusing to accept Cody's story.

"Hey, boys," he hollered to his three companions. "This fellow sitting here is famous. They say he's the fastest gunfighter there is. Billy Pike was one of the best, but this fellow took him easy. Come on over. I want you boys to meet this famous gunfighter."

Only one of his companions rose and walked over to stand beside Cody's table. The other two sat where they were.

The café owner heard what was going on and hurried out of the kitchen. "You boys got a problem, take it outside. I don't want any trouble in my place. Why don't you leave him alone? He's already told you he ain't the man you think he is."

"Mind your own business, old woman. I don't make mistakes. He's the Hondo Kid, sure enough. This fellow's known all over."

Cody could see where this was going and he didn't like where it would end up. *I've tried my best to get around what*

I know is coming. I don't want no trouble here. I'm gonna try one more time to talk him outta this.

"Look mister. I've already told you. I don't want no trouble. Why don't you just let me finish my coffee and I'll leave?"

"He don't sound like no famous gunfighter," the ugly fellow's companion said sarcastically. "Fact is, he sounds more like a coward to me."

Cody stood and fished money from his pocket and handed it to the café owner. "Good meal. I'll be back," he said, turning and heading for the door.

Just as he suspected, they followed. As he stepped outside, he thumbed the traveling thong off the hammer of his Remington. *If this comes to a fight, I sure wish I had my Colt and belly holster, but wishing don't change anything. Reckon I'll have to make do with what I got.*

It was dark. Only lamplight from store windows lit the darkened street. He had gone no more than a few feet when a voice from behind him called out.

"Hey, you. Hondo'. Turn around. I think I can take you."

Cody stopped.

He knew it had gone too far. There was no way out of the fight. He just hoped when he turned around he would be facing only the ugly one, not two, and especially not all four of them. Four to one odds would mean almost certain death. He might be able to take two of them, maybe even three if he got lucky, but four would be impossible. He took a deep breath, let it out slowly, and turned around.

Two men stood facing him with their legs spread apart and their hands hovering just above their side arms.

"Want to know who it is you're facin'?" the ugly one asked, his voice filled with bravado.

"Couldn't care less," Cody said. "Far as I'm concerned, you're just another dead man."

That's all it took. Both men slapped leather. The ugly one was faster. His gun was close to level when Cody's slug punched a hole just below the Bull Durham tag that dangled from gunman's left shirt pocket.

He swung his Remington and shot the second man just as his gun cleared leather. The man's shot plowed a furrow at Cody's feet. Both men toppled into the dusty street. By the time Cody stepped over to them, they had both breathed their last breath.

In mere minutes the sheriff pushed through the crowd that gathered.

Hickman leveled a look at Cody. "It's you again."

"They drew first, sheriff."

"Any of you folks see what happened?" he asked the crowd.

The café owner stepped forward.

"He's telling it like it is, sheriff. Those two fellows kept pestering him, saying he was somebody else. He told them he wasn't, but they wouldn't let it drop. They followed him outside and drew first."

"Thank you, ma'am. Anybody else see it?"

The older couple stepped forward.

"Yes, sheriff, we both saw it. It happened just like that lady said it did."

"Anybody see it different?"

No one spoke up. The two companions stood silently.

"Then I guess you're in the clear. Sure hope that telegram comes in pretty quick, though. I've got enough going on in town without more shootings. Try to stay out of trouble."

* * *

Two days later, Ben Hickman knocked on Cody's hotel door.

"The telegram came through. The reward has been authorized. Here's the voucher for two thousand dollars. You can cash it at the bank."

"I'm obliged, sheriff. Sorry about the shootings the other night. I tried everything I could to get out of that."

"Just tell me one thing for my own curiosity. Are you the one they call the Hondo Kid?"

"Used to be."

The lawman nodded his head. "I understand. It's hard leaving a reputation like that behind, ain't it?"

It was Cody's turn to nod his head and he did.

The next morning, Cody walked out of the bank with two thousand dollars in his pocket. He went directly to the livery, saddled his horses, looped the lead line to his packhorse around his saddlehorn, and booted a stirrup.

"Come on, Cincinnati, let's make some tracks. I got me a *lonesome* on for Colorado."

Chapter XVI

Ray heard them coming long before they arrived.

The chuck wagon was a mere speck on the distant prairie, but his heart leaped inside his chest at the sight. He didn't know whose herd it would be. He had lost track. Didn't matter. Help had finally arrived.

When old Joshua, the cook for Buster Keene's herd, spotted him and pulled the wagon to a stop, the big black man hurried over with worry written all over his face. He took one look at the wound and shook his head.

"Mister Ray, you shore got yourself one bad leg there."

"You should have seen it a couple days ago."

"I gots some medicine in the wagon. Let me fetch it."

"Hope you got something to eat," Ray told him. "I haven't had anything except beef jerky and water for three days."

"I's got some leftover cold biscuits and molasses if'n that'll do you till supper."

"That sounds so good."

"Junior," the cook called to his helper, "bring them leftover biscuits and a jar of molasses fer Mr. Ray."

The lead riders of the herd galloped up and swung to the ground. Buster Keene, the trail boss of the herd, hurried to Ray's side.

"What happened, Ray?"

"Some Indians jumped me five days ago. One of 'em got an arrow in me." Ray told him, picking up the arrow and handing it to the foreman.

"How'd you get it out?"

"Had to cut it out."

"*You* cut that arrow out of your own leg? Never heard tell of such a thing."

"Neither did I, but it was either that or get my ticket punched."

Buster looked closer at the wound the cook was doctoring and shook his head.

"Yeah, maybe so, but I ain't sure I could do that."

"A man can do a lot of things he don't think he can do when he's got no other choice."

"What can we do to help?"

"Joshua, reckon you could find room in the supply wagon to make me a pallet? Don't think I can fork a horse just yet."

"Yes, sir, Mr. Ray. We can shore do that."

Buster flicked a look at the sun. "It's not long till stopping time anyway and we got water here. We'll stop here for the night. We'll water the herd and circle 'em over yonder. Mitch, ride back and tell the others."

Joshua finished doctoring the leg while Ray wolfed down four cold Dutch oven biscuits sopped in molasses.

By the time the drovers had the herd watered, circled, and bedded down for the night, Joshua and his helper had coffee hot and supper almost ready. Twenty tired cowboys straggled into camp. They picked up a tin plate and coffee cup and waited in line for the cooks to ladle their plates full.

Buster filled an extra plate and brought it to Ray.

"How're things going up ahead?" the foreman asked.

"Fair to middlin'," Ray told him. "We had trouble with the first herd. Had a stampede. Lost way too many cattle."

"Yeah, we saw the bones back a ways. Too bad, but those things happen now and again."

"Market's strong though. Rest of the herds made the drive without much trouble. We ought to be running into Smokey's crew heading back home in a day or two. I'll hitch a ride with them back to the ranch."

"Boy, that's somethin'," Buster said, shaking his head as he sipped on his coffee.

"What's something?"

"Man diggin' an arrow outta his own leg. Something to tell my grandkids about."

"Grandkids?" Ray said. "Didn't even know you was married."

"Ain't, but I'm gonna be someday. If I can find a woman that would have me, that is. Gonna have me a whole passel of young'ens. Then I'm gonna sit on the front porch and tell 'em stories about times like this."

"Reckon most every man dreams of something like that."

On June 20, 1869, Buck gaveled the Texas State Congress into adjournment. He hurried to his office, finished some last minute business, and shook hands with his secretary.

"You're actually going home and leave all this work to me for almost a year?" Miss Johnson kidded.

"Yep. Leaving it in your capable hands. I'll see you next April."

"Well, maybe I'll have things straightened out by the time

you get back. Goodbye, Congressman Cordell. You're the best thing that's happened to politics in Texas."

"I'm obliged, Ms. Johnson. You still seeing that guard, what was his name?

"Wilbur. Wilbur Hughes. And yes, we're still seeing one another. He's a very nice man."

"I'm sure he is. Well, time's wasting. I've got a long ways to go. I'll be seeing you."

"Take care of yourself, congressman."

Buck's two security men had the team hitched to his buggy and were waiting on their horses when he emerged from the capitol building.

"Let's make some miles before dark," Buck told them, as he unwound the reins and popped the team's rumps.

A mental image of Rebekah flashed into his mind. He crooked a thin grin and urged his two black horses into a trot.

They were less than a block from the capitol building when a shot rang out. Something slammed into Buck's left arm just below his shoulder. A sharp pain stabbed through his arm and shoulder. The blow slammed him sideways. He lashed the team into a gallop with his good arm.

His two security men, one riding in front and the other behind, immediately jerked their Spencer Carbines from their saddle boots and spurred their horses toward the alleyway where the shot came from.

The buggy bounced along the street, putting distance between Buck and the shooter. He pulled the buggy to a stop a block away and looked down at his arm. Blood had already soaked through the arm of his jacket. He jerked his bandana from his pocket and twisted it around his arm just above the bullet wound.

Back up the street, the distinct sound of two carbines going off within a heartbeat of each other told Buck his men had spotted the shooter. He turned the buggy around and headed back the way he had come.

Wade Thomas, Buck's chief of security, walked from the alley carrying his Spencer rifle.

"We got him, boss. Here's all he had in his pockets."

Thomas handed Buck twenty double-eagle gold pieces and a handwritten note. He unfolded the short note and read it.

Here's your money. He will be leaving the capitol building sometime after noon, heading south. See it's done like we agreed. I want him dead.

"Who'd want to kill you, Boss?" Thomas asked.

"I can think of a few."

The police arrived.

"What's going on here?" the big officer with sergeant's stripes wanted to know.

"Some fellow took a shot at me," Buck told him. "My security men got him. He's over in that alley."

"Ain't you Congressman Cordell?" the officer asked.

"Yes. Here's a note my men found in his pocket along with twenty double-eagle gold pieces. Looks like somebody paid that jasper to kill me."

"We'll look into it. Right now, looks like you need a doctor."

Buck's two security men escorted him to the hospital. After carefully cleaning and examining the wound, the doctor looked up over his spectacles.

"You were very lucky. The bullet passed through the fleshy part of your arm without hitting any bones or vital muscles. I can repair the damage and sew it up. Don't use it for a couple of weeks and you should be fine."

"I'm obliged, doctor."

When Buck emerged from the doctor's office he

encountered three newspaper reporters insisting they needed to know what happened. A police captain was also there.

"I'm sure after the authorities have had an opportunity to do their job they will be happy to keep you informed."

"Yes, I'm Captain McNeil. We have nothing to say at this point. As the congressman said, after we have had sufficient time to investigate this incident, we will be glad to issue a statement. Until then, we will have no further comment. Good day."

Buck pulled the captain aside.

"Is there any reason I should delay my plans to return to my ranch?"

"No, congressman. We will do everything possible to get to the bottom of this and keep you informed of our findings."

"Good. Thank you, captain. Ms. Johnson, in my office, will know how to reach me."

Buck hurried from the hospital accompanied by his armed security men. He climbed into his buggy.

"I'm gonna ride on ahead a ways and look things over before you come through," Thomas told Buck. "We don't want any more surprises."

Part II

Chapter XVII

Cody reined Cincinnati and his packhorse to a stop in a small clearing on the shoulder of a mountain overlooking the Higgins Ranch. His backside felt like it was grown to his saddle. The ride from Waco, Texas had taken the best part of two months.

"Won't be long now," he said aloud to his pinto. "I know you and Sadie are as tired as I am. Right down yonder is a nice stall and plenty of feed just waiting on you."

Cody gazed down at the sprawling ranch. It was a pretty picture. Cattle grazed peacefully on early spring grass. Young colts scampered about playfully near their mothers. Cowboys went about their daily chores near the barn.

His gaze swung to the big house. It stood like a gleaming-white castle in the morning sun with the white picket fence surrounding it. Suddenly the front door opened and Juliana emerged.

Cody's heart leaped inside his chest at the sight of her. She wore dark riding britches and high-topped riding boots.

A white blouse was tucked into her britches. He was surprised to see a gun belt and holster strapped around her waist. A pearl handled gun rested inside the holster.

Why is she carrying a gun? Has something bad happened?

She hurried from the porch and headed toward the stable. Cody heeled his pinto down the mountainside. By the time he got close, Juliana was already in the saddle of her snow-white mare and riding away from the barn.

She spotted him and let out an excited scream. She heeled her mare into a lope and raced to meet him. When they met, they leaned from their saddles and embraced. Happy tears coursed down Juliana's cheeks as they held one another. She laughed through the tears.

"Oh, Cody, you're here! It's so good to see you. You've come back to me."

All he could do was nod. Words were unable to get past the lump lodged in his throat. Their hands clasped and refused to let go as they rode stirrup-to-stirrup to the stable.

The Mexican stableman took charge of their horses. Cody and Juliana walked hand-in-hand toward the house.

"I can't believe you're here," she said, squeezing his hand and pressing against his shoulder as they walked. "I've worried so much about you. Wondered where you were or if I would ever see you again."

"It's good to be back," he said. "I missed you. Missed being here."

"Well, you're here now. That's all that matters. Did you find out anything?"

"Yep. Got some things settled that needed settled."

Over several cups of coffee they talked the day away and far into the night. He explained about his trip and what he had learned, leaving out the parts about the gunfights.

"I noticed you are wearing a gun now," he said. "Has something happened while I was gone?"

She told him about her encounter with the saddle tramp.

"I decided to start wearing it in case something like that ever happened again."

Cody was uneasy about her carrying a gun, but he nodded agreement.

"It's late. I best be heading for the bunkhouse. Don't want to wake the boys while I'm trying to find a bunk."

"Why don't you stay in the extra bedroom?" she asked. "It's silly you sleeping in the bunkhouse when there's a perfectly good bed right upstairs."

"I couldn't do that. It wouldn't look right."

"You're a hardheaded cowboy, Cody Cordell," she told him, leaning over and brushing his lips with a playful kiss.

He rose, stretched, and clamped his hat in place as he headed for the door.

"Yep, reckon you're right about that. See you in the morning, pretty lady."

A week passed, then two.

During the day Cody and Juliana rode the ranch, inspecting the new cattle she bought, looking over new pastures, and checking on the progress of the new worker cabins being built.

Nightly they enjoyed their supper together. Afterward, they sat together, talked, laughed, and just enjoyed one another's company.

They sat together on a leather sofa in front of a warm fire.

"I'm so glad you're here," she told him, as she snuggled

deeper into the hollow of his shoulder. "I want you to stay forever."

"Juliana, there's nothing I would like better, but I can't. You're somebody. You own a big ranch. I'm nobody. I've got nothing to offer you."

She lifted her head and looked deep into his eyes.

"Cody, I don't care about that. I don't care if you have a nickel to your name. All I want is you," she said, her voice going quivery. "We could be married. You can help me run the ranch. Together we can be happy and build something we both can be proud of."

Cody's eyes clouded and went blurry. His face saddened. He slowly shook his head.

"I couldn't do that, Juliana. Don't you see? About all I've got is my pride, and that won't let me live off of you. I've got to make something of myself before I could ever ask you to be my wife."

She buried her face in his shoulder and wept silently. For a long time he held her because he needed to hold her and she needed to be held. She had learned that a man did what he had to do.

"I'll be leaving come morning," he told her quietly. "I'll be staying at Miss Molly's until I can figure out what I'm gonna do. I'll ride out now and then to see you, if that's okay?"

"Of course, it's okay," she whispered hoarsely.

Cody rode into Trinidad at mid-afternoon. He reined up in front of Miss Molly's boarding house and tied his pinto and packhorse to the hitching rail. He climbed the two steps to the front porch and pushed open the front door.

Molly walked into the wide hallway and saw him. Her face lit up like a summer sun.

"Well, would you lookie here. When did you get back? If you ain't a sight for sore eyes," she squealed, hurrying her large frame down the hall to meet him. She wrapped him in a huge bear hug.

"Howdy, Miss Molly. I've been out at Juliana's ranch a few days."

"Hope you're back to stay. We've been missing you around here. The town's hired a new marshal. He's doing a right good job, too, far as I hear. Not as good as you, mind you, but he's a nice enough fellow, I reckon. Stays right here. I gave him your old room. Didn't have no idea you was coming back or I'd a saved it for you. Hope you're gonna be staying with us?"

"Yeah, if you got another room."

"I've always got a room for you, 'Kid. Bring your gear and follow me. Your room is right down the hallway. Land sakes alive, it's good to see you. Didn't know if we'd ever lay eyes on you again in this lifetime, maybe the next one."

Cody followed Molly down the hallway and into a room.

"This room ain't got a window like your other room, but the bed's a good one. Reckon you can make do with it?"

"It'll be just fine," he assured her.

"My, my," she said, shaking her head. "Folks are gonna be happy to see you. You're a genuine legend hereabouts."

"I go by my real name now," he told her. "It's Cody Cordell. I'm trying to put all that behind me. So, if you can, don't let on to anybody that I used to be the Hondo Kid."

"Cody Cordell," she said, repeating it over and over several times. "I'll try to remember. Oh, you haven't seen Mary Ann yet, have you? Her and the kids are living here with me, those little darlings. Mary Ann is like my own daughter. Always wanted a daughter. Well, I know you need some time to get things put away. Don't forget, supper is at six."

After Miss Molly left, he unpacked his saddlebags and put his spare clothes in the big dresser. He stashed his belly holster and gun belt in one of the dresser drawers.

He felt the bed. It was soft. It would be good to sleep in something besides his bedroll for a change. The bunk at Juliana's was an improvement, but nothing like this one.

He needed to take his horses down to the livery and get them situated, so he left the house and rode down the street. His presence went unnoticed until he reached the livery. It took a minute for ole Pete to recognize him.

"Didn't know you, 'Kid. You look different. It's mighty good to have you back."

"Good to be back. Do me a favor, will you, Pete? I'm trying to leave the Hondo Kid buried up yonder in the graveyard. I'm Cody Cordell now."

"I gotcha. Cody Cordell. I'll keep the other to myself."

"Good. Take care of my horses, will you, Pete?"

"Shore will, Mr. Cordell. Welcome to Trinidad."

Next, Cody walked back up the street to Hamilton's Mercantile. Ed was on a ladder stocking shelves when Cody walked in. The storeowner offered his usual welcome smile, obviously not recognizing Cody right off. He wrinkled his forehead and did a double take.

"Is tha...yeah, it is! Well, if it ain't— He jerked a quick look around to make sure no one was around. "Cody Cordell."

"How are you, Ed?"

Hamilton hurried down from the ladder and reached a welcome hand. They shook hands like family.

"I'm fine. Just fine. When'd you get into town?"

"Just rode in. Staying over at Miss Molly's."

"Well, it's good to see you. You back to stay?"

"Hope so. If I can find some way to make a living."

"Guess Molly told you we hired a new marshal. His name

is Ollie Gardner. He's a good man. Doing a good job. He's from Texas, too. Somewhere around San Antonio, I think he said."

"Glad to hear it."

"So, what you plan on doing? I always kinda figured you and Juliana would get together."

"Maybe someday. I've got to make my own way. I'll find something. I'm gonna make the rounds and see a few folks. Ed, if you wouldn't mind, kinda spread the word that I want to leave the Hondo Kid buried. I'm Cody Cordell now."

"I'll sure do it. Be seeing you around."

Cody made the rounds, explaining to everyone about his new identity and his desire to keep the Hondo Kid buried. Everyone understood and agreed to his secret.

The last place he stopped was the marshal's office. He opened the door and stepped inside. The new marshal was writing a letter. He looked up.

"I'm Cody Cordell. I'm new in town and wanted to stop in and introduce myself."

The marshal stood to his feet and stuck out a work-hardened hand. He was a head shorter than Cody, but his shoulders were Texas wide. He was a clean-cut looking fellow that Cody judged to be straddling thirty. He had a strong handshake.

"Howdy, Mr. Cordell. I'm Ollie Gardner. I'm the town marshal here in Trinidad. Where you from?"

"Oh, been mostly tumbleweeding around a lot. Reckon I'd call Texas home. Over near San Antonio."

"You don't say? I'm from San Antonio. Small world, ain't it? What brings you to Trinidad, Mr. Cordell? Trinidad ain't a place you just happen onto. A fellow's might near got to come here on purpose."

"I was here for awhile, not too long back. Liked it. Figured

I might settle down here if I can find something to do to make a living."

"Well, not much here except mining and a few cattle ranches scattered around. You ever punch cows?"

"Some. I worked on the Brazos River Ranch over near Waco for a time."

"From what I hear, most of the ranches around here are having a rough time of it. I doubt they'll be looking to hire help."

"I'll find something. Just wanted to stop in and meet you."

"Glad you did. Stop in again sometime."

"Miss Molly says you're staying over at the boarding house."

"Sure am. She sets a good table."

"Then I reckon I'll see you at suppertime," Cody said, turning toward the door.

"Wouldn't miss it."

As usual, supper at Miss Molly's was something to write home about. Conversation was cordial and friendly with most doing more eating than talking. It was obvious Molly had talked to the others about keeping Cody's identity secret because they acted as though he were a stranger.

The marshal didn't linger after supper. He hurried back to make his rounds. After the others left, Mary Ann refilled Cody and Sammy's coffee cups and left them alone. She headed for the kitchen to help with the dishes.

"Juliana told me about you helping with the saddle tramp thing," Cody told the big German. "I'm obliged for your help."

"Miss Juliana is a nice lady."

"Yes, she is. It's good to see Mary Ann happy again. You've been good for her."

"We're planning on getting married as soon as I hit pay dirt."

"How's it going?"

"It's slow. It's hard working a mine by yourself. Mary Ann's got her hopes up about us getting married. I haven't said anything to her and I wouldn't want her to know, but I've run out of money. I've used up everything. Don't even have money to pay Miss Molly room and board. Don't know what I'm going to do."

"Were you a miner before you came to this country?"

"Yes. My father and his father before him worked in the coal mines in Germany. When I was old enough, my father sent me to mining school. I studied all sorts of mining. Coal, gold, silver, zinc, lead and many other metals. I have a degree in mine engineering. Mining is all I've ever known."

"Don't know anything about mining myself. You looking for gold or silver?"

"Silver."

"How do you know where to dig?"

"It's mostly to do with the terrain of the land. There are signs to look for. There are likely silver deposits in most of these mountains. But I believe Sugar Loaf Mountain has more potential than any of the others in this part of Colorado."

"I've always wondered about that. Seems to me, men are just digging holes in the mountain in blind luck hoping to find something."

"Some are. I'm going to find a vein. It's just a matter of time."

"Why did you pick silver? Gold seems to be what most are looking for."

"That's true. But so far, all the signs suggest silver holds the best chances in this part of the country."

"Interesting."

"Ride out and look around sometime."

"Might just do that," Cody told him.

That night after he went to bed, the conversation with big German came to his mind. He felt sorry for him. He made up his mind that come morning, he would pay Sammy's room and board for a month.

Before breakfast, Cody cornered Molly and paid Sammy's room and board for another month.

"Don't say anything to anyone about this," he instructed.

Over breakfast, Cody asked the big German, "Is that invitation to ride out and look around your mine still good?"

The man looked surprised at his question.

"Yes, of course."

"Then if it's okay, I'll ride out with you this morning. I'd like to see what you do."

After breakfast they saddled up and rode to the mine together. It wasn't that far, maybe three or four miles. They climbed a steep trail up the side of Sugar Loaf Mountain, not far from town. The German talked steadily, obviously excited about his work. By the time they arrived, Cody's knowledge about mining had expanded dramatically.

"Did you have to file a claim or something on where you're digging?" Cody asked.

"Yes. I have several claims. Usually they only allow you to stake a claim on a spot a hundred-fifty foot wide, but since there haven't been any discoveries in this part of Colorado, they granted a waiver allowing me to file on as many claims as I was willing to pay for. All my claims are registered and certified by the assay office in Denver. My claims cover this whole mountain all the way to the top."

Cody was disappointed when they arrived at the mine. To him, it was nothing but a hole in the side of the mountain with a large pile of dirt and busted rock Sammy had hauled out of the opening.

"I call it the Quicksilver Mine," Sammy told him.

"How deep are you?" Cody asked.

"Right now, I'm about sixty feet. I hit some color a few days ago that looks promising, but it'll take more digging to see if it amounts to anything."

"What you using to dig with?"

"Pick and shovel. I've laid a track for the cart I use to haul the dirt and rock out. That's the hardest part, bringing that out by myself."

They picketed their horses in a small clearing nearby that had a fresh running mountain stream splitting the middle. They walked into the mineshaft together. Sammy paused to light a lantern and carry it with them into the darkened hole. It was the first time Cody had ever been underground and he felt a little uneasy.

They arrived at the face of the tunnel and Sammy hung the lantern on a steel peg driven into the wall. He picked up a nearby pick and scratched at the face of the tunnel. Reaching down, he picked up a handful of yellowish soil and held it up for Cody to see.

"Smell it," Sammy said, holding it up to Cody's nose.

Cody sniffed the sickening-sweet soil and wrinkled his nose.

"That's sulfur," Sammy said. "Where you find sulfur, you usually eventually find the lead mineral called cerussite. And where you find cerussite, you usually find silver. That's why I say that it's just a matter of time and digging. Just don't know how long it will take. But I've run out of time and money. Guess I'm going to have to abandon the mine and find something else to do."

"How much money would it take to keep you going?"

"Oh, not much. Just living expenses and supplies now and then. The claims are already filed and paid for."

"I'd be willing to grubstake you awhile if that would help."

"I couldn't let you do that. Don't suppose you would be interested in buying half interest in the mine?"

"Might. How much would you sell half interest for?"

Sammy thought for a minute.

"I'd sell you half interest in the mine and all my claims for five hundred dollars."

"How about I'll buy half interest and help you work the mine? I've got nothing better to do right now. That way we could get more done faster."

Sammy broke a wide smile and stuck out his big hand. "You just bought half interest in the mine and all my claims. We'll call it the Schroeder/Cordell Mining Company. We can write out the papers and sign them tonight."

"We've got a deal, partner. Now let's get to work. We've got a lot of mountain to move."

They worked steady the rest of the day. They swung the heavy picks, pulling loose rocks and dirt, then loaded it into the iron cart. One of them slipped the makeshift rope harness over their head and pulled while the other pushed. As he was slipping the harness over his head for the second load, Cody asked his new partner a question.

"Is there a reason we can't use a donkey to pull this cart out of the mine?"

"No, no reason. I just didn't have the money to buy one."

"Well, how about we knock off a bit early this afternoon and go see ole Pete at the livery? I saw a couple of donkeys when I was stabling my horses a couple days ago. We could build a small corral straddling that little stream outside and maybe a little lean-to to keep it out of the weather."

"Good idea. That would sure save us a lot of work."

"Something else I wanted to ask you. What do we do with the ore once we find it?"

"When we find a silver vein it will be mixed with lead in

a rock formation. The silver has to be extracted from the rock and lead."

"How do we do that?"

"We can't. It has to be processed in a smelter that's built for that purpose. It's a complicated process."

"I hate to sound dumb, but then what good will it do us to find it if we can't get the silver separated from the waste material?"

"We will have to send it to a processing plant. It's usually used to extract gold, but they do silver, too. The closest one is in Denver."

"You mean we have to haul the rocks with silver in it all the way to Denver to be processed?"

"Yes."

"What is the silver worth after it is processed?"

"The price goes up and down. Right now silver is selling for about thirteen dollars an ounce."

"Sounds like a lot of expense before we realize a profit."

"That's true, but once we find our silver vein, even after all the expenses, we will be wealthy men."

"Then I reckon we better quit jawing and get to work."

Load after load, they hauled up the steep grade and dumped it over the steep slope in front of the mouth of their mine opening.

After each load Sammy would climb down to the pile, fall to his knees and scratch at the material, searching for some sign of silver. After searching, he would sadly shake his head before they went back down for another load.

At mid-afternoon they called it a day and climbed on their horses to head for home. Cody discovered he had muscles he didn't know he had, and they were all sore.

Arriving in town, they went directly to the livery and bought a dark gray, floppy-eared donkey named Gertie.

"This little lady is gonna save our backs lots of strain," Cody said, as they headed for the boarding house.

They washed up, ate supper, and Cody went directly to his room for some much needed rest.

The long days turned into weeks. Each day was the same as the day before. Still they found nothing except a lot more rocks and dirt.

Just as she had done after Cody left, Juliana poured herself into her work. But her mind refused to stop thinking about him. Finally, after a month passed without hearing anything from him, she couldn't stand it any longer. She decided to ride into Trinidad.

Saddling Snowflake, she slid her Henry rifle into the saddle boot and checked the load in the Colt strapped around her waist.

"I'll be back in a couple of days," she told Roy. "I'm going to ride into Trinidad."

"Be careful, Miss Juliana," her foreman told her. "We're making the final roundup and tally. We ought to be ready to start the drive to Denver in about two weeks or so."

"Do you have everything you need?"

"Yes, ma'am. The new hands we hired are working out just fine. The trail cook says he's got all his supplies loaded and ready. Looks like we're as ready as we can be."

"Do you know how many head we'll be taking?"

"We ain't got the final count yet. Right now it looks like it'll be in the neighborhood of two thousand head."

"Good. Thanks, Roy. You're doing a good job."

"Much obliged, ma'am," the foreman said, touching finger and thumb to his hat brim.

She heeled the white mare and rode away. It was early June and the mountains were beautiful. She loved springtime in the mountains. The majesty of the high mountains never ceased to overwhelm her. Their lofty peaks poked holes in the cottony-white clouds and spread their green carpet of pine trees down the mountainside, inviting all comers to enjoy their beauty.

The ride into town took five hours. She thought about Cody the entire trip. *Where is he? What could he be doing? Why haven't I heard from him?*

She reined up in front of Molly's boarding house and tied Snowflake to the hitching rail. May Ann saw her and ran out to meet her. They shared a friendly hug.

"It's good to see you," Mary Ann said.

"Is Cody here?"

"Yes, well, he isn't actually *here*, he's at work."

"Work? What kind of work?"

"Oh, didn't you know? He bought half interest in Sammy's mine. They've been working it ever since Cody came back."

"No, I didn't know. I haven't heard from him and I was worried. So Cody is working with Sammy in the mine?"

"Yes, Sammy says they're gonna hit pay dirt any day now. Isn't that exciting?"

Juliana found it hard to get excited about digging a hole in the side of a mountain. She'd heard stories about men spending months or even years digging and ending up with nothing. No one had hit anything worth a plug nickel in these mountains that she had heard about.

Still, she decided that if Cody thought the mine was a good idea, there was no way she was going to discourage him. She made up her mind to encourage and support him in whatever he decided to do.

"Yes, yes, it is exciting," she said, trying to make her voice confirm her words.

"They usually get back just before dark, certainly in time for supper. Those two can eat more than a half-dozen ordinary men."

"How are the children?" Juliana asked.

"They're growing like weeds. I've never seen them so happy. Sammy is so good with them. You'd think they were his children."

"You look happy, too."

"I am. I've never been so happy in my whole life. Sammy is the best man in the whole world."

"Well, I might argue with you about that. Cody is quite a man, too."

"Oh, I'm sorry. I didn't mean to say anything bad about Cody, but I just love Sammy so much. I can't believe anybody could be so sweet."

"Is Molly in the kitchen?"

"Yes, as soon as I check on the kids I was going in to help with supper."

"You go ahead and see about the children. I'll go help Molly with supper."

Juliana walked into the kitchen where Molly was peeling potatoes. She looked up and broke a wide smile.

"Well, lookie here. If it ain't the pretty ranch lady. How you doing, girl? Glad to see you. Hope you're staying for supper. I swear to my time, seems like I peel a peck of potatoes every night. Them men can eat a poor woman out of house and home. Guess you heard your man was a miner now? I tell you, he and Sammy are working their heads off digging in that mountain. Sure hope they find something worth something."

Juliana found a knife and began peeling potatoes.

"Yes, I ran into Mary Ann out in the hall. She told me about the mine. Sounds like she and Sammy are hitting it off."

"I'll say they are. Both of them are moon-eyed over one another. They're like two peas in a pod. Did you notice Mary Ann's face? She just glows when Sammy is around."

"Yes. It's good to see her happy. She's had enough unhappiness to last a lifetime."

"Did I hear my name mentioned?" Mary Ann asked as she walked in.

"We were just saying how happy you are lately," Juliana told her.

"I can't believe I'm so lucky to find Sammy. I pinch myself every morning to make sure this ain't all just a dream. Sometimes I'm afraid I'll wake up and find I'm still married to Harvey."

"Mary Ann, how about putting the skillet on for the chicken while we finish up these potatoes? Better fry up at least three. Those men will be as hungry as bears coming out of hibernation when they get home. I've already got the corn shucked and cleaned. We can put that on to boil after the chicken is frying. The yeast rolls are ready to put in the oven, too. Looks like we're gonna have things ready in plenty of time. I hate to keep hungry men waiting on supper."

When they heard Cody and Sammy ride up, Mary Ann and Juliana hurried outside to meet them. Sammy leaped from his horse and swept Mary Ann off her feet, swinging her around and around. Mary Ann giggled and planted a long kiss squarely on Sammy's mouth.

Cody stepped from his saddle. Juliana rushed into his arms. After a long hug, she pulled back to look at him closer.

"I thought you two were supposed to be working in a mine? I was expecting you to be dirty from all that digging.

Both of you look like you just stepped out of a bathtub and your clothes are spic and span."

"We always take a bath in the mountain stream and change clothes before we come home. You wouldn't want to see us before we clean up."

"Well, you sure look good to me," she said, hugging him again. "Supper's ready and waiting."

As they walked arm in arm into the house Juliana leaned against his shoulder.

"I missed you. I got worried when I hadn't heard from you. I didn't know what happened."

"I know. I'm sorry I didn't get word to you. The day after I got here I started working with Sammy. We've been working every day since."

"Well, it's about time you took a day off. Tomorrow is Sunday. Could the four of us go on a picnic or something?"

"Don't see why not. I'll talk to my partner and see if we can afford a day off."

Supper was a happy occasion with lots of good food and laughter. The three other boarders, two miners and the new marshal, joined into the festive mood.

"I'll say one thing for you, Mr. Cordell, you sure don't waste any time getting to know the pretty ladies," Ollie Gardner said around a mouthful of fried chicken.

"Well, fact is, I've known these folks a while."

"Oh, I see. I assumed you were a newcomer to the area. So you and Sammy are working a mine together, is that right?"

"Yep."

"Finding anything?"

"Finding a lot of rocks so far."

"Seems to me that's a mighty hard way to make a living."

"Haven't found an easy way yet."

"Well, that's true enough. Hate to leave good company,

but I need to be getting on. The rowdies will be kicking up their heels before long."

The marshal rose and clamped his hat in place and left. The other two boarders finished meals and went to their rooms.

"I was afraid he was gonna start asking too many questions," Molly said, crooking a look toward the door.

"It's okay," Cody said. "He was just being a lawman. Say, partner, Juliana reminded me that tomorrow is Sunday. Reckon we could take the day off? Maybe the four of us could go on a picnic or something?"

Mary Ann giggled. *"Yes.* Could we, Sammy? Could we, please?"

"Guess we could afford to take a day off. We've been working pretty hard lately."

"Oh, good!" Mary Ann shouted. "We've got enough fried chicken left over for a picnic basket."

"Why don't I keep the children so the four of you can have some time together?" Molly suggested.

Cody and Sammy sipped coffee and talked mining talk while the girls helped with the dishes. Afterward, the four of them sat on the front porch and visited. It was late when they all said goodnight and went to their separate rooms.

Darkness still held the land in its grasp when Cody smelled the coffee. He swung legs to the floor, dressed, stomped on his boots, and run fingers through his hair before slipping quietly from his room.

He made his way to the kitchen where he found Miss Molly slicing ham from a large slab.

"Morning," Molly greeted with a smile.

"Morning."

"Coffee's hot. Pour yourself a cup. It'll be a bit before breakfast is ready. I'm an early riser myself. Always was. My papa always said if you ain't up before daylight, you're sleeping your life away. Just something about early morning; kinda like the good Lord is giving us another chance to get it right. Glad to see you up and around. I like to see a young man with get up and go about him."

"Looks like it's gonna be a pretty day."

"Did you hear all the shooting going on last night?"

"No, didn't hear a thing. Reckon I slept like a log. What happened?"

"Don't know. It was real late when the marshal got home and he's sleeping in. Guess we'll find out after he gets up."

"Think I'll take my coffee and go out to the porch," Cody said.

"I'll call you when breakfast is ready."

Cody walked outside to the front porch. He leaned against a post and sipped his coffee. A faint grayness was beginning to color the eastern sky over the mountains.

Quite a difference from the flat plains where I grew up. But there's something about the mountains that soothes a man's soul. Like maybe God put them there to remind us how big He is and how small we are.

He watched as the grayness slowly turned pink, and then gold, as the sun peeked its head over the mountaintop. Puffy white clouds floated leisurely across a soft blue sky. He remembered when he was a young boy how he use to lay on the grass and watch the clouds, imagining they were white dragons floating across the sky.

A sound behind him crooked his head around. Juliana stood there with a white robe over her nightgown. Her hair was fresh-brushed and eyes still puffy from sleep. Her beauty took his breath away.

"Beautiful, isn't it?" she said, glancing up at the sky.

"Yeah, it is. I was standing here enjoying the morning. Is the picnic still on for today?"

"Yes, I'm really looking forward to it. Where are we going?"

"I was thinking we might ride up to the mine. There's a little clearing and a mountain stream. I think you and Mary Ann would like it."

"Wonderful. We'll get to see the mine, too."

"Well, there ain't really much to see except a hole in the ground and a big pile of rocks and dirt we've hauled out."

"I don't care. It's *your* mine, and that makes it special. I can't wait to see it. I came to get you. Breakfast's almost ready."

They walked together into the dining room. The other boarders were already seated around the big table. Molly and Mary Ann carried platters of food in from the kitchen. Juliana and Cody took their seats. Marshal Gardner was seated next to Cody, sipping his coffee.

"Molly said something about some shooting last night," Cody mentioned. "Anybody hurt?"

"A gambler rode into town a couple days ago. Some fellow accused him of cheating and pulled a gun. The gambler shot him. One of the man's friends took it up and got himself shot too."

"What was the gambler's name?"

"Says his name's Lyle Cooper. Looks to be thirty-something. Dapper sort of fellow. Black hair. Talks real smooth. Real handy with a gun, too. From Texas, like me and you. He's real chummy with another newcomer, a big shot land speculator from back east that moved into town recently. You know this Cooper fellow?"

"Don't reckon so. Texas is a big place. Besides, I ain't much of a gambler."

"Seems to me digging in the side of a mountain looking for silver is a pretty big gamble."

"Maybe. We'll see."

A platter of fried eggs got passed around and Cody raked three into his plate to join the thick slice of ham. He added two biscuits and spooned a generous helping of fresh honey onto the hot biscuits.

"Sure looks mighty good," one of the miners commented.

Everyone around the table nodded. They were too busy eating to put words to their agreement.

"There was another stranger in town a few days ago, too," Marshal Gardner said around a mouthful of biscuit. "A gunfighter from Missouri named Charley Haden. He was looking for the Hondo Kid. I told him he was too late. Told him the 'Kid was already dead and buried. He seemed disappointed that he had ridden that far for nothing, but he left town the next morning. That Hondo' must have been some kind of man to stand up to a gang of killers like he did."

Juliana flicked a quick glance at Cody. "Yes, he was."

"Say, come to think about it," the marshal continued, looking over the rim of his coffee cup at Juliana. "Wasn't it your pa who was killed in that same raid?"

Juliana only nodded and said nothing.

"Folks all over are still talking about that one. I heard about it clear down in Texas. Well, a lawman's work don't stop just because it's Sunday. Guess I better be moseying along."

It was quiet after the marshal left.

Chapter XVIII

The guard sounded the special bell announcing Buck's arrival. Rebekah heard it and flew from the house to welcome him home. She rushed across the compound yard to meet him. She immediately saw his arm in the sling and stopped a step away.

"Oh, Buck. You're hurt. What on earth happened?"

"It's nothing. I'll tell you about it later. Right now I want a hug."

Rebekah wrapped her arms around his waist and pulled him to her. She lifted her face to his and their gazes met in a long look of love. He lowered his face. Their lips met.

"Welcome home, my husband."

"It's good to be home, wife."

Arm in arm they headed toward their house.

Suddenly the front door flew open. Little Cody raced across the wide yard as fast as his little legs would carry him, followed closely by his Mexican caretaker.

"Papa! Momma, Papa's home!"

Buck scooped the boy up with his good arm. The boy wrapped both arms around Buck's neck and hugged his father tightly.

"Reckon I need to go away more often," Buck said, as he put his son down and took the boy's hand. The three of them headed to the house together.

"You're gone quite enough, thank you, Mr. Cordell. We need you here at home some, too. Oh, guess what? Selena had her baby."

Buck jerked a quick look at her. "She did? Is she all right? Is the baby healthy? Is it a boy like Chester was hoping for?"

"They are both fine. It was a beautiful little girl. They named her Dakota Selena Colson."

"A girl, huh?"

"Yes, and you should see Chester. He dotes over her like you won't believe."

"He'll be a good father. I can't wait to see the baby. Soon as I get settled in, I'll walk over and see them. How are things here at the ranch?"

"As far as I can tell, things are going well. Chester takes care of the outside operations. Jewel oversees the day-to-day activities inside the compound, and I take care of all the expenses and bookkeeping."

"A girl, huh? I bet that was a shock to Chester. He had his heart set on a boy."

"No, actually, he seems quite pleased that it was a girl. I don't think his feet have touched the ground since the baby was born."

Buck deposited his valise in the bedroom, washed up while both Rebekah and Cody stood nearby watching. It was difficult doing even the simple things using only his good arm. He noticed their presence and slanted a questioning look.

"What?"

"Nothing," Rebekah replied. "We just love to watch you. It's so good to have you home." She took the cloth from his hand and washed his face for him. Tell me how you got hurt."

"It's nothing to worry about. It's like General Sheridan told me not long ago. When anyone rises to a position of power and influence, you develop enemies that are opposed to what you're trying to accomplish. I reckon I've picked up a few along the way."

"And they tried to *kill* you? Who are these people?"

"That's what the police are trying to find out now. Whoever they are, they paid a back shooter to kill me. We found a note and twenty shiny double-eagle gold pieces in his pocket. I must be accomplishing something. Somebody wanted me out of the way real bad."

"Oh, Buck, that's *scary.*"

"Naw. They'll find out who it is. Come on, let's go see that new baby."

Chester sat in a rocking chair beside Selena's bed. He held their new baby in his arms. She was wrapped in a white blanket with a white crocheted cap on her head. Buck leaned over and took a long look at their baby.

"Welcome home, Partner. Look what the stork brought us while you was gone."

"Yeah, I heard about it. Congratulations," Buck said, shaking hands with Chester and leaning over to hug Selena. "But your wife did all the hard part."

"Yes," Selena agreed, smiling broadly. "It is true."

"Good to see she takes after Selena instead of you."

"You're just jealous cause I got a girl and you haven't. What happened to your arm?"

Rebekah cut a quick look at Selena and smiled. "Fellow took a shot at me."

"Looks like his aim wasn't off much."

"No. I was lucky."

"You get him?"

"My security men did. The police are looking into it now."

"Think I'll stick to ranching. Appears to me it's safer."

Suddenly the bell in the guard tower sounded announcing an arrival. Chester handed the baby to Selena. He and Buck clamped hats on their heads and hurried from the room to see what was happening.

A covered chuck wagon pulled through the gate escorted by two Longhorn riders.

Buck and Chester hurried over.

"It's Ray," one of the riders told them. "He took an arrow in the leg. He's inside the wagon."

They rushed to the back of the wagon and pulled aside the canvas flap. Ray Ledbetter lay on a pallet. He rose to a sitting position and propped himself on his elbow.

"Howdy, Boss," the foreman said. "My leg got in the way of an arrow."

"Looks like it. How's the leg?" Buck asked.

"Better'n it was a couple weeks ago."

"Couple of you boys help Chester get him outta the wagon and into the medical room. I want Jewel to take a look at that leg."

While the large black woman examined Ray's leg, he related the events surrounding his battle with the Indians and his wound.

Buck and Chester listened, grimacing when he told about cutting the arrow out and cauterizing the wound with his red-hot knife blade.

"That's more'n likely what saved you from getting that

leg infected, too," Jewel said, peering up from bandaging the wound. "If'n you hadn't done that, blood poisoning would'a set in and you'd be a dead man before anybody found you."

"Boss, got something else to tell you, too. Don't know any other way to say it except straight out."

"What is it, Ray?"

"We had a bad stampede with the first herd. Nothing we could do except let 'em run themselves out. When it was all over and the count was done, we lost nearly five hundred head. I know I was responsible for the herd and that's a lot of money lost. If you want to let me go, I wouldn't blame you none."

"You did your best, didn't you?" Buck asked.

"Yes, sir."

"Then we couldn't ask more of a man than that. Was anybody hurt in the stampede?"

"No, sir."

"Good. That's all that's important. We can replace the cattle. We can't replace a man's life. You did a good job, Ray. We're mighty proud to have you riding for the Longhorn."

Both Buck and Chester shook their *segundo's* hand.

"You stay off that leg until it gets well. You're way too valuable to the ranch to have you all crippled up."

That night after little Cody had been put to bed, Buck and Rebekah shared one of their private times together in the large bathtub. For a long time they lay together in the warm water in one another's arms, basking in the feeling of love. Rebekah's head was resting on his good shoulder.

"Buck, remember what Chester said this afternoon?" she said without looking up.

"Don't know what you mean."

"Remember when he said you were jealous because he got a little girl and you didn't?"

"Yeah, so?" he said, lifting his head and gazing down at her.

She lifted her face to look deep into his eyes.

"Well, that may be about to change."

For a moment her words didn't sink in. When they did, his mouth dropped open and his eyes widened.

"You mean?"

She nodded.

"We're gonna have another baby?" he exclaimed, a wide smile splitting his face.

Again she nodded.

He kissed her.

Buck and Chester leaned on the corral fence looking over a new batch of mustangs that had just been delivered when they saw the soldiers coming a ways off. Buck studied the approaching army column from under an eye-shielding hand. They rode in columns of two. It was a full platoon followed by three canvas-covered supply wagons. An officer with captain's bars led the procession.

The officer reined his horse to a stop and stepped to the ground. He saluted smartly.

"I'm Captain Alexander Marshal, Fifth Calvary Regiment, United States Army. Could one of you gentlemen direct me to Congressman Cordell?"

"I'm Buck Cordell. How can I help you?"

"My mission is to construct a new fort in this part of Texas to protect the new homesteaders moving into the area.

After the fort is completed, Major George Bingham will arrive with a full company. Our mission is to round up any hostiles in the area as well as deal with the cross-border raids by bands of Mexican bandits that have become more frequent in recent months.

"My orders instruct me to consult you for your suggestions as to the location of the fort."

"I see," Buck said, taken by surprise at the captain's words. "Could you join us for dinner this evening? Maybe we could talk in greater detail after dinner."

"It would be my pleasure, sir. If you have no objections, we will setup a temporary camp down by the river. The Sycamore, I believe it's called."

"That would be fine. Would six o'clock be convenient?"

"It would," the officer said, saluting again. "Until six, then."

He toed a stirrup and swung into the saddle. He lifted a hand and motioned. The column moved out.

"A fort, huh?" Chester said, watching the soldiers ride away. "We're getting downright civilized."

"I knew they were gonna build one, just had no idea it would be in this neck of the woods."

"Sounds like you got a lot to say about where it's gonna be built. Guess I didn't realize how much influence my partner's got these days."

"You got any idea where a good location would be for a fort?"

"Maybe west of Del Rio a ways. Over toward the Big Bend country might be a good place. There's some pretty wild country up that way. Lots of timber and fresh streams."

"Yeah, kinda where I was thinking about, too. I might take a ride up that way with the captain tomorrow and take a look around.

"I got some good news last night."

"Oh?"

"Rebekah is in a family way."

"Really? That's great news. So you're gonna be a papa again, huh? What you hoping for this time, another boy?"

"Don't matter, as long as Rebekah and the baby are healthy."

"I was hoping for a boy at first, but now I'm kinda glad it was a girl."

"She's sure a pretty one. Looks a lot like Selena."

"She does, don't she? Selena's the best thing that's ever happened to me."

"Same here. I reckon we could both say that. Can you and Selena have dinner with us tonight?"

"Don't see why not. That'll give us a chance to hear what the captain's got to say."

As usual, Rebekah outdid herself. The dinner was fit for a king. Thick, juicy steaks, baked sweet potatoes, corn on the cob, and hot yeast rolls had everyone bragging on the meal.

"The army certainly doesn't prepare us for a meal like this one, Mrs. Cordell. Don't believe I've ever enjoyed a meal more."

"Thank you, captain."

"Where's your home?" Buck asked.

"Pennsylvania. But unfortunately, I haven't been back there in years."

"Do you have a family?" Selena asked.

"No. I'm afraid not. The army moves us around a lot. It's just not conducive to having a wife and children."

"It must be a lonely life."

"Yes, it is, but one has to choose what he wants to do. The army is the life I've chosen."

"So you're new to Texas?" Chester asked.

"Yes, sir. This is the first time I've been west of the Mississippi River."

"Then you've never had any dealings with Indians?"

"No, sir."

"Hmm," Chester breathed, cutting a quick glance at Buck.

"Let's move into the den so we can have a cigar and talk," Buck suggested.

"If you men will excuse us," Rebekah said. "Selena and I need to get the children to bed."

The men all stood to their feet as the ladies left the room. Buck ushered the captain into the den. Chester followed closely. After they were seated and the cigars were lit, Buck asked the captain to explain more about the fort they were sent to construct.

"I took the liberty of bringing along a set of plans. Would you gentlemen like to take a look at them?"

He reached inside his dress tunic and withdrew a folded drawing. They spread it out on a nearby table.

"As you can see," the captain explained. "It's a rather small fort. It's only three hundred feet by four hundred feet. It's a log structure designed to quarter a full Company."

"Will a Company, once it arrives, be the extent of your strength?" Buck asked.

"Yes, sir."

"And the army expects forty to fifty men to *round up* the Indians and send them to a reservation a thousand miles away in the Indian Territory?" Chester questioned skeptically. "This area of Texas is used as a hunting ground for the Lipan Apache, Comanche, and Kiowa. Any of these tribes can field three hundred or more warriors at a moment's notice.

"If they're pushed, there's a better than likely chance they could join forces. If that happens, you and your soldiers could be facing a thousand or more seasoned warriors."

"It seems you and your ranch are doing rather well," the captain commented. "How do you survive in this area against the Indians and Mexican bandits?"

"We've got two hundred heavily armed men on the Longhorn payroll. Even so, the only way we survive out here is because we live inside this walled compound. Over time, the Indians have learned if they kill one of our men, we spare nothing to hunt down the ones that did it and hang 'em, no if's, and's or but's about it."

"All that may be true, but I still have my orders."

"I don't envy your job," Buck told him. "You've got your work cut out for you."

"Do you have a recommendation as to the location of our fort?" the officer asked.

"If you want, I'll ride with you tomorrow and we can take a look at an area that might work for you."

"Thank you, sir. I would appreciate your help."

"Believe me, captain, you're gonna need all the help you can get."

Chapter XVIV

Cody and Sammy saddled the horses while Juliana and Mary Ann prepared the basket for their picnic. The girls talked excitedly about their special day.

"I'm so glad the men decided to take the day off," Mary Ann said. "They've been working so hard in the mine. Sammy really likes Cody. He says he's a hard worker."

"Yes, he is," Juliana, agreed. "I tried to get him to help me run the ranch, but he's dead-set on making it on his own."

"Sammy says they're getting closer to finding a silver vein. He says it's just a matter of time and hard work."

"Have you ever seen their mine?"

"Sammy took me up there once. I wouldn't want him to know I said this, but it was a little disappointing. It's just a big hole in the mountain, but just knowing that my man dug it was exciting."

"That's the way I feel, too," Juliana said. "If it makes Cody happy, then I'm all for it."

"He really loves you, you know?"

"What do you mean?"

"I see the way he looks at you. Miss Molly sees it, too. You and I have been friends a long time, Juliana. Cody worships the ground you walk on. Don't tell me you haven't noticed."

"Well..."

"See, you've seen it, too. I can tell you love him. Take a word of advice from an old friend and slap your brand on that man before he gets away."

"We'll see."

"You ladies about ready?" Sammy asked, walking into the room followed closely by Cody. "We have the horses all saddled and waiting."

"We're ready," Juliana said, picking up the picnic basket and cutting a look at Cody. He looked at her. Their gazes held for a long moment.

"Here," he finally said, his word breaking the trance-like moment and jerking her mind back to reality. "Let me carry that."

She glanced quickly at Mary Ann to see if she had been watching. She was, and lifted a knowing smile.

The ride to the mine was fun. Mary Ann and Juliana were in a giggly, schoolgirl mood. It was one of those times when *everything* seemed funny. Sammy and Cody were soon infected with the mood and joined in. The four of them laughed and talked as they rode slowly up the mountain.

It was a bright, sunny morning, a near perfect day for a horseback ride and picnic. It was nearing noon when they arrived at the mine. *Mary Ann was right,* Juliana thought at first sight of the mine. *It's disappointing.*

"I know it don't look like much right now," Sammy said, apologetically, "but the important part isn't on the outside, it's down there in the mine."

"How deep is it?" Juliana asked, staring at the gaping hole in the mountain.

"We've made a lot of progress since me and Cody became partners. We're about a hundred twenty feet now, wouldn't you say, partner?"

"Yeah, something like that."

"Could we go down to where you work?" Juliana asked.

"It's too dangerous," Cody told her.

"If it's too dangerous for us, why isn't it too dangerous for you and Sammy?"

"Well, that's different. That's our job. Besides, it's real dirty down there."

"I don't see how it's any different. I'd like to see where you work. I'm not afraid to get dirty."

"Okay, if you're sure you want to, we'll take you down later."

"So that's the *Gertie* I've been hearing about?" Mary Ann asked, pointing at the little gray donkey with her head over the top of the rail fence peering back at them.

"Yes, that's Gertie. She was Cody's idea. She pulls that iron cart full of dirt and rocks out of the mine for us. She saves us lots of backbreaking work. We built the small shed for her so she could get out of the weather.

"We talked about someday building a small cabin over there by the mountain stream for one of us to sleep in after we hit our silver vein. We'll need someone to be here to watch after things."

"When you get ready, I've got just the man for the job. He's building several log cabins for me right now."

"When the time comes we'll talk to him about it," Sammy said.

"Where's a good place for our picnic?" Mary Ann asked. "I'm starved."

"There's a nice grassy spot over by the stream. We wash up there every day before we head home," Sammy told her.

They headed that way. The girls unpacked the picnic basket and spread the food on a red and white-checkered tablecloth while Cody and Sammy built a small fire and put water on for coffee. They all sat down and had a nice meal of fried chicken, potato salad, and oven-baked beans.

After lunch they lazed around, talking, laughing, and relaxing.

"Let's go wading in the water," Juliana said, impulsively slipping off her boots. Mary Ann quickly did the same. Side by side they hurried to the edge of the stream.

"Should we warn them?" Sammy asked, smiling broadly.

"Naw. Let them find out for themselves."

They watched as Juliana tested the icy water gingerly with a toe.

"Eek!" she screamed. "That's cold!"

For the next half hour Cody and Sammy laughed, sipped their coffee, and watched as Juliana and Mary Ann waded and played in the shallow stream, wading further and further upstream. They picked up pretty rocks and splashed water on one another with their bare feet.

Cody saw Juliana reach down and pick something up out of the water. She examined it closely and then quickly climbed from the stream and hurried toward Cody. She handed him what she had found.

"Is that what I think it is?" she asked, excitement apparent in her voice.

Cody looked closely at what she had found and held it out for Sammy to examine. It was a nugget the size of a thumbnail. Sammy's eyes saucered wide and his mouth dropped open.

"That's gold!" he near shouted. "That's a pure gold nugget! Show us where you found it."

Sammy and Cody leaped to their feet and raced to the edge of the stream. Juliana was right behind them. She pointed out the spot where she found the nugget. Without even pausing to remove their boots, both men waded quickly into the water.

By sundown, the four of them had collected a double-handful of gold nuggets, most much smaller, but several even larger.

With shadows lengthening, they reluctantly returned to their picnic site. They were all so excited they couldn't eat the leftovers from lunch that remained.

"How much you figure what we found is worth?" Cody asked.

"Hard to tell how many ounces we've found today, probably at least twenty to thirty. Right now, gold is bringing forty-two dollars a troy ounce. That means we've found at least a thousand dollars worth just today."

"We're rich!" Mary Ann shouted.

"Not yet," Sammy told them, "but might be well on our way. What we found today came from a vein of gold and washed down from somewhere upstream. What we've got to do is find the source. When we do that, then we *will* be rich."

"I can't wait to tell everybody what we found," Mary Ann said, her voice shaking with excitement.

"That might not be a good idea just yet," Cody told them. "I think we best keep this to ourselves for awhile. We go talking about this and folks will be swarming all over Sugar Loaf Mountain. Sammy, you right sure you have the claims for this whole mountain sewed up legally?"

"I filed all the claims and paid the fees. I've got all the legal papers signed by the assay office in Denver."

"Before we breathe a word of this, let's get Judge

Goodson to take a look at those claim papers just to make sure everything is on the up and up," Cody suggested.

"Good idea," Sammy agreed.

"Right now we best be heading back," Cody said. "It'll be dark before we get home."

The next morning Cody and Sammy stood waiting at the judge's office when he arrived.

"Morning, Cody. Morning, Sammy. You boys are out mighty early this morning. Something wrong?"

"No, we'd just like for you to take a look at something."

"Be glad to. Come on in the office."

Cody and Sammy followed the judge into his small office and took chairs across the desk from him.

"Me and Sammy went in partners and started a mining company. We'd like for you to take a look at our partnership agreement and the claims we hold papers on, just to make sure everything is done right."

"Be glad to. You got all the papers with you?"

"Yes, sir," Cody told him, handing the papers across the desk.

Judge Goodson examined the papers closely, nodding agreement as he read. Finally, he handed the papers back to Cody.

"Nothing wrong as far as I can see. That partnership agreement needs to be notarized. I can do that for you right now if you want, seeing as how I'm the only notary within two hundred miles."

"You're the judge, undertaker, doctor, and now a *notary, too?*" Cody commented. "Is there *anything* you don't do?"

"Yep. I don't dig holes under ground like you boys. Seems to me a mighty hard way to make a living."

"I can't see that you boys have a problem at all. Them papers are as legal as you could make 'em. It's a little unusual for one man to be able to file claim on as much land as you boys hold, but that waiver signed by the assay office is legally binding."

"Good. We're much obliged, Mr. Goodson," Cody told him. "We just wanted to do things right. What do we owe you?"

"Don't owe me a thing. Glad to do it for you boys. Calling your company the Schroeder-Cordell Mining Company, huh?"

"Yes, sir."

"Well, I wish you boys luck. Offhand, I'd say you're gonna need a whole passel of that."

Leaving the judge's office, they hurried to Hamilton's store. They were anxious to get their business completed and get back to the mine.

"Morning, Mr. Hamilton," Cody greeted, as they entered the large mercantile store.

"Morning, Cody, Sammy. Figured you fellows would be working your mine this morning. Molly was in a couple days ago. She told me you boys had partnered up in the mining business."

"Yes, sir. We had some business to take care of this morning. We're headed back to work soon as we pick up a few supplies."

Sammy browsed around the store, selecting another pick and some extra pick handles and two scoop shovels while Cody picked out two pair of work gloves.

"Reckon you heard about the big shooting a couple nights ago?" the storekeeper asked.

"Yep. Marshal Gardner is staying over at Miss Molly's," Cody replied. "He told us about it."

"The marshal's a good man. He's working out right good. You met Haig Jessup yet?"

"I ain't been in town in a while. Who's he?"

"He moved in a couple weeks ago. He's from somewhere back east. Boston, I think it is. He calls himself a land speculator. Opened an office and everything. Already buying up land left and right. Seems to have a barrel full of money."

"Better be careful. He'll be after your job as head of the town council."

"He can have it. It's a thankless job anyway. Ain't no way to keep everybody happy. Will that be all for you boys?"

"Reckon so," Cody said, pulling money from his pocket and paying for their supplies.

They picked up their purchases and walked back to the boarding house. Juliana, Mary Ann, and her two children were sitting in the porch swing when Cody and Sammy walked up. Cody noticed Juliana's white mare was already saddled and tied to the hitching rail.

"Get your business all taken care of?" she asked.

"Yep. The judge said everything was in order."

"That's wonderful. I'm excited for you and Sammy. I've got to return to the ranch this morning, but I wanted to wait and see what you found out before I left."

"Do you have to go?"

"Yes, I'm afraid so. We're leaving with our trail herd for Denver in a couple more weeks. I need to get back and make sure everything is ready."

"You ain't thinking about going on the drive, are you?" Cody asked, concern evident in his voice.

"No. Roy will be handling the drive, but I'm having cabins built for my workers' families and I need to check on those, too. Will you come out as soon as you can?"

"Yes, but it might be a while with all we've got going on right now."

"I understand. Just promise me you'll be careful."

"I will. You, too."

Cody walked with her to her horse and stood nearby as she mounted. She looked down. Their gazes met. She leaned over. He lifted his hands to her face and caressed it. They kissed. It was long and soft and wonderful. He didn't want it to end. Her fingers trailed along his cheek as she finally straightened in the saddle.

Cody and Sammy labored from daylight to dark for the next week working their way upstream. They walked slowly, keeping their gazes fixed on the rocky bottom of the shallow, but swift-running stream.

They camped in the small clearing near their lean-to, deciding the time spent traveling between their mine and Molly's boarding house could be better spent searching for the source of the gold nuggets.

Their labor was rewarded. They found enough nuggets that week to fill two Mason fruit jars. But still their efforts to find where the nuggets were coming from eluded them.

On the eighth day, they came upon a waterfall. The mountain stream spilled over the edge of a rock shelf about forty feet above their heads and created a large pool of crystal-clear water at least thirty feet across.

It was a hot, May afternoon. Despite wading in the stream all morning, they were tired and sweaty.

"How about taking time out for a swim?" Cody suggested.

He didn't have to ask twice. Sammy immediately shucked his shirt and britches right down to his long johns. Cody wasn't far behind. They both plunged into the cold water.

The ice-cold pool took Cody's breath away. He came up sputtering and shivering. They quickly adjusted to the cold water and spent several minutes washing the dirt from their bodies and relaxing.

Cody decided to see what it would be like to move underneath the water as it fell forty feet from the rock shelf and plunged into the pool. He swam over until the water pounded down on top of him. The weight of the water beat upon his head and shoulders. It felt good.

Treading water, he chanced opening his eyes. What he saw pricked his curiosity. He moved farther underneath the curtain of water to make sure he actually saw what he thought he saw. Time and untold tons of water had eaten out a shallow cave in the wall of rock behind the waterfall.

We found it!

Sunlight filtered through the wall of water and reflected off the wide veins of gold. Cody's heart leaped up into his throat.

We found it!

He tried to scream to Sammy but the thunderous roar of water and the knot he couldn't swallow drowned out all sound from his throat.

He dove under the water and swam until he got past the pounding water above him. He came up sputtering and yelling at the top of his voice.

"We found it!"

Sammy had been floating leisurely on his back, enjoying the relaxed time. Cody's outcry caused him to roll over quickly.

"What?" his German partner hollered.

"We found the mother lode!" Cody yelled again. "Right there behind the waterfall. You won't believe it!"

Sammy raced through the water, swimming as fast as he could. Together they plunged underneath the water and came up behind the waterfall. When Sammy saw the streaks of gold glimmering in the dim sunlight, his eyes went wide and his mouth dropped open.

He made his way over to the rock wall. His hands reached out. His fingertips traced along the wide veins of gold lodged in the solid wall of rock.

For long minutes he stared at the golden streaks and shook his head in disbelief. Finally, he nodded.

"We found it, partner. We really found it."

The two men clasped hands in a long, firm handshake.

Chapter XX

"I'm gonna take Captain Marshal over to the location where we're suggesting he build his fort," Buck told Chester after their breakfast meeting with the foremen. "Wanna come with me?"

"No, with that trail herd pulling out tomorrow, I'd like to be here to see 'em off."

"I should be back in two or three days. I'm taking a packhorse and enough trail supplies for a week, just in case."

"Good idea."

"Ray says his leg is healing good," Buck said. "I saw him up and around on crutches yesterday."

"Yeah, that was a close call. Not sure I coulda done what he did."

"A man does what he has to do. Did I tell you I met with General Sheridan up in Austin?"

"No. I thought the powers that be had moved him."

"They did. They claimed he was too severe in his treatment of all the ex-Confederates that returned to Texas after the war. They returned to find they had lost everything. The carpetbaggers had taken over their farms; they had no jobs, no way to make a living. Lots of them hit the outlaw trail just to survive.

The general's enemies used all that to attack him and succeeded in getting him removed from his assignment in charge of reconstruction. It's the same bunch who's trying to get President Andrew Johnson impeached. And it's most likely the same bunch who tried to have me killed.

"The meeting with the general was very hush-hush. He wasn't even supposed to be in Austin. He told me something interesting."

"What was that?"

"He's known about the ambush we were involved in right from the get-go. He even knew that it was us who took the Union Army payroll."

Chester's wide eyes reflected his shock.

"I can't believe he didn't have us arrested and hung, or shot."

"Me, either. I asked him why he didn't. He said I was more valuable to him alive than dead."

"Well, if that ain't something. I thought we got away with it."

"Looks like we did."

"What'd they do with him when they relieved him of his command, give him a desk job in Washington or something?"

"No, they put him in charge of rounding up the Indians and sending them to a reservation in the Indian Territory. He's putting together his force right now. I'm afraid it's gonna be bad before its all over, real bad. Captain Marshal and his platoon are just the beginning of that effort."

"Well," Chester said. "Like you told him, he better have more than one platoon or he won't last long enough to build his fort. The Indians will run through them like a dose of Castor Oil. There's just something about an army uniform that makes their blood boil."

"Yeah, I'm afraid you're right. I'm concerned for them, but maybe they can hold out until the army decides they need a larger force down here."

"Don't count on it. You know how slow the army is about doing things. They're slow as cold molasses."

"Well, I better go say goodbye to Rebekah and Cody. See you in a few days."

"Ride careful," Chester told his friend and partner, sticking out a hand.

Buck took it and they shook hands like family.

He found his wife dressing little Cody. When Buck walked into the room, his son rushed into his arms.

"How's my big boy this morning?" Buck asked, hugging him close.

"He's rambunctious, as usual," Rebekah answered. "That boy has more energy than a dozen wild mustangs."

"You feeling okay?"

"I'm fine."

"Well, be careful. You work too hard, especially now that you're expecting."

"Don't worry about me, Buck. Women have been having babies since the beginning of time."

"I'll be gone a couple of days," Buck told her. "I'm gonna ride with Captain Marshal over to the Big Bend country to look at a place to build his fort."

"Can I go with you, Papa?"

"Not this time. I'll take you riding when I get back."

Buck sat the boy down and took Rebekah in his arms for a long hug.

"See you in a couple of days," he said, kissing her a long goodbye.

"Be careful," she told him as he left.

Captain Marshal and his platoon's temporary camp was set up on the bank of the Sycamore River in the shade of large trees of the same name. Three rows of two-man tents with five tents in each row were spaced precisely four steps apart in typical army formation. It was clear the captain was regulation army right down to his skivvies.

Buck quickly spotted the captain's tent by the Regimental Fifth Cavalry colors flying on a pole in front of his tent. A corporal stood guard in front of it. He came to attention and saluted as Buck reined up and stepped to the ground.

"The captain is expecting you, sir."

Buck pulled aside the tent flap and stepped inside. Captain Marshal sat behind a small desk, studying a map of the area.

"Good Morning, Mr. Cordell. Thank you for taking time to accompany me. I'm sure a ranch the size of yours keeps you very busy."

"Yes, but I've got lots of good help."

"Could you show me on the map where you're suggesting we build the fort?"

Buck spent a few moments studying the map before pointing a finger.

"The Rio Grande River swings into a horseshoe bend right there, that's why they call it the Big Bend country. It's a rugged country, very mountainous, heavily wooded area with numerous fresh streams that run into the river.

"The area I'm suggesting is right about there," he said, stabbing the map with a finger. "It backs up to a sheer cliff that will offer some protection. There's a mountain stream with plenty of fresh water and lots of timber to build your fort. It's only a dozen miles from Del Rio."

The captain nodded agreement as Buck talked.

"If you're ready, we can go take a look at this place," Buck said.

"I'm ready," the officer said, rising and clamping his cavalry hat in place. "I've arranged a small squad to accompany us."

As they rode, Captain Marshal peppered Buck with a steady stream of questions about Del Rio, about the Longhorn Ranch and why they chose to locate it right in the middle of the Indian hunting grounds.

Buck answered the captain's questions, but was careful not to elaborate. They arrived at the location in mid-afternoon. They reined up and sat their saddles as the captain looked around, nodding his approval.

"You were right," Mr. Cordell. "This is an ideal place to build the fort. I'll leave the squad here and return with my platoon tomorrow."

"Captain, not trying to tell you how to run your army, but I wouldn't do that if I were you. We've been watched for the past two hours. Your squad might not be here when you get back."

The captain quickly swiveled his head all around, searching for hostiles.

"Where? I don't see anything."

"Captain, out here, when you see them it's most likely already too late."

"Oh, I see. Very well, I'll accept your recommendation. The squad will return with us to our camp.

"This seems to be a suitable location for the fort: lots of trees, good water, not far from town to replenish supplies. You're right, Mr. Cordell, it's an excellent location. This is where we'll build."

"Is there anything else you want to look at before we head home?" Buck asked.

"No. I believe I've seen everything I need to see."

"Then let's head on back. Having Indian eyes on me makes me nervous. We'll stop by town and I'll introduce you to John Walker. He owns the local mercantile store. I expect you'll be doing business with him."

"Yes. Yes, that will be good."

As they rode, Buck got more and more nervous. He felt that old familiar tingling in the back of his neck that usually meant trouble. They passed through an area of thick woods hugging the thin trail on both sides. The eight-member squad of troopers fell into a single file line.

This would be a good place for an ambush, Buck thought.

He suddenly got that tingly feeling on the back of his neck. Instinctively, he reached a hand and slid the Spencer carbine from its saddle boot. The captain noticed his actions.

"Something wrong?"

"Something. Don't know what, but something. Might think about having your men ride with their rifles at the ready."

Captain Marshal gave the whispered order.

"How do you know? I haven't seen a thing."

"Captain, in south Texas, you live by your instincts. Death comes sudden and when you least expect it. I got a bad feeling about this area we're riding through. Keep your eyes peeled."

No sooner had the words left his mouth than a sound like that of a dozen sparrows in flight reached their hearing. Buck flicked a look backwards and saw several arrows bury deep into three of the troopers. They slumped in their saddles, but managed to hang on.

Buck slammed the Spencer to his shoulder and fired at a movement in the heavy timber. Captain Marshal and his other troopers began firing blindly into the bushes on either side of the trail.

Buck spurred his mount. His black gelding leaped into

a full gallop within two jumps. The sound of hoof beats close behind assured him the troopers were following his lead. The black weaved in and out and around trees. Buck guided his mount with the pressure of his knees and ducked and dodged low limbs that tore at him. He twisted in the saddle to fire at a dozen or more mounted Indians charging after them.

One painted warrior threw his hands into the air and somersaulted backwards over the back of his pinto as Buck's heavy slug tore into him. Others bent low over their mustang's neck to offer a more difficult target.

An opening in the trees loomed ahead.

"Do what I do!" Buck shouted over his shoulder.

As his gelding broke into the clearing, Buck pulled his mount to a sliding stop and leaped from the saddle. He hit the ground running and immediately dropped to one knee with the Spencer jammed against his shoulder. He laid the sight on the chest of a warrior and squeezed off a shot. The Indian slid sideways from his mount and tumbled along the ground.

By the time Buck levered another shell, Captain Marshal and his five unwounded troopers were beside him, laying down a steady barrage of lead at the pursuing Indians.

Before the surprised warriors could turn their mounts and flee, the heavy rifle slugs tore them from their mounts. In the space of a dozen heartbeats, all of the attackers lay dead or dying. Riderless horses fled wildly past Buck and the troopers, trailing the single rawhide bridle rein used by most Indians. The acrid smell of gun smoke hung thick like a cloud in the still afternoon air.

One by one the troopers rose and moved cautiously among the downed Indian warriors, checking for any that remained alive.

Buck slanted a look at the captain. The officer's face was chalky-white. Drops of sweat hung on his forehead. He gripped the wooden stock of his rifle tightly.

"This your first encounter with Indians, captain?"

"Y-yes," the officer stuttered an answer.

"You and your men done good," Buck told him.

"I need to see to my wounded," the captain said, suddenly embarrassed by the fear he had displayed. He pushed quickly to his feet and headed toward the three wounded troopers, still clinging to their army-issued McClelland saddles.

Buck followed the captain. Two of the troopers were hit bad. The third only had a flesh wound.

"I need to get these men back to camp so our corpsman can tend to them," the captain told Buck.

"There's a doctor in Del Rio," Buck told him. "It's a lot closer."

"Yes, that would be much better. We'll take them there. Thanks for helping us back there," Captain Marshal said, as they rode side-by-side.

"Glad to help."

"You were in the army, weren't you?"

"Yep."

"Mind me asking which side?"

"South."

"Good thing they didn't have many like you or we might have lost the war."

Riding slowly, and with troopers helping to hold the wounded men in their saddles, they made it to Del Rio before sundown.

Marshal Cauthorn saw them ride in and hurried over to the doctor's office. Buck met him outside.

"What happened, Buck?"

"We got jumped by a band of Comanche west of town a ways. Three of the troopers took arrows, two of them pretty bad."

"What's the army doing this far from Fort Clark, anyway?" Bud asked.

"The army sent a platoon to build a new fort west of here over near the Big Bend country. Captain Marshal is in charge of the project. Once the fort is complete, a full company will be stationed there under the command of a major. The captain's inside with his wounded men."

"I'll wait around and make his acquaintance."

"When you see him, tell him I headed on back to the ranch. Tell him if we can be of help, just send word."

"I'll do it."

Chapter XXI

Cody and Sammy worked feverishly from daylight until dark for the next week. They searched every inch of the bottom of the pool. By week's end they had gathered two saddlebags full of gold nuggets.

As they sat around their campfire near the mouth of the mine, they discussed what they should do next.

"We've pretty well cleaned the stream and pool of nuggets," Sammy said, sipping on his coffee. "We're going to need more than a pick and shovel to get that gold out of the solid rock wall behind the waterfall."

"What will we use?"

"We can use hammers and chisels for awhile, but before long we'll have to use a steam engine jack hammer. One of us needs to go to Denver and change the gold we have into money. I think you should be the one to go. I'd feel safer with you carrying all that gold."

"Where do you cash it in?"

"At the assay office. As much gold as you'll be cashing

in, the news is bound to get out, but we need to keep it quiet as long as we can. Claim jumpers will be swarming all over Sugar Loaf Mountain when the word gets out."

"Since we've got the claims sewed up on the whole mountain we shouldn't have any trouble," Cody said.

"That won't keep them out."

"We'll just have to cross that bridge when we get to it then," Cody told his partner.

It was decided that it would be safer if Cody rode along with Juliana's herd that was headed for Denver.

"They should be heading out any day now." Cody said. "I'll ride out to the Higgins Ranch tomorrow. I'll join up with the drive and have the added protection of the other cowhands. If I'm lucky, nobody will know I'm carrying two saddlebags full of gold."

Cody tied the heavy saddlebags containing their gold securely behind his saddle. He took up the lead line to his fully loaded packhorse and forked his pinto.

Sammy Schroeder stood on the front porch of Molly's boarding house and lifted a hand in goodbye. Cody touched the brim of his Stetson with a thumb and finger as he reined Cincinnati around.

A graying dawn pushed aside the darkness and gave birth to a new day, a day full of excitement and anticipation.

The past two weeks had been like a dream. Each morning Cody and Sammy had waited anxiously for dawn, lying awake for hours waiting for daylight so they could resume their search for more gold nuggets. With each nugget they plucked from the cold waters of their mountain pool, they became more and more excited. It was like a dream, a dream from which neither of them wanted to wake.

Now, as Cody rode along the trail toward the Higgins

Ranch, the possibilities of a future life with Juliana seemed within reach. Though his love for her caused his heart to ache, he had refused to allow himself to consider marriage as long as he had nothing to offer her. His pride wouldn't allow him to ask for her hand in marriage until he had made his own way.

Now, all that seemed about to change.

An early morning breeze slid down the mountainside and brought with it the tangy, sweet aroma of mountain pine. He loved the cool freshness of early morning. The mountains were a sharp contrast to the flat, dry plains of west Texas.

The thought caused his mind to flash back to his childhood home and to his ma and pa. A lump crawled up the back of his throat and his heart hurt as he recalled the bloody scene of their mutilated bodies after the Comanche finished with them.

He remembered each shovelful of dirt as he dug their grave. He swallowed and drew a long breath as he remembered lowering his parents into the single grave and covering his mother's naked body with his shirt. The sound of the dirt falling on them still haunted him. He slammed his eyes shut. Tears seeped from his eyes and coursed down his cheek. He shook his head and swiped them away with a gloved hand.

The sun was noon-high when Cody arrived at the Higgins Ranch. He rode past two large herds of Longhorns tended by several Higgins riders. They recognized him and waved. He lifted a hand in return.

He reined up near the barn and swung to the ground. Roy Self emerged from the barn leading a young colt.

"Howdy, Cody," the Higgins foreman greeted.

"Howdy, Roy. Is Miss Juliana up to the house?"

"Think so. She headed that way awhile ago."

"Saw your trail herds when I rode in. When you boys heading for Denver?"

"At first light, tomorrow."

"Thought I might ride along if you have no objections?"

"Be mighty glad to have you."

"I'll check with Miss Juliana and make sure it's agreeable with her."

Cody tied his two horses to the corral fence and headed toward the big house on the hillside. He pushed open the gate and stepped up onto the porch. Juliana jerked the front door open and greeted him with a beaming smile. She hurried across the porch and into his open arms. He pulled her to him with a long hug.

"I saw you coming," she said happily. "I'm so glad to see you. Come on in. I'll make some coffee."

"I'm headed for Denver. Thought I might ride along with your trail herd, if it's all right with you."

He followed her into the kitchen.

"You're going to Denver? Is something wrong?"

"No, nothing. Just between you and me, we found the source of those gold nuggets. The one you found in the streambed washed down from upstream. We discovered the mother lode by accident. It was behind a waterfall.

"We've accumulated so much gold we need to cash it in for money to buy supplies and equipment. We decided one of us needed to make a trip to Denver. Sammy thought I ought to be the one to go."

"Really? Oh, Cody, that's wonderful news."

"I thought if I rode along with the trail herd, it might not arouse anybody's curiosity."

"That's a good idea. It will be safer, too. While I'm thinking about it, after I get the money for my herd, what do you think about me buying a couple of those super bulls you suggested I need? Remember the ones you told me about down in Texas? How much did you say they cost?"

"According to what my old foreman down in Waco said, they cost five thousand dollars apiece."

"Would you make the arrangements for me when you get back?"

"Be glad to, if you're sure that's what you want."

"Wish I could go with you on the trail drive," Juliana said, as she busied about the kitchen making coffee. "

"A trail drive ain't no place for a lady," he told her.

"I know, but I still wish I could go. I can ride and shoot as good as any man on the ranch."

"Maybe we can take a trip to Denver together someday," he told her.

"I'm going to hold you to that one, cowboy." She paused long enough to brush his cheek with a kiss.

"I ran into Roy down by the barn. He said they were pulling out with the herd in the morning."

"Yes, that's the plan."

"From what I saw when I was riding in, looks like they've got everything ready to go."

"Actually, I'm glad you're riding with them. Roy's a good foreman, but I'm not sure how well he could handle things if they ran into trouble."

"Any reason to believe they might?"

"No, not really, but renegades of the *Jacarilla Apache* tribe roam the area you'll be traveling through. They've been on the warpath since 1853 when the Governor of New Mexico broke the treaty they signed."

"Well, we'll keep our eyes peeled," Cody told her. "Did

Roy say how long he expected the drive to take? I've never been to Denver."

"He said it's about four hundred miles, said they would skirt most of the mountainous country the way he plans on going."

"He'll be lucky to get ten to twelve miles a day," Cody said. "It's gonna take forty days or so at best."

"I need to ride out and see how the cabins are coming along. Want to ride with me?"

"Of course."

Cody and Juliana rode side-by-side. It was a beautiful day. They talked, laughed, and enjoyed one another's company. As they rode she told him of her experiences growing up on the ranch and pointed out places where memorable childhood events took place.

"I use to slip off and go swimming right over there," she told him, lifting an arm to point to a wide pool of the river. "I had to sneak off even to do it. My father was a hard man. My brother was his favorite. He never had much time for me," she told him sadly.

"Juliana, I'm real sorry what happened to your brother and your pa."

"I know. It wasn't your fault. I don't blame you. You just did what you had to do. It's ironic, isn't it, that I would fall in love with the man that killed both my brother and my father?"

Cody couldn't answer. He just nodded his head.

Up ahead, Cody saw what looked like a small town. All along the river new log cabins lined the bank. Children ran to and fro, laughing and playing childhood games. Goats grazed peacefully in the tall green grass. Chickens scratched the dirt, searching for their next meal. Women toiled over washtubs and hung their wet clothes on a line stretched between nearby trees. It was a peaceful scene.

"Are all these folks the families of your ranch hands?" Cody asked.

"Yes, well, most of them anyway. We have several widows whose husbands have died that still live with us. A few are just close relatives of our workers."

As they rode past the new cabins, the women and children all stopped what they were doing and shouted happy greetings to Juliana. It was clear to Cody they all loved and respected her.

"It's mighty nice, what you're doing here," he told her.

"They're like my family. I've known many of them most of my life."

They reined up in front of a partially built cabin. Ian Fritz and his two boys were lifting a notched log into place near the top of one wall of a cabin.

"Good Morning, Mr. Fritz," Juliana greeted.

The big German nodded a reply. His two boys hardly paused long enough to glance their way. They fitted the notched portion of the large log into another notched section of the previous log. The two logs molded together with hardly a crack between the two.

"How many cabins have you completed now?" Juliana asked the builder.

"This will make eight," the German replied.

"They look good," Juliana told him. "You're doing a fine job."

"*Danke Vielmals,*" the big German replied, touching the brim of his floppy hat.

"How many are you gonna build?" Cody asked.

"At least twelve, maybe more." Juliana said.

"Looks like they build a good cabin. When he gets finished here, I'd like to get him to build a cabin near the Quicksilver mine over near the little mountain stream. I think me or Sammy one will need to stay there pretty much all the time."

"Why?"

"Somehow, someway, word will get out about our gold strike. When it does, I'm afraid we'll have all kinds of unwanted visitors to Sugarloaf Mountain."

"You think there'll be trouble?"

"Hope not, but I think it's better to be safe than sorry."

"I suppose you're right. I think the cabin is a great idea. You're having dinner with me tonight. I'm going to fix you a dinner you will never forget."

"You'll get no argument from me."

They rode back to the ranch house. Juliana went to start dinner while Cody looked up Roy Self. He found the foreman in the barn repairing harness for the chuck wagon team.

"Juliana gave her permission for me to ride with you on the drive."

"That's good. Be glad to have you along. I believe you said you've been on a cattle drive before?"

"Yeah, several of them, matter of fact."

"Never been on one myself," the foreman told him. "Leastwise one that lasted more'n a day or two. What cattle Mr. Higgins sold was mostly to the mining camps scattered in this part of Colorado.

"To tell it like it is, I was dreading this drive, not knowing much about what I was doing. With you along, maybe you can help me keep from making some bad mistakes, that is if you don't mind helping?"

"Be glad to help any way I can. How many drovers you got?"

"Just hired three new ones for the drive. We got ten, not counting the cook. I figure we'll need two to handle the remuda, so that leaves eight drovers."

"That ought'a be about right. Any of them ever been on a drive before?"

"Two of the new ones say they have, the rest are mostly ranch hands."

"Well, we'll make do. Just didn't want to butt in where I didn't belong."

"Unless I miss my guess, you'll be bossing this outfit one of these days anyway, I figure you and Miss Juliana will tie the knot before long."

"Well, we'll see."

Juliana was right. The dinner she fixed was one he wouldn't soon forget. She went all out. Fried chicken, mashed potatoes and sawmill gravy, biscuits, corn on the cob, and a peach cobbler for dessert. Cody felt like he was about to pop when he pushed back from the table.

"Where'd you learn to cook like that, Juliana?"

"Before mother got sick she was a wonderful cook. She took delight in teaching me."

"Well, she shore done a good job. I reckon that was the best meal I ever sat down to."

"Thank you, cowboy. Want to sit on the porch awhile?"

"Can't think of anything I'd rather do."

It was one of those nights a woman will treasure for the rest of her life. A million stars dusted the black sky like gold dust sprinkled on a velvet background. A full moon hung high and proud in a cloudless sky. Juliana breathed the cool, green scent of the mountain pines. Somewhere not far away, a whippoorwill called out to a mate, sending its sweet, sad song into a darkening night.

The feeling that passed between them was warm, comfortable, and at the same time, exciting. Cody's hand reached out to take hers. That simple touch sent shivers tingling from her head to her toes. Ripples of awareness raced through her. She turned her head to look at him. His gaze was fixed on hers.

Suddenly, she felt an irresistible urge to kiss him.

Without stopping to rationalize the right or wrong of it, she closed the distance between them. Her open lips met the sweet tenderness of his mouth. He tasted of manliness, and loneliness, and yearning, of confusion and need.

She felt his strong arm encircle her shoulders and draw her to him. Juliana curled her fingers into his shirt where it strained across his shoulders, needing to draw him closer. She opened her lips wider to drink him in, to quench a thirst she had never felt before.

When the kiss ended, she buried her face into the hollow of his shoulder. Her face flushed. Her chest filled. Her heart flickered and picked up speed. She drew a long, slow breath and swallowed hard before she could squeeze words past the knot in her throat.

"I love you, Cody. I love you with all my heart."

"And I love you, Juliana. One day I will make you my own."

She closed her eyes and gave herself over to the beauty of the moment, savoring his words, committing them to her heart. She curled into the protective strength of his arm, nestled closer, and breathed him in.

Chapter XXII

It was the middle of the night when the alarm bell sounded. Buck jerked awake and sat up in bed.

"What's wrong, Buck?" Rebekah asked, concern evident in her sleepy voice.

"Don't know. Something. I'm going to see. No need for you to get up."

He swung quickly to the floor and jerked on his britches. He stomped on his boots and sleeved into his shirt. He grabbed his holster from the wall peg beside the door as he hurried outside.

All over the Longhorn compound, half-dressed men were rushing toward the main gate with rifles in their hands.

A wounded Longhorn rider Buck recognized as one of the night wranglers, stood beside his horse talking to Wade Thomas, the head of security for the ranch. Chester and Buck reached them at the same time.

"What's going on?" Buck asked.

"Mexican bandits," Thomas told them. "They hit our

remuda. Killed two of our wranglers. Got off with over a hundred head of those high-blooded black horses we bought down in Mexico."

"We tried to fight 'em off," the wrangler explained. "But there was too many of them. They killed Luke and Ed. They got me in the shoulder, but I managed to get away in the dark."

"How many of them was there?" Chester asked.

"Don't know. A dozen, maybe more. Some of them were Indians. It happened so fast."

"Take him over to the infirmary and get him patched up," Buck instructed. "Chester, Wade, get some men together. Let's go get our horses and the ones who did this. They'll likely head across the river to Mexico. We'll need to take along enough trail supplies for a long chase."

"We'll have the packhorses loaded and be ready to ride in half an hour," Thomas said, turning to carry out Buck's orders.

"We better tell the girls what's going on," Buck told Chester. "I'll meet you at the stable in fifteen minutes."

They both headed quickly toward their houses.

Rebekah was up and already had coffee perking in the pot when Buck hurried in.

"What is it?" she asked anxiously. "What's happened?"

"Mexican bandits raided us. Killed two of our men and stole the remuda. We're going after them. One of our riders is shot up. He's over at the infirmary. See if Jewel needs any help tending to him."

Rebekah nodded and sleeved into a robe. She knotted it around her waist as she pulled on her boots.

"Buck, are you sure you're up to a trip like this? It's only been four months since you were shot. Is your shoulder well enough?"

"It'll do," he said, dismissing her concern.

"Coffee's ready. Pour yourself a cup before you go. How long you think you'll be gone?"

"Got no idea. It might be a long chase. They're bound to be smart enough to know we'll come after them, so they're liable to head deep into Mexico."

Rebekah went to him. Tiptoeing, she wrapped her arms around his neck and pulled him close.

"Be careful, cowboy."

Chester, Wade Thomas, and twenty heavily armed Longhorn security men stood beside their horses as Buck strode up. His spurs rattled with each long step as he approached. The long-tailed canvas duster he wore flapped about his legs from a gust of wind. He carried a Spencer carbine under one arm and his bedroll under the other. His face was hard. His mouth was drawn into a tight line.

Horses stamped their hooves impatiently, swishing their long tails.

Without a word, he cinched his saddle and tied his bedroll behind the saddle of a big, solid black, high-withered gelding and slipped the rifle into his saddle boot.

Pausing, he let a slow gaze crawl over each of his men. These weren't ordinary cowboys. They had been chosen carefully because of their skills. These were hard men: men who had been up and down the trails more than a few times, men who most likely lived on both sides of the law at one time or another, men who knew how to use the guns strapped around their waists.

Low-pulled hat brims mostly hid their faces. Their bodies were shrouded by dusters identical to the one Buck wore.

"Time we covered some country," he said, toeing a stirrup

and swinging his big frame into the saddle. "That bunch will cover forty miles a day, even driving our herd of horses. I'd like to catch them before they get too deep into Mexico. I don't want trouble with the Mexican army if we can avoid it. Mount up. Let's ride."

A hundred hooves pounded out of the compound at a gallop and quickly disappeared into the darkness. The riders set their faces toward the river. The Longhorn cowboys were like family. When you messed with one, you riled the whole crew. Two of their own had been killed and another wounded. Somebody had to pay for that.

A silver moon hung overhead in a star-sprinkled sky. A small dust cloud lifted from their horses' hooves and was swept away by a cool breeze from the north. It always amazed Buck how it could be so cool during the night and so blazing hot in the daytime. From May through October, the temperature usually hovered above one hundred degrees. Come daylight, it would be another hot, south Texas day.

As the sun peeked over the horizon, they drew rein on the bank of the Rio Grande River.

"Couple of you boys ride the bank in both directions," Buck said. "See if you can spot where they crossed. Two more do the same on the other side. The rest of us will wait here. Fire a shot when you find something."

They didn't have long to wait. A single shot rang out to the west. They swung into saddles and headed that direction.

A long, dry wash cut it's way through the countryside and ended up at the edge of the river. A Longhorn rider sat his saddle on the high bank. As Buck and the others rode up, the security man lifted an arm and pointed toward the bottom of the wash.

A blind man could see that a hundred or more horses had recently traveled along the wash. The caliche crusted sand showed clearly the passage of the herd of horses.

"No doubt about it," Chester said. "This is where they crossed."

Buck and his men urged their mounts down into the dry wash and into the muddy waters of the Rio Grande. The river flowed sluggishly along at this point, no more than belly deep, and they walked their horses across without difficulty.

They followed the tracks that came out of the water on the Mexican side into an offshoot canyon. It was bone-dry, barren of all but the hardiest of vegetation. Cactus and agave clung to the sandy topsoil. Gnarly mesquite dotted the canyon floor, their thorny branches bent by countless swirling winds.

The Longhorn men rode cautiously. Their searching gazes examined every rock, every wash, every cluster of mesquite trees, lest they ride into an ambush. This was empty country. Harsh, desert-like, and untamed, a land where only the strongest survive. This was the land they rode into.

Buck reined his mount to a stop and raised his arm to signal a halt.

"Couple of you boys ride on ahead and scout the canyon."

One of the riders Buck knew as Bill Fallon reined his mount alongside Buck.

"I'll go, Mr. Cordell. I've been tracking men as a bounty hunter for ten years."

"I'll ride with him," another security man the Longhorn boys called Brickshy Loggins said. They joked that he was *one brick shy of a full load,* but few had the nerve to say that to his face. Brickshy would fight a grizzly bear barehanded.

Buck fixed the two with a look and nodded. They urged their mounts forward in a slow walk and disappeared around a bend in the canyon.

A short time later, a shrill whistle echoed down the canyon. Buck spurred his gelding forward in a lazy trot. The winding switchback canyon meandered along for more than three miles, finally growing shallow and spilling out into a rocky, desert countryside.

The hoof prints were clearly visible as the horse herd wound around fields of ocotillo and cactus beds and headed due south.

Buck lifted an arm and motioned it forward. As they moved south under a boiling mid-morning sun, Buck considered what they were facing.

We're riding into unfamiliar country. We have no idea how many of these bandits there are or where they're headed with our horses. I'm leading my men into what's likely to be a bloody fight in the emptiest part of Mexico.

The deeper into this country we have to go, the less I like it. But there's no turning back. If we let these bandits get away with killing our men and stealing our horses, we might just as well pull up stakes and go someplace else. No use worrying about it now. There'll be plenty of time for that once we find them.

No, we'll follow them to the devil's gates if we have to, but we'll do what we gotta do.

"Where you think they're headed?" Chester asked, reining his mount alongside Buck's gelding.

"No telling," Buck replied. "One thing for sure, they're riding like they got someplace in mind. Wherever they're headed, we'll find them."

They rode steady, sparing their horses, but holding them to a ground-eating short lope. By mid-afternoon, they reached a long, narrow, rock strewn valley. The hard-baked caliche gave unmistakable signs of the horse herd's passing.

They reined to a stop. Bill Fallon stepped from his saddle and knelt beside the tracks. He fingered the outline of the shod hoof prints.

"Bill can read sign like most men read a newspaper," Wade Thomas told Buck.

A dry wind swept through the narrow valley and kicked up a swirl of dust. The boiling sun cooked into the ground. Shimmering waves of heat rose from the sandy surface, baking man and beast.

They waited. Buck settled against the cantle of his saddle and allowed the bounty hunter all the time he needed to read the signs.

Finally, Fallon stood and pushed back the flat brim of his sweat-soaked hat and looked up at Buck.

"They're pushing the herd hard. Holding them to a gallop. These tracks are three, maybe four hours old."

"Can you tell how many bandits are herding the horses?" Chester asked.

"Hard to say. The tracks are all jumbled up together."

"Three or four hours. Don't sound like we're gaining any ground on 'em," Chester said.

"Let's hurry these horses some," Buck shouted, irritation evident in his booming voice. He touched the rowels of his spurs to the black's ribs, asking the gelding for speed. They settled into a steady, ground-eating short lope.

Just after good dark, they reached a narrow muddy stream that snaked across the barren land.

"Let's let the horses slake their thirst," Buck said.

The Longhorn riders stepped stiffly to the ground, having been in the saddle half the night and all day. They knelt upstream from the horses and ducked their sweaty heads in the warm water, shaking their long hair like a dog when they emerged.

From somewhere in the distant darkness, a coyote sounded.

"That coyote sounds mighty lonesome," Chester commented. "I can sure understand how it feels. This is the loneliest place I've ever seen."

"That wasn't a coyote," Bill Fallon told him in a voice no louder than a whisper.

"You sure?" Buck asked.

"I'm sure. A coyote barks four times before it howls. That cry had five barks before the howl. That was an Indian."

Squatting on their haunches to rest a bit, they scanned the darkness uneasily. Another cry from the darkness made tiny hairs stand out on the back of Buck's neck and his mouth went dry. He listened intently. Sure enough, he counted five barks before the howl. He stood to his feet and slipped the Spencer from the saddle boot and levered a shell. The other men did the same.

They waited.

After a time, the 'coyote' cries stilled and silence settled in around the twenty-three Longhorn men. Buck decided the cutaway bank with huge rocks scattered along the streambed would be as good a place as any to spend the night. He couldn't ask his men and horses to travel all night again. They needed rest.

"Let's make camp right here and take up the chase at first light," he told his security chief.

"What about a fire for coffee?" Thomas asked.

"Why not? They already know where we are."

Working together, they soon had the horses watered, unsaddled, picketed nearby, and a small fire built for coffee.

"Let's post some guards tonight," Buck suggested to his security man.

Buck hardly slept a wink all night. He lay awake, listening intently, drowsing off from time to time, but waking instantly at every sound. An anxious hour passed, then two. Finally the grayness of dawn pushed darkness aside. After a quick cup of coffee and some cold biscuits they hit the saddles.

They followed the tracks all day and the next. By sundown of the third day they reined up on a hillside overlooking a small Mexican village. They looked down at a makeshift corral of broken mesquite bushes that held thirty or so Longhorn horses.

Another dozen horses stood hipshot, tied to a hitching rail in front of a flat-roofed cantina. The saddles told Buck the horses in front of the cantina belonged to the *federales*.

"I was afraid of that," Buck told Chester and Wade Thomas. "Looks like the bandits have left part of our horses and paid off the Mexican army to watch after them.

"What are we gonna do?" Thomas asked.

"We're gonna do what we came here to do," Buck said. "We're gonna get our horses back and deal with anybody who tries to stop us."

"You got it, Boss. That's all I wanted to know."

They all slid their Spencer carbines from the saddle boots and levered shells into the chambers. Chester opened his double-barrel shotgun and thumbed two shells into the twin holes. He closed it with a flick of his wrist.

Buck eased his gelding forward down the sloping hillside. The Longhorn men scattered as they rode into the small village. With rifles ready, they rode along both sides of the narrow, dusty street.

Small adobe huts sat scattered along the street. Old men and young children peered from open doorways at the strangers as they rode into town. Skinny goats looked up briefly from the few sprigs of grass and then resumed their grazing. Red chickens scratched at the dusty ground, searching for some morsel of food.

Buck, Chester, and Wade Thomas reined up beside the

horses belonging to the Mexican soldiers. They stepped to the ground, examining every doorway and every rooftop carefully.

Buck nodded his head in the direction of the front door of the cantina. Chester and Wade both acknowledged understanding and stepped through the open doorway. Buck followed.

The sickening smell that greeted them assaulted their stomachs. The stench of stale whiskey, vomit, cigarette smoke, and unwashed bodies was overwhelming. The large room was stifling hot.

A dozen soldiers in various combinations of dirty uniforms slouched around the three tables in the place with drinks in their hands. Clouds of flies circled puddles of beer on their tables. They glanced up, seemingly unconcerned, as Buck and his two men stepped inside, almost as if they had been expected. A deadly silence settled over the room like a cloud.

A bearded bartender with a dirty apron leaned on a makeshift bar made from a plank stretched between two upended wooden barrels. He stared disapprovingly at the three *gringos* as they entered.

"Anybody speak English here?" Buck asked loudly.

A man in officer's uniform swung a critical look at Buck.

"*Si*. I am Captain Ruale Hernandez. I am the commandant of this part of Mexico. How can I be of help to you?"

"Those horses outside in the corral belong to me. They're part of a herd that was stolen a few nights ago over across the border. The bandits who stole them killed two of my men and wounded another. We've come to get our horses back and the men who stole them."

"Oh, *señor*. I'm afraid you are mistaken. Those horses belong to my friend, *Señor Antonio Sanchez*. He is a very wealthy landowner in this part of Mexico. They were left in my care by some of his *vaqueros*."

"No, commendant. Those horses belong to me. They're wearing the Longhorn brand. Make no mistake, when we leave, the horses go with us."

Some of the *federales* stood to their feet and reached for their rifles that were propped against nearby chairs. Chester lifted his shotgun and trained it on the soldiers. The sound of both hammers being clicked into place froze the soldiers' hands.

"Be better if you told your men to keep their hands away from those guns," Chester told the commendant.

"How dare you threaten the army of Mexico?" the man shouted angrily. "I will have you shot!"

"Maybe, maybe not," Chester said. "Right now, we'll just gather up those guns so you won't be tempted to do something you'd be sorry for. Wade, wanna collect those rifles and the comendant's sidearm?"

The security chief stepped forward and gathered up all the weapons.

"Now, commendant. If you would be so kind as to direct me to where I can find this *Antonio Sanchez*, I would be grateful," Chester asked.

"I will tell you *nothing, gringo pig!*"

"I doubt you'll get anything out of him," Buck said.

"Oh, he'll come around. All he needs is a good talking to. Won't you, comendant? We can do this the easy way or the hard way, but I wouldn't recommend the second option."

The Mexican officer hawked from deep in his throat and spat directly into Chester's face. Chester wiped the spittle from his face with the back of a hand and glared.

"Wish you hadn't done that. I really do," Chester said. "Tie him up with his hands in front," he told Wade Thomas.

In mere moments, the *federale* officer was trussed up with a rope. Chester withdrew the big Bowie knife from his belt scabbard. Reaching a hand, he grabbed the comendant's little finger and stretched it out on the tabletop. Holding it down with his left hand he placed the razor-sharp knife blade just above the knuckle.

"I'm gonna ask you one more time. Where do we find this man called *Antonio Sanchez?*"

The comendant's wide-eyed gaze lowered to the knife blade on his finger. He licked suddenly dry lips. Beads of sweat popped out on his forehead and trailed down his face.

"He would kill me," the man said, closing his eyes. He clamped his lips together and slowly shook his head.

The ear-piercing screams shattered the silence as the knife blade sliced through the man's finger as easily as if it were hot butter. Blood gushed out of the stub and puddled on the table. Chester grabbed another finger and stretched it out. Again he placed the knife on the second finger just below the knuckle.

"Once more, commendant. Where can we find *Antonio Sanchez?*"

Through choking sobs, the comendant gave rapid directions to the *Sanchez hacienda*.

"One more thing. We'll be back for our horses. They'd *better* be here. Get my meaning? Nod your head if you understand."

The broken officer slowly nodded his head.

Chapter XXIII

Juliana walked with Cody down to the barn. His black and white pinto stood saddled and waiting. He took up the reins and fiddled with them as he looked down at the toes of his boots. He was at a loss for words.

"I'll miss you," she said softly. "Please be careful."

Cody nodded.

"I'd better be going," he said. "It's almost daylight. The others will be waiting."

Juliana reached a hand and pulled his face down to her. Her lips parted. They kissed. He wrapped his arms around her and hugged her close.

Turning, he booted a stirrup and swung into the saddle. He reined Cincinnati around and rode away without looking back. He couldn't. She would see the tears in his eyes.

The trail herd was gathered in the north pasture. They milled about, grazing on the lush, green grass. The drovers were gathered in a wad near the chuck wagon when Cody rode up. He stepped to the ground and walked over to join the others.

"Like I said before," Roy was telling them. "We'll drive from daylight till dark. I'm planning on ten to twelve miles a day. The first couple of days we'll push 'em hard until they settle in. Watch out for bunch quitters. Some of them will want to turn around and head back home. It's your job to see they don't.

"This young fellow is Cody Cordell. He'll be riding with us. He's experienced with cattle drives, so if he asks you to do something, it's the same as me asking. Any questions?"

"Yeah, I got a question," a big, burly fellow spoke up. "Are you the boss or is this fellow? I don't cotton to taking orders from some snot-nosed kid that ain't dry behind the ears yet."

Cody knew trouble when he saw it and this fellow was trouble. Cody decided right off that he didn't like this fellow and he figured the feeling was going to be mutual.

"What's your name, mister?" Cody asked.

"Name's Whit Barlow."

"Well, Mister Barlow. I ain't here to boss anybody around. I'm here to carry my own load just like everybody else. The day I don't do that, I'll fork my saddle and ride out. Fair enough?" Cody stuck out his hand.

The man glanced around at the other drovers, obviously looking for others to side him. Finding no one, he reluctantly took Cody's hand and shook it.

"No offense intended," the big man said.

"None taken," Cody replied.

"Well, then," the foreman said. "Let's head 'em up and move 'em out."

"Where do you want me, Roy?" Cody asked as they climbed on their horses.

"Work wherever you want to," the foreman replied.

"I'll ride drag."

"You don't have to do that. I'll have one of the other men work drag and eat dust."

"I'll do it. Like I told Barlow, I'll pull my own weight."

Cody dug his old serape from his pack and slipped it over his head, figuring it would keep some of the dust off him. He decided to go ahead and replace his regular holster and gun with his belly holster while he was at it. He pulled out the familiar black, hand-tooled holster and strapped it in place. He thumbed the Colt full of shells, except for the one directly under the firing pin. He left it empty. He pulled the serape down to cover the belly gun.

He loosed his coiled lariat and reined Cincinnati around. He circled around the herd and crowded the stubborn longhorns into movement, swatting them with his rope until he had them all moving.

He rode back and forth along the backside of the herd, swinging his coiled rope, yelping, and shouting at the slow movers. An old mossy-horn turned and headed back toward the familiar pasture she knew as home. He reined his pinto to cut her off, leaning to swat her across her tender nose. After a couple of licks she decided to rejoin the herd.

All day the long line of cattle plodded along, winding between towering mountains and through valleys where the grass grew belly-deep. The longhorns simply followed the one in front of them, grabbing a mouthful of the lush grass as they moved along.

There was no let up. By late afternoon, Cody's arms felt like they would pull from his shoulder sockets every time he swung the coiled lariat.

Just before sunset they came to a clear creek. They allowed the trail herd to pause during the crossing long enough to slake their thirst. A wide valley on the other side of the creek was a perfect place to bed the herd down for the night.

Roy had chosen well. The old cook already had the chuck wagons in place and supper cooking.

Cody rode a hundred yards upstream and swung down on the creek bank. He ground-hitched his pinto and knelt at the edge of the water to wash off some of the trail dust.

Roy rode up on his big buckskin. For a minute, the foreman sat his saddle watching Cody wash up.

"You're a hard man to figure," Roy finally said. "Everybody knows riding drag is the worst job there is on a trail drive. Why'd you volunteer for that dirty job?"

Cody stood to his feet and wrung out his bandana that he had just washed in the creek. He studied his boot toes for a minute before answering.

"First job I ever had on a ranch, the boss handed me a scoop shovel and told me to clean out the outhouse. I did. Then he told me to clean out the horse stalls. I did that, too. I earned his respect that day because he saw I wasn't afraid of work.

"You said the other day that, someday, I might be the boss of the Higgins Ranch. If something like that should ever happen, I'd want these men to respect me."

The foreman slowly nodded his head in understanding.

"You'll do," he said, before reining his horse around and heading toward camp.

Cody rode drag every day for a solid week. Each evening he bathed, ate supper, and crawled into his bedroll dog-tired. He was always careful to place the saddlebags containing gold on the ground next to his bedroll and tie a leather thong from the bag to his wrist.

Over breakfast on the eighth day he asked if anyone would

trade places with him for a few days. Every man in the crew except one volunteered. Whit Barlow sat with his head down, refusing to even look up.

That night, Cody unsaddled his pinto and lifted the heavy saddlebags onto his shoulder. He walked the short distance to the camp. He felt eyes on him. Barlow's gaze was following every step Cody made.

He chose a spot near the edge of the jagged circle of light from the campfire to spread his ground sheet and shake out his bedroll. He hefted the saddlebags from his shoulder and covered them with a blanket.

Barlow's gaze followed Cody as he walked to the fire and poured a cup of coffee from the blackened pot. The camp cook spooned Cody a plateful of beef stew and handed him two sourdough biscuits.

Cody found an empty spot on a log near the fire and settled down to eat supper.

"Been watching you for a week," Barlow said, over the lip of his coffee cup. "I notice you keep them heavy saddlebags within arm's reach day and night. I'm asking myself, *what could he have in them bags that's so all fired important?* You know what I decided?"

Cody chewed and swallowed a spoonful of stew before he answered. It was clear the man was on the prod.

"I figure you're about to tell me."

"I decided you got something in them bags you don't want the rest of us to see."

"You're right. Now forget it."

"See, I knew it. What you got in them bags, Cordell?"

"It ain't none of your business what I carry in my own saddlebags."

"You heard him, Barlow," Roy Self spoke up. "Let it drop."

Anger crawled up Cody's throat. *Looks like Barlow is gonna push this to the limit.*

"Ain't dropping nothing," Barlow said firmly, pushing to his feet and heading toward Cody's bedroll. "I'm gonna have me a looksee at what he thinks is so important."

The big man reached Cody's bedroll and jerked the blanket off of the saddlebags. Cody set his plate of stew and cup of coffee on the log next to him and rose.

Casually, Cody flipped the corner of his serape back over his shoulder exposing the bone handled Colt.

Barlow's hand was halfway to the saddlebags when Cody spoke. The words came out calm, clear, and deadly.

"Touch them saddlebags and I'll kill you."

Barlow's hand froze. For a long moment he paused, not moving a muscle. Straightening up, he turned to face Cody. Their gazes fixed on one another. Barlow's lips stiffened with cold fury. Pure hatred boiled in his eyes. His meaty hand hovered only a hair's breath above the gun in his holster.

"*Nobody* threatens me and lives!" he shouted, clawing his gun from its holster.

Cody waited.

He waited until Barlow's sidearm cleared leather and was leveling before he made a move. When it happened, it happened in less than a heartbeat. Cody's hand flashed in a blinding arch and the Colt was in his hand. It bucked once, twice, three times in the space of an eye blink. Three holes the size of a man's little fingertip punched into Barlow's chest. The slugs nailed Barlow in the chest one after the other, each shot slamming him a step backward. All three holes could be covered with a single hand span.

Barlow's face was a mask of shock and hatred. His eyes went wide, and then rolled back in his head. He was slammed backward from the force of the three heavy .44 slugs and bounced when his body hit the dirt.

Cody replaced his Colt in the belly holster and pulled

the serape down to cover it. He calmly picked up his plate and coffee and resumed his supper. Between mouthfuls he glanced up at the foreman who stood staring wide-eyed at Cody.

"I'm sorry, Roy. I didn't want trouble. Now we're one hand short."

The foreman didn't reply. He just shook his head in wonderment.

"Couple of you boys dig a hole over yonder a ways. We'll bury him come first light."

Later, every drover who saw it would swear Cody's draw was so fast they saw nothing but a blur. The shooting was the subject of conversation for the next week.

They had been on the trail for three weeks. Cody figured they should be about halfway to Denver. They were traveling through a narrow valley between two heavily wooded foothills. Thick pine trees stood straight and tall and proud like giant soldiers standing at attention, guarding the towering mountains behind them. Off in the distance, the Rocky Mountains sat like giant majestic kings reigning over their lowly subjects below, their white, snow-capped peaks punching holes in the clouds. The sheer enormity of the mountains took Cody's breath away.

He was riding point alongside Roy Self. The trail herd plodded along fifty yards behind them. Their remuda of thirty horses followed the chuck wagon. It was a low, darkly overcast day with no rain. Only the sounds of the cattle behind them marred an eerie stillness.

Out of the tail of his eye he saw them. At least a dozen half-naked Indians on paint mustangs thundered out of the heavy timber and headed directly for the herd of horses. Red pieces of cloth were bound across their foreheads and held their long, loose hair in place.

"Apache!" Cody shouted at the top of his voice, as he reached a hand backward and jerked the Henry rifle from its saddle boot.

"They're after the horses!" he shouted again, spurring his own pinto to intercept the horse thieves.

The sound of pounding hooves behind him told him the foreman had reacted, too. Cody levered a shell into the chamber and ducked low instinctively as he saw one of the attackers swing his rifle in Cody's direction. A puff of smoke bellowed from the end of the Indian's rifle and a hot nugget of lead singed close enough to his face that he felt the heat from it.

Cincinnati galloped full out and belly to the ground. Cody stood up in his stirrups and slammed the Henry to his shoulder. He laid the sights square on the chest of the shooter and squeezed the trigger.

The Indian arched backward and somersaulted over the back of his charging paint. Cody saw him bounce and tumble end over end on the ground.

Cody levered another shell and used the barrel of his rifle to lash the rump of his pinto, urging him to greater speed. He heard Roy Self's rifle bark behind him and saw an Apache tumble from his horse. Other Higgins' drovers raced their mounts toward the horse thieves.

Cody saw one of the Higgins horse wranglers grab chest and slide from his saddle. The other one, a young fellow named Sid, fired his rifle wildly, as fast as he could lever shells into it. Cody saw two more Indians ripped off their horses by the Higgins riders' gunfire.

Another Indian loomed in front of him. Cody threw his

rifle to his shoulder and fired. The Apache grabbed his stomach and toppled from his speeding pony.

But the attackers were already circling the horse herd and driving them toward the thick woods. Roy Self and Woody Childs rode nearby.

"We've got to stop them before they reach the woods!" Cody shouted.

Roy nodded his understanding and reined his mount alongside Cody. Five Indians drove the horse herd. They leaned low along the necks of their racing ponies and shouted at the frightened horses.

Cody leaned over Cincinnati's neck and allowed his body to match the rhythm of the pinto's long strides. The stolen horse herd was no more than three hundred yards from the trees. He knew if they reached the safety of the woods, the likelihood of getting their horses back were slim and none.

He slid his Henry rifle back into his saddle boot and jerked out his Colt. The distance between Cody and the fleeing Apache closed swiftly. An Indian glanced back and saw Cody gaining rapidly. He swung a rifle and fired. Cody returned fire using his Colt. His first shot missed, but the second shot spun the Indian out of his saddle.

Another Apache got within range and Cody took him out with a single shot. Only three Indians remained driving the horse herd.

Cody felt a presence pulling up alongside him. He shot a quick glance. Unbelievably, Roy's big buckskin was outpacing Cody's pinto. Another few strides and all Cody could see was the buckskins rump and long tail flying in the breeze.

Roy did as Cody had done. He slid his rifle into his saddle boot and grabbed his sidearm from his holster. The foreman overtook another Apache and put a slug in the Indian's back, causing him to wheel from his pony and slide along the ground.

One of the two remaining Indians reined his pony to the right, away from the horse herd. Cody followed. It took only a few strides to overtake the smaller Indian mustang and bring Cody within range of his Colt.

The Apache glanced back over his shoulder. When he saw Cody closing the distance between them his eyes got big. He lunged forward along the neck of his pony. Cody pulled alongside him. He extended his arm. The nose of the Colt was only a few feet from the frightened Indian when Cody feathered the trigger.

The heavy .44 slug struck the Apache's rib cage, slamming him sideways. He flew from his mount with arms windmilling the air.

Cody pulled back on Cincinnati's reins and swung a look over his shoulder in time to see the last remaining Apache disappear into the heavy woods. Roy had pulled alongside the leaders of the horse herd and turned them away from the timber.

By the time Cody got to the remuda Roy already had them circled and headed back toward the trail herd at a trot.

"Good job," Cody said, reining up alongside the foreman.

"Same to you. If you hadn't been here we'd a lost the remuda. I'm much obliged."

Chapter XXIV

It was an hour's ride to the *Sanchez* ranch. A river watered the desert country as they neared the ranch and turned the terrain into a lush, green oasis. Large herds of fat longhorn cattle grazed peacefully.

Off in the distance, a collection of barns, corrals, and adobe workers' cabins were set some distance from a large walled compound. This was the *Sanchez* hacienda. They reined to a stop on a hillside overlooking the layout and sat their horses.

"Looks like our black horses yonder in that corral," Chester said.

"Yep. How you think we ought to handle this?" Buck asked Chester and Wade.

"I say we just ride in, clean house, collect our horses, and go home," Chester said.

"Judging by the number of worker cabins, that might take some doing," Wade Thomas suggested. "Offhand, I'd say he's got at least forty gun hands on his payroll down there."

"Yeah, and some of 'em killed our men and stole our horses. I want those fellows bad," Chester said.

"Maybe he'll listen to reason," Buck suggested. "I'd like to at least talk to him before we just ride in and start shooting."

"Waste of time, partner. A man who would send his *vaqueros* across the border to shoot our men and steal our horses ain't gonna listen to reason. The only talk he'll listen to is gun talk."

"Maybe, but I'd still like to give it a try. Wade, me and Chester will ride in. You and your boys keep the dogs off us. Nobody goes in or out. If you hear shooting, come a runnin'."

"You got it, boss. Watch your back."

Accepting Buck's decision, Chester retrieved the sawed-off double barrel shotgun that hung from his saddlehorn and thumbed two double-aught shells into the twin barrels. He closed it with a flick of his wrist and checked to assure his Colt was fully loaded.

He dug a handful of shotgun shells from his saddlebags and stuck them in his righthand duster pocket. He had cut out the lefthand pocket of his duster so he could stick his hand inside and hold the shotgun underneath his duster, hidden from view. Once he had the shotgun out of sight, he gave Buck a nod. They heeled their horses down the hill.

Little plumes of dust lifted from their mounts' hooves and swept away in a gust of wind. The breeze flapped the tails of their long, open canvas dusters. Flat brim hats shaded the week's stubble on their faces. Neither one said a word. Each man was lost in his own thoughts as they mentally prepared themselves for battle.

Approaching the walled compound, they rode past a large pole corral. Inside the corral were the seventy black horses with Longhorn brands on their hips. Several Mexican *vaqueros* paused from their work to stare, but none made a threatening move.

As they drew near the wide, double doors of the walls surrounding the *hacienda,* Wade and his twenty security men fanned out, essentially surrounding the walled compound.

Buck and Chester rode through the gates.

Three tough looking Mexican *pistoleros* stepped from underneath a covered veranda and walked out to meet them. Each wore low slung guns. Bandoleers chocked full of ammunition criss-crossed their chests. As they approached, they spread several yards apart.

Buck judged the swarthy fellow in the middle to be the leader. He was tall for a Mexican, tall and dark and ugly. A deep purple knife scar ran from his right ear down below his chin. His eyes were evil looking and hard. His penetrating gaze fixed upon Buck and never wavered.

"We're here to see *Señor Antonio Sanchez,*" Buck said.

"Why you want to see *Señor Sanchez?*" the leader questioned.

"I'll tell him when I see him."

The man's eyes slitted with obvious anger and a cruel snarl curled his lips. For a long moment the *pistolero* said nothing. His intense stare said it for him. The man obviously had a short fuse and Buck had just lit it.

From long years of fighting together, Buck knew he didn't have to worry about the ugly fellow's two companions. If it came down to gun trouble, Chester would handle the other two.

Buck tensed and kept his unblinking gaze locked on the leader, searching his ugly face for any sign the *pistolero* was about to go for the two pearl handled guns he wore.

After a minute the muscles in his face relaxed a bit.

"Follow me," the ugly one said, turning his back and walking toward the sprawling main house.

Buck stepped to the ground and followed the *pistolero.*

He swung a glance over his shoulder and saw Chester dismount and wait for the other two to walk ahead before he followed.

The ugly leader opened a large, dark, oval-shaped door and stepped through it, leaving it open. Buck followed the man into a sprawling main room with elaborate, colorful furnishings. They passed through the room and came to another door. The *pistolero* paused and tapped lightly.

From the other side of the closed door a voice spoke a single word.

"*Entente.*"

The man opened the door and closed it behind him, leaving Buck standing outside the room. After a few moments, the ugly one returned and opened the door for Buck to enter the room. Chester and the three *pistoleros* followed him in.

A heavy Mexican, dressed in traditional dark vest and white shirt, sat behind a large, dark desk with a polished top. His long, coal-black hair was pulled straight back and tied with a leather cord. His face was pockmarked and he sat smoking a fat cigar.

His hard gaze followed Buck as Buck crossed the room to stand in front of the desk. There was no other chair in the room.

"Are you *Señor Sanchez?*"

The man stared at Buck with unwavering eyes for a moment before answering.

"*Si.*"

"I'm Buck Cordell. My partner and I own the Longhorn Ranch across the river in Texas. A few nights ago some bandits raided our ranch, killed two of our men, wounded another, and stole a hundred head of horses.

"We found thirty of our horses in a small village guarded by some *federales*. The rest of them are outside in your corral.

We've come to get our horses and the men who did this. We won't go home without them."

The Mexican landowner glared at Buck. He took a long, slow puff from the cigar and, leaning his head back leisurely, blew the blue smoke out in a long, thin trail.

Buck waited. Anger crawled up the back of his neck and reddened his face.

"I know nothing of these *banditos* that stole your horses. I purchased the horses in my corral and those in the village only two days ago."

"Who sold them to you?"

The man stuck out his hands, palms up, and pursed his fat lips in a gesture of veiled ignorance.

"Who knows? Men come. Men go. I purchase many things. I do not know the men who sold the horses. But now, the horses belong to me."

Then the man's face darkened. He leaned forward with his hands leaning on the desk. He glared at Buck and his voice took on a threatening tone.

"Go home, *gringo,* while you still can."

Buck took a single step. His strong arm reached across the desk and gathered a handful of the man's shirt and jacket. He jerked, pulling the fat landowner halfway across the desk. At the same instant, his .44 Colt filled his other hand. He placed the nose of the gun against the Mexican's nose and thumbed back the hammer.

"Now you listen, 'cause I ain't gonna say this but once. We *are* taking our horses. And we *are* gonna hang the ones who killed our men."

Behind him, Buck heard the familiar twin clicks of hammers on Chester's shotgun being locked into place, and heard Chester's voice above the clicks.

"First one goes for those guns and you all get blowed away. Now just relax and stand *real* still,"

Somebody didn't listen.

The next sound Buck heard was the sound of a gunshot behind him, followed closely by a blast from Chester's shotgun. Twisting a look, Buck saw the three *pistoleros,* or what was left of them anyway, sprawled on their backs with most of their faces blown away.

"The ugly one drew on me," Chester explained

Glancing at the three dead men, Buck saw one of them had his gun clutched in his lifeless hand.

"Let's get out of here," Buck said, dragging the landowner the rest of the way across his desk. "We're taking this fellow with us. The order to steal our horses likely came from him."

Buck shoved *Sanchez* in front of them as they hurried out the door of the office. The front door suddenly burst open. Several Mexicans with guns in hand rushed in. Buck jerked the landowner backwards through the office door just as a gun blasted. A slug gouged a large chip from the door-facing only inches from his face.

"You will never get out of my *hacienda* alive," the smirking Mexican said. "My men will kill you."

"Maybe. But if we die, you die," Buck told him.

Buck loosed his grip on the Mexican for a moment to shift his gun to the other hand. *Sanchez* seized the opportunity and made a lunge for the door, but Chester saw what was happening and swung his shotgun backhanded. The heavy barrel caught the Mexican across the nose. The impact flattened the landowner's nose. It sounded like a dead limb breaking. Blood splayed through the air. *Sanchez* dropped like a sack of feed.

Running boots in the other room told them more of *Sanchez's* men had arrived. Chester returned to his position with his back pressed against the wall only inches from the open office door. He thumbed a shell into his shotgun to replace the used one, thumbed back a trigger, and jerked his head around the doorjamb for a quick look. He quickly stuck the nose of the shotgun around the door and fired.

A choking scream from the other room told them his shot had struck at least one target. The sound of running boots told them several men were rushing the open door. A bearded Mexican with bandoleers across his chest charged through the opening with guns in each hand.

Chester swung the shotgun and fired point blank. The man's chest exploded in a shower of blood and leather. Another appeared. Buck jammed his .44 into the man's ribs and fired. The muffled explosion sounded strange. The heavy slug traveled completely through the attacker and exited the other side, leaving a hole the size of a man's fist.

As Chester reloaded his shotgun, a third man plunged through the door, leaping over the lifeless bodies of the first two. He twisted in the air, swinging his gun around for a shot. Buck shot the man twice before he landed. His body jerked each time the heavy slug tore into him.

An eerie quietness settled over the room. Buck and Chester waited. Buck's hand made sweat on the handle of his Colt.

The stillness was shattered by the sound of shots coming from outside the house. It was the unmistakable sound of Spencer rifles. Wade Thomas and the Longhorn security men arrived and joined the fight.

They made short work of the remaining *Sanchez* fighters. Within minutes, the remaining Mexicans gave up and threw down their weapons.

When Buck and Chester emerged from the house half-dragging a dazed landowner, Wade hurried up to meet them.

"Sorry it took so long for us to get here," the security man said. "Turned out most of his fighters were in a barrack already inside the compound. It took a few minutes for us to fight our way to you."

"You got here just in time," Buck told him. "It was getting pretty hairy in there."

"We took eight prisoners. I questioned them. They say they've been raiding across the river for more'n a year. Their boss was behind it all. He ordered the raids."

"Pretty much what we figured," Chester said. "What you want to do with *Sanchez?*"

"Hang him," Buck said bluntly.

They did.

When they gathered their stolen horses and headed up the road toward the Mexican village, they left *Antonio Sanchez* hanging from the crossbar over the entrance to his sprawling *hacienda*.

CHAPTER XXV

The Higgins trail herd arrived in Denver on June 18, 1869. Once they completed the count and moved the herd in the stockyard pens, Cody shook hands with Roy.

"I won't be traveling back with you. I've got some business regarding our silver mine I have to take care of. If you get back before I do, tell Miss Juliana I'll stop by as soon as I get back."

"I'll do it. I'm obliged for all your help."

"Don't mention it."

Cody rode to the livery stable and arranged for his two horses to be fed, curried, and stalled with plenty of hay. He hefted his two sets of saddlebags over his shoulder, slipped his Henry rifle from the saddle boot, and headed for the Sargent House Hotel he spotted earlier.

The hotel was a sprawling three-story red brick building with a covered porch in front that extended the length of the building. Cody pushed through the front door and walked up to the counter.

The fellow who greeted him was a heavyset, balding man who wore horn-rimmed glasses and an easy smile.

"Good afternoon, sir. I'm Ned Sargent, owner of this hotel. May I be of assistance to you?"

"Yes, I need a room."

"Very good, sir," the man replied, turning to select a key from a board containing at least forty keys. "If you would kindly sign the register. You will be in room number 201. It's on the second floor facing the street."

"How much?" Cody asked, as he scribbled his name in the book.

"That will be four dollars a night. How many nights will you be staying with us?"

"Not sure yet, two or three, most likely. I'll pay for two now and see how it goes."

He dug the money out of his pocket and paid the man.

"Could you tell me where the assay office is located?"

"Certainly. You will find it two blocks to your left. You will see the sign."

"Obliged."

Cody scooped the key off the counter and headed for the stairs. He found room number 201 and used the key to open the door.

It was the grandest room he had ever seen. What looked like an imported floral rug covered most of the polished wooden floor. Wine-colored wallpaper covered the walls, with oil paintings well placed on them.

A wine-colored covered chair and sofa sat near a large dresser with a mirror. A floral pitcher and matching washbasin sat on the dresser. Floral towels and wash cloths hung on a nearby rack.

The bed was larger than a normal bed. It was covered with a white bedspread. He walked over and punched the bed with a finger. His finger sunk into the softness up to his knuckle. A featherbed.

Pretty fancy place.

He stashed his saddlebags containing his extra clothes and gun rig under the bed and headed for the door. *I'm anxious to see how good this gold is and what it's worth.*

Cody easily found the Colorado Assay Office, so the sign on the front of the single square brick building said. He opened the door and stepped inside.

A short, squatty fellow who looked like he hadn't missed many meals glanced up from underneath a green visor.

"What can I do for you?" the man asked.

"Are you the assay fellow?"

"I am the official assay officer for Colorado, yes, sir."

Cody withdrew one of the larger gold nuggets, about the size of a good chew of tobacco. He transferred it from the saddlebags to his pocket while in his hotel room. He laid the nugget on the small desk in front of the assay man.

"Can you tell me what that's worth?" he asked, folding into a small chair in front of the man's desk and setting the heavy saddlebags on the floor beside him.

The assayer picked up the nugget. His eyes bugged wide. He glanced up at Cody with amazement showing on his face. He quickly scooped up a small eyepiece and

secured it over one eye, held there by the layer of fat underneath his eyes.

For a long moment the man examined the nugget.

Cody waited.

Finally the man looked up with his eyes wide and his mouth wider.

"Where did you get this?"

"I'd rather not say just yet," Cody told him. "What's it worth?"

"Young man, this is the purest gold I've ever seen. I haven't seen gold this high grade since the Pikes Peak discovery back in 'fifty nine."

"Again, what's it worth?"

"Easily forty-five dollars a troy ounce," the assayer said.

He turned to a small scale on a back table behind his desk and weighed the nugget.

"It weighs eight ounces. It's worth three hundred-sixty dollars. Is this the only one you have?"

Cody reached down and lifted the heavy saddlebags and set them down on the man's desk without a word. The man looked puzzled until he opened a flap and saw the contents inside. His eyes almost bugged out of his shocked face.

"Oh, my!" he exclaimed. "Oh, my!"

He looked from the gold in the saddlebags to Cody and then back again and again. He seemed speechless. It took awhile for the fellow to recover from his shock.

"Young man, I don't know where you found this, but you have undoubtedly uncovered a major gold discovery. This will be another gold rush even bigger than the Pikes Peak discovery, and that drew a hundred thousand people from all over the country to this area."

"That's what I'm afraid of," Cody told him.

"Then I take it you want to exchange this gold for money?"

"Yes, sir."

"Well, I'm afraid that will take some time. I'll have to grade it, weigh it, and arrange for a bank draft from the Denver Bank."

"How long will all that take?"

"Couple hours, maybe more."

"I'll wait."

"You mean you want to sit right here while I do all that?"

"I got no place to go."

"Very well."

Cody figured at forty-five dollars an ounce, even if just a little of his gold got misplaced, it would amount to a lot of money. He watched carefully as the man weighed each batch and recorded the exact weight. It was well after dark before the man came up with a final tally.

"All the gold checked out to be the exact same grade. Obviously, it all came from the same vein. The total weight was forty-eight pounds, four ounces. At forty-five dollars an ounce, your gold comes to thirty-four thousand seven hundred forty dollars.

"Unfortunately, the bank is already closed. If you will meet me at the bank when they open at nine, I'll arrange for a bank draft in that amount."

"Can I trade the bank draft for money?"

"Of course. A bank draft is as good as cash, better in most cases. But surely you don't want to carry around that much money. There are lots of unsavory characters in Denver."

"Seems to me they have kinfolk most places," Cody said, standing to his feet. "One more thing. You *will* keep this quiet, won't you? About the gold, I mean."

"Why, yes, of course."

"Of course," Cody said. "I'll be over at the Sargent Hotel. I'll see you in the morning at nine."

"Yes, sir, Mr.— I didn't catch your name?"

"I didn't give it. But it's Cordell."

"Yes, yes, of course, Mr. Cordell, sir. Until morning then."

"One more question. Who's the best attorney in town?"

"Arthur J. Winfield, no question about it. But he's quite expensive."

"Where can I find him?"

"His offices are just across the street from the Denver Bank on Boulder Street, next street over on the corner."

"Obliged," Cody said, turning and walking out the door.

Cody felt a bit self-conscious still wearing the serape. Folks were staring at him real funny like. *Reckon I better buy me some clothes that don't attract so much attention,* he decided. *But right now I'm plumb tired. I'm gonna find some supper then go try out that feather bed. Thirty-four thousand dollars. That's more money than I ever heard of, let alone knowing that half of it belongs to me.*

After a good night's rest, Cody washed, shaved, dressed, and went downstairs.

"Where's a good place to eat breakfast?" he asked the hotel owner.

"There's a good place up the street, two blocks on your left called Sadie's. The best place is three doors down. It's called the *T-bone*. Food's good either place."

"Obliged," Cody told him.

Somehow the T-Bone sounded a little too fancy for his taste. He walked the two blocks to Sadie's. The place was crowded, but he spotted an empty table over to one side. He walked over and sat down.

A pretty red-haired waitress hurried up with a pot of coffee and an empty mug. She greeted him with a happy smile.

"Good morning."

"Morning," Cody replied.

"Coffee?" she asked, fixing him with a lingering look.

"Yes, ma'am. No better way to start a day than a pretty lady pouring coffee."

"Well, thank you. You're not from Denver, are you?"

"No, ma'am, but how did you know?"

"Just something about you. I'd say you are from Texas."

"Right again. Next thing I know you'll be reading my thoughts."

"If I could, would I be pleased?"

"Yes, ma'am, you surely would," he said, wrinkling a small grin.

She smiled. It looked good on her.

"What can I get you for breakfast?"

"I trust you. Bring me what you think a fellow from Texas ought to have for breakfast."

"Coming right up, Texas."

She hurried toward the kitchen.

Cody was sipping his coffee when a fellow rushed in and joined three other men at a nearby table. Cody couldn't help overhearing.

"Did you hear the big news?" the man asked his companions.

"What big news?" one of the men asked.

"Gold! That's what! Some fellow rode into town yesterday with two saddlebags full of high-grade ore. Word is it could be a bigger strike than the Pike's Peak discovery a few years back."

Cody swung a look at the talker. He'd never seen the man before.

"Where is this strike?" another of the man's companions asked, excitedly.

"Don't know yet. The fellow's name is Cordell. Nobody seems to know where the strike is, but we'll find out pretty quick. News this big won't be a secret long."

"You can say *that* again. I'm gonna go pack my knap sack and saddle my hoss so I'll be ready to head out soon as I find out where this strike's at."

All four men jumped up and hurried from the café.

Sure didn't take long for the news to leak out. I figure the assayer spilled the beans. I should 'a known. Oh, well, like that man said, news that big was bound to leak out sooner or later.

The pretty waitress brought his breakfast and sat it in front of him. Cody looked down at a thick beefsteak, a half-dozen fried eggs, a wooden basket full of hot biscuits, and a jar of fresh honey.

"Ma'am, if I didn't already have a lady waiting on me back home, I'd most likely ask you to marry me," Cody joked.

"Just my luck," she laughed, smiling broadly and hurrying off to another customer.

He dug into his breakfast. It was delicious. While he was eating, Roy Self walked in. Cody saw him and motioned him over.

"Morning, Roy. How's it going?"

"Going good. Sold the herd yesterday. Got a good price for them, too."

"Figured you would. They are good cattle. What'd they bring?"

"Forty-four dollars a head. Got the bank draft right here in my pocket."

"That's a good price."

"When you gonna quit fooling around and marry that lady? A blind calf could see she loves you."

"We'll see. We both got a lot going on right now," Cody told him. "Want some breakfast? I'm buying."

"Let me buy yours. After all you done to help on the way up, it's the least I could do."

"You better look at what I'm eating. Might cost you your whole bankroll."

"I'll charge it to my expenses. I doubt the boss would turn that expense down."

The red-haired waitress hurried up and poured Roy some coffee.

"You know this fellow?" she asked Roy.

"Shore do."

"Trying to get him to stay in Denver, but not making much headway."

"Well, ma'am. He's got a lady waiting on him that's *almost* as pretty as you are."

"Ain't you a smooth talking cowboy? No wonder you two are friends. What can I get you for breakfast?"

"Whatever he had, bring me one just like it."

They ate and talked cattle talk until their second cup of coffee was just a memory.

"When you heading back?" Cody asked.

"First light. What about you?"

"Day or two. Might run into you boys on the trail."

"You're welcome to ride with us, you know."

"I know. Still got some business to take care of before I head out."

"Yeah, I heard about it this morning, first thing. The news is spreading like wildfire. Everybody in Denver is talking about the big gold strike. Now I know what was in those saddlebags."

"Sorry I couldn't tell you before."

"I understand. Gold does strange things to a man. Whit Barlow's an example of that. So you and your partner found the mother lode, huh?"

"Seems like it."

"Well, I'm happy for you. You're a good man. Just the kind of man Miss Juliana needs."

"She's a fine lady."

* * *

Cody walked into the Denver Bank at exactly nine o'clock. He gave his name to the clerk behind the counter. The man's eyes rounded and started stuttering.

"Ri-right...th-this way Mr. Cordell. Mr. Sylvester is expecting you."

The clerk ushered Cody through a frosted glass door to a private office. The assayer was already there. They both rose to their feet when Cody walked in.

"You must be Mr. Cordell," the big, heavyset fellow said, hurrying around his desk to greet Cody. "I'm Henry Sylvester, president of the bank. Have a seat, please."

They shook hands before Cody sat down in the only vacant chair in front of the bank president's desk.

"Mr. Barnes has just been telling me about your strike. He said it was some of the richest grade gold he's ever seen, even better than the famous Pike's Peak discovery. Congratulations. Looks like you are well on your way to being a very wealthy man."

"Well, don't know about that, but we're happy about it."

"I would think you should be. I'll have my treasurer draw up a draft for, let's see, yes, here it is, thirty-four thousand-seven hundred and forty dollars. That's a lot of money."

"Yeah, it is, more'n I ever heard of. But actually, I'd like to have ten thousand of that in cash, if you don't mind. The rest I'd like to have kept in an account so we can issue drafts against it. Can we do that?"

"Of course, you can. What name would you like on the account?"

"The Schroeder/Cordell Mining Company."

The banker wrote the name down on a piece of paper and showed it to Cody.

"Is that correct?" the banker asked.

"Yes, sir."

"Excellent. Then that's how it will be done. If you two gentlemen will excuse me for a moment, I'll go take care of this and be right back."

"Guess you already heard the news leaked out?" the assayer asked sheepishly.

"Yeah, I heard," Cody said coolly.

"It wasn't my fault. It just kinda come out accidentally."

"Yeah, well, what's said can't be unsaid. Reckon you *accidentally* gave 'em my name, too?"

The assay man dropped his head and nodded. The banker hurried back in carrying a leather satchel and some legal papers.

"Mr. Cordell, there's ten thousand dollars cash in this satchel. Here are the papers establishing your account and some bank drafts. Just fill these out as you see fit. They are as good as money. If you will, just sign this paper establishing your account."

Cody signed the paper.

"Is there anything else I can do for you gentlemen today?"

"Reckon that about covers it," Cody said, standing and picking up the leather satchel.

He found the attorney's offices and opened the door. A stern faced lady sat at a desk. The rest of the office was filled with file cabinets and a line of chairs along one wall.

"May I help you?" she asked.

"Yes, ma'am. I'd like to see Mr. Winfield."

"Do you have an appointment?"

"No, ma'am. Didn't know I needed one."

"Ordinarily, Mr. Winfield doesn't see anyone without an appointment. Have a seat for a moment. I'll see if he might have a spare minute."

She disappeared into an adjoining office. Cody sat down in one of the chairs and waited. The lady emerged in a couple of minutes and held the door to the adjoining office open.

"Mr. Winfield will see you."

Cody stepped through the open door into a plush office. The desk the attorney sat behind was the biggest desk he had ever seen, even larger than the bank president's desk. The office was decorated to perfection. One wall was lined from floor to ceiling with legal books.

"Come in," Winfield invited. "Have a seat. I'm A.J. Winfield." The attorney stuck out his hand for a firm handshake. "How can I help you?"

"Got a question before we start," Cody said, releasing the attorney's hand and sitting down in an overstuffed leather chair.

"Ask it."

"Can I be sure anything we discuss will be kept just between me and you?"

"Absolutely," the man said, looking Cody directly in the eyes with an unwavering stare. "That's called *attorney/client privilege*. I'm obligated by law to keep anything we discuss in strictest confidence. I could be disbarred and lose my license to practice law if I should breach that confidence."

Though he had never met the man before this moment, he somehow trusted him immediately. He struck Cody as a man of his word.

Cody reached into his pocket and withdrew the legal papers he and Sammy had shown the judge back in Trinidad. He handed them to the attorney.

"Me and my partner are working a silver mine near

Trinidad, Colorado. We call it the Schroeder/Cordell Mining Company. We signed those papers and had them notarized. They say we are equal partners. Do they look all right? Is there anything else we need to do to make it legal?"

The attorney took several minutes to examine the papers, nodding his head in agreement every minute or so.

"I can't see anything wrong whatsoever with this partnership agreement. It would stand up in any court in the land."

"The other papers there are mining claims. They show they've been filed with the assay office. Do those look all right, too?"

Again, the attorney took his time examining the claims.

"I see no problem. They've been properly filed and stamped by the assay office. You have a valid waiver for the extra claims you hold. I see nothing wrong. What's the problem?"

"There's no problem, we just wanted to make sure there wasn't one sometime down the road. You see, we've been mining for silver, but we struck gold. Seems it's very high-grade. The assay officer says it's the highest grade gold he's seen since the Pike's Peak discovery back in 1859."

"Oh, yes. I read about it in the newspapers of course. Well, well. I can see why you wanted to dot the I's and cross the T's."

"Would you consider being our attorney?"

"I'm sure you realize my services don't come cheap?"

"Most things worth having don't come cheap."

"Well said. Very well. My retainer will be one thousand dollars a year. I charge ten dollars an hour for my services. Is that acceptable?"

"Agreed. I just left the Denver Bank. We have an account there. I'll give you a bank draft, if that's agreeable?"

"That will be fine. Any time I can be of service, don't hesitate to let me know."

"I'll have any bills or legal stuff directed to your office, if that's okay with you?"

"Of course. I'll make sure it's taken care of."

Cody took one of the bank drafts, filled it out and signed it. He stood to his feet and stuck out his hand. They shook hands, sealing the agreement.

"One more question?"

"What is it?"

"Do you know where I might find a good mining engineer?"

The attorney rubbed his chin in silent contemplation. After a minute, he nodded his head.

"Yes, perhaps I do at that. He's a bit eccentric, but word is, he's the best in the business. His name is Sid Peters. I understand he can usually be found at a saloon over on Benton Street. The place is called, appropriately enough, the Golden Nugget Saloon."

A grin wrinkled Cody's features.

"Yeah, that's appropriate, sure enough. I'll look him up."

Cody left the attorney's office and headed for Benton Street. He found the Golden Nugget Saloon and pushed through the batwing doors. It was better than the saloons in Trinidad, but not much. The dozen or so tables were mostly empty. Only a few customers were whiling away their time nursing drinks. A large man, even taller than Cody, stood behind a well-worn mahogany bar that had seen better days. He wore an apron around his waist that most likely was white at one time long ago. Cody walked to the bar.

"I'm looking for a fellow named Sid Peters. Know him?"

"Reckon I do. He's sittin' right over yonder," the man said, lifting a stubby finger to point.

Cody's look followed the barkeep's finger.

A heavily whiskered old fellow sat alone, slumped over a table. His clothes were worn and tattered. He wore a floppy hat that sat cock-eyed on his head. From all appearances, he was passed out.

"That's Sid Peters?" Cody questioned.

"That's him. Spends most every day sitting right there."

"Is he a heavy drinker?"

"Likely would be, if he had the money. Don't remember him having any of that in a while. Somebody feels sorry for him and buys him a drink now and then, but mostly he just sits there waiting to die. There sits a fellow that's given up on life before life gave up on him."

Cody was sorely tempted to turn and walk out. *How could a man like that be the best mining engineer around? Could we depend on him to stay sober? I got my doubts.*

But instead of walking out he walked over to the old man's table and pulled out a chair. Sid Peters lifted his head an inch or two off his arm and slanted a look up at Cody.

"Wanna buy me a drink?" Peters asked. Cody was surprised that his voice was not slurred.

"No, I want to talk with you, if you're Sid Peters?"

"That's me. Has been for forty-two years."

Cody was shocked into silence. The man looked much older than forty-two.

"Somebody told me you use to be a mining engineer?"

"Still am. Fellow don't change his occupation just because he's out of work."

"Yeah, reckon you're right. You looking for work?"

"Do I look like I'm looking for work? No, sonny, I ain't looking for work, but I never run from it in my life. What you wanting to talk to me about?" The man finally sat upright. He looked Cody in the eyes. The man's eyes weren't bloodshot or puffy, they were clear as a crystal.

"Ever worked a silver or gold mine?"

"Yep."

"Which one?"

"Both."

"Interested in working another?"

"Maybe. Which one?"

"Both."

"You just looking or have you struck pay dirt?"

"Both."

The man called Sid Peters studied Cody for a long minute, obviously taking his measure.

"Where's your mine located?"

"About four hundred miles from here."

"Long ways. What you paying?"

"What you charging?"

That brought a small smile.

"How would I get there? Long ways to walk."

"I'll buy you a horse. I'll be leaving in a day or two. You can ride with me."

"Tell you what I'll do, sonny. I'll go have a look at your mine and let you know then what my services will cost you."

"Got any idea what kind of equipment you'll need?"

"Not until I look around your place. I'll let you know after I decide if I'm gonna take the job or not."

"Fair enough. You got a place to stay?" Cody asked, afraid the fellow might be sleeping on the street, judging from his appearance.

"Yep. Just don't like staying there."

"I'm staying over at the Sargent House Hotel, room 201. My name's Cordell."

"I'll be ready to go anytime you are, sonny."

"I'll arrange for a horse for you. It will be at the livery stable down the street. Plan on leaving at first light, day after tomorrow. I'll meet you at the stable."

"I'll be there, sonny, rain or shine."

When he left Sid Peters, Cody found a jewelry store.

"How can I help you?" the nice, well-dressed lady greeted him.

""I'd like to look at some wedding rings."

She smiled broadly.

"Come right over here," she invited, leading him to a glass enclosed case. "Did you have anything particular in mind?"

"No, ma'am. I've never done this before. What would you suggest?"

He saw her brief glance take in the ragged serape, dirty britches, and scuffed boots.

"What price range were you thinking about?"

"Start with the best you got and work down."

Her smile brightened.

"Very good," she said, reaching into the case and withdrawing a small, wine-colored case. She opened the top. The diamond caught light from an overhead lantern. Brilliant white rays exploded from the large stone and sent fingers of light flashing around the room.

"This is our finest set of rings. It's a combination engagement and wedding ring set."

"What do you mean by engagement?"

"Well, when a young man asks his lady to marry him, that means they are *engaged,* or *promised* to each other for marriage. It's the time between when he *proposes* and the actual marriage. It's becoming a very popular tradition."

"I'll take two of them," Cody told her.

"Two? No, I'm afraid you misunderstood. The rings come as a set. They go together."

"Yes, ma'am. I understand. I'll take two sets. My partner's getting married, too."

"Oh, I understand. What size is your lady's finger?"

He looked at the sales lady's hand.

"About the same size as yours, I reckon."

"These rings will fit my finger perfectly," she said, slipping the rings on the third finger of her left hand and holding her hand out for Cody to see. "They're absolutely breathtaking aren't they?"

She was right. They were the most beautiful rings Cody had ever seen.

"Yes, ma'am, they are that sure enough. Like I said, I'll take two sets."

"Don't you even want to know what the cost? These are our very best rings. They're very expensive, I'm afraid."

"How much?"

She paused for a moment, appearing embarrassed to tell him the price.

"They are three hundred dollars a set."

"Could you wrap them up in some kind of pretty paper for me?"

That wide smile stretched from ear to ear this time.

"I'd be happy to. It will only take a few minutes."

Cody pulled the folded bills from his pocket and counted out six hundred dollars and laid it on top of the glass case. The lady hurried to a back counter and began wrapping the ring sets.

Cody browsed around the store while he waited. A gold pocket watch caught his eye. The cover was engraved with pretty scrolls. A long, gold chain was attached.

"Don't mean to bother you, ma'am," he called out. "But could I look at this gold pocket watch?"

She hurried over, took the watch from the glass case, and opened the front cover. Soft, soothing harp music filled the room. After a moment she closed the cover and handed the watch to Cody. He examined it carefully.

"That's a fine-crafted Swiss time piece. It will last you a lifetime."

"Oh, it's not for me. It's for my business partner. I'll take it."

"It's fifty dollars."

He paid her.

Minutes later he left the store with three wrapped packages.

Chapter XXVI

A dry wind howled through the tiny village of *Jaumave* as Buck and his men drove their seventy stolen horses, recovered from *Antonio Sanchez* and his murderous crew, north up the dusty road. Buck, Chester, and Wade Thomas sat their horses on a hillside overlooking the village. Buck tented his big shoulders, his hands resting on top of his saddlehorn.

"I don't like it," Chester said. "It's too quiet. No movement in the village at all. Nothing. Even the *federales'* horses are nowhere in sight."

Buck's eyes narrowed, examining the village with a critical look. The village sat in the bottom of a bowl shaped terrain with hills completely surrounding it. Chester was right. Not a living soul could be seen. It was as if the village was completely deserted. The remaining thirty of their stolen horses milled restlessly around in the small rail corral near the cantina.

"You know me, Buck," Chester said. "I get this feeling when something ain't right. I got that feeling real strong right now."

Buck felt a growing uneasiness, too. The hairs on the back of his neck stood out. He swept his sweat-stained hat from his head and sleeved perspiration from his forehead. Replacing his hat, he drew the Spencer carbine from his saddle boot and levered a shell into the firing chamber.

"Wade, send ten of your men to the left and the other ten to the right of the village. I want it boxed in. Me, you, and Chester will drive the horses real slow to the edge of town, and then stampede them. I'd rather round up our horses later than ride into an ambush. We'll ride in behind our horses."

Wade rode away to share the plan with his twenty men. Buck and Chester heeled their mounts down the hillside and fell in behind the horse herd.

The heat was merciless, moving in hot blasts by the gusting wind. Their horses suffered, as did Buck's men, wrapped in their canvas dusters.

"Maybe everybody's staying inside outta this blasted heat," Chester suggested.

"Yeah, maybe. Let's hope that's what it is," Buck said.

The herd plodded along. When they were within a hundred yards of the village they shouted and drew their pistols, firing into the air. The horses bolted. They broke into a dead run, heading up the dusty road toward the village. Buck, Chester, and Wade were right behind them with their carbines ready, their eyes searched every window, every doorway for anyone lying in wait.

Dust from the horses' pounding hooves gave cover to Buck and his two companions. As a result, they were almost through the village before the first shot rang out. The slug tore through Wade's duster sleeve, but failed to strike flesh.

Blue gun smoke lifted from the window of a small adobe hut, swept away quickly by the wind.

Buck jammed the butt of his carbine to his shoulder and

drew a bead on the shape of a man's head above the windowsill. He fired. The man's head exploded in a spray of blood, bone, and hair.

"Good shot," Chester shouted.

Another shot rang out. The rumble of galloping horses sounded from the hills. A barrage of gunfire that sounded like a young war came from both sides of the village. Buck swung a quick look. Dozens of *federale* soldiers charged down the hills on either side of town.

"The cantina!" Buck shouted. "Take cover in the cantina!"

Chester and Wade must have heard him because they spurred their mounts toward the largest, sturdiest building in the village. Buck beat his companions there, and ducking his head, rode his mount through the open front door right into the large saloon.

Two *federale* soldiers knelt at the windows. They leaped upright, shocked by Buck's sudden entry. They swung rifles in his direction for a shot. Holding his carbine in his left hand, Buck fired from the waist. The force of the heavy slug somersaulted the soldier backwards. The second *federale* soldier fired too quickly and missed. Buck could feel the heat of the bullet as it singed past his cheek.

Chester and Wade followed Buck's lead and rode their horses through the door. An explosion from Chester's shotgun caught the second soldier in his stomach. Parts of him splayed through the dim light inside the room, coloring the wall behind him in crimson.

Buck nodded his thanks as he leaped from his saddle with the carbine in his hand. He slid to a stop beside the window.

The rattle of gunfire outside the cantina told them the *federales* had either broken through the Longhorn security line or had ridden around it. They spurred their mounts along the street, firing as they passed. Heavy rifle slugs whacked into the adobe walls beside the window where Buck squatted, while others ricocheted and whined off into space.

A hard charging soldier raced past Buck's window. He laid his sights on the man's back and feathered the trigger. The slug tore the rider from his saddle. His rifle flew from his hands as he tumbled along the dusty street.

Chester and Wade had taken up positions at the other window and the front door. Their Spencer carbines barked again and again.

Buck swung his rifle and found the chest of another rider, triggering off a shot that tore the rider from his saddle, arms askew, hands clawing empty air.

Another rider broke from the cloud of dust in the street, his rifle aimed squarely at Buck. Only a dozen yards separated the two men when Buck fired. He saw a crimson splatter gush from the bare skin just below the rider's full beard. A strangled cry sounded above the rattle of gunfire and the man flew backwards over the back of his horse, limbs thrashing as he landed.

The back door slammed open. A bearded *federale* with a rifle held waist high charged in. Chester swung the double-barrel shotgun and fired. The blast shook the room. A swarm of angry double-aught pellets slammed the soldier and sent him staggering back through the open door.

All along the street, riderless horses trailing their reins galloped to and fro, frightened by the gunfire. The sound of more horses drew nearer, but this time it was Wade's Longhorn security men. They had obviously regrouped and galloped hell-bent-for-leather down the street, firing as they rode.

Within minutes, it was all over. The few *federales* remaining alive stood in a small huddle with hands raised, guarded by four Longhorn riders.

Buck, Chester, and Wade Thomas walked from the cantina. They paused to look to the right and left before stepping into the dusty street, stopping in front of the huddle of prisoners. Chester stepped over and grabbed one of them by the arm and pulled him from the wad of soldiers. It was the *federale* captain.

"You should have left well enough alone," Chester told him.

"What are you going to do, gringo, murder the rest of us?"

"No, we're gonna strip you naked, boots and all, and set you afoot. You've got a long walk in the hot sand ahead of you."

Within an hour they had gathered their stolen horse herd, along with the *federale* horses, and headed home, home to Texas.

Rebekah was worried. Buck and his men had been gone over a week. He had told her they might have to go deep into Mexico, but she was still concerned. She jumped at every sound and ran anxiously to the front door every time she heard riders coming in or going out of the compound.

"When is Papa coming home?" Little Cody asked over and over.

"He'll be back soon," she tried to reassure him. "Very soon."

But her words didn't reflect her true feelings. *Mexico is a bad place. Bad things happen to good folks there.*

Someone tapped on the front door. Rebekah hurried to the door with a lump in her throat. Selena stood there. A questioning look swept across her face.

"Rebekah, what's wrong? You look like you've see a ghost."

"I'm worried sick, Selena. I don't know what's come over me. I'm not usually this way when they're gone. Something's wrong. I just know it."

"I'm sure they're okay. We've got two of the best men alive. They've been through thick and thin together. They'll be home soon, I'm sure."

"Wish I was as confident as you are. Want some coffee? I just made a pot, hoping it might settle my nerves down. Come on in."

After a cup of coffee and some *woman talk*, Rebekah felt better.

"Guess I just get uptight sometimes. I've never told Buck this and never would, but I worry every time he's gone. I love him so much I just don't know what I would do if something should happen to him."

"Nothing's going to happen. He's a young man and the strongest man I've ever met, and that includes my husband. I know what you mean, though. I would be completely lost without Chester."

"We are both so lucky," Rebekah said, staring down at the bottom of her coffee cup.

"Yes, we are," Selena agreed.

A day passed, and then another. Two more crawled by slowly. Rebekah grew more worried as each day passed.

She was giving little Cody a bath when she heard the security bell sound just once. It was Buck! She just knew it! She hurriedly wrapped her son with a towel and rushed out the front door just as Buck and Chester rode through the front gate.

Rebekah raced to meet him with little Cody's legs swinging in the air as she ran. He screamed excitedly.

"Papa's home! Papa's home!"

Buck crawled stiffly from the saddle and waited with open arms. She filled them. They hugged for a long moment, maybe two, before she pushed him back a step so she could look at him.

"Are you all right? Oh, Buck. We're so glad you're home safe."

"Me, too. It's been a long, hot ride."

Chapter XXVII

Sid Peters, the mining engineer, waited at the livery just as he promised he would be. Cody was relieved. He was more than a little concerned the man might have had second thoughts about the trip and job.

"Glad to see you made it," Cody told him.

"Sonny, you'll learn when Sid Peters gives a man his word, it's his bond. In some folks eyes I may be a drunkard and no-account, but if I tell a man I'm gonna do something, I'm gonna do it."

"Good to know. I won't doubt you again. Your horse is all saddled and waiting. You can stow your belongings on the packhorse, there's plenty of room. I've got a few more things I bought to add to the pack."

It was just coming good daylight when they rode out of the livery and headed south.

"How far you say it is to your mine, sonny?" Peters asked.

"Long way. Riding steady we ought to make it in two weeks, maybe a little less."

"Tell me about your setup."

"Well, my partner already had the claims filed and was digging for silver when we threw in together. We worked the mine for a few weeks. Found traces of sulphur and something he called *cerussite*. He said when you find that, there's a better'n average chance silver ain't far behind."

"Well, maybe, but not necessarily," Peters agreed.

"Well, one day we were having a picnic when—Juliana, she's my girl—found this shiny object in the little mountain stream near our mine. Turned out to be a gold nugget. We kept looking and found a whole passel of 'em.

"Me and Sammy kept working our way upstream. One day we came to a waterfall with a good pool of water under it. The whole bottom of the pool was littered with nuggets.

"I got curious and looked behind the waterfall. That's when I found it. The rock wall behind the waterfall had seams as wide as two fingers put together. We counted four seams like that."

"Did you try to get any gold from the seams?"

"No, by that time we had two saddlebags full of nuggets and decided one of us needed to come to Denver and see what we had found."

"Gossip that's going around says it was high-grade gold, maybe the best that's been found in Colorado."

"That's what the assayer said, too. That's where the gossip came from. He is the one who spilled the beans."

"Figures. I've known Mel Barnes for years. He likes to talk."

"Seems so."

By nightfall, Cody figured they had traveled forty miles or so. They camped beside a small mountain stream. Peters proved to be a good travel partner. He jumped right in and helped care for the horses and set up camp.

After a supper of beans, bacon, and cold biscuits brought from Sadie's café, they settled down beside the campfire to enjoy a cup of coffee. The night was chilly and Cody threw a couple more logs on the fire.

"You know how to shoot a gun, Mr. Peters?" Cody asked.

"Yeah, why?"

"Cause we've been followed most of the day. Far as I can tell, there's two of 'em. I figure they're fixin' to rob us. They most likely won't make their move until we're asleep."

"What are we gonna do?"

"We're gonna have a little surprise waiting for them."

They had picketed the horses just outside the circle of light from the campfire. Cody knew Cincinnati would warn him if the intruders got too close.

Cody pumped the mining engineer with a hundred questions about mining for gold and silver. Peters seemed happy to share his knowledge and experience about the subject. After an hour or so, Cody suggested they turn in.

Since Cincinnati hadn't yet sounded the alarm, it was a pretty safe bet the intruders weren't close enough to see what they were doing. Cody used his Bowie knife to cut some pine branches from a nearby tree. He used those to place underneath their blankets to look like two sleepers. They put their hats at the head of their pallets to round out the charade.

Once he had the decoys in place, he handed Peters his extra Remington. They took up a position behind some low-growing bushes nearby with a clear view of their camp and waited.

An hour passed, then two. Cody was beginning to question whether the robbers would make their move the first night out, or wait for a better opportunity, when Cincinnati let out a low rumbling snort from deep in his chest.

Cody tapped his companion on the arm and crossed his lips with a finger. They hunkered down.

From the edge of darkness, a figure stepped quietly into the dim light of a dying campfire. Another man followed. The first man was a tall, skinny fellow who looked to be straddling thirty. He had a gun fisted in his right hand.

The second man was short and heavy with a full beard. He, too, carried a gun in his hand. They approached the decoy sleepers carefully, taking one slow step at a time, like they were stalking a deer.

When the robbers were a few yards from the decoys, they stopped, raised their guns, and fired point-blank into the decoys. Cody and Peters stepped into the circle of light behind them.

"Don't move!" Cody ordered.

Both men spun around, deciding to gamble instead of giving up. They lost.

Cody shot both of them before Peters could get off a shot. The would-be killers doubled over and toppled to the ground. Cody walked over and kicked their guns away before kneeling to check their condition. The one with the beard was dead. His companion wasn't far behind.

Peters walked over and looked down at the two men with a shocked look on his face.

"You killed them. Both of them."

"That's a fact," Cody replied.

"Why would they do that?" he asked.

"Money," Cody told him. "They most likely heard about the gold and figured I had changed it into cash. They wanted it."

"The good book says money is the root of all evil," Peters commented, still staring at the dying man.

"You a Bible reader, Mr. Peters?"

"My father was a traveling preacher. He was always quoting scripture to my mother and me."

"Sounds like some of it stuck."

"Not near enough, I'm afraid. What are we gonna do with these men?"

"We'll dig a hole and bury them come morning. This one will be dead before then."

It took them twelve days to arrive at the Higgins Ranch. They reined up near the corral. Roy Self came out of the barn as they stepped to the ground.

"See you made it. We rode in yesterday," the foreman said.

"Run into any trouble on the ride home?" Cody asked.

"Nope. None at all."

"Roy Self, this is Sid Peters. He's a mining engineer. He's gonna be working with us at the mine. Roy is the foreman of the Higgins Ranch."

Peters and Roy shook hands.

"Miss Juliana up at the house?" Cody asked.

"Yep. She's been looking her eyes out watching for you."

"I'll only be a few minutes," Cody told Peters.

Cody dug two packages from their packhorse and tucked them under his arm as he headed for the big house on the hill. Juliana somehow saw him coming and burst from the house, running as fast as her legs could carry her. Cody met her with open arms. She filled them.

For a long moment neither spoke. They basked in the joy of being together again, of the knowledge that the other was safe in their arms.

"Oh, Cody, I missed you so much. It's so good to have you home."

"I missed you, too. It was a long, but very successful trip."

"Let's walk up to the house. I've got a million questions to ask."

"Some of those will have to keep. I've got to ride on into Trinidad today. I've hired a mining engineer to work with me and Sammy. He's down at the barn talking with Roy."

"Then you sold your gold," she said excitedly.

"Sure did. It brought forty-five dollars an ounce. We had forty-four pounds of gold. That worked out to almost thirty-five thousand dollars."

"Really? Oh, my goodness. That's *a lot* of money."

"Yes, it is. And that's just the beginning. It's hard to believe. The assayer in Denver said it was the highest grade gold he's ever seen."

"Yes, that's what the newspaper said."

"Newspaper? What newspaper? What do you mean?"

"You haven't seen the Denver newspaper? It's front-page headlines about your gold strike. Trinidad is already flooded with prospectors and more are pouring in every day."

"Oh, *no*. I was afraid of something like this. I've got to get to Trinidad as soon as I can. I've got lots of things we need to talk about, Juliana, but right now, I need to get back to our claim. Sammy's gonna need all the help he can get."

"I understand. Go do what you need to do. I'll come into town as soon as I can. We'll talk then."

Cody wrapped her in his arms. They kissed.

"Soon," he promised. "Very soon, we'll talk."

Cody and his traveling companion made the trip to Trinidad in record time. Their horses were exhausted when they slowed to a walk and rode down the street. Cody couldn't believe what he was seeing. Trinidad was busting at the seams.

The boardwalks were so full of people, many were walking in the street dodging the wagons, buggies, and riders on horseback. All seemed in a big hurry to get wherever it was they were going.

"What's going on?" Cody wondered out loud. "Where did all these people come from?"

"It's gold fever, sonny," Peters told him. "I've seen it before. Makes folks plumb crazy. You ain't seen nothing yet. When news got out about Sutter's Creek in California, it set off the biggest gold rush in history. Folks flocked there from all over the world.

"Same thing happened when they discovered gold at Pikes Peak. More'n a hundred thousand folks from all over the country come a runnin', hoping to get a piece of the pot of gold at the end of the rainbow. Might as well get ready, same thing will happen here."

"But how'd they find out? I was careful not to say where we found it or even give my full name."

"You can't keep something this big a secret. Not for long anyway. They have ways to find out."

"Seems so. They even beat us here."

"There'll be more coming, sonny. Lots more."

"We'd better get up to the mine as fast as we can," Cody said anxiously. "No telling what we'll find there."

They crowded their horses through the busy street and coaxed them into a trot as they reached the edge of town. They passed several men with tow sacks over their shoulders trudging up the trail to Sugarloaf Mountain.

As they drew near the mine, Cody spotted a spanking brand new log cabin sitting only a few yards from the mountain stream where they found the first gold nugget.

"Would you look at *that*." he exclaimed.

The cabin was beautiful. It had a covered front porch

that spanned the front of the building. A rock chimney rose above one end. From the size of the cabin, Cody guessed it had several rooms.

Something else caught his attention out of the corner of his eye. A growing huddle of men was gathered in front of the entrance to their mine. Sammy stood with his feet apart with a rifle in his hand. Cody heeled his pinto that way and swung down beside his partner.

"What's going on?" he asked Sammy.

"Claim jumpers," he said angrily. "They're crawling all over our mountain. It's been like this for the last three days. I've told them we have claims on this whole mountain, but it don't seem to make a difference to them. They refuse to listen."

A huge, grizzly fellow who stood a full hand taller than Cody stepped from the midst of the crowd.

"Out of our way!" he bellowed in a bullfrog voice, advancing menacingly. "We got as much right to this mountain as you do."

Cody's gaze hardened and his eyes narrowed to thin slits. He flipped the serape back over his shoulder revealing the bone handled Colt in his belly holster.

"Now listen to me, all of you. It's like my partner has already told you. We've got legal claims filed with the assay office in Denver for this whole mountain. There's lots of other mountains in Colorado where you can look for whatever it is you're looking for. This *ain't* one of 'em. All of you are trespassing on our property. You got five minutes to clear out, starting right now. I'll shoot any man I find on our mountain after that."

The men looked at one another and then back at Cody. First one, then another, turned and grudgingly started down the mountain.

The grizzly fellow and two other tough characters stood their ground.

"You're bluffin'," the big man croaked.

" I don't bluff and you're wasting time," Cody told them. Still they refused to move.

His hand was nothing but a blur. In less than a heartbeat, Cody drew and fired. The bullet caught the big man in the fleshly part of his leg, just above the knee. The force of the heavy .44 slug spun the giant around. He dropped to one knee, blood coloring his britches leg.

"You shot him!" one of the man's companions shouted.

"Did what I said I'd do. The next shot's gonna hit about waist high. Like I said, I don't bluff. Now get him up and get off our mountain."

The big fellow's two companions helped him up and started hobbling down the mountain, one of them shouted over his shoulder.

"We'll get you for this! That's a promise!"

Cody turned to his partner. They shook hands.

"I like the new cabin. How'd we come by that?"

"A fellow named Fritz and his two sons just showed up one day and said you hired them to build a cabin. He said you told him I'd show them where we wanted it built. I decided that was the best place."

"Right where I had in mind. I can't wait to look around inside. Got some good news for you, partner. I sold our gold. We had forty-four pounds of nuggets in them saddle bags. Got forty-five dollars an ounce for it. The fellow at the assay office said it was high-grade gold, maybe the best he's ever seen."

"Really?" Sammy shouted excitedly, slapping Cody on the back and slapping his knee. "I figured it was good, but that's even better than I thought!"

"Yep," Cody continued. "It brought thirty four thousand, seven hundred dollars, all told. I opened an account in the Denver Bank. Put all except ten thousand in the account. Kept out that for us. Five thousand for you and five thousand for me. I figured we'd earned some fruits for our labor. I've got the money right here," Cody told his partner, patting the money belt around his waist under his shirt.

Sammy was so happy he couldn't stand still.

"Reckon you've already figured out that somebody let the cat out of the bag, though, from all the prospectors flocking to town. I tried my best to keep it quiet, but they found out anyway."

"Well, somebody would have figured it out sooner or later. Just don't know how we're gonna keep them off our mountain."

"Maybe now Mary Ann and I can get married. I promised her we would as soon as we stuck pay dirt."

"Figured that was coming. As soon as things settle down a bit, I'm gonna ask Juliana to marry me, too. Matter of fact, I took the liberty of buying two wedding rings while I was at it. I'll show them to you as soon as I get a chance to unpack."

Cody called Sid Peters over and introduced them.

"Mr. Peters here is a mining engineer. He's gonna take a look at our mine and the other place as well. He's gonna decide if he can help us. If so, I've promised him a job."

"We can sure use the help," Sammy said. "I studied mining in my country, but it's altogether different here. I'd welcome the help."

"How about showing Sid the mine while I take a ride up the mountain. I want to see if we've got any more claim jumpers nosing around."

In less than half an hour, Cody found two more prospectors. They were standing knee-deep in the mountain stream. They each had a large, shallow pan. They scooped a shovel full of gravel from the bottom of the stream, sloshed water around inside the pan, washing away the dirt and sediment, hoping to find any heavier gold nuggets that remained.

Cody pulled rein beside the stream and watched them for a minute.

"Sorry to have to tell you, but you fellows are trespassing. Me and my partner have claims filed on this whole mountain. You fellows are gonna have to find you another stream to do your panning."

"Say's who?" one of them asked.

"The Schroeder/Cordell Mining Company. I'm Cody Cordell."

"I know the law. You can't file a claim on anything but a hundred-fifty foot of streambed, not a whole mountain."

"You can if you've got a waiver and we've got one. Now I'm asking you nice-like. Gather your stuff and light a shuck down the trail."

"And if we don't, then what?"

"I just shot a stubborn fellow a few minutes ago. I can do it again, if need be."

The two men looked at one another, hesitated for a moment, and then waded to the bank. Gathering up their gear, they started down the mountain trail. Cody rode for another hour, but found no one else. He returned to the mine.

Sammy and Sid Peters were just emerging from the mine when Cody rode up. They both had long faces.

"What's wrong?" Cody asked anxiously.

"Well, the long and short of it is, you boys got a deep hole leading nowhere."

"You saying there ain't no silver down there?" Cody asked.

"That's what I'm saying. Oh, you got traces of sulphur, shore enough, and even some cerussite. But in this part of the country that don't mean beans. Sorry, boys.

"You ready to take a look at our other operation?"

"I'm ready."

The three of them mounted and rode along the bank of the mountain stream. It was slow going. They picked their way around large boulders and around growths of pine trees so thick they were impassable on horseback. They climbed steadily. It took the best part of an hour before they reached the waterfall, and the large pool below.

"And you say your gold strike is behind that waterfall?" the mine engineer asked skeptically.

"Yep. Ready to get wet?"

"Ready as I'll ever be. Me and water's got an aversion to one another."

"Well, might just as well get better acquainted," Cody told him. "You'll likely be spending a lot of time behind this waterfall."

The three of them shucked their clothes down to their long johns, and then plunged into the cold water. They came up sputtering and shivering. They adjusted quickly and swam over to the waterfall. The roar of water impacting the surface of the pool was almost deafening.

Cody motioned and all three ducked under the water and came up behind the waterfall. The moment Peters saw the rock wall behind the waterfall his eyes saucered wide. For a long moment he stared, obviously finding it hard to fathom.

"Never in all my born days saw veins that wide!" the mining engineer hollered above the roar. "You boys sure 'nough got yourselves a humdinger of a gold strike."

For several minutes, the mining engineer examined the rock facing containing the veins of gold. He measured with his hands the distance between the parallel veins.

"The thing about it," Peters said, so excited he could hardly speak, "those veins don't stop at the edges of the cave, they run on into the mountain. No telling how far they go."

"Does that mean you'll work with us?" Cody asked.

"You ain't just whistlin' Dixie. Things are liable to get real excitin' around here before this string runs out. I wouldn't miss it."

"What's your time gonna be worth?"

"Sonny, you boys can't afford what I'm worth, but I'll leave it to you to decide. If I'm making you boys' money, I figure you'll be more'n fair. If I ain't, then you don't need me around anyway. Fair enough?"

"Fair enough," Cody told him.

"Then, in your opinion, we've got a good strike. Is that what you're saying?" Sammy asked.

"Good strike? Boys, I'd say you hit the mother lode of all mother lodes!"

CHAPTER XXVIII

Almost a week after Buck, Chester, and their men returned from Mexico with the horses they recovered, the bell in the guard tower rang, announcing a visitor.

Buck and Rebekah were working in the office going over some account books when they heard it.

"I'll go see who it is," he told her.

Walking to the front door, he was pleased to see Richard King, of the King Ranch, pulling through the gate in his buggy. Buck hurried to meet his rancher friend.

"Richard, my friend. It's good to see you. Welcome to the Longhorn."

"Sorry to drop in unexpected, Buck, but I was in San Antonio and wanted to drive on down and visit with you a bit."

"Glad you did. You're welcome here anytime. Hope you know that."

"I do, indeed. Just as you would be at the King Ranch."

"Climb down and come on in. Rebekah will be happy to see you again."

"Wish I could have brought the missus, but she hates to travel."

They walked side by side up to Buck's house. Rebekah met them at the door.

"Good to see you again, Mr. King. Can I get you men some coffee?"

"Coffee would be good," Richard said. "It's been a long trip. I'm not as young as I used to be."

"Come on into the den, Richard," Buck said.

After they were seated, the owner of the largest cattle ranch in Texas leaned forward in the chair.

"What I wanted to talk with you about," he said, "is that we just dropped our first crop of calves sired by the offsprings of your *El Toro*. They are a wonder to see. I've never seen anything like them and I've been in the cattle business for a long time."

"Glad you're pleased with the bulls you bought from us."

"I'm more than pleased. The truth of the matter is, I'd like to buy some more."

"That might be a problem, my friend," Buck told him. "Last I heard, all this year's bulls are already spoken for. We can put you on the waiting list for the ones that will be ready for next year. I've already made the commitments. I couldn't go back on my word."

"I wouldn't ask you to. A man's word is his bond. I respect that. Reckon I'll just have to wait until next year. Do you suppose you could let me have at least four of next year's crop?"

"Don't see why not. I'll put you down for four of our very best for next year."

"How are things in Austin?"

"Like I've said many times about politics, when it's all said and done, there's a lot more said than done."

They shared a good laugh at that. Rebekah came in carrying a tray with coffee.

"Rebekah, I swear you get more beautiful every time I see you," King commented.

"Why, thank you, Mr. King. I'm still looking forward to visiting with Mrs. King again soon. You will stay the night with us, won't you?"

"If it wouldn't be putting you out, I'd love to. Oh, by the way, Buck, you don't happen to have any kin folk up in Colorado, do you?"

A knot suddenly formed in Buck's stomach at the question. His mind flashed to his late brother, Cody, and to the tragic news of his death.

"Not that I know of. Why do you ask?"

"I was just reading in the San Antonio paper about some fellow named Cordell who struck gold. They're saying it could be the biggest gold rush since the Pike's Peak discovery back in fifty-nine, maybe even bigger than the California gold rush."

"You don't say."

"Just thought it might be a long lost uncle or something. Kinda odd it being the same name and all."

"Well, don't reckon the Cordell name is all that uncommon."

"Guess not."

The conversation turned to cattle talk. After a while, Rebekah excused herself and said goodnight. The two men sipped coffee and talked until the wee hours of the morning before calling it a night and turning in.

Rebekah was asleep when Buck slipped quietly into bed, careful not to wake her. Though it was late, sleep eluded him. For a long time, he lay awake, staring through the darkness at the ceiling.

It's odd the fellow in Colorado who discovered gold is

named Cordell. If it weren't for the Pinkerton report about my brother being killed...

Buck and little Cody went for their morning ride. Cody sat in the saddle in front of his father. They made their usual rounds of the corrals that held the young bulls sired by *El Toro*.

The young boy, with his inquisitive mind, asked a steady stream of questions. Buck patiently answered each one, knowing this was an important part of his son's learning process.

They rode for an hour before ending up on top of the high plateau overlooking the ranch. They climbed down and sat on a large rock.

"See that herd of cattle down there?" Buck asked, leaning close and lifting a finger to point. "Those are our brood herd."

"What's a brood herd, Papa?"

"Well, a brood herd is the cattle we have picked out as our *special cattle*. They are the ones that have the calves we're going to keep."

"Why is my name *Cody*?"

His son's question left Buck speechless. A large lump crawled up the back of his throat and lodged there.

"I use to have a brother by that name. We named you after him."

"Where is he?"

It took a few moments before Buck could answer. He stared at the ground for a time.

"Where is he, Papa?"

"He's, he's in a good place. A place called Heaven."

"With Uncle Pappy?"

Buck nodded. "Most likely."

"Tell me about him, Papa? Do I look like him?"

Buck closed his eyes, but the tears seeped under his eyelids. He swallowed, then swallowed again, but the words still wouldn't come. It took a few minutes.

"Yes, son, you look a lot like him. You've got the same color hair, the same eyes, and the same inquisitive mind. He was always asking questions, just like you."

"Did you and him go riding like we do?"

"No, we didn't have horses until later."

"I sure wish I could' a knowed him."

"Me, too, son. Me, too."

"Do you miss him, Papa?"

Buck choked up. He couldn't say a word. He just ducked his head so little Cody couldn't see the tears, and nodded his head.

Chapter XXIX

Cody, Sammy, and Sid all stayed in their new log cabin that night. They made some coffee and sat around talking. They were all too excited to sleep anyway.

"With all the claim jumpers sneaking around, we best keep a close eye out," Cody told them.

"What are we gonna do about all of them?" Sammy asked.

"I'm riding into town tomorrow and get some signs made, maybe that will at least keep the honest ones out and be a warning to the others."

"Might help," Sid added. "But I doubt it. When a man gets the gold fever, he don't think like he would if he was in his right mind."

"I'll talk to Mr. Hamilton at the store. He might know somebody we could hire to help us keep watch. We're gonna need somebody to help us mine that gold, too, ain't we?"

"Sure would speed things up," Sid told them.

"Reckon we can trust anybody not to stick some in their pocket?" Sammy asked.

"We'll have to figure out someway to keep that from happening, too. It sure might get tempting," Cody agreed.

"Oh, I've got something for you," Cody told Sammy as he lifted his shirttail and pulled a money belt from around his waist. "With all the commotion going on, I haven't had a chance to give you this."

Cody handed Sammy a thick wad of folded bills.

"There's five thousand dollars there, partner."

Sammy unfolded the wad of money and fanned the bills out in his hands. He stared silently at it for a few moments, shaking his head in disbelief.

"I've always dreamed of striking it rich. Reckon most men have, but now that it's actually happening, it's hard to believe."

"Yep, I know what you mean. This is a really nice cabin," Cody said, letting his slow gaze examine the German builder's handiwork. "I may get him to build me a nice log home upstream by the waterfall. What would you think about that?"

"Sounds like a good idea. Mary Ann wants us to build a house in town. She's a town-type girl."

"Oh, that reminds me. I've got something else for you," Cody told his partner.

He dug around in his pack and handed Sammy a small package wrapped in white paper.

"Go ahead. Open it. See if you like it."

Sammy unwrapped the package. When he opened the lid he went bug-eyed.

"Woowie! That's gotta be the most beautiful rings I've ever seen. But why is there two of them?"

"The sales lady said that was the latest thing. One of them is called an engagement ring. You're supposed to give her that one when you ask her to marry you. The other one is a wedding ring you give her at the wedding."

"I can't wait to give it to her. We've already talked about getting married, but I didn't want to until I could take care of her."

"I know how you feel. I felt the same way. I couldn't offer Juliana anything but a forty dollar a month cowboy. I'm not much, but I'm too proud to let her and her ranch support us. This gold discovery changes all that. Soon as I can, I'm gonna ask her to marry me."

"That's good. She's a fine lady."

They drained their coffee cups.

"Well, it's late and we've had a long day," Cody said. "I'm gonna spread my bedroll and crawl in it."

"Me, too," Sid said, pushing to his feet.

Cody got up before daybreak. He built a campfire outside near the stream and started putting water on to boil for coffee when Sammy and Sid came out of the cabin to join him.

"Mornin'," he greeted.

"You're up mighty early for a young fellow," Sid told him, squatting near the fire and holding his hands out to the warmth. "It gets mighty chilly at night up here on the mountain, don't it?"

"Can," Cody acknowledged. "How's it feel to wake up a rich man?" he asked his partner.

"Don't think it's sunk in good yet," Sammy said, squatting next to Sid. "What's our plans for today?"

"Well, like I said last night, I'm gonna ride into town," Cody said. "You fellows do whatever needs to be done."

"I think we ought to abandon working the silver mine for awhile and concentrate on getting as much of that gold out as we can," Sammy suggested. "What do you think?"

"I think you're right," Cody agreed.

"That's what I'd do if it was me," Sid also agreed.

"Well, keep your eyes peeled, you're liable to have more visitors today. Been thinking about something. If you fellows go up to the waterfall and happen to find a couple of small nuggets, what would you think of dropping them in our sliver mine near the face of the tunnel? That way if somebody's nosing around when we're not here, maybe they'll think that's where we found the gold."

"Might fool some, wouldn't if they know beans about finding gold," the mining engineer said.

"We'll see if we can find a couple of small nuggets," Sammy said. "Might be good if we divided up the work. Sid and me could handle the mining operation if you could handle the business end of things."

"Good idea," Cody agreed. "I'm not much good when it comes to mining."

Cody decided with all the claim jumpers around, he might better start wearing both of his guns. He buckled both his belly-holstered Colt as well as the Remington in its regular holster, but left the serape in his saddlebag; he was afraid it might identify him as the *late* Hondo Kid.

He saddled Cincinnati and cinched the girth tight. He flipped the stirrup down and stepped up into it and swung into the saddle. His big pinto seemed rested and rearing to go.

The early morning air was crisp. A few puffy white clouds floated lazily in a soft blue sky. The fresh smell of mountain pine drifted on a small breeze. He walked his pinto slowly down the steep path, enjoying the morning.

Though it was early, the single street of Trinidad was already bustling with activity. Prospectors on foot, leading donkeys loaded with supplies, trudged along headed to the mountains to find their own pot of gold at the end of the rainbow. *Who knows? They just might...we did.*

Cody reined up in front of Ed Hamilton's store. He stepped to the ground and half-hitched Cincinnati's reins to the hitching rail. He paused and touched thumb and finger to his hat brim as two ladies hurried by.

A whiskered old timer sat on a wooden bench in front of the store. He looked up from his whittling as Cody stepped toward the door of the store.

Marshal Gardner came from the store as Cody started inside.

"Glad I ran into you, Cody. Just about to ride up the mountain and have a word with you."

"Oh, what about?"

"Got a complaint about a shooting up that way yesterday. Wanted to hear your side of the story."

"Nothing worth talking about."

"That ain't the way they're telling it. They're saying you flew off the handle and chased everybody off the mountain. They said you shot one fellow without provocation."

"That ain't exactly the way it happened, Marshal. We've got a legitimate claim to that mountain. It's all signed and notarized. A bunch of claim jumpers were trying to force their way into our mine. They were trespassing. I told them so and told them to get off our claim. Three of them refused. I shot one in the leg to sorta convince them to leave."

"Kinda figured it was something like that. The fellow hem-hawed about the details when I questioned him about it."

"Fact is, I'm in town to have some signs made warning claim jumpers to stay out. Got any more questions on your mind, Marshal?"

"Nope. It's a settled matter, far as I'm concerned."

"Glad to hear it."

Ed Hamilton stepped out of his store as the marshal turned and walked away. "Good morning, Cody. Good to see you. Heard you boys struck pay dirt up on Sugarloaf."

"Yeah, got lucky, I reckon."

"Wouldn't call it luck, as hard as you boys worked at it."

"Well, like somebody said, the harder we worked, the luckier we got."

"One thing about it, you boys sure brought a passel of folks to Trinidad. I've done more business in the last week than I did in the rest of the year put together."

"I need to buy some tools: picks, shovels, chisels, that kind of thing. Reckon you could get your helper to bring them up the mountain in the wagon tomorrow?"

"Sure can. Just tell me what you need and I'll see it's delivered."

"Know anybody in town who could make me up some signs?"

Hamilton scratched his chin in thought.

"You remember Elmer Cox, who runs the little cabinet shop down the street? He's a fair to middlin' painter, too. I reckon he could paint up about anything you want."

"I'll stop and see him. One more thing. We're looking for some men to work in our mine. If you run across anybody who wants to work, tell them we'll be talking to them tomorrow at the mine."

"I'll sure do it. Shouldn't have much trouble finding help with all the men in town."

"We're also gonna need a few security men, in case you think of anybody that might work out," Cody added.

"Now there I might be able to help you. There's a young fellow named Bret Allison who came to town a couple of months back. Clean cut, handles himself well. In fact, we considered him for the town marshal's job before Ollie

Gardner came into the picture. We felt like Gardner had more experience, but I think Allison would be a good man for the job you're talking about."

"If you don't mind, try to get hold of him and tell him we'd like to talk with him. Something else, when you get time, how about sending your boy up to Mr. Fritz's place and ask him to stop by and see me. I'd be obliged."

"I'll do it today."

Cody turned down the street. He dodged between wagons, buggies, and riders on horseback as he crossed the busy street. He opened the door to the small cabinet shop.

"Howdy, Mr. Cox," Cody greeted the shop owner, who was sanding a cabinet door.

The man looked up. Recognition swept across his face.

"I thought you were...oh, howdy, Mr. Cordell."

"Ed Hamilton, over at the store, said you might could make me up some signs?"

"Be glad to. Cabinets and furniture are my main business, but I do a few signs now and then. What kind of signs are you needing?"

"I need a plain white sign with big red letters that says:

—WARNING—
PRIVATE PROPERTY

NO TRESPASSING!
VIOLATERS WILL BE SHOT ON SIGHT!"

The cabinet owner's eyes widened.

"How big do you want the signs?"

"Oh, I'd say three foot by four foot."

"How many signs you needin'?"

"About twenty, I reckon. How much will they be?"

"Oh, about three dollars apiece, I reckon."

"When can I get them?"

"Can you give me a week?"

"How about three days?" Cody countered.

"That's awfully fast, but I'll get 'em done for you some way."

Cody paid the man sixty dollars.

"I'll have somebody pick them up in three days."

"They'll be ready."

Cody left the cabinet shop and went by the telegraph office. He remembered he had promised Juliana he'd send a telegram to that big ranch down in Texas and order two of those high powered bulls he'd heard about.

After leaving the telegraph office he walked down the street to the livery and blacksmith shop.

"Mornin', Pete," Cody greeted the liveryman.

"Mornin' to you, 'Kid." Then, quickly looking around to make sure no one heard him he corrected himself.

"I mean, mornin', Mr. Cordell."

"I know. It's hard to make the switch in names, ain't it? I'm obliged. We're gonna be needing some new wagons and good teams of mules. Reckon you could come up with some?"

"Why, shore. What kind of wagons you lookin' fer?"

"Heavy duty. We'll be hauling ore to Denver."

"Well now, that's a horse of a different color. You'll need something with strong axles and extra large bed that will hold up fer a trip like you're talkin' about. How many you reckon you'll need?"

"Probably a dozen to start with, more later."

"That's a tall order, but I think I know where I can lay my hands on that many. You'll want good strong mules that'll be able to hold up to a trip like that. Let me go to work on it. How soon will you be needin' 'em?"

"Sooner the better. Just let me know when you can deliver and we'll pay you."

"I'll shore do 'er," the liveryman said, smiling from ear to ear. "That right there is the biggest order I ever got."

Cody gathered the reins to his pinto and booted a stirrup. "See you around, Pete."

Cody returned to Hamilton's General Mercantile and tied Cincinnati to the hitching rail in front. He dismounted and walked into the store. Ed was waiting on a customer. Cody browsed around until the lady left.

"I was thinking about something I wanted to throw out to you and see if you might be interested," Cody told his friend. "You were telling me earlier that your business had grown in the last few weeks.

"Before long, we'll be running wagons between here and Denver hauling the ore from our mine. Most of the time our wagons will be returning empty. I was wondering if we could work out something to haul back the supplies you need for your store?"

The storekeeper slapped his knee with a hand. A big grin broke across his face.

"By doggie, that solves a problem I've been worrying about. I'm already running short of a lot of stuff. I couldn't figure out how I was gonna get all the supplies I'll be needing. You just solved that problem for me. When you reckon you'll start hauling?"

"It'll likely be a couple weeks, maybe three. Pete's looking for some wagons and teams for me. But the round trip is gonna take some time."

"Just let me know when you're ready and I'll line up a load of supplies for you to haul back."

It was nearing suppertime. Off in the west, the sun hung low over the dome of the mountains, it's fiery mantle streaking the sky. Cody decided to stop by Molly's Boarding House and spend the night. He stalled his pinto in the little shed out back and went to the house.

"Well, lookie here." Molly greeted him as he walked in. "Lord-a-mercy, if it ain't Mr. Money bags himself."

"How are you, Miss Molly?"

"I'm just tolerable. My arthritis's been acting up lately. But even all crippled up, I'm better'n most women half my age. Where you been keeping yourself? Can you believe all the people that're pouring into town? They've been about to drive me crazy looking for room and board. Hope you're staying for supper. We're having your favorite, fried chicken."

"Thought I'd spend the night, if I still got a bed?"

"Land sakes, you'll always have a bed at my house. Your room is just like you left it. By the time you wash up, supper will be on the table. Seen anything of Juliana lately?"

"Yeah, I stopped by the ranch on the way back from Denver."

"Wish you'd hurry up and marry that pretty lady."

He cut a thin smile.

"The thought's crossed my mind some," Cody told her.

"Would you listen to me, poking my nose in where it don't belong. Go ahead and wash up. I'll finish setting supper."

Mary Ann greeted Cody with a wide smile when he walked into the dining room to take his place at the long table.

"How are you, Cody?"

"I'm just fine. How are the children?"

"They're a handful. How's Sammy? I was hoping he'd come down for supper."

"Things are pretty hectic on the mountain right now. I'm sure he'll be down in a day or two."

"I hope so. I really miss him."

The other boarders shuffled in and took their seats. Cody nodded howdy and answered their probing questions about the gold strike with as little conversation as he could. Two of the men asked about jobs and Cody told them to come up the next day and talk to Sammy.

Marshal Gardner walked in and took a seat across the table from Cody.

"Heard you're looking to hire some security men?" the marshal asked.

"Yep."

"What's it pay?"

"Depends on the man. You looking for a job?"

The lawman chuckled over his coffee cup.

"Not me. Got about all I can handle. Thought I might run into somebody along that line, though."

"If you do, I'd be obliged if you'd send them up to talk with me" Cody told him.

After supper, Cody strolled onto the front porch with a third cup of coffee. It was full dark. He leaned against a post and gazed off into forever. It was a beautiful October night. A small breeze drifted down from the high mountains and brought with it an early chill. A thumbnail moon hung in a clear, cloudless sky. Tiny specks of light winked against a dark, velvety sky like nuggets of gold flung from the hand of the creator. Cody breathed in the night.

His mind flashed to Juliana.

Wonder what she's doing right now? Maybe she sitting in the porch swing looking up at our star.

A sudden urge to be with her swept over him, overwhelming him with the need to hold her, to look into her face, to feel her nearness. The memories of their all too brief times together flashed on the walls of his mind.

Reckon that's mostly what life is made of, dreams and memories. Soon, he knew. *Soon we will be together.*

He swallowed the last of his coffee and headed for his

room. His last conscious thought before drifting off to sleep was of Juliana.

Cody didn't wait for breakfast. Before the first hint of light colored the darkness he was up had Cincinnati saddled, then rode up the trail to Sugarloaf Mountain.

Sammy and Sid were already up and had coffee perking. Bacon and fried potatoes sizzled in the frying pan as Cody reined up near the campfire.

"Peel an extra potato," he told his friends.

"About time you showed up," Sid kidded. "We thought you'd gone and flew the coop."

"Had some things in town to take care of. Stayed at Molly's last night so I wouldn't have to listen to your snoring."

"I don't snore. Do I snore, Sammy?"

"You sound like a grizzly bear with a thorn in his paw."

"I been hearing somebody snore, but I thought all time it was you."

They all shared a big laugh. Cody unsaddled his pinto and turned him into the small corral. Picking up a tin cup, he poured a steaming cup of coffee.

"How are things in town?" Sammy asked.

"Busy. It's like a bunch of ants running this way and that. Everybody seems to be in a rush to get somewhere, but can't figure out where they're all going or how to get there."

"I don't cotton to crowds," Sid said, slicing another potato into the frying pan. "They give me the willies."

"Well, better get used to it," Cody told him. "I expect we'll have a bunch of men coming up the mountain today looking for work."

"What're we supposed to do with them?"

"You and Sammy talk to them one on one. Look them over and hire the ones you think are the best ones. Make sure they all understand they'll be searched at the end of every shift. Anybody caught stealing will be fired and put in jail."

"How much do we pay them?" Sammy asked.

"Let's start them off at seventy-five dollars a month," Cody suggested. "That's almost twice what they could make at most jobs nowadays."

"We ought to be able to get some top men for that salary," Sammy said.

"The man from Hamilton's store is supposed to deliver some tools this morning, too. I ordered picks, shovels, chisels, pry bars, and gloves. If you think of anything else we need just tell the deliveryman. He'll see we get it.

"I also ordered some wagons and mule teams to haul the ore to Denver. They should be here in a couple of weeks. Made a deal with Mr. Hamilton down at the store to haul supplies on the return trip back. Figured there wasn't any use in the wagons coming back empty. Bought some signs to put up, warning claim jumpers to stay away."

"Sounds like things are gonna start poppin' around here," Sid commented.

"Yep," Cody said, blowing steam from his coffee. "Gotta make hay while the sun shines."

They were still eating breakfast when the men started arriving. They came on foot and on horseback. First it was one or two, and then a steady stream began pouring into camp.

Sammy and Sid set up a makeshift table in the cabin to interview the men looking for work. The line stretched thirty deep with more arriving all the time.

A tall, thin, wide-shouldered fellow rode into camp on a long legged buckskin gelding. Cody saw him coming and knew without asking who he was.

Cody judged him to be in his late twenties to early thirties. His clean-shaven face was the color of seasoned leather from long hours in the sun. His hair was coal black and touched his shoulders. His black eyes darted to and fro, taking in his surroundings with a single glance. He wore a bone handled Colt in a low slung holster tied to his left leg.

"Climb down and pour yourself a cup," Cody motioned with his own coffee cup. "If I was a betting man, I'd wager you're Bret Allison."

"Then you must be Cody Cordell? Mr. Hamilton said you wanted to talk to me."

"Yep."

Allison climbed down from his buckskin and dropped the reins. He took three long steps, picked up a tin cup, and poured it full from the blackened coffee pot over the fire.

"You looking for work?" Cody asked.

"Maybe. What you got in mind?"

"You any kin to Clay Allison?"

The man flicked his dark eyes up over the coffee cup and fixed them on Cody.

"Will it make a difference if I am?"

"Nope. Just kinda wondering is all."

"He's my cousin. You know him?"

"Only by reputation. Word about a gun fighter like him travels fast and far."

"Seems so. Mr. Cordell, I'm my own man. I stomp my own snakes. Just so we understand one another up front. If I go to work for you, I'll ride for the brand. I'll do the job I'm paid to do."

"Wouldn't have you no other way. Let's lay our cards on

Longhorn III: The Prodigal Brother 349

the table face up. As I'm sure you already know, we struck gold. I'm looking for somebody to head up our security. Mr. Hamilton says you're a good man.

"We need somebody to keep the claim jumpers off our mountain. If you're the man we're looking for, you'll be in charge of seeing our workers don't get sticky fingers and help themselves to our gold when their shift is over.

"We'll be hauling the ore to Denver in wagon trains. Part of your responsibility would be to see they get there like they left here. All that's a tall order, I know. You think you could handle the job?"

"Not by myself, but I can handle it."

"Good. I think you can, too. I like your confidence. Hire as many men as you need. Mount them on the best horses you can find and equip them with the best rifles money can buy. We'll start you out at two hundred a month, if that's acceptable? Start the men you hire out at a hundred a month."

A grin wrinkled Allison's lips. He lifted his cup in a left handed salute and stuck out his right hand for a handshake to seal the bargain.

"That's more'n I'd a asked for," he grinned.

"That's less than I'd give," Cody told him, lifting his own grin as they shook hands.

"When do I start?"

"You just did."

By the end of the day, they had hired twelve workers for the gold operation behind the waterfall and four more to do odd jobs around the camp. They also hired a black cook. Ironically, his name was Isaiah Black, but called himself *Blackie*.

The wagonload of tools arrived from the store and their

new workers unloaded them. Sid took the workers up the mountain to the waterfall and put them to work.

Mr. Fritz and his two sons arrived at mid-morning, Cody walked with them to a fairly flat spot behind the log cabin.

"I'd like to have a log bunkhouse built right there," he told the German builder. "Make it big enough for forty bunks and with two rooms on one end. One room big enough for tables where the men can eat and the other for a kitchen. When can you start?"

"Right away," the builder said, studying the ground carefully.

"Would it speed things up if you had more workers?"

"Yup."

"Good. I'll get Sammy to hire a few more men to help you."

One of the German's sons went to pull their wagonload of tools up to the new building site.

"After you get started on that, I've got another job for you, too," Cody told the builder. "I'll take you up and show you later what I've got in mind."

Chapter XXX

It was late October. All the cattle drives were over and the Longhorn cowboys had returned home from Kansas. Three weeks passed since Buck and his men recovered the stolen horses from Mexico.

Buck and Chester were summoned hastily to the front gate of the compound.

"Something I thought you ought to hear," Wade Thomas told them. "Tell them what you saw," Wade told the line rider.

"Well, it's like I told Mr. Thomas. I was riding the line of the Longhorn property, like always, when I saw this long line of Mexican Army crossing the river. I've never seen them cross into Texas like that and thought I best tell somebody about it."

"Could you tell which way they was headed?" Chester asked.

"Well, not exactly. Looked to me like they was headed here."

"By *here,* you mean the ranch?" Buck asked.

"Yes, sir. Looked like it to me."

"Anything else?"

"No, sir. That's all I saw. Figured you'd want to know."

"You done right," Buck told him. "We're much obliged."

After the Longhorn rider left, Buck, Chester, and Wade Tomas got their heads together, trying to figure out what the news meant.

"The *federales* crossing the river into Texas?" Chester said, puzzling over the unusual event. "Never heard of it happening before, least not since the war with Mexico."

"Whatever it means, can't be good," Buck said. "This could spark another war."

"Might be wise for us to get ready, just in case they come calling," the security man suggested.

"I think you're right, Wade," Buck agreed. "Rather be safe than sorry. Sound the alarm. I want every Longhorn rider armed and at their posts on the wall."

Wade Thomas hurried to sound the alarm and pass the word to prepare for an attack. Within minutes, two hundred Longhorn men were armed with Spencer carbines and two bandoleers full of ammunition each. They took up positions on the catwalk along the high adobe walls of the compound. Even Ray Ledbetter, with rifle in hand, limped to a place on the wall.

"Pass the word," Buck instructed. "Tell every man to stay hunkered down out of sight until I give the signal. I'll take off my hat."

"Here they come," the guard in the tower shouted.

Buck and Chester stood in the wide opening in the front wall beside their saddled horses. Two Longhorn men stood beside the heavy double doors, ready to close and bar them when the order was given.

Shielding his eyes with the palm of his hand, Buck saw a

long line of mounted *federales* riding up the well-worn road directly toward them.

"Looks like they brought enough help," Chester said.

"Yep. Looks like half the Mexican Army. I can't even see the end of that column."

They watched as the large column drew closer. When they were about five hundred yards from the compound, one of the leaders of the column gave a signal. The four-wide column split, two soldiers swung left and the other two *federales* swung to the right.

"They mean business," Chester said. "They're forming a skirmish line."

They watched as the Mexican Army completely encircled the compound with a double line of mounted *federales* with rifles in hand.

Three officers separated themselves from the column and walked their horses forward toward the open gate where Buck and Chester waited.

"Let's go see what kind of burr they got stuck under their saddle," Buck told his partner.

They booted stirrups and swung into their saddles. They walked their horses toward the oncoming Mexican officers.

"Recognize the four-fingered *federale* captain?" Chester asked.

"You mean the one you cut off his finger?"

"Yep. That's him riding beside the one wearing a general's bars. The other one is a colonel."

"Surely they ain't risking an all-out war over a little finger," Buck said. "Let's rein up here and make them come to us. If it comes to a shootin' situation, I'd like to be as close to the compound as we can get."

They reined to a stop and sat their horses. The *federale* officers continued walking their horses toward them and reined up. Only a few yards separated them from Buck and Chester.

"Buenos Dias, señor," the one wearing colonel's bars greeted.

"You speak English. Speak it." Buck said, clamping down hard on his anger and fixing the colonel with a look.

"Very well," the colonel said in near perfect English. "Are you *Señor* Cordell?"

"I am. You fellows are a little off your beaten path, ain't you?"

"This is General *Miguel Juarez Cortez*. He is commandant of all *federale* forces of the army of Mexico. He would have a word with you."

Buck swung a look at the general. The man's cold, cruel black eyes were fixed directly on Buck with an unwavering stare.

"I'm listening," Buck said, intentionally failing to acknowledge the man's rank.

The general said nothing. He sat still as stone for a moment and continued to stare at Buck. Finally he spoke.

"You are an obstinate, crude *gringo*," the general said, allowing the edge of anger to be evident in his voice.

"Did you ride all the way over here to trade insults or do you have something worthwhile to say?" Buck said evenly.

"You and your men came into *my* country. You insulted one of my officers by cutting off his finger and turning him and his men into the desert naked. You stole horses and hung one of our leading citizens.

"For this, you must be accountable. We have come to arrest you and the one called Colson."

"You've had your say. Now I'll have mine," Buck said. "Your *so called* leading citizen sent his men into Texas and stole those horses you mentioned. They also killed two of my men. We tracked them down and got our horses back and hung the man responsible.

"Your captain, sitting right there, was paid off to guard part of our horses. He laid an ambush for us and tried to kill us. We dealt with them, end of story.

"Surely you know you're risking an all-out war with the United States by bringing your army into our country. If you got a beef, take it up with the United States Government. I'm through talking. Turn your men around and get them off my land and I mean *right now!*"

The dark-skinned general's face turned a high shade of red. He clamped his lips tight. His jaw muscles pulsed. His eyes squinted in anger.

"If you will not surrender peacefully, you leave me no alternative but to use force."

"You better have more men than I'm seeing now," Buck told him.

"You are a stubborn *gringo pig!*" the general shouted, clawing for his sidearm. "I'll kill you myself!"

It was all the provocation Chester needed. He palmed the .38 caliber Colt from his holster and shot the general square between the eyes. He swung the nose and plugged the four-fingered captain with two bullets in the chest.

The colonel jerked his mount around, bent low over his saddle, and high-tailed it back toward his line of soldiers. Buck reined around quickly and swept the hat from his head. Two hundred Longhorn fighters showed their heads and Spencer rifles over the top of the wall of the compound.

As Buck and Chester raced through the gates, slugs slammed into the thick walls of the compound around them. The Longhorn guards quickly swung the heavy gates shut and dropped the sturdy bar in place.

The Mexican *federales* opened up with everything they

had, firing madly at the vague targets above the wall. The Longhorn men calmly used the top of the thick adobe wall to steady their aim as they emptied saddles. Buck and Chester climbed a ladder to the catwalk and filled a space on the wall.

Buck fired meticulously, taking time to make sure of his target before he fired. His sight found a burly Mexican with a rifle to his shoulder. Buck paused, took a breath, let it out, and fired. The slug dug into the soldier and swept him from his saddle like a giant unseen hand.

Again and again he fired. He emptied his Spencer of the seven shots it held. Someone handed him a bandoleer full of .52 caliber cartridges. He reloaded and continued firing.

The Mexicans obviously knew only one way to fight. They sat astride their horses in plain view, no more than three hundred yards distance. They were easy targets for the Longhorn fighters with their long range Spencer rifles.

The battle raged for more than a half an hour. The battlefield littered with the dead and dying *federales*. Riderless horses galloped frantically about, their iron-clad hooves doing further damage to the wounded lying helpless where they fell. Blue gun smoke hung like an angry cloud over the battlefield. Screams of the wounded could be heard all the way to the Longhorn compound.

Finally, Buck spotted a white flag tied to the end of a rifle, waving back and forth.

"Hold your fire!" he shouted.

The Longhorn fighters stopped firing. After a moment, a rider carrying the white flag walked his horse toward the compound. Buck and Chester climbed down and mounted their horses. The gates were swung open far enough to allow them to ride out.

It was the colonel. He rode slumped in his saddle. Blood

colored his left sleeve. He reined to a stop in front of Buck and Chester.

"It was a mistake coming here," he said. "I tried to tell the general that. He wouldn't listen."

"Many men have died for no reason," Buck told him. "Gather your wounded and go home. If you want, we'll bury the dead."

The colonel nodded sadly. He reined his mount around and rode back to his lines, which were now no more than a few scattered soldiers here and there.

Buck and Chester reined around and rode back through the gates of the compound. Buck stepped wearily to the ground, and for a long moment, held to his saddlehorn with a hand.

"You okay, Buck?" Chester asked.

Buck nodded, just once.

"That just brought back some bad memories of the war. Such a waste of the lives of good men."

Chester nodded agreement.

Wade Thomas hurried up.

"How many Longhorn men did we lose?" Buck asked.

"Four. Six more were wounded, but will recover."

Buck lowered his head sadly, shaking it from side to side.

Chapter XXXI

The Schroeder/Cordell mining operation was in full swing. After only a week under Sid's guidance and leadership, the new crew managed to mine a full wagonload of ore. Two full-time guards were posted beside the growing pile of gold-laced ore.

The large bunkhouse began to take shape and Allison's security team had grown to thirty men.

"I've been real selective on who I hire," the security chief told Cody. The two men sipped coffee and watched workers lift logs in place for the bunkhouse. "I'm having all my security men wear a gold armband to identify them so there'll be no question who they are."

"Good idea. Still having trouble with claim jumpers?"

"Some, but nothing we can't handle."

As they spoke, two men approached the camp.

"Here comes trouble," Allison said.

"You know them fellows?"

"Yeah, I know them. The one on the right is Lyle Cooper.

He calls himself a gambler, but he's nothing but a hired gun. The other fellow is new in town. He's a known man, if you know what I mean. His name is Sonny Boy Slade. Rumor is, he's got more'n a dozen notches on his gun handle. He's a bad one. They both work for Haig Jessup."

"I've heard of Jessup. Supposed to be some kind of land speculator or something of the sort."

"Watch out for him. He's crooked as a barrel of snakes."

The two newcomers rode right up to where Cody and Allison stood.

"One of you gents named Cordell?" the one called Cooper asked.

"Something I can do for you? I'm Cody Cordell."

"Boss wants to see you."

"Who's this *boss* you're talking about?"

"Haig Jessup. He sent us to get you. He wants to talk with you."

"You found me. So can he."

"You ain't listening, *boy*," the other fellow said, sarcastically. "We're Mr. Jessup's *associates*. He sent us to get you."

"Your name Slade?" Cody asked, growing anger evident in his voice.

"That's right."

"Well, Mr. Slade. I'd like you to meet *my associates*. This one is Mr. *Colt* and this one is Mr. *Remington*," Cody said, patting his two guns resting in their holsters.

"You go tell your *boss* if he wants to talk to me he knows where to find me. You've worn out your welcome. Get off my mountain."

Unbridled anger colored Slade's face a dull crimson. His eyes flicked a slanting look at his partner. Cody braced himself, ready in case the gunman decided to accept his clear challenge.

"Let's go, Sonny Boy," Cooper said. "We can settle this later."

"Why later?" the gunman demanded bitterly. "Let's settle it right here, right now."

"You heard me. I said, *let's go*."

Sonny Boy swung a glaring gaze on Cody.

"Mister, you just bit off more'n you can chew. I'll be seeing you again *real soon*."

"I ain't gonna say it again. Get off my mountain." Cody pushed the words between clenched teeth.

The two gunmen yanked their horses around and trotted them back down the trail.

"There goes one mad *hombre*," Allison said, watching the two gunmen ride away.

"Sonny Boy's a hot head. Cooper is the dangerous one."

"He might be a hothead, but the word I get is he's a born killer and enjoys it. They say he's lightning quick with a gun.

"A friend once told me no matter how fast you are, there's always somebody faster."

"Yeah, too bad the Hondo Kid ain't still around. From what I hear, he could've cleaned Sonny Boy's plow. Reckon what Haig Jessup wanted?"

Cody shrugged his shoulders.

"Who knows? I don't cotton being sent for."

"Yeah, I kinda got that idea."

The days passed quickly and turned into weeks. The cabinetmaker lived up to his promise and delivered the signs on time. Bret's security men posted them at the mouth of every trail leading up Sugarloaf Mountain.

Pete sent word the new wagons and mule teams had

arrived. Cody sent some men down to pick them up. The workers already stockpiled up to fill three of the twelve wagons.

The bunkhouse was finished and the workers moved into the comfortable new quarters. Even Blackie was happy with his new kitchen and stove.

The days were long and hectic. Each day began well before daylight and ended when it was too dark to see.

Mr. Fritz and his boys started work on the new house Cody wanted built beside the waterfall and pool. It was to be a glorious log home with five large rooms and a front porch that stretched the length of the front and overlooked the waterfall. Cody wanted it to be a surprise for his future bride.

Cody, Sammy, Sid, and Bret Allison were sitting at one of the tables in the bunkhouse sipping coffee and going over the day's production.

"Another couple of days and we'll have enough ore to fill four wagons," Sid promised. "The new crew is working out good."

"The veins of gold in this ore are the richest I ever heard of," Sammy told them. "It's gonna yield a good percentage when it's smeltered out."

"Glad to hear it," Cody said. "With all the expenses we're running up, we're gonna need it."

"Speaking of expenses, I've hired six more security men in the last few days," Allison told them. "When you've got enough ore for six wagons, my men will be ready to make the run to Denver."

"How many guards you thinking of sending to escort the wagons?" Cody asked.

"I figure we need at least twenty. I'm going along on this first run myself."

"Good. I'd rest easier knowing you're along. A wagon

train load of gold ore is gonna be a mighty tempting target for somebody looking to get rich quick."

"I've got to ride into town tomorrow," Cody told them. "Ed Hamilton and the judge sent word they wanted to talk with me about something. They didn't say what it was about."

"Most likely want to make you the mayor or something," Sid joked, yawning as he said it. "Daylight's gonna come mighty early for these ole bones. I'm gonna hit the sack."

The others agreed and retired to their bunks.

Cody ate an early breakfast with the workers before saddling Cincinnati and heading for town. He arrived at Hamilton's Mercantile just as Ed opened for business. Several customers were already lined up waiting for him to open.

"Let me take care of these folks and I'll be able to talk," the storeowner told him.

Cody loafed around the store while Hamilton waited on his customers.

"Let's walk down to the judge's office," Ed suggested. "My man can handle things here."

They walked side by side down the street.

"How are things going up at the mine?"

"About like they are here in town. Busy," Cody told him.

"Yeah, that's what I hear. No doubt about it, your mine is gonna put Trinidad, Colorado on the map."

"What is it you and the judge wanted to talk to me about?"

"I'll wait and let the judge explain it all. It's sorta complicated."

They arrived at Judge Goodson's office and stepped inside. The judge, sitting at his desk, motioned them into chairs.

"Morning, Cody. Morning, Ed," the grim-faced judge greeted.

"You look like you bit into a green persimmon," Cody said. "What's going on?"

"There's been a lawsuit filed against you and Sammy and the Schroeder/Cordell Mining Company. The suit contends your mining claims are invalid. The plaintiff charges the assay office didn't have the authority to grant the waiver for the extra claims you hold.

"Another party has subsequently filed on those extra claims and is claiming that they, indeed, now belong to him."

"I thought you told me our claims were good and would stand up in court. Just cut the legal mumbo-jumbo and give it to me in language I can understand," Cody said.

"Okay, here it is in a nutshell. The complaint has been legally filed so it has to be settled in court. I still think your claims are good, but here's the kicker. They want the trial to be held in the Denver court. I've got no choice but to grant their motion for a change of venue. They don't want me trying this case."

"Who filed the suit?" Cody wanted to know.

"Haig Jessup."

"Him again," Cody said, nodding his head. "He sent two of his goons up to bring me down for a talk with him. Reckon it's about time we had that talk."

"I wouldn't advise that, Cody," the judge said. "If you go over there, there'll likely be trouble. That might look bad against you when time comes for the trial."

"Maybe. If there's trouble, I won't be the one to start it. But if it comes, I'll sure as shootin' try to finish it."

Cody pushed from his chair and stormed from the office. He headed up the street to Jessup's new office. The spanking new brick building was impressive. The sign over the door was even more impressive. *HAIG JESSUP-LAND DEVELOPER.*

Cody opened the door and stepped into an outer office. A gray-haired lady with spectacles looked up when he entered.

"Can I help you, young man?" she asked in an uppity tone.

Cody spotted a door that obviously led to another office. Without a word, he strode to the door and opened it over the loud objections of the woman.

A huge, sweaty fellow sat behind a large desk. His salt and pepper hair was more salt than pepper. Cody judged him to be on the sundown side of forty. He had a large cigar clamped between his teeth.

The two gunnies that rode up the mountain to get him jumped from their chairs when Cody burst into the room. Jessup held up a hand and the two *associates* settled back into their chairs.

"You would be the one and only Mr. Cordell," the fat man said, taking a long, casual inhale on his cigar and blowing lazy smoke rings toward the ceiling.

"Yeah, I'm Cody Cordell. You wanted to talk with me?"

"Yes, well, I'm afraid it's a bit too late for talk, *young man*. I had intended to offer to buy those worthless claims of yours to avoid the unpleasantness of a lawsuit, but you so rudely refused to come and discuss it with me. You left me no alternative except to contest those claims in court."

"Our claims are good and you know it."

"I'm afraid they are no longer your claims. I've filed on the specific claim that just happens to be the one your mine is located on. As soon as the proper papers arrive from Denver, I'll be taking possession of the mine."

"Over my dead body, you will." Cody said through clenched teeth.

"That can be arranged, too, if necessary," the fat man said, smiling and winking at Sonny Boy Slade.

The hotheaded gunman let out a cackle.

"Yeah, just say the word, Mr. Jessup. I'm looking forward to this."

Cody swung a hard look at Sonny Boy.

"Anytime, anyplace." Cody said evenly.

Slade leaped from his chair and kicked it backwards. His hand hovered a hairsbreadth from the pearl handled Colts tied to both legs. Unbridled anger swept across his face. His eyes went bug-eyed.

"Touch those guns and I'll kill you," Cody said, his words barely above a whisper.

"Now, now, gentlemen. There's no call for gunplay," Jessup said, "we'll settle this in a court of law."

"Jessup. I'll say this just once. You send anybody up the mountain to try to take over our mine and I'll send them back to you in a pine box. That's my final word on the matter."

Cody turned on his heels and strode from the office.

After Cody left Jessup's office, Cooper and Slade turned to leave.

"Sit down!" Jessup bellowed. "I want to know who that fellow is. He's way too sure of himself to suit me."

"He's a nobody," Sonny Boy said. "I could'a took him easy if you hadn't stopped me."

"Maybe, maybe not," Lyle Cooper said, settling back into his chair. "I make my living at poker by being able to read men. To know when they're bluffing and when they ain't. That fellow wasn't bluffing. If you had gone for those guns, he'd of killed you just like he said."

"That's bull!" Sonny Boy screamed. "I ain't never met the man that could outdraw me!"

"You just did," Cooper told him. "I don't know who he is, but if you brace him he's gonna kill you."

"I know all the fast guns from here to Texas," Sonny Boy bragged. "I ain't never heard of a gunny named Cody Cordell. I think we ought to just kill him and get it over with."

"I don't pay you to think!" Jessup yelled. "I want to know *who* that fellow is and I want to know real quick. Find out! Now both of you get outta my sight."

The Higgins Ranch house came into view just as the sun kissed the western horizon and sent golden streaks shooting across the sky. Cody hurried his horse.

He reined up near the barn and was met by the old Mexican stableman.

"How are you, Marcos?" Cody greeted.

The old man bowed slightly and swept off his straw sombrero. Cody swung from his pinto and stepped stiffly to the ground. The ride from Trinidad had been a fast one.

The stableman took the reins to his horse. Cody knew Marcos would curry and brush Cincinnati before he watered, fed, and stabled the pinto for the night. Cody headed quickly toward the house.

Juliana must have seen him coming because she jerked the front door open and met him before he got to the front steps. She rushed into his arms with a mixture of happy tears and a long hug.

"I've missed you, cowboy," she whispered into his ear.

"I've missed you too. I couldn't stay away any longer. I had to see you."

"Good. Come on in. Supper is almost ready and you know how I hate to eat alone."

Arm in arm they walked slowly into the house.

"I thought you were never going to come," she said, pursing her lips in a fake pout.

"I've thought about you every day," he told her.

"I know. Me, too."

"Have a seat right there at the table, Mr. Cordell. I'll pour you some coffee and you can fill me in on what's been going on while I put supper on the table."

"Lots of things are happening. All at once, it seems like," he told her, as she poured a cup of coffee. "We've hired a good crew of workers and some security men. We've got almost six loads of ore loaded and ready for a trip to Denver. Something's come up regarding our claims and I've got to make the trip to Denver to talk to our attorney. I'll be riding along with our first wagon train of ore. We'll be leaving in a few days."

"Oh, no," she said, disappointment evident in her voice. "How long will you be gone?"

"Can't say for sure. A few weeks, most likely."

"You said *something has come up* regarding your claims. What's wrong?"

"Seems a new fellow in Trinidad named Haig Jessup has filed a lawsuit against our company. They're saying the waivers Sammy got are no good. Now, Jessup filed a claim, and someway got a claim on the very spot where the Quicksilver Mine is located. He's trying to take possession of it now. We've got to stop him."

"But I thought Judge Goodson said your claims were good?"

"He did, and he still says they are, but it's out of his hands now. It's gonna be decided by a court in Denver because that's where the claims were issued."

"But that's not right." Juliana said angrily.

"No, it ain't, but it could be worse. Far as I can tell, he thinks the Quicksilver Mine is where we struck gold, because that's the only spot he filed a claim and lawsuit on."

"And your engineer said there wasn't even silver in the mine, right?"

"Right, but I'm afraid after he discovers all he's got is a deep hole in the ground, he'll try to somehow get hold of where the *real* gold deposit is."

They talked steadily about all that was going on all through supper.

"Let's take our coffee and go into the den. There's something else I need to talk with you about," Cody said, his voice thick.

His serious sounding words sent a ripple of fear running the length of Juliana's spine. Her throat was suddenly full. She felt jittery. Apprehension simmered in the pit of her stomach. *Something else is wrong. I could hear it in his voice. I've never heard him sound that serious before.*

Not another word passed between them as they carried their coffee into the den and sat on the leather sofa in front of the fireplace.

The soft crackle of the fire was the only sound to break the building silence. She heard Cody clear his throat as he stared at the floor in front of his boots.

Juliana took a deep breath and let it out in a ragged sigh.

"Cody, there's something else wrong, isn't there? I can feel it. What is it?"

"Juliana," finally managing to get out the single word before his breath ran out.

"What is it, Cody? You're scaring me."

"I don't know no other way to say this but to just come right out and say it."

Her heart climbed up her throat. She could barely breath.

Is he going to tell me that he doesn't love me after all? That he's found someone else? She blinked away unwelcome tears.

"I love you," he finally managed to put sound to the words. "I reckon I've loved you since the first time I saw you. If you'll have me, I'm asking you to be my wife."

His words sounded fragile and pure. All the worry and fear was stripped from her in that instant. All of her hopes and dreams were granted with his simple words.

She threw herself into his arms, laughing and crying happy tears.

"I love you, Cody. Of course, I'll marry you!" she cried excitedly.

Pulling the little box from his pocket he opened it and handed it to her.

"The lady at the jewelry store said this was an *engagement* ring. She said I was supposed to give it to you when I ask you to marry me. I reckon this is the time."

Juliana's eyes widened and her mouth fell open.

"Oh, my! Oh, my! That's the most beautiful ring I've ever seen. That must have cost a fortune."

She slipped it onto her finger and held it out for him to see.

"It looks good on you," he told her. "Nothing is too good for you."

Chapter XXXII

It was mid-November, 1869. Darkness still held the land captive. Not even a hint of dawn colored the eastern horizon. A chilly wind crossed the flatlands of southwest Texas and sent a shiver through Buck as he, Chester, and Ray Ledbetter stepped into their saddles.

As they rode past one of the large barns, Smokey and three Longhorn cowboys emerged leading two large, haltered, black bulls. Another half-dozen Longhorn security men fell in behind the cowboys.

"Delivering a couple of *El Toro's* finest?" Buck asked his foreman.

"Yes, sir," Smokey replied, reining up near Buck, Chester, and Ray.

"Where these two going?"

"We're taking them to a ranch up near Waco called the Brazos River Ranch. Fellow named Nate Swenson owns it. He's got another big spread down in south Texas somewhere around Corpus Christi."

Buck nodded. "Long trail. You boys ride easy. See you when you get back."

Smokey touched thumb and finger to his hat brim and heeled his mount to catch up with the others.

"Good looking bulls," Chester commented.

"We still getting five thousand apiece for them?"

"Yeah, and got 'em standing in line waiting," Ray answered. "All this year's bulls are already spoken for and next year's crop is going fast. We're getting orders from all over the country. Fact, we got a telegram a couple weeks ago from Colorado ordering two of next year's bulls."

"Colorado? Where abouts in Colorado?" Buck asked, his interest suddenly aroused.

"A place called Trinidad. Say, ain't that the place where your little brother's buried?"

Buck nodded and was quiet for a minute.

"Yeah. Yeah, it is. Remember who ordered them?"

"Higgins, as I recall. The Higgins Ranch."

Buck nodded his head in silent contemplation before he replied.

"That's good. Small world, I reckon. That monster bull's making us lots of money. Them leg hobbles we put on him still working good?"

"Sure are. We take 'em off when we're breeding him, but other that that, he wears them all the time."

"Sure wish we'd thought of that before he killed Pappy."

"Yeah, me too." Chester agreed.

"How're things shaping up for next year's drives?" Buck asked as they rode.

"Carlos says it's getting harder to find good stock in Mexico. He says we've bought up most of the Mexican ranchers' extra stock, leastwise the cattle that's worth anything."

"Where we gonna get enough cattle to make the drives next year?"

"We're hoping to make up the shortfall from Mexico by increasing the catching crews along the rivers. There again, we're having to go farther up into the Big Bend country to find the numbers we need.

"I think we can come up with enough for next year's drives, don't know about the year after that." Chester told him.

"Maybe by then, we'll have our brood herd big enough we can cut back a little and still make some profitable drives," Buck said. "We'll see."

"Talked to your pa lately?"

"Yeah, me and Selena took the baby to see them a few days ago. They're doing good. He said the bank was growing so fast he could barely keep up with it."

"Glad to hear it."

They rode out to the north pasture to take a look at their brood cattle. They reined up on the shoulder of a hill and gazed down into the valley at the vast herd of longhorns.

"How many we got in our Longhorn herd now?" Buck asked.

"Last count we took, it was over six thousand."

"We don't have enough pasture land to handle many more than that, do we?"

"Not the way I see it, we don't."

"What would you think about approaching *Antonio Rivas* again about buying this land outright instead of continuing the lease arrangement? Who knows, maybe something has happened that he would consider selling it to us now." I think we ought to see if he has any more tracks of land nearby too.

"Sure couldn't hurt anything. All he can say is, no," Chester agreed.

"Next time I go into San Antonio, I'll talk to that attorney of his. Maybe we'll make him an offer he'll have a hard time refusing. Leasing this land was good for us at the time, but now I'd sure rather own it outright instead of leasing. Good chance he's got some more land nearby that we could buy, too."

"Looks like we're gonna need it," Chester agreed.

Chapter XXXIII

Six heavily loaded freight wagons pulled out from the Schroeder/Cordell Mining camp just before sundown on November 18, 1869. White canopies, lashed tightly, hid the gold ore inside.

The plan was to leave the Trinidad area under cover of darkness in order to attract the least amount of attention possible. They would travel all night the first night. After putting some miles between them and Trinidad, they would make the rest of the trip during the day.

Since Cody had to make the trip to Denver to meet with their attorney, and given the trouble brewing with Haig Jessup, it was decided that Bret Allison would remain at the camp in case Jessup tried to take control of the Quicksilver Mine claim.

Four mounted security men had heavy ropes tied to the backs of each wagon and half-hitched around saddle horns to aid the wagon brakes while going down the steep trail of the mountain. A chuck wagon brought up the rear of the wagon train.

Cody led the wagons down the mountain. Twenty-four security men provided protection for the ore wagons during the long trip to Denver. Cody carried a list of supplies waiting in Denver to be picked up for Hamilton's store.

The wagon train headed due north, moving steadily all night. By mid-morning the next day, they reached the Cucharas River. Cody figured they had covered close to fifty miles and called a halt. Both men and animals were exhausted.

They made camp beside the river and rested the rest of the day and that night. By daylight of the second day, they started rolling again.

A security man named Walt Seals was in charge of the security detail. He was a stern-faced, no nonsense fellow that Cody judged to be in his forties. Allison had told Cody the man fought for the Confederacy as a captain and later worked as a Deputy United States Marshal in Fort Smith, Arkansas for Judge Isaac Parker, known widely as the *hanging judge*. Cody rode up alongside the security man.

"We're making good time," Cody said, making conversation.

"Yep," was the man's only reply.

"Bret tells me you fought for the south?"

"Yep."

"My brother was killed in the war," Cody told him. "He was a captain in the Confederate Army."

"Lots of good men died who shouldn't have. What was your brother's name?"

"Benjamin Cordell. He was a captain, like you. He rode for Colonel Mosby's raiders."

"I heard about them. Tough bunch."

"Wish I knew where my brother was buried."

"Most of the time, they didn't have time to bury the dead proper. It was a bad war. One that was lost before it even got started."

"Don't reckon there is such a thing as a *good* war," Cody said.

"I'll say *amen* to that." Seals said.

"Well, it's good to have you riding with us, Walt. We need men like you."

"I'm obliged."

For the next twelve days they pushed hard, traveling from dark to dark, averaging thirty miles a day. On the thirteenth day, December 1, the wagon train pulled into the Denver Smelting & Refining Company yard.

Cody climbed from his horse and found the office. He tapped on the door. A voice from inside invited him to come in and he opened the door and stepped inside.

A short fellow with a partially bald head and a white shirt with the sleeves rolled up greeted him.

"Something I can do for you, young fellow?"

"Yes, sir. I'm Cody Cordell from Trinidad, Colorado. I've got six wagonloads of gold ore I need worked out. Are you the one I need to see?"

A look of surprise swept across the man's face. He stuck out his hand.

"Name's Frank Spicer. I'm the owner. It's good to make your acquaintance. Read about you in the newspaper. Likely about everybody in the country has."

"Yeah, I reckon."

'Well, let's go take a look and see what you've got."

Cody walked with the smelter owner out to the first wagon. One of his security men untied the back of the canopy.

Spicer reached a hand and scooped it full of the ore-laced dirt. He rubbed it vigorously between the palms of his hands. He stared at the remains for a long moment while shaking his head in amazement.

"Been in this business a long time, Mr. Cordell. Never

seen anything like this before. It's the richest ore I've ever seen. Offhand, I'd guess this ore is going to yield six, maybe seven percent. Have your drivers back the wagons up to that door over yonder, one at a time, and we'll get you unloaded."

"How long will the smelting process take?"

"Not long, couple of days at the most. Let's see, today's Tuesday. Come back on Friday. We should be finished by then."

"Never done this before so I don't know what I need to do."

"You don't need to do anything. The assay official will inspect the gold and test it to verify our results. After verification, he'll sign the report and authorize the Denver Bank to make payment. You've done the important part, discovering the gold and transporting it here. We'll do the rest."

"Looks like we'll have regular shipments like this about every six weeks or so," Cody told him.

"Excellent. We're happy to work with you and will look forward to your shipments. Will you have an office in Denver where I can send a copy of our report along with an invoice for the work?"

"Yes. Our attorney is Arthur J. Winfield. He'll be taking care of stuff like that."

"Aw, yes. We've dealt with Mr. Winfield on a number of transactions. He's a fine attorney. The best in Denver, most folks would say. In fact, he was very instrumental in helping get Colorado admitted into the Union as the thirty-eighth state. He's quite well known, especially politically."

"Well, I'm much obliged for your help, Mr. Spicer. I'll look forward to seeing you again."

Cody walked over to where Walt Seals was talking with some of his security men.

"Walt, Mr. Spicer asked us to back the wagons up to that door yonder. After you get unloaded and the drivers have seen to the teams and wagons, take all our men to the Sargent House Hotel. I'll arrange for lodging and meals for everybody. I expect you'll want to start back in the morning."

"Yes, sir. The men will appreciate sleeping in a soft bed for a change."

"I'll see you and the boys at the hotel."

Cody stepped in a stirrup and mounted. He rode to the Sargent House Hotel and tied his pinto to the hitching rail. Pushing through the door, Cody strode up to the check-in counter.

The same, heavyset, balding fellow Cody remembered from before, looked up. Recognition swept over his face.

"Mr. Cordell, isn't it?"

"Uh, yes. Yes it is. But how did you remember? I've only been here once."

"I make it my business to remember our customers. Besides, it isn't every day we have someone stay with us who recently discovered gold."

"I see. How many vacant rooms do you have?"

"Well, let me look," the hotel owner said, turning and counting the keys in a shelf with divided compartments.

"Right now, I have twenty-one rooms available. Why do you ask?"

"I'll take 'em," Cody told him, scribbling his last name on the register.

"You mean you want them all?" Mr. Sargent asked, surprise sounding in his voice.

"There'll be thirty-two of us, counting me. My men will be here after a bit. Suppose you could come up with cots for the extras?"

"Yes, sir, Mr. Cordell. I'll see to it. We'll take good care of you and your men."

Cody scooped up one of the keys the hotel owner laid out on the counter and walked out the front door.

Outside, Cody turned up the street. He walked two blocks to Sadie's, the small café where he had eaten earlier. The redheaded waitress, he remembered from before, saw him come in and hurried over.

"Welcome back, Texas," she said, greeting him with a teeth-showing smile. "I thought you didn't enjoy your food when you were in before since you waited so long to come back."

"I live four hundred miles away, but I got here as soon as I could," Cody joked.

"Oh. Where might that be?"

"Place over west called Trinidad."

"Isn't that where somebody struck gold?"

"That's the place."

"Some people have all the luck."

"Ain't it the truth?"

"I never got a chance to introduce myself. I'm Rachel."

"I'm Cody."

"Have a seat, Cody. I'll see if I can fill you up."

"Actually, I've got some more business to take care of, but I wanted to see if you could feed thirty-two of us?"

"Thirty-two? Wow! If I start cooking now, I could. When will you be here to have supper?"

"It's about three now, I reckon. What about six? Could you be ready for us by then?"

"I'll be ready. In fact, I've got an extra room I use sometimes for large groups. I'll set it up for you and your friends."

"Sounds good. These fellows have been on the trail for two weeks or so eating chuck wagon food. Feed 'em good, okay?"

"Don't worry, I'll lay it on thick."

From Sadie's, Cody made his way to his attorney's office. The sourpuss secretary looked up with an expressionless look when he walked into the office.

"Is Mr. Winfield in?"

"Yes, sir. Mr. Cordell, isn't it? Shall I tell him you're here?"

"That would be good, I reckon."

The secretary rose from her desk and tapped slightly on the attorney's door. She waited a moment before opening the door only far enough to allow her to step inside and closed it behind her.

Why do I get the feeling she don't like me? Cody wondered.

Arthur Winfield jerked the office door open and hurried to meet Cody with his hand outstretched.

"Mr. Cordell. Good to see you again. Come on into the office."

He stepped aside to allow Cody to walk in front of him and closed the office door behind them.

"I get the feeling your secretary don't like me," Cody said.

Winfield laughed.

"It's not you. She's that way with everyone. She has shortcomings in the customer relations department, but she's the most efficient secretary I've ever seen. I'm surprised to see you back in Denver so soon."

"Well, seems we've got a problem."

"Oh?"

Cody pulled a copy of the lawsuit from his pocket and handed it to the attorney. Winfield studied the legal paper for several minutes before looking up.

"Looks like this Haig Jessup is out to steal your mine."

"Yep."

"Cecil Haddock is his attorney."

"You know him?"

Winfield chuckled.

"Oh, yes, I know Mr. Haddock well. We've opposed one another in court several times. I've never lost a case to him. He doesn't like me very well."

"I met with Judge Goodson in Trinidad. He said they didn't want him to hear the case. He said they were asking for a *change of venue*, or something like that, to have the trial here in Denver."

"Yes, these papers, here, are to that effect. He's already granted their request. I'll contact Judge Littlefield, here in the Denver court, and get all the information they have about it. Don't worry, Cody, they don't have a leg to stand on. We'll get this thing settled without a problem."

"According to Jessup, he's already filed on the very claim where our mine is. He says the law gives him the right to take possession."

"I'll get the judge to issue a *stay* on his fraudulent claim so he can't. You going to be in town a day or two?"

"I can, if need be."

"Let me see what I can do. Where are you staying?"

"The Sargent House Hotel."

"Good. I'll get to work on this right now. I'll be in contact with you shortly."

Cody rose, shook hands with Winfield, and turned to go before he remembered.

"Oh, one more thing. Mr. Spicer over at Denver Smelting and Refining will be sending you an invoice and some papers from time to time as we bring in our ore. Could we set up an account so you can go ahead and pay the invoices?"

"Of course. We'd be glad to handle that for you. You'll need to set up a special account over at the bank just for that purpose. Mr. Sylvester will be happy to set that up for you."

"Good. I'm obliged for your help."

"Don't worry. We'll get this all straightened out for you."

"I hear you had a hand in getting Colorado admitted to the Union?"

"Well, I'm not sure how much I was able to contribute, but I worked on it. I ended up being appointed as chairman of the Railroad Commission as a result. Guess you've heard we're finally getting a railroad?"

"No, I hadn't heard that."

"Yes, it should revolutionize the entire area. It will open Denver up for trade goods from all over the country."

"Where will it go to? This railroad."

"Most anywhere. St. Louis, Kansas City, Chicago. Just imagine. We'll only be twenty-eight hours by train from Chicago and fifty-two hours from New York. Denver is finally joining the rest of the world."

"When will it be open for business?"

"The first train of the Denver-Pacific will pull out from the Denver terminal on June 12 of the coming year."

"That's good news for Colorado," Cody agreed, though he wasn't sure how the coming of the railroad would help him.

Cody left the attorney's office and walked the two blocks back to his hotel. Walt Seals and the rest of his men were already there lounging around the lobby.

"You and the boys get checked in?" Cody asked.

"Yes, sir. Some of the boys are already upstairs trying out those feather beds."

"We're all set up for supper at six o'clock. We're eating at a place called Sadie's Café. It's up the street a couple of blocks. Think I'll go wash up before supper. I'll meet you and the boys there at six."

"I'll make sure they're there on time."

Longhorn III: The Prodigal Brother

Cody made his way up to his room. He washed and shaved before putting on a clean pair of pants and shirt. The bed looked mighty inviting, but he decided to go downstairs and visit with his men until time to go to supper.

They sat around the lobby on the sofas. Cody found an empty seat and folded into it.

One of the men told some tall tale about when he used to catch longhorns out of the thickets along the east Texas rivers.

"So there we stood, looking at one another eyeball to eyeball. That big ole longhorn had horns that must'a been ten foot wide. He was snortin' fire and pawing the ground with those razor-sharp hooves. I knew if he charged, I was in a heap of trouble.

"Well, sir, I made up my mind right then and there. Weren't no longhorn bull gonna buffalo Rowdy Abel. My momma didn't name me Rowdy fer nothin'."

"What'd you do, Rowdy?" another of the security men asked anxiously.

"What'd I do? I done what any Texas cowboy worth his salt would'a done. When that big ole bull charged, I did me a little Texas shuffle. When that critter tore past, I grabbed two handfuls of horns and threw him to the ground, that's what I did. From that day 'till this, they call what I did *bulldoggin'*."

All the cowboys just shook their heads and laughed. They were still laughing and poking fun at Rowdy for his story when they all walked into Sadie's Café.

Rachel greeted them and drew a loud chorus of whistles and good-natured flirting. She ushered them through a door and into a large room. The tables were set with plates, silverware, and a coffee cup beside each plate.

Two of Rachel's friends came from the kitchen carrying large coffee pots. That brought another round of whistles and loud joking.

For the next hour, Cody's men feasted on pot roast with potatoes and carrots, corn on the cob, hot yeast rolls, and apple pie.

"Think I just died and went to Heaven." one of the cowboys said loudly.

"Ma'am, it just ain't right for somebody who can cook like that to still be a single lady." Rowdy Able told Sadie.

"Is that a proposal, cowboy?" Sadie shot back.

The laughter drowned out his answer, if he even had one.

After they all finished eating and enjoying a last cup of coffee, Cody walked up to settle up with Rachel for the meals.

"What do I owe you?" he asked.

"Six bits apiece. That'd come to twenty-four dollars."

Cody laid two, twenty dollar gold pieces on the counter.

"Keep the change. It was a fine meal, Miss Rachel."

"Thank you, Cody. I found out from one of your men who you are. You forgot to tell me that it was *you* who discovered the gold over in Trinidad."

"Didn't forget. Just didn't think it was important, that's all."

"Whoever that girl is that's waiting on you is one mighty lucky lady."

Cody's face blossomed crimson.

He walked back to his hotel room, feeling tired. He shucked his clothes down to his long johns and crawled into the soft feather bed. He went to sleep thinking about what Rachel had said. *I think it's the other way around, though. I feel like I'm the lucky one.*

Walt Seals and his men pulled out early the next morning. They were to go by the warehouse and pick up Ed Hamilton's supplies before leaving town.

Longhorn III: The Prodigal Brother

Cody slept until after daylight, something very unusual for him. He had been an early riser since he was a young boy. His father's words kept ringing in his ears. *A man that sleeps after daylight will never amount to a hill of beans.*

Feeling guilty, Cody finally got up, dressed, and made his way downstairs. He was still full from the previous night and decided to forgo breakfast. Instead, he found a barbershop.

"I need a shave and haircut," he told the barber, as he settled into the barber chair.

"Beautiful day," the barber said.

"Yep."

"You live in Denver?"

"Nope."

"Lived here all my life," the man said, still trying to make conversation. "Ain't been more'n a hundred miles from Denver since I was born."

"It's a big world out there," Cody told him. "Lots to see."

"I reckon. Just never was much of a traveler. Reckon I'm what most folks would call a homebody."

The rest of a half hour passed without another word passing between them. Cody paid the man and headed up the street. He felt like walking a spell.

The brand new railroad depot came into view up the street. An idea struck him and he headed that way.

A small, sickly looking fellow with a green visor on his forehead stood behind a counter.

"I understand Denver is getting a railroad?" Cody asked.

"We sure are," the fellow said excitedly.

"When will it make its first run to St. Louis?"

"June 12. You want to buy a ticket?"

Cody paused for only a second.

"Yeah, I do. Fact, I need two tickets to St. Louis for June 12."

"First class or coach?"

"What's the difference?"

"If you go first class, you have a private compartment with sleeping accommodations. Coach is just a seat in the regular passenger car."

"Give me two first class tickets."

The clerk stamped two long tickets and handed them to Cody.

"That'll be twenty-four dollars."

Cody paid the man and stuck the tickets in his pocket.

Next, he stopped by a men's clothing store and bought himself two suits of clothes, a new pair of boots, and a brand new Stetson hat. *Reckon I ought to start dressing better,* he decided, remembering the saloon woman from long ago making fun of the way he was dressed. *Guess I'll never get over that.*

As he was paying the sales clerk, the man put his purchases in a sack, handed it to Cody, and said cheerfully, "Merry Christmas."

Christmas? Is it almost Christmas?

"What's the date?"

"It's the second of December."

Good. He smiled. *I can still make it home in time for Christmas.*

He went by the jewelry store. The nice lady who sold him the wedding rings was there.

"Remember me?" he asked, as he walked into the store.

"Of course. You're the young man who bought the wedding ring set. Did you give her the engagement ring yet?"

"Yes, ma'am. She seemed to really like it."

"I would think so. That was the very best ring set we carry. It's the only one of its kind I have ever sold. Is there something else you might be interested in?"

"Yes, ma'am. I'm looking for something to give her for Christmas."

"Hmm. Step over here and let me show you something you might be interested in."

She walked over to a glass enclosed counter and selected a large velvet case. She held it in front of Cody and opened it. It was a diamond necklace and earring set. Light from the sun bounced off the diamonds and sent rays of light shooting in every direction. Cody blinked his eyes in wonderment.

It's beautiful. But is it practical? What kind of occasion would she likely attend that she could wear it? No, it's just too much. I think Juliana would be embarrassed to wear that.

"No, I had something more like a simple heart necklace in mind. Do you have something like that?"

"What about something like this?" she asked, pulling a beautiful, but simple heart locket from the glass display case. The locket was on a gold chain.

Cody examined it, turning it over in his hand.

"Yep. That's just what I had in mind. I'll take it."

The nice lady placed the necklace in a little velvet-covered box and wrapped it with pretty paper. Cody paid her and thanked her for her help.

Cody got up at first light on Friday morning. He washed, shaved, and dressed in one of his new outfits he bought the day before. Looking at himself in the big mirror over the dresser, he combed through his long wheat-colored hair before adjusting his new gray Stetson. Satisfied, he walked up the street to Sadie's for breakfast. Rachel greeted him with a wide smile.

"Well, look at you." she said. "Don't you look spiffy this morning?"

"Mornin'" he said, scraping out a chair and folding into it.

"Where you headed, all dressed up?"

"Got a meeting at the bank and with my attorney, then I'm headed back home."

"You and your lady set the wedding date yet?"

"No. Most likely, sometime next summer."

"You'll have to bring her with you sometime," Rachel said, pouring him a cup of coffee. "I'd love to meet her."

"I'll do that."

She brought his breakfast and got busy waiting on other customers. He ate leisurely, enjoying the delicious food. He had another cup of coffee, paid for his meal, and said goodbye to his friend.

"See you the next time I'm in town," he told her.

She waved goodbye from across the room.

He walked to the livery and saddled Cincinnati. "I'll be back later today for my packhorse," he told the liveryman, as he paid what he owed. He swung into the saddle and headed for the Denver Smelting & Refining Company.

He tied his pinto to the hitching rail outside the office and strode inside. Frank Spicer rose from behind his desk and greeted Cody with a wide smile and a handshake.

"Been expecting you," the owner said, picking up an official paper from his desk. "We finished your ore yesterday. Got the report right here."

"How'd we come out?" Cody asked, studying the paper in his hands.

"Best ore I ever seen. Worked out at eight percent. That's much higher than normal. You've got a good, high-grade gold."

"What does that mean?" Cody asked.

"Well, you had a total of six thousand eight hundred pounds of ore. It worked out at eight percent. That means you ended up with Five hundred forty.five point six pounds of gold. That's eight thousand seven hundred twenty-nin point six troy ounces. At forty-five dollars an ounce, that comes to three hundred ninety two thousand, eight hundred and thirty-two dollars."

Cody went white-eyed. His mouth dropped open. Never in his wildest dreams had he imagined it would come to that much. It took a few minutes for his mind to absorb what he was just told.

"That's an awful lot of money," Cody finally managed to say.

"Yes, that's an awful lot of money," the smelter owner agreed. "Just take this paper to the Denver bank and they'll arrange for the transfer of funds. I'll submit my invoice for the smelting to your attorney."

"Yes. Yes, you do that. I've arranged for him to handle things like that."

Cody walked out of the smelter office in a trance. He wanted to leap into the air and let out a loud cowboy yell, but he managed to control himself until he got out of hearing.

His attorney was waiting in Mr. Sylvester's office when Cody arrived. They both rose to their feet when he entered.

"Good morning, Mr. Cordell," the bank president greeted, extending his hand. Cody shook hands with both men.

"Morning, Cody," Arthur Winfield said.

"Good morning, gentlemen" said Cody, returning the friendly greetings.

"Judging by the smile on your face, you have good news," his attorney said.

"Yes, it worked out good." Cody handed the paper Spicer had given him to Sylvester.

The bank president studied the paper for a moment, nodding his head the entire time.

"Eight percent. My goodness! That's excellent. You are a very wealthy young man."

"Well, I've got a partner."

"Yes, but if your mine holds out, you'll both be millionaires in no time."

Millionaires. First time I've heard that word connected to me. I still can't believe this is happening. Millionaires!

"Do you want this credited to your account?"

"I need to set up a separate account so Mr. Winfield can pay our local bills. Do you think ten thousand dollars will be enough in that account?" he asked his attorney.

"That will be more than sufficient." Winfield replied. "I'll give you a certified audit of the account each quarter."

Cody nodded agreement.

"I'd like twenty thousand in cash," Cody said.

"Very good," Sylvester said, rising to make the transaction.

Mr. Winfield pulled an official document from his inside pocket and handed it to Cody.

"That's a *stay*, signed by a Federal Judge, Honorable Henry Wofford, a friend of mine. That order by the court prevents your friend from seizing possession of the mine until after the matter has been settled in court.

"But I assure you, the trial is merely a legal formality. You have nothing to fear. Your claims will all be upheld."

"That's good. Much obliged for your help," Cody said.

Mr. Sylvester returned carrying a leather satchel. He handed it to Cody.

"There's twenty thousand dollars in there, Mr. Cordell." "Here's a certificate of deposit for the balance."

"Our loads ought to be coming in about every six weeks or so." Cody rose to his feet. "I've asked Mr. Spicer, over at the smelter, to turn in the certificates to my attorney. He'll arrange for the deposits."

"Very good," the bank president said, shaking hands with Cody. "It's a pleasure doing business with you, Mr. Cordell."

"See you the next time you're in town," Mr. Winfield added.

Cody left the bank and went to his hotel. He gathered his belongings and transferred the twenty thousand dollars to his saddlebags to avoid attracting attention. He double-checked his room and went downstairs.

"Are you leaving us?" Mr. Sargent asked, as Cody laid his key on the counter.

"For this trip, anyway," Cody told him, as he paid for his stay. "I'll be back from time to time, though."

"It's always good to have you," the hotel owner told him.

Cody walked outside, gathered the reins to his pinto, and stepped into a stirrup. He rode to the livery and girthed his packsaddle on the packhorse, and nodded a goodbye to the liveryman.

"Let's make tracks, big fellow," he told his pinto as if he was talking to a friend. "We've got a long way to go and a short time to get there."

Averaging fifty miles a day, Cody made the return trip home in eight days, arriving December 10, 1869. He reined up in front of the imposing Higgins Ranch house and stepped stiffly to the ground. It had been a long and hard ride from Denver.

Juliana ran from the house into his open arms.

"Welcome home, cowboy." she whispered with no small difficulty.

She wrapped her arms around his neck and pulled his face down to her. Hot tears breached the rims of her eyes. Tiny sobs escaped her lips. Cody silenced them with a kiss that left her head spinning. She felt feverish and was trembling when he raised his mouth from hers.

"I missed you," Cody whispered, staring deep into her eyes. "I missed you every minute of every day."

"I can tell," she whispered through a smile. "Come on in the house. Tell me everything."

They talked the rest of the day and half the night away. It was late when Cody made his way to the bunkhouse, very late.

For a long time he lay in the darkness, staring at the ceiling through what little light seeped from the big potbelly stove in the corner of the bunkhouse. Cody's thoughts mostly drowned out the loud snoring from a dozen cowboys in the small room.

So much is happening so fast. Just a few short months ago I was nothing but a nobody. I was running from the Pinkertons and every wannnabe gunfighter looking to build his reputation by putting a bullet in me.

If somebody had asked, I couldn't have named one person who gave a flip whether I was alive or dead. All that has changed. I have folks who depend on me. I have friends who respect me. I have somebody who loves me.

With those thoughts clutched close, he drifted off to a peaceful sleep.

The first snow of the season greeted Cody as he stepped from the bunkhouse. A soft, white blanket covered the land. Large snowflakes fell silently from a wintry dawn. He paused, stretched, and breathed in the scent of the morning.

Juliana had breakfast on the table and coffee poured when he entered.

"Good morning," she greeted cheerfully. "Isn't the snow

Longhorn III: The Prodigal Brother

beautiful? I love the first snow of the season. It's so clean and fresh, like a newborn baby. Can we make some snow ice cream this afternoon?"

"Wish I could, but I need to get on into town. I'm a little worried that Haig Jessup might try to take control of the mine without knowing the judge has issued a stay on his lease."

"I'm excited about making the trip we talked about last night. I've never been to Texas. Of course, I've never been married, either," she said, sitting down next to him and smiling broadly. "I can hardly wait until June."

"It'll be here before you know it," Cody told her, forking a slab of ham into his plate beside the scrambled eggs.

"I know, but I just want it to hurry up and get here. Can we spend a couple of extra days in Denver so I can do some shopping? I'm going to buy the prettiest wedding dress you have ever seen."

"If it's on you, it will be pretty no matter what it looks like."

"You're a smooth-talking cowboy. I like that." She squeezed his arm.

"When do you think Sammy and Mary Ann will get married?" he asked.

"It wouldn't surprise me if it happened right away. One thing for sure, they won't wait until June. I've never seen her so excited before."

"Yeah, June seems like a long way off, but I'd sure like for us to be married in that little chapel where my ma and pa were married."

"I know. That will be so special."

"I'm anxious to see those high-powered bulls we ordered, too. The way Del Horton talked, they must really be something."

"Yes, to cost five thousand apiece, they *must* be something. How are we going to get them back to Colorado?"

"We'll ship them back the same way we get down there."

"What's the name of this ranch where the bulls are?"

"The Longhorn Ranch. It's on the Rio Grande River that separates Texas from Mexico."

"Isn't all this so exciting?"

"Yeah, it is," Cody agreed. "So many good things are happening, I keep waiting for something bad to come along."

Breakfast was over. It was time to go. Cody stood with hat in hand, staring down at the toes of his boots. He hated goodbyes. Seemed like he was always saying goodbye to someone.

"I better be getting on, Juliana." He managed to squeeze the words past the knot in his throat.

She nodded sadly.

"Wish you didn't have to go."

"I know. Me, too."

She filled his arms. He held her tight for a long while.

Chapter XXXIV

Cody knew something was wrong even before he reached the mine; strangers he had never seen before were coming and going as he made his way up Sugarloaf Mountain.

He hurried his horse.

When he saw six strange guards with rifles standing in front of the Quicksilver Mine he had a pretty good idea what was going on. His fears were confirmed when Bret Allison stepped from the log cabin. His face told the story before his words explained it.

"We've got problems, Cody," his security chief told him.

"Seems so," Cody replied, stepping down from his pinto.

"They had a court order. They brought the law with them. There was nothing we could do."

"How long they been working our mine?"

"They just took over yesterday."

"They find anything yet?" Cody asked, lifting a thin grin.

"Don't think so, but they've sure been hauling lots of dirt outta that mine."

"Has Haig Jessup been here?"

"Oh, yeah. He shows up two or three times a day. Left just a little while ago madder than a wet hen."

"Where's Sammy?"

"He's up the hill. He shut down the operation up there when Jessup took over the mine. He said he didn't want them to know we weren't getting the gold out of the mine."

"Good thinking. Tell him I'll be back in an hour or so. Don't do anything until I get back."

Cody toed a stirrup and swung back into the saddle. He pointed Cincinnati's nose toward town.

Judge Goodson was in his office when Cody opened the door and walked in.

"Howdy, Cody," the judge said with guilt sounding in his voice.

"Howdy, Judge."

"Cody, I hated what happened up at the mine yesterday. Jessup had a court order from Denver saying he had a legitimate claim to the property where the mine's located. There was nothing I could do."

Cody withdrew the legal document his attorney had given him from his pocket and handed it to Judge Goodson.

"Look that over," Cody said.

The judge spent several minutes going over the order issued by Judge Henry Wofford in Denver. Finally, judge Goodson looked up with a wide smile on his face.

"I've heard about Judge Wofford for years. He's a powerful Federal Judge. Don't know how you convinced him to sign this stay, but it's the final word on the matter."

"I'll be right back," Cody said over his shoulder as he hurried out the door.

Cody went directly to Marshal Gardner's office and walked inside.

"Marshal, got time to walk over to the judge's office with me?"

"If it's about Haig Jessup's claim, there's nothing I can do to help you, Cody. He had a court order. I was bound by law to enforce it."

"I know. I'm not blaming you, Ollie. Just come with me for a minute."

Cody and the marshal walked together to Judge Goodson's office and stepped inside.

The judge handed Gardner the court document and allowed him time to look it over.

"This is a *stay* signed by a *Federal* Judge," Goodson said. "It makes the previous court order null and void until such time as a trial can be held to decide the matter in a court of law."

The marshal looked confused.

"Okay, so what are you saying?"

"I'm saying we've got to undo what we done yesterday," Goodson told him.

"I want Haig Jessup and his men off my claim and I want them off now," Cody said emphatically. "If you can't do it, I'll do it myself."

"I'll do it if that's what the judge says I ought to do."

"That's what a *Federal Judge* orders you to do as an officer of the court," Judge Goodson told him.

"Then that's what I'll do," Gardner said. "Let's go."

Cody and Ollie Gardner walked to their horses.

"Give me a minute," the marshal said.

He hurried into his office and emerged with a sawed-off double barrel shotgun. He thumbed two shells in and closed it with a flip of his wrist.

"Just in case they take some extra persuasion," he said, as he climbed into his saddle.

Bret Allison must have guessed what was about to happen, because he had twenty of his security men, fully armed with rifles in hand, waiting by the cabin when Cody and the marshal rode up.

"Is your boss here?" Gardner asked one of the Jessup guards.

"No, he left a little while ago."

"Go get him. We'll wait."

The man hesitated only for a moment before turning to one of his companions.

"Go get Mr. Jessup," he instructed. "And be quick about it."

The man walked to a nearby horse and climbed quickly into the saddle. He left camp at a hard gallop.

The other Jessup workers emerged from the mine, saw what was happening, and picked up nearby rifles.

It was a Mexican standoff. Both factions, armed to the teeth, faced each other. Cody knew that even one aggressive move by anyone would set off a small war. He motioned to Bret and told him quietly.

"Pull your men back. Have them wait by the cabin until Jessup gets here. I'm afraid somebody will make the wrong move and start the dance."

Allison pulled his men back as Cody had instructed.

They waited.

It didn't take long. Pounding hooves coming up the trail told Cody that Jessup was on his way. Cody, Sammy, Sid, Marshal Gardner, Bret Allison, and his twenty security men walked forward to meet them near the mine with rifles ready.

Jessup rode in the lead. Close on his heels rode Sonny Boy Slade and Lyle Cooper. Another group of hard looking hombres brought up the rear. Cody didn't count them, but he judged there was another dozen or so, all heavily armed.

Jessup wore his anger all over his face. He reined down from a fast canter near the huddle of his men at the entrance to the mine.

"I'll have a word with you, Marshal!" Jessup shouted.

"Say your say," Gardner replied calmly.

"What's the meaning of this?"

The marshal withdrew the legal document from his coat pocket.

"I've got a paper here, signed by a Federal Judge in Denver, nullifying the court order you showed me yesterday. As of now, your men are trespassing on Mr. Cordell's property. I'm ordering you to gather up your men and leave. Right now."

"*You're ordering me?*" Jessup yelled. "You don't *order* me to do nothing! That's *my* gold mine and *nobody's* taking it away from me!"

Bret Allison closed the distance between him and Jessup with a few steps. He raised the shotgun and settled the barrel directly on Jessup's big belly. When he spoke, the words came out cold and hard, like a pronouncement of a death sentence.

"Jessup, you can ride down the mountain in your saddle or across it. Your choice."

For a long moment there was complete silence. Only the creak of saddle leather broke the thickening quietness. Somewhere somebody coughed. A horse snorted. You could have cut the tension with a knife.

"Don't know about the rest of you," Lyle Cooper spoke up. "I'm a gambler, but I know when I'm holding a losing hand. Deal me out," he said, reining his horse around and heading down the mountain. Several others followed the gambler.

"Come back here!" Jessup shouted. "I'm ordering you to come back!"

One by one, the Jessup men toed a stirrup and rode out until only Sonny Boy Slade and a handful of others remained.

"Looks like your men are smarter than you are," the marshal said. "You got thirty seconds to turn your horse around and ride, or I'm placing you under arrest for trespassing."

Jessup looked Marshal Gardner in the eyes for a moment before jerking his reins around and heeling his horse into a gallop toward town.

Sonny Boy walked his horse over to where Cody stood.

"I'm calling you out, *Cordell*, or whatever your name is. Unless you're the yellow bellied coward I say you are, meet me in town at sundown. We'll settle this *my* way."

"I'll be there," Cody replied.

It began snowing just before sundown.

By the time Cody rode into town, the ground was already covered. News about the gunfight must have spread like wildfire, because the street was two deep and shoulder-to-shoulder from one end of Trinidad to the other.

Men stood hunched over in their heavy coats with their collars pulled tight against the falling snow. Every window was crowded with faces pressed close. Even small boys lay underneath the boardwalks, hoping to see the most exciting event in their young lives.

When Cody reached the edge of town, he squinted a look through the snow. He could barely make out the figure of a man standing in the very middle of the street.

Sonny Boy Slade.

Cody reined up in front of Hamilton's store. He stepped slowly down from his pinto and tied it to the hitching rail. He sleeved out of his heavy Mackinaw and hung it on his saddlehorn. Adjusting the belly holster, he lifted the familiar bone handled Colt in his hand, opened the loading gate, and double checked the shells. Satisfied that it was fully loaded, he replaced it in his holster and turned down the street.

A small ripple of whispers quickly became a rising crescendo of voices spreading from one end of the street to the other.

"It's the *Hondo Kid!*" somebody shouted. "I'd know that serape anywhere. I saw him in a gunfight down in Waco. It's *him* all right."

"It's him!" Another fellow shouted at the top of his voice. "It's *really* him!"

"But it couldn't be!" another questioned. "He's supposed to be dead!"

"If Hondo ain't dead, who's that buried up yonder in Boot Hill?"

Cody ignored the waves of recognition that swept the crowd. Slowly, with even steps, he closed the distance between him and the gunfighter.

Sonny Boy must have heard the shouts of recognition, too, because he twisted his head from side to side, and then back toward Cody.

"Is it true?" Sonny Boy shouted from twenty yards away.

Cody didn't bother to reply. He kept walking.

"But, but, you *couldn't* be the Hondo Kid! You're dead! I saw your grave!" the gunfighter shouted, his voice frayed and shaky.

Cody kept walking. Only fifteen yards separated them. The snow was heavier. A strong wind slanted the large flakes into Cody's face. He blinked them away and kept walking.

Sonny Boy was visibly shaken. His head twisted from side to side as if searching for somebody, anybody, to confirm what he was saying.

From the corner of his eye, Cody saw Haig Jessup standing in the open door of his office. He quickly dismissed the presence and focused his attention on the hothead gunfighter in front of him.

"I don't give a hoot who you are!" Sonny Boy shouted, obviously wanting the spectators to hear his words. "I can take you! Nobody's ever beat me. I've killed more'n twenty men better'n you!"

But the nervous look written on his face belied his boisterous words. Despite the driving snow and cold, large drops of sweat stood from his forehead. His eyes flicked about nervously. His top lip quivered. His tongue made a circle along his lips.

Cody spoke his first words. They came out casual, self-assured. "You don't have to die today, Sonny Boy. Walk away while you still can."

For a fleeting moment, Cody thought the gunfighter was going to do what he suggested. But suddenly Slade's expression changed. Cody saw it on his face. The man shook his head defiantly and lifted his left hand to sleeve sweat from his forehead. Cody noticed he was left-handed.

Cody decided to try once more.

"Walk away or I'm gonna kill you," he said, lifting his own left hand to flip the edge of the serape back over his right shoulder. This time, Cody's words came out like daggers, each one stabbing the gunfighter in the heart.

Time stood still. Cody waited.

Cody's mind flashed back once more to the words of his friend and mentor, *El Diablo*. It seemed like a lifetime ago.

If there is no way to avoid the gunfight, only thing left is to kill him before he kills you. Watch his face, not his hand. His face tells you when he is going to draw. Sometimes a squint, sometimes lowering the eyebrows, sometimes gritting his teeth or clenching his jaw, but you will know.

Cody focused his unblinking gaze on his opponent's face.

Suddenly Cody saw it. Sonny Boy's lips clamped together and his eyes went wide. Cody remembered that look from the time back in Jessup's office when Slade come close to drawing on him.

He's about to draw.

Without actually seeing it, Cody was aware of the gunfighter's hand streaking to grasp the gun on his left hip.

Without making a conscious decision, his hand instinctively reacted on its own. It was as natural as breathing. In one heartbeat, his right hand rested casually with his thumb hooked in his gun belt. In the next, it held the bone handled Colt.

Cody felt the jarring recoil as it raced up the length of his arm, first one and then another.

He saw the familiar look of shock on his opponent's face; he'd seen it before. He watched as Sonny Boy's eyes walled white and his mouth dropped open.

Cody saw the two holes as they punched through the gunfighter's left pocket. He saw the bone handled Colt curl from lifeless fingers.

Sonny Boy's knees buckled. His right hand rose to claw at his chest. Slowly he fell backwards, as if in slow motion, to the snow covered street.

The street of Trinidad was deathly silent. The crowd stood in shocked disbelief.

For a moment, Cody stood motionless, still holding the Colt in his hand, and stared at the man lying in front of him. Sonny Boy's feet made one final jerking motion in false life as his blood stained the white snow around him.

Cody felt sick to his stomach. *It's got to end right here, right now,* he decided.

He slipped the worn serape over his head and tossed it on top of the late Sonny Boy Slade.

Turning, he strode toward the doorway where Haig Jessup stood. The fat man's eyes bugged wide when he saw Cody stop only a few feet from him.

"Jessup, if you're in town come sunup, I'll kill you."

With that said, he turned and walked to where Cincinnati was tied, sleeved into his Mackinaw, and stepped into his saddle.

The residents of Trinidad watched him ride away until the heavy falling snow swallowed him from their sight.

Chapter XXXV

Time sped by. Days became weeks and weeks months.

The yearly trail drives were in full swing and Rebekah had come to full term.

Kristianna Cordell was born on May 20, 1870. Jewell finally emerged from the bedroom with a smile as wide as Texas.

"It's the most prettiest little girl I ever did see," she announced proudly.

"How's Rebekah?" Buck asked anxiously.

"That lady beats all I ever seen in all my born days," the black midwife told him. "She be fit as a fiddle."

Buck, Chester, and Selena all let out a sigh of relief and burst into happy laughter.

"Can we see them?" Selena asked.

"Shore can. I expect they be as anxious to see you as you be them."

Buck led the way. The others followed. Rebekah lay propped up on two pillows. Her face was pale, but a smile lifted one corner of her mouth. Their new daughter, wrapped in a pink blanket, lay in her mother's arms.

"How are you, Pretty Lady?" Buck asked, leaning over to brush her lips with his.

"I'm fine," Rebekah said, widening the smile. "You got yourself a beautiful little daughter, cowboy."

Buck moved the edge of the blanket aside with a curled finger. He looked down into the rosy-red face of the most beautiful baby he had ever seen. Her eyes were closed, but her tiny lips curled up at one corner in a small smile, just like Rebekah's.

A large lump crawled up the back of his throat. He swallowed, and then swallowed again. He choked up and couldn't get a single word to come out. His lips pressed together and he drew a deep breath.

"She's so beautiful," he finally managed. "Just like her mother."

Rebekah smiled, and handed the baby to her father. Buck gathered his daughter and held her out in front of him. For a long moment he studied her face. The bright green eyes, the soft reddish hair, the tiny nose, the barely visible freckles. She was her mother made over again.

"You sure done a good job," he said, glancing up at Rebekah. "She's perfect."

"You mean *we* did a good job. You had *something* to do with it, you know."

"Could I hold her?" Selena asked.

Buck handed his daughter to her. Selena and Chester played with the baby and went on how beautiful she was. Buck's chest swelled with pride as he watched and listened.

"I'm going to get little Cody so he can see his new sister," Buck said, heading for the door.

He found his son with Marie. They were chasing

butterflies in the small, open air courtyard in the center of Buck's hacienda.

"Rebekah's had the baby," he told Cody's Mexican caretaker. "I want Cody to meet his new sister."

Marie smiled and nodded.

"Come on, son. There's someone I want you to meet."

The boy hurried to his father's side. He reached a hand. Buck took it. They walked side by side as they entered the hallway leading to the bedroom.

Selena squatted down so Cody could get a good look at the baby. For a moment a puzzled look crept across his face.

"Son, this is Kristianna, your new sister."

Cody glanced up at Buck, and then to his mother lying in the bed smiling broadly, then back at the baby. A look of understanding changed his expression. He grinned, and bending close, kissed his sister on the cheek.

The adults all looked at one another and smiled.

"I've got to ride into town," Selena said. "Rebekah, is there anything I can pick up for you while I'm there?"

"I don't know of anything."

"When will you be back?" Chester asked his wife.

"It's just my usual trip I take every other day to check on the café. I'll be back before dark."

Chester nodded. "Want me to ride with you?"

"You have your work to do. I'll take two of the security men like I always do. I'll be fine."

She walked over and squeezed Rebekah's hand.

"Get some rest," she told her friend. "Take advantage of this time. Pamper yourself a little for a change."

Rebekah smiled. "I feel good."

Selena left the room and hurried to the stable. On the way, she asked one of the security men near the gate to see who was available to ride with her to Del Rio.

"I'll go ask," he said, hurrying off to talk to Wade Thomas, the security chief.

Thomas returned with two of the security men.

"Miss Selena, this is Larry Steed and Wesley Leeds. They'll be escorting you today."

"Mr. Steed. Mr. Leeds," Selena acknowledged.

"Ma'am," they both said, touching the brim of their hats. "We'll get our horses and be ready in a couple of minutes."

The Mexican stableman led Selena's solid black mare from the barn and handed her the reins.

"Best take a poncho, ma'am," Thomas said, handing one to her. "Looks like rain."

Selena glanced quickly up at the darkening clouds and accepted the rain gear. She tied it behind her saddle and threaded a boot through a stirrup. She swung easily into the saddle.

Her two escorts rode up and fell in behind her as she reined her black mare through the wide gates of the compound.

Six miles from the Longhorn Ranch, three men sat around a small campfire sipping coffee. They were concealed in a shallow swag on a hogback hill overlooking the trail to Del Rio. Large boulders surrounded their campsite, but still afforded a clear view of the trail.

Two of the men were the Bratton brothers, Leon and Rudy. Both started out as low-level thieves when they were barely big enough to walk, but only hit the big time in their criminal career when they joined the Pepper gang.

Lon Pepper was a cold-blooded killer and leader of the gang. His qualifications as leader rested in a leather holster tied to his left leg and his willingness to use it.

He much preferred to ride alone, but found it necessary

to recruit others from time to time in order to pull off certain jobs. This was one of those times. But he had already decided that once this job was over, he would dispose of the brothers as quickly and easily as he would squash a bug.

He was a tall man, rangy and long boned. A hard man, his face looked weathered down to its elements. His pale gray eyes flashed when he spoke. Wolf eyes, most folks called them, at least the few who had looked into them and lived to tell about it.

He killed his first man when he was twelve. Since then, he had lost count long ago.

He had been on the wrong side of the law ever since. *I reckon I've done it all at one time or another,* he freely admitted, but only when he was liquored up, which was anytime he had the money. Right now wasn't one of those times. He didn't have a plug nickel to his name, *but that's about to change.*

"How long we gonna hang around here?" the brother named Rudy complained. "We ain't done nothing but sit here for two days."

The speaker was a round bellied man with bushy whiskers, stained yellow by months old tobacco juice. Neither his clothes nor body had felt the touch of water in weeks, maybe months. As if to emphasize his complaint, he spat a stream of yellow, foul-smelling juice into the fire.

"You got someplace to go, go?" his brother answered angrily. "Me and Lon don't need an idiot like you on this job, anyway. We ought'a have our heads examined for letting you come along."

"Don't call me an idiot!"

"Stop acting like an idiot and I'll stop calling you one."

"Both of you shut your mouth!" Lon Pepper told them coldly, slicing a hard gaze in their direction. "I'm tired listening to your yakking. The next one that opens his mouth, I'm going to stick my gun in it and pull the trigger. You got it?"

The two lowered their heads and nodded.

The plan was simple. They would take care of the two security men who always accompanied the pretty Mexican gal when she rode into town. They would attach a ransom note to her saddle and send her horse back to that big ranch where she lived. Then they would set back and wait for the money to be delivered.

"Keep your mouths shut and do what I tell you to do," he told his companions. "The only reason I picked either one of you was because you're both good shots. I been watching this Mexican lady make the ride into town every other day for over a week. She'll be along."

His companions just looked at him and said nothing.

A sound reached his hearing. Lon Pepper crooked his neck quickly and looked down the trail. Sure enough, three riders cantered their horses up the trail toward them. The Mexican lady rode in the lead.

"It's them," the leader said. "Don't forget what you're supposed to do. Kill the guards. Don't miss or I'll kill both of you."

"Don't worry about me, boss. I can shoot the eye out of a bird when it's flying." Leon bragged, scooping up his rifle and patting it before levering a shell.

Pepper gave the two brothers a hard look before slipping from his hiding place and hurrying down the hill. He ran bent over, slipping from rock to rock, using the large boulders to hide him from the approaching riders. When he was only a few feet from where the riders had to pass, he hunkered down and waited.

Selena rode easy. The trip into Del Rio had become a

routine part of her life. Balancing her time between running the rapidly growing café in town, with her duties of both a wife and mother, would have been impossible for most women. But to Selena Colson, it was a challenge she thrived on. As she rode, her mind was busy arranging the things she needed to do in an orderly manner, as was her custom.

Suddenly two gunshots jarred her back to the present. Jerking her head around, she saw both of her security men blown from their saddles. Their frightened horses shied sideways and bolted.

What's happening?

A hand grabbed her leg. An ugly man with evil looking eyes pulled her from her saddle. Instinctively, she lashed at his face with her riding quirk. He snarled angrily and drug her to the ground. She landed with a body-jarring jolt.

Again, she swung the only weapon at her disposal. The leather quirk struck the man across his cheek. She saw a gloved hand raised, and watched helplessly as it descended.

The blow exploded against her face. Bright pinpoints of light twinkled against a gathering darkness. Her eyes went blurry. A black shroud covered her as she descended into total blackness.

Buck and Chester were leaning on the corral fence when the emergency bell rang. They hurried toward the front gate to see what it was about.

Wade Thomas held the reins of a black mare, Selena's mare.

"One of the line riders brought her in. There was a note tied to the saddle horn," the security chief told them, handing

Chester the note.

"Get my horse!" he hollered, handing the note to Buck. "Somebody's kidnapped Selena!"

In minutes, Chester, Buck, Wade Thomas, and twenty heavily armed security men and Zack Gibbs, their tracker, raced up the trail toward Del Rio.

Chester and Buck rode side by side.

"The note said to bring half a million dollars when we come or they'd kill her," Chester said.

"I think we ought to send a man on ahead to the bank and get the money, just in case."

"Yeah, I think you're right. No telling what we're gonna run into."

They quickly found the two dead security men. Zack dismounted and squatted near the tracks. Chester and the others sat their horses and waited anxiously.

"Soon as Zack gets through, couple of you boys take our men back to the ranch and see they're cared for proper," Buck instructed. "Wade, we'd like you to ride into Del Rio and tell Chester's pa what's happened. Tell him we need half a million dollars. Follow us with it as fast as you can."

"Yes, sir, fast as I can." the security man said, heeling his mount into a gallop and heading for Del Rio.

The old tracker dismounted and squatted. He traced his finger around the fresh tracks and carefully inspected the area surrounding the place of the attack. He followed a set of tracks up the hillside and returned in minutes.

"There was three of 'em," Zack told them. "Two of 'em waited up yonder in them rocks and ambushed our men. Looks like they'd been waiting at least a couple of days. A third man waited behind that rock. He's the one who attacked your wife. From the impression her body made in the dust, it looks like he knocked her unconscious. No doubt hey loaded her on one of the security men's horses and took off that-a-way," he told them, lifting a hand to point northward.

"How much start they got on us?" Chester wanted to know.

"Two, maybe three hours at the most," Zack told them.

"Let's ride!" Chester shouted, spurring his mount.

Zack rode out front, reading the signs as one would read the newspaper. At times, he leaned far over in his saddle, studying the ground. From time to time the tracks completely disappeared. At those times the tracker rode in ever widening circles until he picked up the trail again.

The sun was directly overhead when they reined up on the bank of a running creek. The tracks clearly led into the water, but didn't come out on the other side.

"They're trying to throw us off by riding either upstream or down. I'll head upstream on the far side, somebody take this side. A couple of you ride downstream, one on both sides of the creek.

"I'll go upstream on this side," Buck said, reining his mount in that direction.

"I'll head downstream on the far side," Chester told them. "Kinch, how about you take this side? First one who finds something, give a holler. Rather not fire a shot. They might hear it."

They lost nearly half an hour before a yell rang out upstream. Everybody headed that direction. The kidnappers had come out on a sandy bank, but the tracks were still wet.

"We're gaining on 'em," Zack told them. "We're no more'n an hour behind."

"Reckon what they could be thinking?" Chester asked. "They knew we would be following, their note said as much. I don't like it. They got something up their sleeve."

"Afraid you're right," Buck agreed, "but what?"

They found out shortly.

A *teepee shaped* mountain rose out of the flat countryside. Huge slabs of flat rock stabbed out of the sides of the mountain and lifted their fingers toward the sky, creating an impassible barrier. The peak of the mountain reached several hundred feet into the air.

The tracks led to a single, narrow trail that wound steeply upward.

"Look yonder," Zack said, pointing toward the top.

Selena was plainly visible, tied to a flat, upthrust rock at the top of the trail. Three men were partially visible, mostly hidden behind nearby rocks.

"Just so you'll know," a voice yelled down, "there ain't but one way up. Anybody tries coming up that trail and we'll kill her, no ifs, ands, or buts about it."

"You harm her and I'll rip your dirty heart out with my bare hands!" Chester shouted, anger like he had never known evident in his voice.

That brought a loud laugh from the top of the mountain.

"Did you bring the money?"

"We sent a man for it. It'll be here!" Buck hollered. "Don't hurt her!"

"You got no idea what we'll do to her if we don't get that money!" the talker hollered from above.

"Just hold on! It'll be here."

"What're we gonna do?" Chester asked, his voice shaky.

"Let's not take his word there's no other way up that mountain. Let's send Zack around it and look it over."

Chester just nodded his head sadly.

"Zack, take a few of the boys. Circle the mountain. If there's another way up it, I want to know about it."

The old scout spat a long stream of tobacco juice and toed a stirrup.

"If it's there, we'll find it. Ed, Toby, Slim, Shorty. Come with me."

Longhorn III: The Prodigal Brother

The five Longhorn riders rode away, headed around the edge of the mountain to search for another trail. The other Longhorn men squatted near their horses or sat down on one of the many rocks scattered around.

There was nothing they could do now except wait.

Mid-afternoon sun bore down on them with a vengeance. The sandy soil radiated heat and cooked into anything or anybody that invaded its domain. Nothing to offer the slightest hint of shade could be seen. The Longhorn men wiped sweat and sipped tepid water from their canteens.

Zack and his companions returned. The looks on their faces gave Buck and Chester the answer to their question before it was asked.

"Anything?"

Zack shook his head. "Nothing. A Texas jack rabbit couldn't get up that mountain any other way."

Wade Thomas galloped up. His horse was heavily lathered and winded from the hurried trip in the afternoon heat. Wade tossed a brown leather zippered valise to Buck.

Buck unzipped the leather bag and looked inside. Bundles and bundles of hundred-dollar bills lay stacked in neat piles wrapped with a paper strap showing the amount in each bundle.

"I got here as fast as I could."

"Is that the money?" the kidnapper hollered down from the mountain.

"It's here!" Buck hollered. "Whadda we do now?"

"One man brings it up. No guns! If I see a gun, we'll gut her like a hog!"

"I'm taking it up," Chester said through clenched teeth.

Buck slanted a glance at his friend and partner. What he saw rounded his eyes. For a fleeting moment, he stood in shocked silence.

I've known Chester and rode with him for most of a lifetime. We've seen things and done things no man ought never to see and do, but in all that time, I've never seen him like this.

"You sure that's a good idea, Chester? Maybe—"

"I'm going." Chester said emphatically, stripping off his gun belt.

"Surely you ain't thinking about going up there unarmed?" Buck asked.

"No," his friend said, removing his .38 Colt from its holster and tucking it into his right boot. He pulled his pant leg down over it to hide it from sight.

"Hey! Look at this!" one of the Longhorn cowboys shouted, leaping up from the rock he was sitting on and scrambling to safety. "Look at the size of that sidewinder!"

A desert sidewinder rattlesnake lay coiled in a shady crack under the edge of the rock the cowboy sat on. Its head was in the air and its dangerous mouth was open wide. The long, curved fangs protruded from its mouth. It was only about two and a half feet long, but everybody knew it was one of the deadliest rattlesnakes alive.

The cowboy pulled his Bowie knife from its belt scabbard, obviously intending to rid the world of one of its most deadly reptiles.

Suddenly an idea flashed into Buck's mind.

"Hold it. Don't kill it. I want that critter alive. Anybody here know how to catch a snake without getting bit?"

Without a word, Zack, the old scout, stepped forward. He walked over to the rock where the cowboy sat. Everybody crowded around and watched, fascinated by what was taking place.

Zack squatted near the coiled snake. He reached his left hand out and moved it slowly back and forth in front of the snake, his hand extending farther and farther to the left with each pass.

The snake's head swayed back and forth, following Zack's hand as it moved. On the next pass, the scout extended his hand farther to the left than before. The snake's head followed the hand.

Zack's right hand shot out, grasped the tail of the deadly rattler, and held it high in the air. His left hand curled around the tail of the snake and quickly slid up its body until it grasped the snake just behind the head.

All the Longhorn men let out a big sigh of relief.

"Remind me to give you a raise," Buck told the old scout.

"Count on it," Zack said, spitting a stream of tobacco directly in the snake's eyes. "Now what you gonna do with him?"

Buck opened the zipper bag containing the money and held the top wide apart.

"Put him in there."

Zack walked over and put the snake inside the bag tail first. When he turned the snake's head loose, he wasted no time getting his hand out. Buck quickly zipped the bag closed.

"There's your diversion," Buck said, handing the bag to Chester. "That ought to get their attention for a minute or two."

Chester nodded and took the bag Buck handed him.

"Good luck up there," Buck told his friend, extending his hand.

Chester took it and they shook hands like family. Chester turned and started toward the mountain.

He paused at the foot of the trail. He twisted his head and glanced back at his Longhorn companions. They all stood with eyes peeled, watching intently. He turned, took a deep breath, and started the climb.

It was hard going. The trail was steep and narrow. He often had to turn sideways to squeeze through the narrow opening between the large rocks. It was so steep he sometimes lost his footing and slid backwards several steps.

His lungs screamed out for air. He gasped in great gulps. He paused to catch his breath, but happened to glance upward. His gaze looked directly into the beautiful face of his wife.

Her face was badly beaten. Her right eye was swollen shut. Dried blood trailed from her split lip down her chin and stained the white blouse she wore. A rope was wrapped again and again around her, binding her securely to the finger of upthrust rock.

Volcanic anger boiled in Chester's stomach. His eyes blazed. He clamped his teeth together to stifle the scream of protest that raced up his throat.

This isn't the time to lose my head, his mind told him. *I've got to control myself. Selena's life depends on it.*

He shook his head to clear his thinking, took a deep breath and started climbing again, purposely avoiding looking at his wife.

"Come on up, *Mr. Colson*," the man taunted. "Your beautiful woman is waiting on you."

Chester gritted his teeth and kept climbing. Finally, he reached a small flat spot beside the rock where Selena lay tied.

A tall, hard-eyed fellow stepped from behind a nearby rock. Two more emerged from the other side of his wife. Both had rifles resting in the crook of an elbow.

"Raise your hands over your head and turn around real slow," the obvious leader told him.

Chester only lifted his right hand because he held the heavy leather bag in his left. He slowly turned a complete circle. Obviously satisfied that Chester was unarmed, the man turned his attention to the bag in Chester's hand.

"Well, lookie here what *Mr. Colson* brought me. Pitch that bag over here. I wantta see what half a million dollars looks like."

Instead of obeying the kidnapper's order, Chester took a step toward him and set the bag on the sandy ground between them. He stepped back a couple of steps.

The man holstered the gun in his hand and fell to his knees beside the bag. Chester held his breath and tensed as the kidnapper anxiously grasped the zipper and slid it along the top of the leather valise. He grasped both sides of the opening and leaned close as he jerked it open.

Like a flash of lightning, the angry rattlesnake sprung its head out of the bag. He clamped its long, deadly fangs in the kidnappers throat an inch to the right of his Adam's apple.

The kidnapper let out a high-pitched, blood-curdling scream. He leapt to his feet and staggered backward. The rattler refused to loosen his bite and hung onto the man's throat. The reptile stretched past the kidnapper's hips.

Chester swung a look at the man's two companions. Their gazes were locked on the snake. Chester jerked up his pants leg and grasped the handle of his Colt. He swung it up and shot the two men to his left. They both dropped their rifles and staggered backwards, grasping the holes in their chests.

Chester swung back to the third man, but saw quickly there was no danger from him. He had collapsed to his knees. He had hold of the snake with both hands, tugging with all his remaining strength to pull it loose from his neck. His eyes walled white. His mouth gaped wide open with another scream.

Chester watched for a fleeting moment as the man toppled over onto his face. His feet and legs thrashed the ground as life drained from his body.

Chester quickly turned to his wife. Her eyes were

fixed on the dramatic event being played out only short feet from her.

Chester used his Bowie to cut her loose and gathered her weakened body in his arms.

Chapter XXXVI

Juliana sat in the saddle in front of Cody. The big pinto climbed the trail up Sugarloaf Mountain with ease, even carrying the two riders on his back.

When they neared the Schroeder/Cordell Mining camp, Cody pulled Cincinnati to a stop. He reached into the saddlebag tied behind the saddle and withdrew a white dishtowel he borrowed earlier from Miss Molly.

"What is it?" Juliana asked. "What are you doing?"

"I'm going to blindfold you," he explained, as he placed the dishtowel over her eyes and tied it behind her head.

"What are you *doing*, Cody? Why are you blindfolding me?"

"Never mind. Just relax. I'll take it off in a little bit."

Cody heeled his pinto forward. The workers and security men stopped what they were doing and stared as Cody and Juliana passed through the mining camp. The pinto continued to climb the mountain trail for another half hour before he halted.

Cody reached up and loosed the blindfold.

Juliana blinked a couple of times to clear her vision and then let out a loud gasp.

Sitting on the mountainside before her, and overlooking the waterfall and pool below, was the most beautiful log home she could imagine.

Her eyes widened and her mouth dropped open.

"You like it?" Cody asked anxiously, like a child would ask about a Christmas present given to their father.

"What? What do you mean? Of course, I like it. It's the most beautiful home I've ever seen. But I don't understand."

"It's ours. Come on. I'm anxious for you to see inside," he said, sliding from the pinto and reaching hands to help her down.

"What do you mean, it's ours?"

"I mean *it's ours,*" he said, tugging her along as he hurried them toward the house.

"Really? Do you mean it? I don't believe it. It's so beautiful."

"Wait until you see the inside," he said excitedly, as he pulled her up the wide steps.

Cody opened the front door and swung it open. He reached down and scooped Juliana off her feet and into his arms. Carrying her, he stepped through the door.

"Welcome home," he said softly.

She pulled his head close and hugged him before planting a long kiss upon his lips.

"Oh, Cody, you're the sweetest, most wonderful man I could ever imagine. I can't wait until we are married."

"Won't be long now," he said. "We leave for Denver tomorrow."

They spent the next two hours touring the house. The furniture maker in Trinidad had outdone himself. The entire house was complete with beautiful furniture, made specifically for the spacious log home.

Juliana rushed from room to room, letting out tiny squeals of delight at what she was seeing. Cody soaked it all up, grinning from ear to ear.

When the tour was finally over, they walked out to the front porch. A large swing hung suspended by two chains.

"Let's sit for a minute," Cody told her.

They folded side by side into the swing. Juliana nestled her head on Cody's wide shoulder as they swung gently back and forth. A soft, sweet-smelling breeze drifted down from the pine-covered mountain. They looked down at the waterfall and the pool below.

For several minutes they basked in the surroundings, soaked up the sounds and smells, and reveled in the closeness and love they shared.

The gold train, as it had become known, pulled out at daybreak the following morning. It was May 24, 1870. Six heavily loaded ore wagons, plus a chuck wagon, lumbered out of the Schroeder/Cordell Mining Company camp.

Once down the steep mountain trail, they stretched out and began the long, thirteen-day journey to Denver. Twenty-four heavily armed security men rode alongside the wagons, four more than usual.

Cody and Juliana rode in a covered buggy in the lead. Their saddle horses were tied behind the buggy. Two security men with rifles propped upright against their legs, rode on either side of the buggy.

"How many loads of ore have you taken to Denver now?" Juliana asked.

"This is our tenth load."

"How's the gold mine holding out?"

"Sid and Sammy say the veins are still as rich as the day we started. They say it ought to continue producing for some time yet."

"It's almost beyond belief, isn't it? It's like a fairytale come true."

Cody nodded his head.

"Yeah, it is. We've got over four million dollars in the bank, even after expenses. This load will put us well over five million."

Juliana just shook her head in wonderment.

"Will we have time to do some shopping in Denver before we catch the train? I don't have a thing to wear."

Cody lifted a grin.

"Yes, my love. I allowed four extra days for shopping. We're having dinner with Arthur Winfield and his wife one night. They've invited us to be their guests at the opera."

"Oh, good. I've never been to the opera. I'm more of a *pickin' and grinnin'* sort of girl, but I'll try most anything once." She giggled.

"Yeah, I doubt it'll be my cup of tea either, but we'll grin and bear it."

"How long will it take us to get to San Antonio, Texas?"

"Not sure. We'll take the train to St. Louis. From there, we'll ride the steamboat downriver all the way to New Orleans. We're supposed to take an ocean steamer along the coast to Corpus Christi, and then we'll ride a stagecoach to San Antonio. The trip will take a while."

"That's okay," she said, nestling closer. "As long as we're together, I don't care if it takes a month."

"Well, it'll likely take longer than that."

The trip to Denver went well. They arrived on June 7. Cody asked his men to go ahead and take the ore wagons to the smelter and told them he would meet them there in an hour. He and Juliana went directly to the Sargent House Hotel and checked in.

"Good to see you again, Mr. Cordell. Is this Mrs. Cordell?"

Cody flicked a look at Juliana. She smiled and looked a little embarrassed.

"Well, not yet. This is my fiancée, Juliana Higgins. We need two separate rooms, and then I need rooms for thirty-one of my men. They'll be along in shortly."

"Oh, I see. Sorry, ma'am. I meant no offense."

"None taken," Juliana said.

Mr. Sargent produced two keys and handed them to Cody. He handed one of them to Juliana.

"You and Miss Higgins will be in rooms four and six. They're right next to one another, upstairs and to the left. I'll assign rooms for your men when they arrive."

Cody escorted Juliana to her room. They unlocked the door and went inside. Everything seemed to be in order.

"I'll bring our bags up and then I need to ride over to the smelter for a few minutes. Will you be all right until I get back?"

"Of course. I think I'm going to lie down for a few minutes anyway. Let me know when you get back."

"I will," he promised, kissing her on the cheek.

Cody unloaded their bags and set them inside the lobby.

"I'll be happy to take your bags up to your rooms if you like?" the hotel owner volunteered.

"That would be good. I'd be much obliged."

He then took the buggy to the livery and stabled the horses, along with Juliana's white mare. He climbed into his saddle and rode to the Denver Smelting Company. His first wagon was being unloaded when he dismounted and headed for Mr. Spicer's office.

"Mr. Cordell," the smelter owner greeted, as Cody walked into his office. "How are things in Trinidad?"

"Still digging. How are you, Mr. Spicer?"

"Long as we've done business together, call me Frank."

"Only if you call me Cody."

"It's a deal," Spicer said, extending his hand in greeting. They shared a warm handshake.

"Haven't see you in a while," Spicer said. "Everything okay?"

"Yep. Just been busy. I'll be in town for a few days. Me and my fiancée are catching the train to St. Louis on the twelfth."

"That's supposed to be their maiden run, ain't it?"

"Yep. That's what they're saying."

"Going to St. Louis, huh?"

"Well, we're actually going to San Antonio, Texas, but we catch a paddle wheeler at St. Louis."

"Long trip."

"Yeah, it is. We're getting married in San Antonio."

"Well, congratulations."

"Obliged. Things going all right? Guess Mr. Winfield is taking care of your invoices?"

"Sure is. Pays like clockwork. No complaints at all."

"That's good to hear. I'm having dinner with him and his wife while we're here. I'll pass on your good words. Well, reckon I better be getting back to the hotel. I left my fiancée there alone."

They shook hands again and Cody left the office. Several of Cody's men lounged around the wagons waiting to unload. Walt Seals was there.

"Walt, after you boys get unloaded and get the mules stabled, take the boys over to the hotel and check in. I'll arrange for all of us to have supper at Sadie's."

"Sure thing, boss," the head of the security detail said. "We'll catch up with you at Sadie's."

Cody rode back to the livery and stabled his pinto. He walked to the hotel, climbed the stairs, and tapped on Juliana's door.

"It's Cody."

He heard the door unlock and swing open.

"How's that bed?" he asked.

"It's wonderful. I must have dozed off."

"We're supposed to meet the boys at a place called Sadie's for supper."

"What time?"

"Oh, about six, I imagine."

"What time is it now?" she asked.

"The big clock downstairs said four-thirty when I came up."

"Good. That will give me time to take a bath and freshen up."

"I'll go down and arrange for a bath to be brought up."

"Thank you. Let me know when it's time to go."

Cody went downstairs and arranged for a bathtub and hot water to be taken up to Juliana's room. Then he went to his own room and stretched out on the soft feather bed. He relaxed for an hour, rose, washed up, dressed in a clean outfit, then went to Juliana's room where she waited. Together they walked up the street to Sadie's Café.

"Well, would you look what the cat dragged in!" Rachel shouted, as Cody and Juliana walked in.

"Be nice now, this is my fiancée I told you about. This is Juliana Higgins. Juliana, this is Rachel. She owns the place."

They shook hands.

"You're even more beautiful than he told me," Rachel said.

"Thank you, Rachel. It's a real pleasure meeting you."

"Every man in my outfit is in love with Rachel," Cody told Juliana. "Incidentally, all my men will be here for supper in a little bit. Sorry I didn't give you more warning."

"Then I better get busy. I'll send word for my help to get here as quick as they can. You folks have a seat. I'll pour you some coffee."

"You go ahead," Juliana told her. "I'll pour us some coffee, if that's all right?"

"I like her already," Rachel joked, turning and heading for the kitchen.

The meal was wonderful, the conversation loud and happy, and the coffee kept coming. When Cody and Juliana finally gave up and scooted back their chairs, it was past eleven.

"Reckon you'll be pulling out in the morning?" Cody asked Walt Seals.

"Yeah, we got a full load of supplies to pick up for Mr. Hamilton, and then we'll be heading back to Trinidad."

"Well, take it easy and keep your powder dry," Cody told him.

"You do the same, boss. See you when you get back."

"That'll be a while."

They shook hands. Cody paid for the meals and left a generous tip. He and Juliana walked the two blocks to their hotel and climbed the stairs. At her door, Juliana stopped and slowly turned around.

"Someday, we won't need but one room," she said softly.

"I know. Can't be too soon for me."

"Me, either. Goodnight, Cody," she said, tiptoeing to lift her face.

Cody leaned down, gathered her in his arms, and closed the distance between her lips and his. When they finally broke the kiss, his face felt flushed and his breathing was heavy and short.

He reluctantly released her, trailing his hands along her arms until only their fingertips touched. Their gazes held one another until finally she turned and stepped into her room.

Cody stood outside his own door until he heard her key turn and the door lock.

Juliana spent Friday and Saturday shopping. Cody tagged along. He spent hours nodding his head and agreeing the dresses looked great on her. When all was said and done, she ended up buying only three outfits.

On Saturday evening, they met Arthur Winfield and his wife Margaret for an early dinner at a private exclusive club before going to the opera. Juliana was gracious and listened intently as Margaret Winfield went on and on about the *inner workings* of Colorado politics and the important part her husband played in it.

"I'm sure Miss Higgins isn't interested in what I'm doing, dear," he finally told his wife.

"On the contrary," Juliana said. "I think it is very commendable that Mr. Winfield would work so tirelessly to benefit our state."

The evening finally ended. They all said their goodnights and assured the Winfields they enjoyed the evening. Both Cody and Juliana breathed a long sigh of relief when dropped off at their hotel.

"I'm sorry about tonight," Cody told her at her door.

"She was just trying to be *entertaining*," Juliana said.

"You handled it well. I was so proud of you. You looked extra beautiful in your new dress."

"Thank you. Well, it's late. I suppose we better say goodnight."

"Yeah, I suppose. Goodnight, Juliana," he said, leaning to kiss her goodnight.

She wrapped her arms around his neck and pulled him to her. They kissed and held one another close in a long hug.

"Someday," she whispered.

"Someday soon," he whispered back.

Tuesday came quickly. Cody hired a buggy and driver to take them and their luggage to the train station. The place was packed. A large celebration was going on. Colorful flags flew everywhere. A bandstand was set up and the band played patriotic music. It was a festive occasion.

The black carriage man carried their luggage to the train. He showed the conductor the tickets Cody had given him, and took their luggage to their assigned compartments.

As the carriage man came out, Cody gave him five dollars.

"Thank you, Mister Cordell. You folks have a nice trip now."

The train already had a head of steam built up. Smoke boiled from the smokestack. Cody and Juliana made their way to the steps and climbed aboard. The conductor showed them to their compartments.

"Welcome aboard," the conductor said. "You folks will be in compartments number one and two. Right this way."

They were ushered along the narrow passageway between the private compartments.

"Our dining car will be two cars forward. We serve three meals daily. Cocktails and coffee are available anytime. If there's anything we can do to make your trip more enjoyable, just let me know."

"We're obliged," Cody told the man, slipping five dollars into his hand as the man turned to leave.

"Want to walk up to the dining car and watch the sendoff?" Cody asked.

"Sure. Why not?"

They hurried up the narrow passageway like two young children off on a great adventure. Reaching the dining car, they chose a seat by a large window and crowded close to see the sendoff.

The band continued playing, people waved, and young children ran along beside the train as it pulled out of the station, a festive atmosphere.

A waiter in a white waist jacket came and they ordered coffee. They sipped their coffee and watched the countryside slide swiftly past their window.

"This is exciting," Juliana said. "I've never ridden a train before."

"I haven't either."

"Really? I thought you would have. You've been so many places and done so many things."

"Not really. About all I've ever done are things I don't want to talk about."

Juliana's face grew serious. She looked deep into Cody's eyes for a time.

"Cody, I love you with all my heart. I don't care where you came from or what you've done. That's all in the past. You're the man I choose to spend the rest of my life with. All I know is that our love is strong enough to last a lifetime."

Cody swallowed, trying vainly to choke back the tears welling up in his eyes. He didn't answer. He couldn't. He nodded his head.

* * *

It was late. The children were asleep and being watched over by Marie, their Mexican nanny. It had been a long and tiring day.

Buck was already lying in their large bathtub with his eyes closed when Rebekah arrived.

"Sorry I'm late," she said, slipping out of her robe and stepping down into the bathtub. "I just had to look in on Kristianna one last time to make sure she's still asleep."

"Was she?" Buck asked, scooting over to make room for his wife beside him.

"Sleeping like a baby," Rebekah joked, settling down into the warm, soothing water.

She nestled close and pillowed her head on Buck's broad shoulder, her face turned into the warm, whiskery crook of his neck. Her hand splayed across his chest. She felt so safe and protected and loved and needed.

She enjoyed these times. For several minutes they lay quietly, enjoying the peaceful solitude of their special place. It was at these times she felt the closest to her husband.

"Did I hear you tell Chester something about going to San Antonio?" she asked.

"Yeah, we're needing some more land. We decided to talk to Antonio Rivas's attorney to see if there's a chance he changed his mind about selling us the land instead of leasing it. We're running out of room."

"When are you thinking about going?"

"No real hurry, don't reckon. Why?"

"I'd like to go with you, if you don't mind?"

Buck raised his head to look into her face.

"Mind? I'd love having you go with me. I thought about asking, but figured with the new baby and all..."

"She's over six weeks, now, and old enough to travel. I'd like to get away for a few days. I could get Selena and Jewel to watch after little Cody. I'd like to get away for a few days. I think a trip to San Antonio would be nice."

She saw Buck smile. He leaned his head to brush her lips with his in a soft, gentle kiss.

"Then it's settled. I think you're right. We haven't had any alone time since Kristianna was born. When would you like to go?"

"Sooner the better."

"We've got another herd pulling out tomorrow for Abilene. I'd like to be here to see them off. What about leaving day after tomorrow?"

"Works for me. I'll be ready."

"This is great," Buck said. "Good idea. Maybe we could catch a play or something while we're there."

"And *maybe* do some shopping?"

Buck chuckled.

"How'd I know you were gonna say that? Yeah, maybe we could find time for some shopping. Sometime while we're there, I'd like to ride over and put some flowers on my folks' grave, too. It's been a while since I've been there."

"I think that would be nice."

"How's Selena doing since her kidnapping?"

"She's doing well, I think. She says she's still having nightmares about it, but seems to be doing better."

"That was a bad time. We're fortunate it turned out as well as it did. Could'a gone the other way real easy."

"We've survived lots of bad times, but the good far outweighs the bad."

"That's for sure."

"I'm glad you didn't have to stay in Austin so long this time."

"Me, too."

"Know what?"

"What?"

"I love you so much," Rebekah said softly.

He breached the distance between her lips and his.

"I love you, too, pretty lady," whispering the words gentle and featherlike against her mouth.

His fingers rose to stroke her cheek, to slide slowly down the long curve of her throat. Her heartbeat flickered and picked up speed. She felt fresh color bloom in her face.

"I've missed you," she whispered.

The covered buggy sat parked near the front door of Buck's hacienda. Two of the young boys on the ranch carried out the luggage. They loaded bag after bag. Rebekah came out of the house carrying yet another.

"We're only staying a couple of days," Buck commented, looking at the pile of bags on the back of the buggy.

"I know, but I couldn't decide what I would be needing, so I had to take extra."

Buck just shook a single nod and took his wife by the elbow to help her into the buggy.

Down near the front gate, eight security men waited. They would escort Buck and Rebekah to San Antonio.

"It's been a long time since I was in San Antonio," Rebekah said, as Buck clucked the matched black horses into motion.

"It's changing fast. The new army fort is finished and several new businesses have moved in."

"I can't believe how much Del Rio has grown, too."

"Yeah, we sure opened the bank at the right time. Mr.

Colson is doing us a good job. He says he can't believe he farmed all those years when he could'a been banking."

"Well, takes money to make money."

"That's for sure."

The trip to San Antonio proved uneventful. Buck reined the buggy to a stop in front of the Cattlemen's Hotel. A black bellhop met him.

"You checkin' in, sir?"

"Yep," Buck said, climbing out of the buggy and hurrying around to help Rebekah with the baby to the ground.

"I'll get your bags, sir."

"I'd be obliged."

Buck escorted Rebekah inside and walked over to the counter.

"I'm Buck Cordell. I'll be needing nine rooms."

The smallish, sallow-faced man raised his bushy eyebrows in an expression of surprise.

"*Nine* rooms?"

"Yeah, nine rooms. You do have that many, don't you?"

"Well, yes, sir. It's just a bit unusual to have someone request that many."

"Well, I stay here every time I'm in town. I need one room for me and my wife and baby and eight for my men. They'll be in shortly."

"Very well. We're glad to have you. If you wouldn't mind signing the registration book, I'll get your key. You and Mrs. Cordell will be in suite A. That's upstairs."

"Good," Buck said, scooping the key off of the counter.

"Leonard," the clerk said to the bellhop, "Mr. and Mrs. Cordell will be in Suite A."

Buck and Rebekah climbed the stairs and found their

room. Buck used the key to open the door and stepped aside for his wife to enter.

"This one is nicer than the one we had before," she observed, glancing around. "It even has a bathtub behind that screen."

"Bet it ain't like ours at home," Buck said, doffing his hat and hanging it on a bedpost.

"Well, we'll see," she said, slanting a tantalizing look and lifting her, one-corner-of the-mouth grins.

Rebekah spent the next two days shopping and tending her newborn while Buck visited Antonio Rivas's attorney.

Manuel Rodriguez listened intently as Buck explained their problem.

"Understand that we're happy with the lease agreement, but the fact of the matter is, our ranch has grown to the point that we'd like to purchase the ten thousand acres instead of leasing it.

"On top of that, we need more land. If *Señor* Rivas owns other land anywhere close to us, we'd like to make him an offer to buy it. He told me earlier that he owned large tracts of land along the Rio Grande. We'd like to look it over and talk with him about buying some of it.

"The Longhorn Ranch has simply outgrown the land we have. See if Mr. Rivas has some more land he would consider selling."

"I will contact my client right away and let you know what he says."

Buck rose and shook hands with the attorney.

"I'm obliged for your time," Buck said

"Good day, Mr. Cordell. I'll be in touch with you."

Longhorn III: The Prodigal Brother

Buck stopped at a flower shop on the way back to their hotel. He bought two large wreaths for his parents' graves.

"I bought some wreaths this afternoon. I'd like to drive over to Hondo early in the morning and put them on my folks' graves."

"That would be nice. I'd like that," Rebekah told him.

That night, Buck and Rebekah ate dinner in the hotel dining room and attended a touring company play that happened to be in town. Neither Buck nor Rebekah enjoyed the play, but for appearance sake, they stayed until the final curtain came down.

"Let's go back to our room and try out that bathtub," Rebekah leaned close and whispered as they were walking out of the theatre.

Cody and Juliana arrived in San Antonio on Tuesday, July 10. The stage was late. It was after ten o'clock at night when they arrived. The trip from Denver had taken them two days short of a full month.

The stagecoach driver unloaded their baggage and set it on the boardwalk in front of the station. Cody saw a carriage sitting nearby with a Mexican standing beside it. He motioned and the man hurried over.

"Can you take me and my fiancée to the best hotel in town?"

"*Si*, the Cattlemen Hotel is the finest place to stay."

"Good."

Cody helped Juliana into the carriage and climbed in behind her. The carriage driver loaded their baggage and climbed into the driver's seat. It wasn't far to the hotel and it took only a few minutes.

While the Mexican carriage man toted their bags inside, Cody walked up to the registration desk.

"We need two rooms," he told the sleepy eyed fellow.

"*Two* rooms?" the man questioned, darting quick glances at Juliana.

"Yes, *two* rooms."

The man produced two keys and laid them on the counter.

"If you will just register, please, you folks will be in Suite B and C. They're at the top of the stairs."

Cody signed both their names and picked up the keys. The Mexican carriage man carried their bags up the stairs and into their rooms. Cody gave him five dollars and closed the door behind him as he left Juliana's suite.

"Nice place," she said, glancing around. "It even has a large bathtub I'm going to take advantage of."

"Sounds good. I'll go down and arrange for hot water to be brought up."

She kissed him on the cheek.

"That's for the hot water," she joked.

"Hmm, maybe I'll just bring it myself," he said over his shoulder as he went out the door.

He went downstairs and walked up to the clerk.

"I'd like a hot bath sent up to my fianceé's room. She's in Suite B."

"It may be a little bit. I've only got one girl working this late and she's already heating water for another guest."

"Just have her do it as soon as she can."

"Yes, sir."

Cody stopped by Juliana's room and told her it might take some time before the hot water was delivered.

"If you're up to another short ride, I'd like for us to go over to my old home place in the morning and put some flowers on my ma and pa's graves. After the long trip, I know we're both worn out. We can't get the flowers until they open, anyway. I'll pick you up about eight or so and we'll have breakfast, pick up the flowers, and head out. Okay?" "That will be fine. I'll be ready."

They kissed goodnight and Cody went to his room. He was tired after the long trip. He quickly undressed and crawled into bed.

The sun crept through the window and woke Cody. For a brief moment, he couldn't figure out where he was, then remembered. He immediately swung his feet to the floor and looked out the window. The city of San Antonio was wide-awake and going about its business.

He quickly washed, dressed, and hurried to Juliana's room. He tapped lightly on the door. It took her a few minutes before she opened the door.

"I'm so sorry, Cody. I overslept."

"It's okay, so did I. You look beautiful. Are you ready?"

"Ready."

They went downstairs to the dining room and had breakfast. After they finished, Cody asked the man at the desk where the nearest flower shop was.

"You'll find the flower shop two blocks over, then turn left. It will be about three more blocks," the man told him.

"What about a livery where we could rent a buggy?" Cody asked.

"Go outside and to your left. It's quite a ways. You might want to hire the carriage outside to take you there."

"I'm obliged."

They took the man's advice and hired the carriage to take them to the livery stable. The man was right; it would have been a long walk.

Cody arranged for a team and buggy. They finally found the flower shop and bought two beautiful wreaths.

"How far is it to Hondo?" Juliana asked.

"It's about thirty miles or so. We ought to get there shortly after noon."

"Tell me about you. Tell me what you were like when you were young."

"Not much to tell. I was just a tow-headed boy. We farmed, at least as best as we could. We worked hard, but the ground around here is pretty sorry. Always lived hand to mouth, as far back as I can remember.

"Pa was a good man and a hard worker, but we never had nothing but each other. We never knew what it was to have meat, unless we killed a squirrel or rabbit or maybe a turkey now and then."

"Tell me about your mother."

"She was, what I would call, a *saint*. Lots of times when we didn't have enough to eat, she would say she wasn't hungry and give me what was on her plate. But I knew better. We were all hungry most of the time in those days."

"That's what mothers do," Juliana said, her voice rich with emotion. "Didn't you tell me once you had a brother who died in the war?"

"Yes, his name was Benjamin, but we all called him Buck. Everybody except Ma, she always called him by his real name. He went off to war when I was about twelve, I reckon. He never came back.

"I'll never forget. His most prized possession was a pocketknife he had. The day he left, he called me aside and gave it to me. I still have it, to this day."

Cody reached into his pocket and pulled out a small, worn, pocketknife.

"I wouldn't take anything in this world for that knife."

They talked the miles away. Before he knew it they turned into the long, winding lane that led to the old farm. Cody shuttered his feelings and tried in vain to swallow the lump in his throat.

Fresh buggy tracks caught his eye.

"Somebody's been here," he said, "and not long ago. Those are fresh tracks."

It was puzzling. It worried him some.

As they rounded the last curve in the lane, Cody saw a buggy up ahead. Instinctively, he reached a hand to his hip and thumbed off the traveling thong from the hammer of his Colt.

"Can't imagine who would be here," he told Juliana.

Whoever it was, their buggy was pulled up beside the little graveyard where his folks were buried. He guided his buggy in that direction.

A tall man and a red-haired woman stood there, staring at Cody and Juliana. Two fresh wreaths lay on his folks' graves.

That looks like, no...it couldn't be! He's tall just like my brother was. He's got the same color hair.

Suddenly recognition exploded in his mind.

It's him! It's really him!

Cody pulled the team to a stop about forty yards away and leaped from the buggy. He raced forward.

He saw recognition flash across his brother's face. He saw him break into a run. Cody's heart was in his throat. Happy tears blurred his vision. The distance between them closed. They fell into one another's arms, both sobbing out loud.

For a time, they held tightly to one another. Cody was terrified this might not be real and that he might wake up and discover it was nothing but a dream.

"Cody?" Buck asked.

"Yes, is this *really* you? I thought you were dead. I thought you were killed in the war."

"It's me. I heard you were alive. I hired the Pinkertons to find you, but they told me you were killed up in Colorado."

They hugged one another again and again.

Rebekah walked over to the buggy where Juliana still sat. Both women were wiping tears.

"I'm Rebekah," she said. "I'm Buck's wife."

"Hello, Rebekah. I'm Juliana. I'm Cody's fiancée."

Juliana climbed down from the buggy. She and Rebekah hugged one another.

"This is the happiest day of Buck's life. He's been searching for Cody for years."

Buck and Cody walked over to join the ladies. Buck's arm was around Cody's shoulder.

"It's him, Rebekah," Buck choked the words out. "It's really him. My prodigal brother's come home!"

"THE PRODIGAL BROTHER"

Luke 15: 11-24

"And he said, "A certain man had two sons: and the younger of them said to his father, Father, give me the portion of goods that falleth to me. And he divided unto them his goods.

And not many days after the younger son gathered all together, and took his journey into a far country, and there he wasted his substance in riotous living. And when he had spent all, there arose a mighty famine in that land; and he began to be in want.

And he went and joined himself to a citizen of that country; and he sent him into his fields to feed swine. And he would have filled his belly with the husks that the swine did eat: and no man gave unto him.

And when he came to himself, he said, How many hired servants, of my father's have bread enough and to spare, and I perish with hunger!

I will arise and go to my father, and will say unto him, Father, I have sinned against heaven, and before thee. And am no more worthy to be called thy son; make me as one of thy hired servants.

And he arose and came to his father. But when he was yet a great way off, his father saw him, and had compassion, and ran, and fell on his neck, and kissed him.

And the son said unto him, Father, I have sinned against heaven, and in thy sight, and am no more worthy to be called thy son. But the father said to his servants. Bring forth the best robe, and put it on him; and put a ring on his hand, and shoes on his feet:

And bring forth the fatted calf, and kill it; and let us eat, and be merry; For this my son was dead, and is alive again; he was lost, and is found.

And they began to be merry!"

~The End~

About the Author

I was born and raised in eastern Oklahoma, formerly known as the Indian Territory. My home was only a half-day's ride by horseback from old historic Fort Smith, Arkansas, home of Judge Isaac C. Parker, who became famous as "The Hanging Judge."

As a young boy I rode the same trails once ridden by the likes of the James, Younger, and Dalton gangs. The infamous "Bandit Queen," Belle Starr's home and grave were only thirty miles from my own home. I grew up listening to stories of lawmen and outlaws.

For as long as I can remember I love to read, and the more I read the more I wanted to write. Hundreds of poems, songs, and short stories only partially satisfied my love of writing. Dozens of stories of the Old West gathered dust on the shelves of my mind. When I retired I began to take down those stories, dust them off, and do what I had dreamed of doing ever since I was a small boy. writing historical western novels.

Dusty Rhodes loves to hear from his many fans.

WANT MORE? . . .

If you enjoyed this book and would like to read more Dusty Rhodes books simply fill out the order form below, cut out of book and drop it in the mail with your check. Dusty will ship them within three working days. (or) visit Dusty's website listed below at: www.dustyrhodesbooks.com

___ **Man Hunter**	@ $18.00 = $_____
___ **Shooter**	@ $13.00 = $_____
___ **Shiloh**	@ $12.00 = $_____
___ **Death Rides A Pale Horse**	@ $12.00 = $_____
___ **Vengeance Is Mine**	@ $12.00 = $_____
___ **Jedidiah Boone**	@ $12.00= $_____
___ **Longhorn I (The Beginning)**	@ $15.00 = $_____
___ **Longhorn II (The Hondo Kid)**	@ $15.00 =$_____
___ **Longhorn III(The Prodigal Brother**	@ $15.00 = $_____
___ **Shawgo**	@ $15.00 = $_____
___**Chero**	@$14.00 = $_____
Please add $3.00 per book shipping charge	= $_____
Total	= $_____

Ship to: _____
Address _____
City _____**State** _____ **ZIP** _____
Your e-mail address _____

Mail Order to: Dusty Rhodes
P. O. Box 7
Greenwood, AR 72936-007
Website www.dustyrhodesbooks.com

THANKS FOR READING MY BOOKS!